AF605220

NIGERIA

— *An Ancient Secret Becomes the* —

ADVENTURE OF A LIFETIME

TOM WANGLER

First Edition

ISBN-13: 978-1-945587-46-7
Library of Congress: 2019918411
Tom Wangler
Nigeria: An Ancient Secret Becomes the Adventure of a Lifetime
1. Africa; 2. Peace Corps; 3. Nigeria; 4. History

Book Design: Dancing Moon Press
Cover Design: Dancing Moon Press
Cover Art: Lindy Martin
Illustration Art: Philip McDaniel

Dancing Moon Press
Bend, Oregon USA
dancingmoonpress.com

Although the story you are about to read is technically a novel, it is based upon the exploits and experiences of the author, who served in the American Peace Corps from 1974-76 in Nigeria, West Africa.

The history, conditions, ecology, and climate along with most of the locations described in the story, are depicted as they existed in 1975. The ancient Nok civilization, together with its beautiful artifacts, also existed as described.

All of the characters were inspired by the variety of individuals the author met along the way. Any resemblance to actual individuals, alive or dead, is purely coincidental.

"The darkest thing about Africa has always been our ignorance of it."

– George H.T. Kimble

PROLOGUE

The world in the fall of 1975 was far removed from what it is today. There were no personal computers, no cell phones, no music CDs or DVD movies. It would be a long time before GPS would become the norm for navigation as well as for mapping

After twenty years of American involvement, the Vietnam War ended badly for the United States. The movie "Jaws" was a mega-hit, as was NBC's recently introduced "Saturday Night Live" TV show. Muhammad Ali beat up Joe Fraser in the "Thrilla in Manilla" for the world heavyweight boxing title. Two boyhood friends, Bill Gates and Paul Allen, teamed up to form a garage-based company they named Microsoft. It was a time when the average cost of a brand new car was a mere $4,250.

Thanks to South African Prime Minister, Balthazar Johannes Vorster, apartheid was still alive – creating a political, legal, and economic separation between that country's whites and blacks. Leonid Brezhnev was the top official in the Soviet Union. Harold Wilson was the prime minister of Great Britain. In a strange turn of American politics, Gerald Ford became the first unelected President of the United States.

A great many things happened all over the globe in 1975, so it came as no small wonder that many of the lesser stories and events were missed by the world community altogether.

Consequentially, no mention was made of the "incident" in any newspaper, magazine, or on the evening news. No accessible public record of it existed anywhere. As far as the rest of the world was concerned, the event was something that simply never happened.

But something did happen and, as a result, several people disappeared under mysterious, if not bizarre, circumstances. Except for the remains of one person, the rest were never seen again.

Because this event happened in a remote part of the

world, a thorough investigation by way of any government or international agency was never conducted. The disappearances were quietly dismissed as a minor incident not worthy of further effort.

This was especially true for the country in which the occurrence took place. The West African nation of Nigeria, then as now, was suspiciously non-committal, as well as tight-lipped, about the whole affair.

In the end, the friends and families of the victims never received an adequate explanation or subsequent closure for what happened to their comrades or loved ones.

Only after several decades of silence did rumors and unsubstantiated stories begin to emerge. What exactly occurred in that West African nation in the fall of 1975 may never actually be known. But one thing is certain, it could easily happen again.

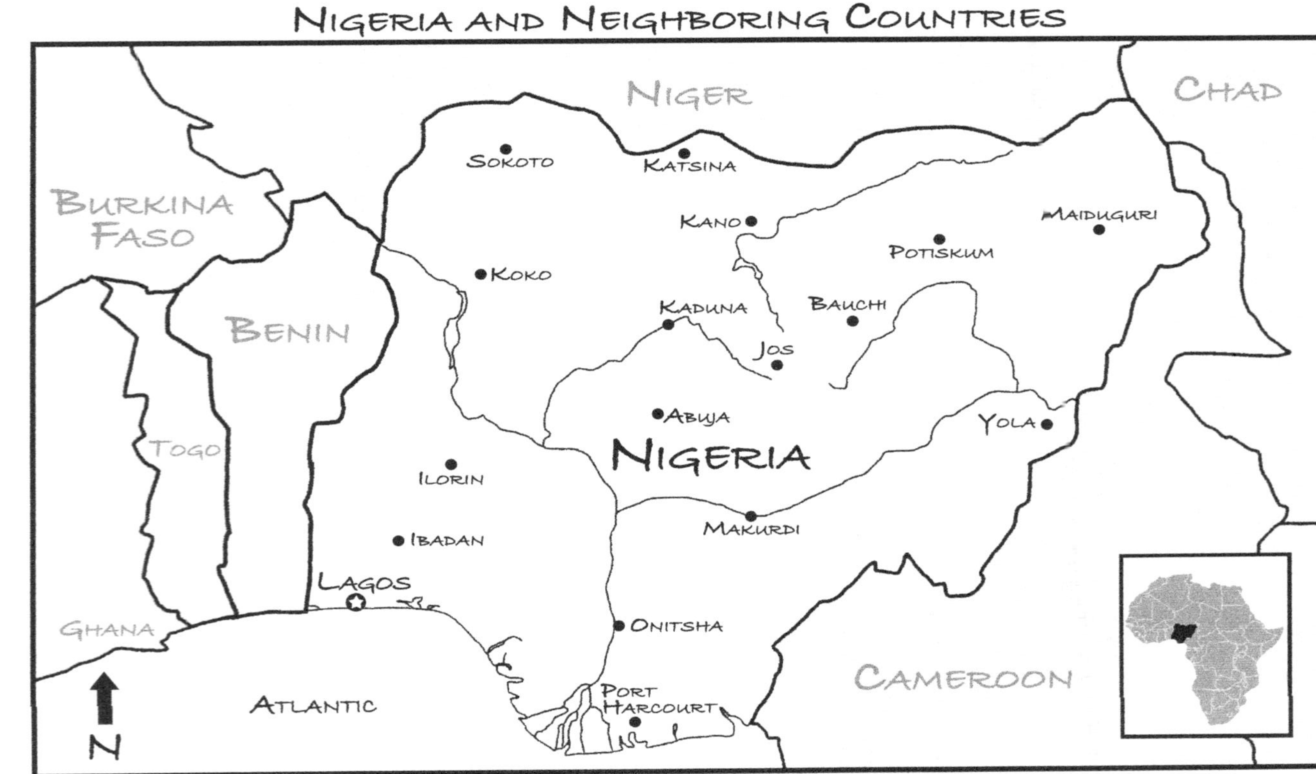
Nigeria and Neighboring Countries
Niger
Chad
Burkina Faso
Benin
Togo
Ghana
Sokoto
Katsina
Kano
Maiduguri
Potiskum
Koko
Kaduna
Bauchi
Jos
Abuja
Yola
Nigeria
Ilorin
Ibadan
Makurdi
Lagos
Onitsha
Port Harcourt
Atlantic
Cameroon
N

CHAPTER I

Saturday Night, September 20, 1975

North Central Nigeria

The blood red moon rose full and ominous over Nigeria's Benue Plateau. Within an hour, it had transformed itself into a bright silver orb, hanging like a lantern in the black African sky.

Normally, a moon of this magnitude would be considered nothing short of supernatural. In scientific terms, this was simply a celestial phenomenon that occurred every two decades or so. This perigee was a time when the distance between the earth and the moon were at their absolute closest and the atmospheric conditions were ideal. The combined events created a moon of rarely seen size, clarity and brilliance.

In Nigeria's central highlands, the moon on this night was especially spectacular. At its zenith, the brightness of this "super moon" was enough to cast shadows, in addition to providing enough light for people to move about without the aid of lamps or torches. Nocturnal predators of the plateau didn't even bother to hunt during this period. To do so would be futile, for it was too bright to effectively stalk prey. Even the contour of the surrounding landscape revealed itself clearly in the pale, silvery light. It was as if the night itself had taken on a life of its own.

American Peace Corps Volunteer Danny Harper—young, fit, and fresh out of college, sat high atop a rock ledge enjoying the sensations this night brought him.

From his perch, and aided by the bright moonlight, Danny could clearly see the idyllic landscape which stretched out in front of him.

He was surrounded by an incredibly beautiful oasis.

With its assortment of ferns, shrubs, flowering bushes, and palm trees, the rain forest below him looked more like a well-maintained tropical garden than something of a natural origin.

The young Peace Corps Volunteer marveled at the fragrant smells emanating from the collection of plants and flowers that adorned this paradise. Adding to the magical effects of his surroundings, Danny was sitting next to a small, spring-fed waterfall which oozed out of the rocks slightly above him. The gentle, cascading stream added a soothing ambience to the evening. Danny enjoyed watching the path of the little stream as it tumbled down into a shimmering pool of crystal-clear water that was approximately six meters (19.7 feet) below. The subtle splashing sounds added a surreal, if not calming, effect to the night.

Danny estimated the temperature to be somewhere around the mid-seventies, or low twenties if one was talking Celsius. The humidity couldn't have been more than sixty percent, making for perfect campout weather.

The awe-struck American absorbed the unspoiled solitude, along with the magnificent view this remote perch afforded. This was perfect. This was heaven. Nothing he had ever known while growing up in central California could ever compare to the wonder of this place.

Danny reached into his small cooler and pulled out a Star Beer, his second since he had set up a modest campsite in the oasis below. *Another one of these,* he ruefully thought, *and I'll be so shit-faced I won't be able to climb back down.* Fumbling for the opener, he smiled to himself as he thought about his first introduction to the mainstay beer of this West African country. He recounted the mind-numbing event with a lop-sided grin.

It was his group's second night in Nigeria, seventeen short months ago. Danny, along with his fellow Peace Corps Volunteers, decided it was time to party. The Federal Palace Hotel, their temporary residence after arriving in Lagos (pronounced LAY-gohs), the country's capital city, had an inviting bar and lounge. Star Beer was not only the cheapest, being a local product, it was also the only beer that was kept chilled. Probably, the group found out, to disguise its taste.

All five of the new Volunteers had decided now was as good a time as any to expose themselves to the local culture. So the colder, principal beer of Nigeria was the beverage of choice for the group that night. The first round was soon followed by a second, and then a third.

Star Beer came in a one-liter bottle, not the standard twelve-ounce container found in the United States. It also had over six percent alcohol, not the three to four percent the young Americans were used to. The beverage was unpasteurized, and quite often not properly aged nor produced in the most hygienic of conditions. The purity of the water used in the brewing process was always suspect. The beverage was, after all, produced and bottled in a third-world country. All things considered, however, it was still beer.

The five young Americans soon discovered they were out of their league when it came to drinking the local's choice. It turned out to be one of the shortest parties any one of the group had ever been to. Not one could remember the trip back to their room that night, nor how much they actually drank. Only the substantial hangover they all suffered the following morning was testament to the previous night's "cultural" experience.

"What the hell," Danny quipped as his reminisce ended. Popping off the bottle's top, he added, "You only live once."

After a quick taste, just to make sure this was an acceptable bottle to drink, he enjoyed a long pull before leaning back against the rock wall. Stretching out, he ruefully thought to himself, *What a way to spend a weekend. This sure beats that shithole I was assigned to upcountry. The nomads along with the scorpions can have the desert. This is where I want to be!*

In late September, Northern Nigeria was on the tail-end of the summer rainy season, so everything in this tropical oasis was green and lush. Additionally, the higher elevation of the Benue Plateau made for cooler temperatures. The rest of the northern territories were just plain hotter than hot. All things considered, the weather was perfect for an impromptu campout.

Danny had another drink, stroked his short goatee, and remembered how he had originally heard of this place.

He had been killing time one evening at his current TDY (temporary duty) location in the small city of Bauchi, in the north central part of Nigeria. Although his primary station (including his home) was in the far northeastern desert city of Maiduguri, part of his job was to travel around the region, working with teachers in the outlying towns and cities. His primary assignment was to train these individuals on how to coach sports the American way. Despite his age and inexperience, he was good at it.

On this one particular evening, he was wandering around in the local open-air marketplace when he came across an unusual sight. An old, haggard Hausa woman selling trinkets in a shabby little stall. This was a not-so-out-of-the-ordinary sight at any marketplace in Africa except for two things: none of the locals went anywhere near her stall and, despite her deep ebony color, the woman had striking amber-colored eyes. Pretty unusual for a black woman anywhere in the world, let alone in darkest Africa.

"*Sannu*," the old woman said in Hausa, and then she broke into halting Pidgin English, inviting the young, pale-skinned foreigner to purchase something.

Danny was intrigued. So he asked what her unusual wares consisted of.

"Spirits," was all the old woman said.

"How much?" Danny expected the typically high price. This was standard for the start of any negotiations in this country. Over the years, Nigerians had turned bargaining into a finely-tuned art form. Danny was poised to do some serious haggling, if for no other reason, than just for the fun of it.

"Ten Naira," was her solemn reply.

Way too much, Danny thought to himself, stroking his little chin beard. *I can get at least three of these trinkets for half that price in any market in Maiduguri.*

"No, sorry. Would you take three Naira?" he asked,

initiating the time-honored bargaining game with the old woman.

"Ten Naira."

"How about four Naira and not a Kobo more?"

"Ten Naira," she said somewhat coldly.

"I can see we won't come to an agreement on a fair or reasonable price," Danny sarcastically concluded. "Thank you for not ripping me off and have a nice day." He gave the old woman a little smirk then turned to leave.

What she said next stopped the young Volunteer dead in his tracks. "What is your life worth, *kodadde abokin fata*?" she hissed, narrowing her eyes.

"Pardon me?" said an astonished Danny Harper as he turned back to the ancient woman, not believing what he had just heard.

"My charms will protect you."

"Really? From what?"

"Evil things."

"What evil things?"

"No more talk, you buy."

"Sorry, not interested," he said with an air of finality. Again, he turned to leave.

"I give you way to paradise," the old woman intoned, reaching out with one upturned palm.

"Paradise?"

Somewhat bemused, Danny again abruptly stopped before turning back to the old woman.

"There is secret place...not far...very beautiful...paradise," the old woman said.

The old hag produced an ancient-looking, hand-drawn map of the region. She carefully unfolded the parchment, then laid it out on the ground so Danny could clearly see it.

"Where is this paradise?" he asked, his curiosity now aroused.

"Here," the old woman whispered, pointing a boney finger to a remote area on the northern edge of the Benue Plateau. "Look for mountain of stones. Paradise inside."

Danny made a mental note of the approximate location as well as what to look for, thanked the old woman, and gave her a one Naira coin.

As he was walking away, the old woman said, *"Sai Sannu."*

The young Peace Corps Volunteer turned around to also say goodbye, but the old woman was no longer there.

When Danny got back to his tiny room at the collegiate guest house, he pulled out his map of Nigeria and noted the spot on it with a small circle. Strangely enough, this so-called "paradise" was way out in the middle of nowhere. There weren't even any roads close to it.

His TDY in Bauchi ended that Friday. Since he didn't have any real commitments back in Maiduguri until the following week, he decided to see if he could find this remote oasis. He became so excited about embarking on a new adventure he completely forgot about the commitment he made to visit a fellow Volunteer in the neighboring city of Kaduna the following day.

Like all of the Peace Corps Volunteers stationed in Nigeria, Danny primarily lived out of a suitcase or, as it were, out of the back of his government-issued Range Rover. So venturing out was no big deal, since he already had a few food items, a couple jugs of water, a sleeping bag, mosquito netting, plus other survival-type items packed and with him at all times. The temptation to explore a new, not to mention, mysterious place was just too compelling.

Danny left Bauchi the next morning after a leisurely breakfast of overcooked eggs, some "mystery" meat, burnt toast, and coffee so bitter no amount of goat's milk could soften it. He paid his bill at the guest house, filled the Rover and two, five-gallon "Jerry" cans with gas, which is popularly called petrol in Nigeria, at a local station, bought extra provisions, then headed southwest on the A3 highway toward the city of Jos. At the little town of Anguwan, he turned off the highway and headed north on a hard-packed dirt road, passing the local landmark of Zaranda Hill far off to his right hand side.

The avid, twenty-two-year-old Volunteer had to make

several stops along the way to get directions. As he made his way toward his destination, Danny couldn't help but wonder how a place called paradise could have earned such an unsavory reputation. Whenever he stopped to ask for directions, he was met with the same foreboding response: "No go, Master...bad, bad place...strong Juju...evil Juju!"

Like most Westerners, Danny was indifferent to the African beliefs of Juju, Voodoo, Vodun, and other mystical notions. To an educated white man, these ancient beliefs, along with their rituals, were nothing more than beliefs or practices resulting from ignorance. Superstitions handed down from generation to generation as a way of explaining away anything unsavory or used for scaring disobedient children. Danny guessed the comments made about this place were simply scare tactics to keep the foreigners away.

Although not indicated on any map but his, Danny guessed that the existence of this place was no secret. Remote and hard to find perhaps, but no secret. To Danny, the warnings were only an affirmation this "paradise" actually existed.

Three and one-half hours after leaving Bauchi, he stopped at a junction in the road, put his Rover into four-wheel drive, and then turned off the dirt road. He was now cutting cross-country in a north-westerly direction. It took him over two hours of slow, rough travel over the open savannah to find what he was looking for.

There, east of the Junguru Hills, isolated and alone, stood a single kopje. The large rock outcropping was virtually in the middle of nowhere. Roughly the size of a college football stadium, it was oddly shaped like one too. The structure consisted of a solid ring of steep granite rocks that rose, almost vertically from the base to the rim.

Tired from over six hours of driving, Danny was eager to find a place to park and relieve himself. Approaching the mass of rocks from the southeast corner, he slowly drove counter-clockwise around the edifice looking for some kind of entrance.

He found what looked like an accessible notch in the rim on the northwest corner. Parking his Rover, he got out and took a look at what appeared to be the only way to get to the inside. Satisfied this spot would work, he unloaded his rig. Then he camouflaged it with some scrub brush. He didn't want anyone to break into it or steal the tires while he was gone. After emptying his bladder, he gathered up his gear, then made the slow climb up the rocky outcropping to the notch in the rim.

It took him half an hour to pick his way through the terrain, find a way to make the climb, and reach the summit. Once on top, the passageway gently ascended on the inside to a flat area. The interior walls looked steep, if not downright sheer. To Danny, this looked more like an ancient volcanic crater than any ordinary rock outcropping.

From his vantage point on the rim, he guessed the floor of the enclosure to be roughly the area of an over-sized football field. But it wasn't so much the acreage of the crater's interior that impressed him, it was the landscape it contained.

Danny just stood there, wide-eyed with his mouth agape. He found it hard to comprehend what he saw below. The interior of this ancient geological wonder contained a beautiful, garden-like grotto with its own tropical ecosystem. This oasis was an anomaly, virtually sealed off and isolated from the dry countryside outside. It was an absolutely stunning sight.

Although he had made several trips in his lifetime to the islands of Hawaii, this place definitely put anywhere he'd ever been to shame. This place was unbelievable and downright majestic.

As he took another swig of beer, Danny conceded that the old woman was right. This was a paradise.

Then the thought struck him: *Why would an old tribal woman lead a complete stranger, a white foreigner no less, to a secret place such as this?*

The thought had barely entered his mind when, inexplicably, the frogs and crickets below suddenly went silent. A cold, sharp shiver interrupted his reverie and abruptly brought him back to the present. The sensation that followed caught Danny completely by surprise. His little garden paradise was suddenly very quiet. Very different. Something was out of sorts and he instinctively felt it.

Danny gingerly set his beer down and slowly got to his feet. "What the hell?" he quietly said to himself. Straining his eyes and senses to the extent the moonlight and the alcohol would allow, he could not see anything amiss in the surrounding rock walls or in the oasis itself. The only noise was the soft splashing of the small waterfall beside him as it tumbled down to the pool below.

Danny's ears caught the faint whisper of something moving through the foliage on the far side of the open area that bordered the pool. Little alarm bells started going off in his head. His heart pounded deep inside his chest. His mouth became dry. The growing lump in his throat made it hard to swallow. His breathing became shallower and he felt hot. Danny's body was giving him all of the classic signs of psychological stress.

Within a few seconds, the effects of two mind-numbing Star Beers had all but disappeared. Thanks to a rush of the stress-produced hormone adrenaline, Danny was now fully alert, not to mention fully conscious, of his surroundings.

The movement in the forested area stopped briefly, then continued. Slowly and methodically, the rustling of the plants worked their way toward the open area next to the pool. Even with the extraordinary brightness of the moon, it was still impossible for Danny to tell what it could be. Especially from this distance. The dense foliage of the oasis coupled with the shadows would camouflage almost anything.

Yes, he concluded, something was definitely down there that wasn't there before. Denial was not an option at this point. He wasn't alone.

As Danny strained to catch a glimpse of the source of the movement below him, his mind raced for an explanation. It couldn't be any of the local natives. They wouldn't be out this late unless they were poachers. If they were poachers, surely, they would be carrying torches or lanterns, perhaps even talking.

No, he thought, *now would be the perfect time for poachers to be out. They would also try to be as quiet as possible and definitely working without lights. Poaching in Nigeria is a serious crime.* So poachers were a possibility, he reasoned. The movement stopped again. Leaving the oasis deathly silent once more.

Danny tensed. Actual panic had not taken hold yet, but it was getting closer. This was not the sort of movement humans would make, he concluded, even if they were out for a night of illegal poaching. If not human, then animal, he thought. Was he being stalked? From his initial in-country training, he remembered a great many of Nigeria's wild animals were nocturnal. They were, in every sense of the phrase, creatures of the night.

He also remembered that tidbit of information also applied to most predators. Several years earlier, a Peace Corps Volunteer in Kenya filmed his own death one evening when he set up his camera to make a self-narrative in the wild. A female lion jumped him from behind and made a meal of him while the camera was still rolling. That film was shown, in parts, to all Volunteers headed for Africa as a reminder not to do something stupid while out in the bush.

As abruptly as it stopped, the movement began again. Whatever this was, it was inexorably working its way through the lush vegetation toward the open area next to the gleaming pool. Realizing he had nothing to protect himself with, Danny broke into a cold sweat. Despite the coolness of his surroundings, he couldn't help himself. In the bright moonlight, the stalker was now close enough for Danny to determine it wasn't walking on four legs.

"This is bullshit!" he said out loud, trying to well up some courage. Someone, he told himself, was deliberately trying to scare him

His mind raced for an explanation. Nigerians were notorious for extorting bribes, payments, and "dashes" from foreigners at every opportunity. No wild animals roamed these parts that he was aware of. The Yankari National Game Reserve was over 150 kilometers (94 miles) away. Some local had probably followed him here from one of the towns or hamlets he passed through, looking for easy pickings because he was foreign, white, and out of place. Anger quickly supplanted his apprehensions.

At the sound of Danny's voice, the movement suddenly stopped, then retreated further into the cover of the dense vegetation.

"Sonofabitch!" Danny exclaimed to himself, "I was right! Some stupid asshole is stalking me!" Now he was pissed. "No backward Nigerian dickhead is going to fuck with me and get away with it!" The now-angry American scrambled down from his rocky perch, promptly reaching the flat ground by the pool.

As he did so, he ran several scenarios through his mind of what he was going to do when he caught up with his intruder. With the peaceful tranquility of his special oasis now ruined, he was determined to teach whoever this was a lesson they would not forget anytime soon. The thought never occurred to him he had left one of the only spots in the entire oasis that offered any hope of protection.

As Danny reached the large clearing next to the pool, he realized he might have overreacted. Perhaps caution, he now reasoned, should have been the better part of valor. The thought he might be at a disadvantage, if not slightly outmanned, crept into his mind.

In the bright moonlight, he could clearly see the ferns, the tall grasses, the assortment of flowering plants and the collection of palm trees that surrounded him But he still could not clearly see who or what he was about to confront. From experience, he knew Africans living in remote areas could be fleet of foot, but this was somewhat of a surprise. How could someone have disappeared so quickly, yet so quietly? Something was wrong here. His misgivings returned, and with them, so did the movement in the forest.

Directly in front of him, in the shadows at the edge of the small clearing, about fifteen meters (forty-nine feet) away, something slowly emerged from the darkness of the foliage and stepped into the pale moonlight.

At this distance, Danny could only make out an outline. He strained his eyes until they hurt. Whatever it was, stood upright. It was also larger than he was. In the shadowed obscurity of the tropical forest, it looked menacing, even sinister. Any notion he may have had about running down a skinny little Nigerian evaporated in a split second.

This was definitely not a man. It didn't look like an animal either. At least nothing like he had ever seen or heard of before. Whatever it was, it just stood there. Silently swaying from side to side. Watching. Waiting.

As fate would have it, the moon suddenly disappeared behind a fleeting cloud. Plunging the oasis into a cloak of velvety darkness. Danny involuntarily held his breath. Beads of sweat broke out on his forehead. His mouth went dry. His hands trembled. Time stood still.

Transfixed and unable to move, Danny strained to see what was at the edge of the clearing. Although his eyes failed him in the dim light, all his senses told him his visitor was slowly, inexorably moving toward him. The youthful Peace Corps Volunteer was neither accustomed, nor trained, to handle situations like this. His decision to fight instead of flight may not have been the smartest of choices. His mind, racing for a solution, screamed at him to run. His body would not comply.

After what seemed like an eternity to him, the small cloud passed. Lifting the veil of darkness inside the kopje. The moon once again bathed the oasis with its luminescent glow, lighting up the area as if a switch had been turned on.

Danny Harper, exposed and defenseless, suddenly found himself standing face to face with the worst nightmare he could have ever imagined. The thing looming before him had the cold, penetrating eyes of a deadly snake ready to strike. They showed no pity. No mercy. No remorse.

In an instantaneous moment of clarity, Danny was certain he was facing death. Frozen and unable to move, his entire body began to spasmodically tremble. His bottom lip quivered as a solitary tear crept down his cheek.

Without warning, a claw-like hand suddenly reached out for him. Danny's ensuing scream stuck in his throat and came out as no more than a faint whisper.

Then his bladder involuntarily released itself.

CHAPTER 2

Saturday Night, September 20

Southwestern Nigeria

Lagos, Nigeria's capital city, lay roughly twelve hundred kilometers (750 miles) to the southwest of the Benue Plateau. Although Lagos was about a fourteen-plus-hour drive by car or two hours by plane, it was still a world away from the drama unfolding in the north.

Fellow Peace Corps Volunteer Cody Armstrong was also enjoying the spectacular African moon this night. Cody, however, was not out roughing it in the bush, nor was he alone with his thoughts or troubles.

As the "coordinator" of the Nigerian Peace Corps program, Cody enjoyed an existence that would have been either the envy or the disdain of most Volunteers. The American public, with its idyllic impression of the organization and its participants, would probably have viewed Cody as a radical departure from what a Peace Corps Volunteer was intended to be.

Since the Nigerian program consisted of only five Volunteers and the program itself was deemed to be "low profile" by the Peace Corps organization, the State Department, and the host country, a fully-staffed PC office could not be justified. Because Cody was the oldest in the group, he was appointed the position of in-country coordinator, with the "official" title of PCVL – Peace Corps Volunteer Leader. As such, he was assigned a small office, complete with a part-time secretary, at the U.S. Embassy Annex.

The office was a remodeled storage area and the annex was a former riding club that backed up to a polo field. The compound was located in the Ikoyi section of Lagos, about three and a half kilometers (two miles) away from the main embassy building, which was located on King's College Road in the downtown area of metropolitan Lagos. Ikoyi, with its grand colonial-style homes and collection of up-scale apartment buildings, was where all of the foreign diplomats and businessmen lived. The neighborhood was high-end, picturesque, comfortable, and had the only real country club in all of Nigeria.

Cody's time was equally split between his duties as PCVL and as a special advisor to the Nigerian National Sports Commission (NSC). He would spend his mornings at his office in the embassy annex, which was close to where he lived, and his afternoons working at the NSC, where he reported directly to the director of the sports commission, Dr. Adeboye "Andy" Kutaya.

The Nigerians furnished him with a car, petrol coupons, and an "official" set of credentials. The U.S. Embassy provided logistical support, the office, the part-time secretary, and a two-bedroom apartment. The U.S. government-provided housing was actually the standby quarters for official embassy visitors or State Department couriers.

The Peace Corps organization provided program support, a living allowance, and plenty of autonomy. Other than filing weekly reports to the deputy chief of mission (DCM) at the embassy, the Peace Corps director in neighboring Ghana, and the West African Peace Corps desk officer in Washington D.C., the only other real duties Cody had were to keep track of the other four Volunteers who were scattered throughout Nigeria. The other half of his job was to do an occasional assignment on behalf of the NSC. It was not what one would call a strenuous or stressful job. It was more like a vacation than actual work.

As the events unfolded in the north that night, twenty-five-year-old Cody Thomas Armstrong was thoroughly enjoying a playful romp in the pool at the American ambassador's residence. With, and courtesy of, one of the ambassador's administrative secretaries.

Ambassador Michael Murray and his family were on vacation in Italy for two weeks and had entrusted his principal secretary, MaryAnn Reed, with the responsibility of "house sitting" the official residence while away. The timing couldn't have been better. Cody had for weeks enjoyed a flirtatious relationship with the ambassador's unmarried assistant and jumped at the invitation for a private swim and a homemade pizza dinner.

MaryAnn, although a good ten years Cody's senior, retained the figure and personality of a much younger woman. She was both wonderfully girlish and yet a mature woman at the same time. The leggy, brown-eyed blonde was popular with most of the embassy staff, especially the men. Everyone found her charming and witty, yet thoroughly professional. MaryAnn also kept a healthy separation between business and pleasure. She took her role and duties at the embassy seriously and avoided any office-type romances.

Professionalism aside, MaryAnn had a different attitude when it came to Cody Armstrong. He was not Foreign Service, State Department, USAID, CIA, military, or anyone with rank. Cody was a young, single, good-looking Peace Corps Volunteer, and to MaryAnn that made him fair game.

Cody was popular with both the embassy group and the people he worked with at the sports commission. Practically everyone who met him liked him. He was sincere, somewhat boyish and made friends easily. With rugged good looks and a smile only years of wearing braces could provide, Cody also carried a muscular, six-foot-two, 190-pound-frame well. A four-year letterman in collegiate football and track, Cody was also highly intelligent. He had graduated from a private college in Oregon with honors. No easy task considering his major was in psychology with a minor in statistical analysis. In every sense of the word, Cody was, as one secretary referred to him, a real stud.

MaryAnn was the type of date Cody enjoyed. She was fun, attractive, easy to talk to, and playful. For this evening's swim date, she was wearing a sexy, one-piece, French-cut swimsuit that left little to the imagination. Needless to say, Cody was having trouble concentrating on the conversation at hand. It also went without saying he was enjoying this date immensely and had high "expectations" for the rest of the evening.

Although the sun had been down for over an hour, the temperature was still very warm, possibly somewhere in the upper-eighties. A relative humidity of seventy percent made the air feel much warmer than it actually was. The cooler water temperature of the pool was a perfect complement to the tepid African night.

The tropical smells and the extraordinary full moon made the occasion even more special, if not downright magical. Here he was, a former farm boy from nowhere, Oregon, enjoying this beautiful tropical evening, relaxing in the pool at the mansion of the American Ambassador with an attractive single woman from the U.S. Embassy. All this, at this time and place, was almost too much for Cody to believe it was actually happening to him.

"This is absolutely wonderful!" MaryAnn remarked. "Thank you for sharing it with me."

Cody gazed over at the shapely, doe-eyed blonde, raised his almost-empty water bottle in appreciation, smiled, and said the first thing that popped into his head.

"Here's looking at you, kid."

MaryAnn laughed and shook her head. "You sure know how to wine and dine a girl," she cooed. "How did you know *Casablanca* was one of my favorite movies?"

"I didn't," Cody said ruefully. "It happens to be one of my favorites too and that has always been one of my favorite lines. I'm a big fan of Bogart. He always seems to know what to say at the time. Or at least, some screenwriter does."

"Yes, someone certainly does."

In the bright moonlight, a grin developed on MaryAnn's radiant face. "So, how do you like to be treated?" Cody asked her rather impishly.

"Like a lady by day and like a woman at night," MaryAnn said with a wink and a wry little smile.

Cody got the distinct impression tonight might be his lucky night. He returned her smile with a lopsided one of his own.

The ambassador's residence was a beautiful estate that included a two-story, 4,150 square foot, colonial-style mansion with sweeping verandas, a tennis court, a tropical garden, a swimming pool (complete with a pool house), a putting green, outbuildings for servants, and a private beach that overlooked the inlet to the Lagos Lagoon. All told, the complex covered approximately two acres of prime real estate on the northeast side of Ikoyi Island.

With the distinctive address of #25 Ikoyi Crescent Avenue, the estate was the envy of many a foreign diplomat. Except for, perhaps, the British ambassador whose official residence was a former palace. Nigeria was, by all accounts, a onetime British colony.

Excluding the beach side that bordered the inlet, the compound was completely surrounded by an eight-foot rock wall topped with razor wire. The primary entrance for vehicles was by way of a massive wrought iron gate with a smaller man-sized gate off to one side. This main entrance faced south onto Crescent Avenue, which was a small loop off the old Colonial Road, the principal roadway that circled the island.

Two more gates existed: another man-sized gate on the east wall by the servant's quarters and a smaller, service-type gate on the west wall that allowed vans and small trucks to pass through to the back side of the mansion.

Inside the walls was an expansive landscaped yard with an ample number of palm trees and tropical foliage. Off to the west side of the oversized back lawn, close to the delivery entrance, were the swimming pool and pool house. On the other side of the lawn, directly behind the mansion, was the tennis court.

The residence was guarded around the clock by two Nigerian foreign security policemen patrolling the compound from the outside and by two U.S. Marines on the inside. One of the marines was always stationed inside of the residence, while the other roamed the grounds outside. They changed places every two hours to keep alert and periodically checked in with their Nigerian counterparts.

The domestic staff of five consisted of two groundskeepers,

two maids who did double duty as cooks/servers, and a staff manager who also served as a pseudo-butler. The cost to keep and maintain this luxury estate in a country where the annual rate of inflation ran 40% was a closely guarded secret.

MaryAnn had only been in-country for approximately four months before she was assigned the job of housesitting the official residence. A veteran of ten years with the Foreign Service, this was her first posting to Africa. She found the climate barely tolerable, the living conditions Spartan but adequate, the social life depressing, the country unappealing, and the selection of attractive single men virtually non-existent. Although it tested her mettle, MaryAnn was a professional and put her best face forward. She knew that Nigeria was classified as a "hardship post" with only a one-year commitment. She had, after all, been promised Paris as her next assignment.

At thirty-five years old, she still had aspirations of settling down someday to a nice home and a family. Time was still on her side, she had convinced herself. Right now, however, she was too busy seeing the world and enjoying all the fruits it had to offer. A serious relationship, with everything that might come with it, was still somewhere in the future.

The reality of her situation never hit home until she arrived in Nigeria. A ticking biological clock was partially to blame for that. She soon felt out of place with the mostly-married, middle-aged embassy staff. Then she ran into the brash young Peace Corps Volunteer during her third week on the job and things started looking up.

Cody picked right up on MaryAnn's sly innuendo. "I can't imagine anyone not treating you like a lady, or a woman for that matter."

A bemused little smile, once again, crossed MaryAnn's face. "Being treated like a lady kind of goes with the gender...and the job. Being treated like a woman is something reserved for special moments...and with special men."

"Well," remarked a slightly aroused Cody, "I think on that note, we should open this fine-looking bottle of wine you brought and expand upon this conversation."

"I think you'll like this," MaryAnn half-whispered, nodding toward the bottle Cody was struggling to open. "But it's not wine, sweetie; it's champagne...imported from France."

"Sorry," quipped Cody as he finally popped off the cork, "my background pretty much limits me to beer and wine with a screw-off top."

MaryAnn couldn't help but giggle. "Well, it's high time, my young friend, you discovered the finer things in life." With that remark and another quick wink, MaryAnn fetched two plastic wine goblets out of her beach bag and held them up for Cody to fill. "Be careful how you pour that," she cautioned. "It has a tendency to bubble and fizz."

Cody couldn't help but feel a little embarrassed and a little outclassed at this point. He'd only had champagne maybe twice in his entire life. The farm and the small town he grew up on back in Oregon wasn't exactly on the *Forbes List* of fancy places to eat and drink.

The cozy feeling, however, as well as the romantic moment, quickly disappeared with the approach of a marine security guard.

"Sorry to interrupt the party, you two, but we may have a problem," announced a serious-looking Lance Corporal by the name of Ramirez.

Cpl. Ramirez had been on duty inside the residence when he received a call from the embassy's swing shift duty officer. A worried Peace Corps Volunteer from Kaduna was needing to reach Cody and asked the U.S. Consulate in that city if someone could track him down through embassy channels.

It was the job of the embassy's duty officer to know, at all times, where the principal members of the staff were. Unfortunately, this did not include any Peace Corps Volunteers. Everyone at the embassy knew who Cody was, however, and with whom he had a date with this night. Embassy grapevines at "hardship" posts were extremely well-greased. Knowing that and knowing where the ambassador's secretary was this night made things easy for the "DO." He simply made a quick call to the ambassador's residence. Corporal Ramirez answered the phone call from the embassy, then strolled out to the pool.

"Cody, the embassy just got a call from our consulate up north. One of your people is trying to reach you. Sounds like some kind of emergency," explained the concerned marine.

Ever since his posting to Lagos as the coordinator of the Nigerian program, Cody had enjoyed a good relationship with all of the members of the marine security detachment. Being slightly older than most of the soldiers in the unit and a great deal younger than most of the embassy staff, Cody was looked up to as kind of an older brother by many in the group. Having a father who served with the Corps in the Second World War didn't hurt either. Cody also enjoyed doing "PT" (physical training) and partied with the marines whenever he had the opportunity. An element of mutual respect and admiration had grown between them. They considered themselves friends and on a first name basis.

"Which one?" Cody asked.

"Jamie Hammer."

"Hammer?" Cody replied, raising his eyebrows. "He's stationed in Kaduna, and if he has an emergency, he knows to go to the consulate there. Why is he trying to reach me here?"

"Cody, he is at the consulate and it doesn't sound like Hammer has a problem. It sounds more like something else," the young soldier replied.

With that, Cody suspected his date with MaryAnn might be over. The champagne, pizza, and whatever followed would have to be put on hold. MaryAnn remarked she was hoping it was nothing serious. Cody was secretly thinking the evening could possibly still be salvaged.

Corporal Ramirez helped each one get out of the pool and handed them their towels. "After you get out of those wet swimsuits, I'll be waiting for the both of you at the front entrance – if MaryAnn is of a mind to join us. There's a dedicated phone at the security station we can use to reach the consulate." Then the ever-professional corporal excused himself and quickly disappeared back into the shadows toward the residence.

The couple looked at each other without saying a word, then

quickly retreated into the pool house, changed, and started up the sloped lawn toward the mansion.

"What do you suppose it could be?" MaryAnn wondered aloud.

"This had better be something important, is all I have to say," Cody said, his stride reflecting his annoyance. "Hammer has a bad habit of overreacting to things. Sometimes I think he just likes to mess with me."

"Surely, he has better things to do on a Saturday night, even in Kaduna, than give you grief."

"You don't know, Jamie," Cody replied, shaking his head. "Once, he pretended to be drowning just to see if I'd jump in the pool to save him."

"Seriously?" MaryAnn laughed.

The conversation abruptly ended there as they reached the front door and the waiting U.S. Marine.

"This way." The corporal directed, leading them into a small room adjacent to the oversized foyer. "I have already established an open line to my counterpart at the consulate in Kaduna. Just press the lighted button on the phone to open the connection."

Cody stared at the white, office-style phone with its row of side buttons for a few seconds before picking up the handset. He couldn't help but notice a similar-style red phone sitting next to it and assumed it was probably a direct connection to the embassy – along with other important places. There was also a large, military-style radio set in the corner of the small room. Cody could only imagine its purpose.

Clearing his throat, Cody punched the lighted button labeled "Kaduna." "Hello?" There was no immediate response.

"There will be a slight delay," Ramirez said, holding up his upturned palms apologetically. "That's how this country's phone system works."

"Cody, is that you?" came the delayed and distant reply. Jamie Hammer's voice sounded weak, anxious.

"Yeah, it's me," replied Armstrong. "What's the emergency?"

After a short pause, Jamie answered. "I'm worried about

Danny. He failed to show up at my place by this afternoon and I haven't been able to locate him anywhere!"

"According to his weekly schedule," Cody said, in a tone meant to portray authority, "he's supposed to be in Bauchi until Friday, then return to Maiduguri. Now, you're telling me he was supposed to meet up with you in Kaduna?"

"He changed his plans," was the curt reply. "He was going to leave Bauchi early this morning and be in Kaduna by early afternoon. We were going to hang out for a couple of days before he went back to Maiduguri. He said he needed a break and wanted to party."

"So he didn't show," Cody snorted. "Maybe he stood you up and went back to Maiduguri without letting you know." Cody suspected Hammer was overreacting once again. "You know Danny," Cody added as an afterthought, "he probably ran into some horny ex-pat and is shacking up for the weekend somewhere."

Both knew Danny was more than capable of doing something like that. Ex-patriots, or "ex-pats" as everyone called foreigners, were individuals not originally from their country of residence. Nigeria was full of them. Europeans, Australians, Canadians, Americans, Chinese, Russians...whoever. They came from a variety of countries with a variety of skills and had a variety of jobs. They were scattered all over the country and a fair number of them were women. Danny had a reputation for enjoying one-night stands and wasn't too picky at times when it came to satisfying his youthful cravings. Hopefully, that is exactly what happened, Cody thought.

"You don't understand," Jamie said, his tone somewhat exasperated. "Danny's been coming to Kaduna a lot these past few months without telling you. He met someone up here he would like to know better, if you catch my drift. No way in hell would he pass up an opportunity to party and see her!"

Cody was momentarily caught off-guard. It was his job to know where his people were at all times in case of an emergency. Danny had broken one of the cardinal rules of his posting. Not only that, but this "missing person" report from a fellow Volunteer had all the indications of actually being something serious.

"So, what should we do?" Jamie asked.

Cody thought for a quick second or two then said, "Have you, by chance, tried contacting someone in Bauchi? Someone who might know what time he left and where he was going?"

"I have...and got nowhere," replied Hammer after another short pause. "It's Saturday; I couldn't reach anyone to talk to. Danny's last call to me was yesterday morning and he said he was planning on leaving Bauchi around seven this morning. He should have been here by noon. I'm worried something bad might have happened to him."

Cody glanced at his watch. It read 9:10 p.m.

"So again, 'Peace Corps Volunteer Leader,' what do we do now?" Jamie sounded like he was beginning to get irritated with his counterpart in Lagos. Cody didn't like the tone of Jamie's last remark either.

Ever since Cody was "pulled from the ranks" and named the coordinator for the Nigeria program, which included oversight of all the Volunteers stationed there, he felt the others somewhat resented him for it. Oftentimes, Cody got the distinct impression that they neither respected nor accepted him as their leader. It was never anything directly said, just implied. Cody was aware of it and was somewhat sensitive to it.

"It's too late and too dangerous to travel anywhere tonight." Troubled, Cody unconsciously rubbed his chin. "I'll catch the first flight up to Kaduna tomorrow morning. Can you meet me at the airport and be ready to hit the road when I get there? Also, let me know if the situation changes between now and then."

"Will do," replied Jamie, abruptly breaking the connection.

"Dammit!" The words shot out of Cody's mouth before he realized it, dropping the handset back onto its cradle. The outburst made both MaryAnn and Corporal Ramirez flinch. Unable to hear both sides of the conversation, both were naturally curious, as well as concerned, by the tone of Cody's conversation.

"What's wrong?" MaryAnn was the first to speak after a

brief period of uncomfortable silence. "Is everything okay?"

"It seems we have a 'missing' Volunteer," Cody said with rising tension in his voice. "Danny Harper, the PCV who's stationed up in Maiduguri, has been missing all day. According to Jamie Hammer, his buddy in Kaduna, Harper was supposed to show up there by early afternoon. As of a half an hour ago, he was around eight hours overdue."

"What are you going to do?" MaryAnn asked, "...is there anything I can do to help?"

"Yeah," Cody nodded. "Since you picked me up, can you also give me a lift back to my place? I need to pack a few things, get a bite to eat, and then get some sleep. If I remember correctly, the first flight to Kaduna leaves somewhere around six. Since it will take me a good hour to drive out to Ikeja airport, I should probably get a move on."

Cody thanked Ramirez for his help and silently walked with MaryAnn back to the pool house to gather up their stuff. Since Cody only lived about one and a half kilometers (one mile) from the ambassador's residence, it was a quick trip. Cody was in deep thought for the entire eight-minute ride.

Upon arriving at Cody's flat, MaryAnn offered to fix them something to eat while Cody threw a few essentials and a change of clothing into a backpack.

They had a meager meal of fried egg sandwiches, potato chips, and Pabst Blue Ribbon beer, the latter courtesy of his Marine Corps connections. Since it was now approaching 11 p.m., the couple decided they would take a rain check on their date until the following weekend so Cody could get a couple hours of sleep. Before she left, he asked if she would give the other two Volunteers stationed in Lagos a heads-up on what was going on if she ran into them

With a long hug and a warm kiss, MaryAnn said goodnight and motored off in her little VW bug back to the ambassador's residence.

Another lost opportunity, Cody thought to himself as he watched her leave. *Hopefully, this will turn out to be a big nothing and I can make up for lost time next week.*

As he climbed into bed ten minutes later, the last thought that entered his mind was about his missing Volunteer up north. *Where in the hell are you, Harper?*

CHAPTER 3

Early Sunday Morning, September 21

Benue Plateau

Ironically, an old poacher from the Bashiri tribe found the body, or what was left of it, shortly after sunrise the following morning. The elderly Nigerian was curious as to what attracted the scavenging birds circling overhead. An assortment of flies and bugs were already on the job.

The remains were partially hidden in a clump of tall grass approximately five kilometers (3 miles) west of the kopje. Instantly recognizable as human because of the bloody outstretched hand reaching for the salvation of the sky, the corpse looked like several kinds of animals had taken turns feasting on the fresh kill. It also appeared as if it had been dragged to this spot. The partially-eaten young foreigner had the look of sheer terror on his face.

The poacher, in all his years of hunting, had never seen anything like this. What once was a living, breathing human being was reduced to a pile of rancid garbage. The sight, along with the accompanying stench, made the old man sick to his stomach and he retched. When he finally collected himself, the elderly Nigerian wrapped up the carcass in an old, ratty plastic tarp. After surveying the scene and uttering something undistinguishable, he tossed the bundle into the back of his small, dilapidated truck and drove off. Since there were no roads to speak of, the journey back to his little town of Kwanbo took over three hours. He arrived on the plateau at mid-morning and the day was getting hot.

The old hunter, after talking with his wife and several friends, decided since this was an ex-pat, he needed to get the body to the authorities as quickly as possible. He thought it would probably be best to take the remains to a police office in Jos, the capital city of the area. That would mean at least another four – hour drive to the south. He put the tarp-wrapped body in a wooden crate, filled it with ice, and put the lid back on. He filled his truck with petrol, grabbed a jug of water and dried meat to snack on, and then headed south.

ꙮ

Cody arrived at Ikeja International Airport shortly after sunup and well before his plane was scheduled to depart. Purchasing a one-way ticket to Kaduna, he was not surprised to hear his flight had been delayed for approximately one hour. "Figures," he mumbled to himself as he settled into one of the ugly plastic seats in the waiting area.

Cody remembered arriving at this airport, Nigeria's largest, when his group first arrived year and a half ago. A somewhat formal reception committee was waiting, consisting of two Nigerian National Sports Commission officials, a representative from the U.S. Embassy, a few photographers, and the two remaining PCVs from the previous group of six Volunteers. The latter of whom were scheduled to be out-processed and leave Nigeria within the next month.

Cody and his cohorts were initially recruited through newspaper advertisements and word-of-mouth. All of the prospective candidates came from America's west coast – Washington, Idaho, Oregon, and California. A total of ten were interviewed in San Francisco that spring with only five finally selected: one swimming coach, one basketball coach, and three track and field coaches.

Cody appreciated the opportunity to leave his teaching and coaching job at a junior high school and do something grand and adventurous. When the offer was made to go abroad and coach on an international level, he accepted the position unconditionally. At the time, he had no idea things would get this dramatic.

At last, the boarding call for his flight to Kaduna was announced and he made his way out of the unattractive waiting area and onto the tarmac. Although one could still consider it to be early morning, the day was already starting to get hot. At times like these, Cody remembered Lagos was only about seven degrees north of the equator.

After climbing the rust-stained, metal staircase into the old Boeing 737, Cody quickly located his assigned seat next to a window. He stuffed his backpack under the seat in front of him and tried to cool off using the ratty, emergency information pamphlet to fan his face. As he settled in, his thoughts again filtered back to that first day in-country and the circumstances which ultimately brought him to this point.

১৩

In 1970, the Federal Military Government of Nigeria (FMG) initiated a $100 million project to renovate and expand an aging soccer stadium in the Surulere section of Lagos into a modern, national sports complex. Completed at the end of 1972, the multi-purpose campus boasted a 55,000-seat stadium, an Olympic-size swimming pool, tennis courts, an expansive indoor arena for basketball and other indoor sports, and a separate building for administrative offices. It was a beautiful and impressive venue. It was also the envy of the rest of the African nations.

In January of 1973, Nigeria hosted the All-Africa Games at this showcase complex with forty independent African countries participating. The apartheid countries of Rhodesia and South Africa were naturally excluded. The high-profile event whetted the Nigerian government's appetite to prepare for, and make a strong showing at, the 1976 summer Olympic Games to be held in Montreal, Canada. To do so, they needed coaches. A lot of them. The Nigerian government was also looking at sports as a way of promoting national unity after the divisive Biafran Civil War that ended two short years prior. Sports and athletic competition were seen as part of the foundation of a new, unified Nigeria.

Cody remembered being told in their pre-arrival training that the Peace Corps role in Nigeria had always been somewhat controversial and complex. This was primarily the result of the 1967 civil war. Volunteers who were assigned to the eastern region called Biafra tended to sympathize with the local cause to secede and said so in a variety of ways. The war had already created a great deal of international attention. Especially since the Nigerian army was accused of various atrocities and other war crimes. As one might suspect, all of this generated negative publicity for Nigeria's military government. Something they didn't like one bit. The international press played all this up big time, especially since the unofficial death toll from the war was estimated to be around two million people and included a large number of noncombatants.

When the fighting escalated and things got ugly, the director of the Peace Corps in Washington ordered all the Volunteers out of that area and the remainder, scattered throughout the country, left at the request of the FMG. For several years thereafter, the governing body of Nigeria would have nothing to do with the American Volunteer organization. Their suspected involvement in the war left a bad taste in the mouths of the victorious Nigerian army who now ruled the country. Engaging in political activities, of any kind, and especially against the host government, was also in direct violation of the Peace Corps' "Prime Directive."

The three-year Biafran Civil War brought about a good many changes to the country, some welcomed and some not. The war left Nigeria completely controlled and governed by the watchful and suspicious eyes of the military. The mere mention of the term "Biafra" was considered somewhat treasonous. A great deal of animosity and "bad blood" still existed between Nigeria's ethnic groups as a result of the war.

A sparse collection of six Volunteers was permitted back into

Nigeria in 1972 to help identify and train athletes in preparation for the '73 All-Africa Games. But, as fate would have it, their activities were restricted and their movements monitored. They were not even allowed to call themselves Peace Corps Volunteers and were simply referred to as American coaches furnished by the U.S. Agency for International Development (USAID).

Initially, the plan to reintroduce the Peace Corps back into Nigeria, via coaching sports, was a noble idea, but soon developed its own set of logistical and political problems which could not be overcome. All of the first group of PC Volunteers knew the program, based upon the country's recent history and the minimal level of support they were getting, was essentially a shipwreck waiting to happen. Four of the Volunteers left the program early due to "low morale, personal matters, and logistical issues." The remaining two were the ones who met Cody and his group when they arrived that first day.

Because the new director for the National Sports Commission, Dr. Adeboye "Andy" Kutaya, received his bachelor's, master's, and doctorate degrees at American universities, he saw firsthand what it took to develop world-class athletes. It was Kutaya's objective to bring coaches from the United States and other developed countries to Nigeria to train his athletes. Understandably, he was under a great deal of pressure by the military government to make an impression at the upcoming Olympics.

When money ran short before he had all of the coaches and equipment he wanted, Kutaya turned to the American Peace Corps for help. Hopefully, the problems that plagued the first coaching group would not affect the proposed, new group. Unfortunately, that was not the case.

The Peace Corps leadership was so anxious to get Volunteers back into Nigeria they literally jumped at the opportunity. The organization didn't even follow their own procedures, standards, or protocols for inserting new Volunteers into a foreign host country. The application and initial interviewing process was primarily the same, but that was where the similarity ended. There was no formalized training, psychological evaluation, cross-cultural or language training, or posting evaluations. No nothing. Cody's group enjoyed a month-long vacation, officially termed as "orientation," in Washington D.C. while they waited for their visas to be approved by the Nigerian Embassy. Except for three days of semi-formal training in Accra, Ghana, that was it.

ꕥ

The one-hour, twenty-minute flight to Kaduna in the twin-engine Boeing was uncomfortable for Cody. The aircraft's air-conditioning system either wasn't working, was set too high, or possibly wasn't even turned on. A departure delay, the aircraft's uncomfortable seats, the airline's policy of allowing all manner of animals in the main cabin, and the bumpy ride all tested Cody's patience. The smell from the chickens, goats, and pigs was a tad much with little or no air circulating.

"Nigeria Airways at its finest," he thought. Cody was in no mood for such unpleasantness. He had enough things to worry about. As the aging jet made its descent toward Kaduna, Cody couldn't help but think Harper's untimely disappearance could possibly lead to the eventual end of the current program.

After a somewhat scary landing, Cody was met in the open-air receiving area by Jamie Hammer, who looked as if he had a bad night himself. After their initial greeting, they headed to the airport's café to get coffee and a quick bite to eat.

The normally-reserved Jamie Hammer was both embarrassed and anxious about the situation. He hoped he wasn't overreacting and apologized to Cody regarding his frantic call, attitude, and comments of the previous night. He was also genuinely worried about his friend and fellow Volunteer. Cody could see Jamie was sincere, as well as somewhat distraught, so he excused Jamie's actions and reassured him that he did the right thing.

Jamie was recruited like most of the other Volunteers. Straight out of college and looking to build his resume, he was convinced to take the big step by his mother, who told him now was the time to see the world. Hammer's specialty was in track and field's throwing events and he could chuck a javelin with the best of them.

Though a little under six feet tall and weighing around 195 pounds, Hammer was solid muscle, yet as agile as a cat. He was also fairly good-looking, in a boyish kind of way. People were always teasing him because he resembled the American actor Tom Selleck with his short-cropped curly hair and trendy mustache. Good-natured with a self-deprecating sense of humor, Hammer was the most down-to-earth member of the group. Always looking for the good side in people, he tended to wear his emotions close to the surface. Which explained his concern regarding the missing Danny Harper.

"Any news?" asked Cody after their initial greeting.

"Not as of an hour ago," Jamie replied, shaking his head. "I thought we should head over to the consulate right after we get something to eat."

Somewhat panicky, Jamie had phoned the local consulate officer at his home late Saturday afternoon when Harper failed to show. He was at a loss as to what else to do. Hammer told the officer his concerns and asked him if he had heard anything or if he could contact someone who might know something. The officer agreed to meet Jamie later that day at the consulate so he could get the details and then let Hammer call the embassy in Lagos. Without realizing it at the time, Hammer had set a few wheels in motion.

"I was thinking the same thing," Cody said. "Are you and your rig ready to go if we have to drive to Bauchi?"

"Yeah, it's ready. But I'm not sure I'm up for this trip." Jamie rubbed his tired-looking face with both hands, his anxiety making him slightly fidgety.

"I hear you." Cody sympathized. "I'm hopeful this will turn out to be a big, fat nothing and at the same time I'm scared to death something bad may have happened to Danny."

The thought had crossed the minds of both Volunteers that Harper might have been in an open road accident. Nigerian highways and drivers were notoriously dangerous. Most of the paved roads that connected the towns and cities were poorly maintained and amounted to no more than a busted-up, single-wide lane with a great many potholes and few shoulders. There were no signs to indicate blind corners, random road hazards, or anything of the sort. In addition, most roads and highways were neither patrolled nor were there any posted speed limits. Nigerian drivers typically drove like the devil himself was chasing them and had no regard for "right-of-way" or any other driving courtesies. Most did not even have any type of driver's training or even a legitimate license. Driving on the open roads of Nigeria was a virtual free-for-all.

To add to the general chaos, pedestrians were on their own when it came to walking along roads or while crossing streets. The reasoning behind this unwritten rule was fairly simplistic: It was easier for an individual on foot to look out for his or her own safety as opposed to expecting a two-thousand-pound vehicle to come to a complete stop and impede traffic flow. Vehicles, not people or bikes, had the right-of-way and simply ruled the road.

As a consequence, accidents usually went unreported. Except perhaps in the towns and cities. As one might expect, the result was a great number of "fender-benders", hit-and-runs, wrecked and abandoned vehicles, and fatalities. One took one's life into their own hands when behind the wheel or when crossing a street or road in Nigeria.

Both Volunteers sat down at a small table in the airport's seedy little café and ordered the "European Breakfast," which consisted of coffee, a hard-boiled egg, toast with an assortment of marmalades, and assorted fruit. The meal was unappetizing, the conversation was subdued, and both boys were primarily lost in their own thoughts. After eating their meager meal, the two young men left the eating area, walked out to the parking lot, climbed into Hammer's NSC-issued Range Rover, and headed into the city.

Kaduna sat on the edge of the Sahel region in north central Nigeria. Located in an area that was partially savannah and partially desert, Kaduna was an ancient city originally populated by members of the Hausa tribe and boasted a variety of beautiful, old world Arabic architecture. Parts of the old city still retained the original mud walls built to protect it. Several areas of the city looked like something straight out of Arabian Nights with its beautiful Mosques, ancient palaces, mud-walled buildings, casabas, palm trees, and colorful open-air markets.

The city was split in half by the muddy Kaduna River and, as a result of its geographical location, was a major trade and transportation hub between the north and the south in this part of the continent, which it had been for thousands of years. With an estimated population of over 150,000 people, the city was home to an eclectic mix of Hausa, Fulani, Yoruba, and several lesser tribes, along with a sizable number of people from all over the world. It was truly an old world, yet international city.

The trip to the American Consulate was fairly quick. Kaduna did not experience the same traffic congestion as some of Nigeria's other major cities and most of the roads and highways were fairly new. This was Jamie Hammer's posting location and he knew the city well. After a couple of roundabouts and street changes, he turned off the avenue aptly-named Independence Way and entered the graveled parking area of the U.S. Consulate. On a Sunday, there was an abundance of places to park. Jamie parked the Rover, then took a deep breath and exhaled slowly.

"Nervous?" asked Cody.

"Depressed," Jamie replied. "I was hoping to hang out at the pool of the Humdalla Hotel today with Danny drinking beer."

Cody had no reply to offer. He pursed his lips and gave Jamie a sympathetic nod. Then Cody slowly exhaled, got out of the Rover, and waited for Jamie to join him.

Normally, the American Consulate in Kaduna would be closed for the weekend, especially on Sunday. However, because Hammer had alerted the Foreign Service officer in charge as to Danny's potential disappearance the previous day, the office was open that morning in anticipation of their arrival.

The two boys exited the aging Rover and strolled into the one-story consulate where they were met by a plainclothes marine security guard.

"We're here to see Kenny," Jamie announced. "I believe he's expecting us."

"He is," replied the guard, a well-built, black corporal from Virginia. "Mr. Wagner is in his office. Go right on in."

Kenneth J. Wagner was a career Foreign Service Officer who had been with the State Department for fifteen years. Despite being thirty-seven years old, he was a young-looking, young-acting, solidly-built, single black man who loved the international lifestyle. Kenny, as everyone called him, was affable, level-headed, and well-liked, but was as professional as it got when it came to performing his duties. A Rhodes Scholar, Wagner was also an excellent soccer player, something he enjoyed doing as a member of a local team. Jamie considered Wagner to be a friend as well as a mentor. He had spent many an evening with the Foreign Service Officer drinking beer and playing poker with other ex-pats.

"Sorry, boys. No news," came the initial greeting from Wagner. "I just got off the phone with a colleague at the U.N. field office in Jos. He checked with the local authorities there, as well as Bauchi, without success. Your boy Danny Harper seems to have vanished into thin air."

Because this was typically a non-work day, Wagner was casually dressed, as was the marine, and neither looked any too happy about the situation or being at the office on their day off.

"So, it looks like we're taking a road trip," remarked Cody, slightly frustrated.

"Afraid so, guys," Wagner chimed in. "You should probably also know I filed a report on this with our embassy in Lagos, who probably also informed the Peace Corps field office in Accra, the State Department, and the main Peace Corps office in Washington. Even though we are not talking about an 'official' disappearance right now, everyone still wants to be kept in the loop on something like this. Sorry to put you boys on the spot, but you know how things work with the government."

Jamie and Cody stole a quick glance at each other. They knew all too well something like this was cause to terminate their work and justify sending them home. No matter how it turned out. A missing Peace Corps Volunteer was a serious matter, especially when missing Volunteers sometimes turned up kidnapped or dead. Cody was hoping Danny either decided to go off on some adventure or was holed up sick somewhere. He hadn't hit the panic button yet, but was starting to get that sinking feeling.

"Good luck and stay in touch as often as you can," requested Wagner. "That way, we can share whatever information we both come up with." Wagner gave the boys his business card with a couple of phone numbers written on the back.

"One last thing, Mr. Wagner," Cody said as they headed for the door. "I'm expected to show up as usual tomorrow morning at the sports commission. I should probably let them know where I am and what I'm doing."

"I'd forgotten about the NSC," remarked Wagner, "and please, call me Kenny. I doubt you'd be able to get ahold of anyone there today. I say go to Bauchi first, find out what you can, and then call the sports commission tomorrow morning. You can give them some excuse, like a sick Volunteer you needed to check up on and say you will be back on the job within a couple of days. That should buy you some time."

"Okay," Cody nodded. "I hope they don't ask too many questions."

"I've also let everyone I work with know I might be gone for the next couple of days," Jamie interjected. "No one at the Kaduna Sports Commission seemed to think that would be a problem. I'm good to go."

Wagner gave Jamie a sympathetic half-smile, knowing what he must be going through.

The two Volunteers thanked the FSO for his help and advice and quietly left the consulate. The mid-morning sun was turning the Nigerian Sahel into a virtual oven. It was going to be a long drive and probably an even longer day. At least it would be cooler in Jos. That is where they intended to begin their search.

Jamie and Cody left the consulate's parking lot at approximately 10:30 and headed south on Independence Way to where it intersected with Constitution Road. Jamie pulled up short at the intersection while waiting for an opening in the slow-moving traffic and handed a five Naira note to a pathetic-looking young woman dressed in rags who was holding a crying infant.

"You know, you're only encouraging them to beg," remarked Cody.

Always the sympathetic and kindhearted one, Jamie simply smiled and said, "I know. But I can't help myself. We have so much and they have so little."

Cody couldn't argue with Jamie's observation. Over the course of his tour in Nigeria, he had witnessed things he thought he would never see. Nigeria, with all its oil and money, was still a developing country that experienced malnutrition, poverty, homelessness, disease, and illiteracy. Although the Federal Military Government had put a high priority on correcting these issues and generally improving the lives of their countrymen, they still lacked the infrastructure to make it happen. Graft, corruption, incompetence, lack of technology, poor communication, and long-standing ethnic rivalries didn't help.

Jamie looked over at Cody, smiled, and then followed up with another sweeping observation. "You know, sometimes, I think as Americans...we take for granted what these people will never have."

The profound remark hit Cody like a cold slap to the face. Jamie had summed up in a single phrase something Cody had never considered.

The United States enjoyed an abundance of everything: clean water and good food, proper sanitation and world-class health care, free public education, comfortable housing, law and order, public safety, and a comprehensive transportation system. Everything was provided, standardized, and safe. People could find a variety of job opportunities and higher education alternatives. For anyone willing to apply themselves and work hard, the possibilities were endless. And yet, Americans mostly squandered away these things. They complained about the ills of their society, how their civil rights were being violated, how unfulfilling their personal situations were, or generally how unfair life was.

Too bad everyone in American can't experience what it's like in a third-world country. Maybe they would appreciate what they have a little more, Cody dolefully thought.

"Yep," he finally replied, "we are definitely spoiled."

Jamie and Cody stayed on Constitution Road as it turned south and crossed the muddy Kaduna River. The road emptied onto the A 235 Highway on the southeast side of the city, so it was pretty much a straight shot from the consulate. The A 235 was the major highway that headed toward the eastern part of the country and away from Kaduna.

Depending on traffic and road conditions, the 282 kilometer (176 mile) drive to their first stop, Jos, should take them approximately three hours, depending on stops. The U-shaped route would take them through, or past, the major towns of Kujama, Samaru, and Vom and put them in Jos somewhere around 1 or 2 p.m. that afternoon, where they would start their initial search for Danny Harper.

Starting off at a semi-arid and hot elevation of 2,080 feet above sea level, where the noon-time temperatures typically exceeded ninety degrees Fahrenheit, the two would slowly climb up to the cooler city of Jos at over 5,000 feet above sea level. In terms of elevation, Jos was the highest major city in Nigeria.

Normally, the two young men would be looking forward to a road trip of this nature. This was not one of those times.

CHAPTER 4

Sunday Morning, September 21

Lagos

The weekend duty officer at the U.S. Embassy that Sunday morning was a twenty-three-year-old Foreign Service officer straight out of stateside training. Weekend duty was a requisite for field training of new officers. It was considered by most of the staff to be onerous duty, but someone had to do it.

Young, cocky, slightly immature, and highly assertive, Mark Duffer had the reputation around the embassy as someone you should keep your eye on, for a variety of reasons. The older, more seasoned staffers referred to him as "Dufus" behind his back, while the younger staffers generally liked him. Not so much because he was part of their generation, but because he was witty, ambitious, always questioned the "status quo," and was the quintessential party animal.

When Duffer checked in with the marine security guard at 7:30 that morning, he was informed a notation in the previous night's shift report should be read. The entry simply stated the possibility of a missing Peace Corps Volunteer who failed to show up in Kaduna as expected.

"Big deal," Duffer quietly said to himself. He was no fan of the Peace Corps in general and especially the crew that was in Nigeria at the time. To his way of thinking, they only got in the way of real Foreign Service work and didn't appreciate all of the attention they received.

Duly informed, Duffer signed the shift report log and went

on his morning rounds to check the floors, various offices, meeting rooms, and storage areas to make sure everything was secure and nothing was out of place. When finished with that little, two-hour chore, he made note of such in the shift report, briefly visited with the security guard, then went to his cubicle on the second floor and read an old copy of Hustler magazine.

The U.S. Embassy in Lagos was one of the largest the Americans had in Africa. With a staff of seventy-five individuals, it incorporated the main embassy building in downtown Lagos, located on King's College Road, and the embassy annex, located over three kilometers (2 miles) away on the neighboring island of Ikoyi. Plans were in the works to build a new embassy on Victoria Island so both could be joined under one roof with room to spare. The Nigerian Mission was considered to be one of paramount importance to U.S. interests in Africa.

ஐ

Lagos was originally built on a collection of four islands: Lagos, Ikoyi, Victoria, and Iddo islands. Originally a deep water port city, the city eventually grew over the years to extend far into the mainland as well. With an estimated population of over three and one-half million people, it was not only Nigeria's largest city and its capital since independence, it was also the hub of a country struggling to come to terms with its own wealth and development. To understand Nigeria, one had to experience Lagos.

The islands that made up the metropolitan area of Lagos were separated by broad creeks that connected the Lagos Lagoon in the north to the Bight of Benin and the Atlantic Ocean in the south. The central part and business district was situated on Lagos Island, the largest of the four islands and home of the original township. The smaller islands of Ikoyi, Iddo, and Victoria were primarily residential, but also contained government offices, army and police barracks, higher-end restaurants, and most of the city's international hotels. All of the islands, as well as their access to the mainland, were inner-connected by a series of undersized bridges.

For centuries, Lagos was nothing more than a typical African coastal town of commerce, ruled by whichever warring tribe that occupied it at the time. In the mid-1400s, the Portuguese and Arab slave traders arrived and the little town quickly expanded.

The Atlantic Slave Trade, as it was called, reportedly began around 1470 and ended by the early 1900s. The business of buying and selling human cargo reached its zenith in the late 1700s before it was finally banned by England and then the United States in 1804. However, the practice continued on in various locations, including the Confederate South in America, until the end of the nineteenth century. The British finally put a stop to Nigeria's slave trade in a military assault on Lagos in 1851.

Contrary to popular belief, the European slave traders didn't go into Africa and shanghai everyone they could get their hands on. The supply end was provided by Africans selling Africans to the traders. It was estimated that over ninety percent of all the slaves who left their homeland in chains were thought to be either criminals or captured enemies from rival tribes.

Those who survived the trip across the Atlantic eventually wound up in a variety of places. The plantation owners in the four countries who colonized the Caribbean and West Indies received around thirty-six percent of the total number. The same amount as for the territory of Brazil in South America. The Spanish Empire acquired around twenty-two percent, all of North American received a paltry four percent, and the remaining two percent wound up in the Arab countries of northern Africa.

The British eventually colonized Nigeria thirty-two years after the 1851 assault on Lagos and remained there for over seventy-five years. When oil was discovered in the delta region in 1956 and independence was granted to the colony four years later in 1960, Lagos became the seat of government and the major trade center for the new nation. The city grew exponentially.

With its resultant expansion over the years, by 1975, Lagos had become the second largest city in Africa, after Cairo in

Egypt, a position which was expected to soon change. By some estimates, the city grew by over 200 people per day – although no one actually knew how many people occupied Lagos and its environs at any given time.

The first impression of Lagos many visitors experienced was that the city was immense, chaotic, dirty, smelly, and extremely crowded. One could experience countless obstacles to impede or stop even the most trivial of tasks. Long lines and bureaucratic entanglements were the norm. A person could stand in queues for over an hour at an international bank to exchange currency or to make a deposit or a withdrawal. To mail or pick up something from the post office requires a similar wait plus a "dash" or two to the right individuals to speed things up along the way.

Oftentimes, the power and telephones didn't work. There was no such thing as safe, potable drinkable water coming out of the tap. It had to be first filtered, then boiled. When it rained, as it so often did during the monsoon season, toilets would back up and the contents of the open sidewalk sewers crept onto the streets. Garbage was often dumped wherever one pleases, feeding a population of rats the size of small cats. Beggars, destitutes, and the homeless seemed to be everywhere.

The daytime temperatures typically hovered around ninety degrees Fahrenheit (33 degrees Celsius) with a relative humidity of 75-80%. One was wet most of the time. If it weren't for air conditioning, Westerners living and working there would probably find the climate totally intolerable.

For those hoping to freely move about in a timely manner, the throng of people and the hectic daily life of the city created excruciatingly crowded venues and crawling traffic jams, commonly referred to as "go slows." The streets and alleyways originally built during the colonial period were woefully inadequate to handle both the pedestrians and the vehicles that jammed the city sunup to sundown. Lingering exhaust fumes was another issue altogether.

Public transportation, except for the ubiquitous taxis, was virtually non-existent. Those same taxis tended to add to the general calamity of the city with their constant honking and rude, aggressive driving. Lagos taxi drivers, who were forever trying to find one more person to squeeze into their overcrowded, smoke-belching vehicles, were typically not even licensed or regulated.

Thanks largely to its oil wealth, Lagos as well as the rest of the country, had also become crowded with foreigners. Businessmen, bankers, professional tradesmen, contractors, sales representatives, educators, foreign service workers, international organizations, and just about anyone from abroad who wanted to get in on the action had flocked to the country since oil was discovered.

Lagos, and for that matter all of Nigeria as well, was not what one would call a typical destination for the international tourist trade.

The U.S. State Department classified the country as a "Hardship Post," requiring its junior Foreign Service staffers to work there for one year before re-posting. The higher ranking officials were expected to stay longer. It was good for continuity as well as for the career. Most, however, never returned for a second tour of duty.

Mark Duffer understood from the beginning, as did everyone on the embassy staff, what life in Lagos as well as Nigeria, was going to be like and accepted it. That was part of the job.

All negatives aside, from a political and economic standpoint, the American mission in Nigeria was considered to be one of the more important postings on the African continent. A tour of duty there was considered a smart move for one's career with the U.S. State Department. The endurance of being at a preeminent hardship post looked good on one's service record.

The extent of U.S. involvement in Nigeria was essentially predicated on the country's influence insofar as the rest of Africa was concerned. Not only was it rich, Nigeria's resume included the largest population of any country on the continent and the second largest standing army. The former British colony had a great amount of clout in all areas of African politics and commerce, all stemming from the fact that in addition to its population and military strength, it was also the world's eighth leading oil producer. Most of which, coincidentally, went directly to the United States of America.

Although the inflation rate in the United States in 1975 had dropped to less than ten percent and the price of gas was holding steady at forty-five cents per gallon, the Organization of Petroleum Exporting Countries (OPEC) had just raised the price of crude oil by ten percent. Oil was selling on the world market for over $13 per barrel and was expected to go higher by the end of the year. To make matters worse, King Faisal of Saudi Arabia, the world's leading exporter of oil at the time, had been assassinated in March.

The United States, understandably nervous about its long-term oil supply, not only wanted to strengthen its relationship with Nigeria, as well as that of all Africa, it also wanted to reduce its dependency on imported oil from the Arab countries. This was the situation which helped spark the construction of the 800-mile Trans-Alaska Pipeline. When completed, the pipeline was expected to move vast amounts of American oil from the Prudhoe Bay reserves in the northern part of Alaska to waiting tankers at the port of Valdez in the south.

Until the pipeline was finished, approximately five years in the future, the United States remained heavily dependent on foreign oil. This included the low-sulfur, Nigerian "sweet crude" which required less refining. America's growing thirst for unlimited cheap gas was apparently a major political motivator.

Simply put, this was the justification for the oversized U.S. Mission to Nigeria. U.S. foreign policy was committed to strengthening the relationship, as well as trade, between the two countries. It became a matter of national security.

Understandably, this commitment required a large number of people on the part of the U.S. State Department and its Foreign Service. It also required key individuals and a rock-solid organization. The close-knit American Embassy community in Nigeria set the standard.

Things were going reasonably well for U.S. relations until Nigeria's leader of nine years, General Yakubu Gowon, was deposed in a bloodless coup in July of 1975. For many in Nigeria's ruling armed forces, Gowon was too pro-American, too slow, and too indecisive to represent their country's best interests.

Being a charter member of the "Non-Aligned Nations," Nigeria also wanted to put some distance between itself and the major world powers. Additionally, a variety of unresolved issues remained between the two countries. These revolved around debt repayment, trade, and the American government's on-going and supportive relations with apartheid South Africa.

After the coup, the relationship between Nigeria's new government and the United States became somewhat tenuous. The Nigerians wanted to renegotiate past debts, raise the price of its oil, and reduce the size of the American presence, as well as its influence, in their country. They were also highly suspicious of possible CIA involvement in their internal affairs. Thus, the stage was set for a challenging remainder of 1975 for the U.S. Mission to this West African nation.

ഇ

Later that morning, MaryAnn Reed dropped by the embassy to see if there was any news regarding the missing Volunteer. She had a restless night thinking not only about Danny Harper, but what Cody must be going through as well. There was also the consideration of their lost opportunity. "Morning Mark," was MaryAnn's perfunctory greeting upon seeing Duffer at his desk with his feet up.

"Well, well, well. Aren't we a bit casual and just a little... hot-looking this morning?" came the coy reply from the rookie Foreign Service officer.

MaryAnn was in no mood to put up with Duffer's adolescent bullshit this early in the day. Especially this day. She knew, by way of the grapevine, that Mark had said on the sly she was going to be his next conquest. Nothing about the lanky, red-headed kid was sexually attractive to MaryAnn and she had rebuffed his advances on several occasions. Not taking the hint, the brash young FSO kept at it and thought it would only be a matter of time before MaryAnn came around. This morning was no exception.

"What's new?" asked MaryAnn, ignoring the comment and trying her hardest to be cordial.

"Well," Duffer casually replied, "I can honestly say life is good. So good, in fact, I think I'm wearing down from too much action, if you know what I mean."

MaryAnn didn't even flinch at the subtle sexual remark and without skipping a beat, responded, "So, you've finally learned how to masturbate, right?"

Mark Duffer, probably for the first time in his life, was at a total loss for words.

MaryAnn had the little bastard by the balls, so to speak, and couldn't resist a follow-up dagger. "How many stains do you have on that edition of Hustler, Mr. I'm Wearing Down?"

Duffer was busted. With a knowing little smile, MaryAnn abruptly walked out of the area that contained Duffer's cubicle in search of the marine security guard. Perhaps the marine would have some news about the missing Volunteer. She wasn't going to waste another second on the "Dufus."

"Good morning, Corporal Simmons," MaryAnn cheerfully said to the guard who was on duty.

"Good morning, ma'am," came the chuckled reply. "And now that the formalities are over, what brings you here on a Sunday morning?"

"Last night, Cody Armstrong got a call from Jamie Hammer in Kaduna saying fellow Volunteer Danny Harper was overdue checking in and might be missing," MaryAnn said as she leaned toward him slightly. "I thought I might stop by and see if anyone has heard anything."

Lance Corporal Jake Simmons knew, all too well, who she was talking about and what was going on. Simmons, as well as the rest of the marine security detachment, knew all of the Volunteers in Nigeria. They had all partied together on numerous occasions, did various activities together, and considered themselves friends.

Since the Peace Corps contingent in Nigeria was relatively small and depended on the embassy for support, all of the Foreign Service diplomats and employees who were posted there regarded the Volunteers as one of their own. All supported the efforts of the young volunteer coaches and looked out for them.

Simmons, along with the rest of his group, had been briefed on the situation the previous evening by their supervisor, a non-commissioned gunnery sergeant by the name of Ripper. They had been told to expect inquiries but were instructed not to give out any information to anyone outside of embassy and consular staff. Jake told MaryAnn what he knew.

"Kenny Wagner, our consular officer up in Kaduna, checked in about a half hour ago to let us know Cody and Jamie stopped by his office and are now heading to Bauchi by way of Jos. Wagner has been in touch with some of his contacts in that region of the country and, although no one seems to have any information, everyone is keeping an eye out. Nothing formal or official has been filed yet, just the notation that this came up and is being looked into. Sorry, MaryAnn, wish I had some good news for you," the marine concluded.

MaryAnn liked Jake, as did all of the marines posted to Nigeria and everyone else at the embassy. As a young black man from the bad side of Los Angeles, he didn't have a chip on his shoulder like one would expect. Raised by his maternal grandmother, he was respectful, polite, disciplined, and appreciative. He also knew the value of hard work, was tough as nails, and "street-wise." He could hold his own in any situation. Rumor had it Simmons was equally good with his hands as he was with a knife. Jake enlisted in the Marine Corps after dropping out of a local community college after just two terms for lack of money and saw the military as his ticket to a better future.

"Do me a personal favor, Jake," MaryAnn asked. "If you hear anything, anything at all, please give me a call. Other than spending a couple of hours at the beach, I plan on staying at the Residence for the rest of the day catching up on my laundry and reading."

"You got it. No problem," replied the corporal.

The marine was envious MaryAnn was going to the beach; that was what everyone on the Embassy staff did on Sundays, if they weren't playing golf or tennis. Simmons decided that since the next day, Monday, was his day off, he might do something similar.

"Oh, one other thing," remarked MaryAnn as she started for the entrance. "Whatever you find out, please keep the 'Dufus' out of the loop unless it's entered into the shift report."

"My pleasure," said a grinning Jake Simmons.

Instead of going directly back to the ambassador's residence, MaryAnn made her way home and prepared a lunch and a beach bag for the day's outing to Tarkwa_Beach. She slipped into one of her favorite bikinis, one with a colorful tropical pattern that was, more or less, appropriate for the venue. Then she slipped on a pair of nylon running shorts and headed out the door. She was hoping to run into the other two Volunteers, Ethan White and Monte Reynolds. A grin crossed MaryAnn's face whenever she thought of Ethan. Everybody loved the funny, outgoing Volunteer, but gave him a bad time about his last name, especially since he was the only black PCV amongst the other four pale faces.

From her flat on the southern side of Ikoyi to the Federal Palace Hotel located on adjoining Victoria Island was about a ten-minute drive, depending on traffic, which was always lightest on Sunday. From the hotel, she caught the late morning motorized launch, aptly named the "Yankee Doodle," across the Lagos harbor to the beach.

Tarkwa Beach was a favorite hangout of the ex-pat community living in and around the Lagos area. Just about everyone who was anyone would hang out there on weekends. After about a fifteen-minute ride across the harbor from the hotel, visitors disembarked onto a small wooden pier. From there, beachgoers made their way along a dirt road for approximately 45 meters (150 feet) before going through a gap in the grass-covered dunes to the isolated beach area.

The weather was a tad on the hot side, but otherwise perfect because of an offshore breeze. The beach was busy on this Sunday. MaryAnn saw a good number of people she knew, many of whom were from the embassy or the American business community. She found a nice spot, spread out an oversized beach towel, and unpacked her beach bag. Although several huts were located on the grassy high side of the beach which offered food and beverages, MaryAnn always brought her own. No sense in paying top price for a semi-cool Nigerian beer when she could have ice-cold PBR from home, she reasoned.

Having settled in, she was applying sun tan lotion when she spotted the two American Volunteers playing volleyball with a couple of off-duty marines down on the beach. She waited until they took a break, called them over, and offered each a beer.

"Have you seen Cody lately?" Monte Reynolds inquired.

"Funny you should ask," was MaryAnn's immediate reply.

CHAPTER 5

Mid-Day Sunday, September 21

Jos, Benue Plateau

Jos was the regional capital of Benue State and was a good-sized city with a population of a half-million people. Fairly modern, by African standards, Jos boasted a university, a zoo, a large venue for a variety of sports activities, three clinics, and two hospitals, all of which were fairly busy. The newer of the two, the Evangelical Church of West Africa (ECWA) Hospital, was the only one that had a morgue with a forensic pathologist on staff. The latter served as the official state coroner as well, which was pretty much a full-time job in this part of the country.

The old Bashiri poacher went directly to the first police station he came across, told them everything he knew, left the body in their custody and quickly headed back home. He had done his duty and was happy to be rid of his grisly burden. The ice-covered remains were delivered by the police to the ECWA Hospital's morgue shortly after noon.

"So, what have we got?" asked the hospital's director, a middle-aged Swiss national by the name of Henrik Kruger.

"The deceased," said the serious-looking pathologist, an Austrian named Hans Gruden, "is a young, Caucasian male. Age is somewhere in the mid-twenties and he looks to be fairly athletic."

"Time of death?"

"Based upon the state of decay and the rate of rigor mortis, I'd say expiration occurred around twelve hours ago."

"Any idea as to the cause of death?" pressed the hospital's director.

"That's an easy one." The pathologist nodded towards the body. "A combination of deep tissue wounds, blood loss, shock, exposure, you name it. From the look of the wounds, probably some type of animal got ahold of him."

"Can you determine what kind of animal?"

"No," The pathologist replied, shaking his head. "Possibly wild dogs, a boar, or even a Hyena. Hard to tell."

Sensing his reply did not satisfy his boss's question, Gruden continued, "I suspect the initial damage was done to his neck and face. I can't tell yet if it was a bite or a claw that did this. At some point during his encounter, I surmise he was so wired with fear and adrenaline he took flight. The ensuing rush probably carried him at top speed for a short distance before the dogs or some other predator caught up with him. That's when the real damage was done. Scavengers probably did the rest."

The director's face winced at the thought. "Any toxicology performed?"

"No, not yet," replied Gruden. "I was going to do a work-up sometime later today or tomorrow."

Kruger asked the pathologist if there was any identification on the body. "No, none," Gruden said. "I can ascertain, however, that our victim was either American, Canadian, or Israeli."

"And how, may I ask, did you come to that conclusion?" Director Kruger asked rather smugly.

"Well, the first clue," replied Dr. Gruden, "is the dental work. It consists of state-of-art applications and the teeth have been straightened. After that, by the way the deceased was circumcised."

"Circumcised?" replied an astonished Kruger. "How in the world did you determine the method used?"

"Well," came the somewhat bemused reply from Gruden, "we know the practice is relatively rare in Europe, Latin America, parts of Africa, and most of Asia. Also, because the practice is common in North America and the Middle East we can, through the process of elimination, determine to some extent, the origin of the victim. The use of the Shang Ring is a modern instrument typically used in only those regions I have mentioned."

"Shang Ring?"

"Yes," replied Gruden. "You see, the 'ring' is a special device which allows for the safest and cleanest way to perform the procedure. It leaves a distinctive and uniform circular scar that separates the head of the penis from the shaft...I can show you illustrations if you like."

"Some other time perhaps," came the terse reply from the director. *So this is what forensic science has come down to,* Kruger thought to himself, *identification by Shang scar."*

Kruger took one last look at the body, pursed his lips, and slowly shook his head. "So we have a dead and mutilated young Caucasian male in our custody who, in all probability, is a U.S., Canadian, or Israeli citizen. Christ, this is not going to work for me. I've got a team of people coming in tomorrow from the World Health Organization to investigate that outbreak up in Lassa. They undoubtedly will take up all of my time and most of our resources."

Director Kruger took a deep breath, glanced up at the ceiling, and slowly exhaled. "Dr. Gruden, I'm assigning you the responsibility of finding out who this poor unfortunate soul is, prepare the body and send it where it needs to be sent. Also, keep this quiet. I don't want to draw any unnecessary attention to us right now. Understand?"

"Understood."

Kruger nodded in acknowledgement, turned, and quickly left the tiled basement room they called a morgue. Hans Gruden, on his first real job since completing his internship in Innsbruck, shook his head and wondered where in the world the director could have possibly learned his people skills.

Gruden wasted no time in having his secretary contact the local international businesses, the local UN office, and the Embassies of the United States, Canada, and Israel. Word got out fast, and in a variety of ways, that the ECWA Hospital in Jos had the mutilated remains of a young white male who was found in the highlands.

ꕤ

Jamie and Cody were not particularly enjoying their drive up to the Benue Plateau. Normally, leaving the hot, semi-arid Sahel countryside with its scrub brush and Acacia trees for a cooler, more temperate climate would be a joy. Not this day. Both boys were preoccupied with thoughts of Danny Harper and what could've possibly happened to him.

Jamie had made this trip several times before and always looked forward to spending time in the high country, as he called it. Cody had been to Jos only once, but not by taking this route. He flew into the airport in Jos on twin prop, "puddle – jumper," and didn't enjoy that plane ride either. At least on this trip, he would be able to see the countryside, stop for breaks, and be in a more comfortable seat.

As the idle conversation ebbed and the landscape sped by, Cody's thoughts trailed off to what they had originally learned about Nigeria during their short training period in Accra. One of their sessions was spent on discussing the diversity of this African country with its distinctive and unique geographical regions and ecosystems, which he was admiring as they drove on.

Four distinct ecological bands that began at the Atlantic Ocean, technically called the Gulf of Guinea, worked their way northward toward the Sahara Desert. In the southern band, along the coastal areas, was where the mangrove swamps existed. This area was hot, wet, and inhospitable except for a couple of nice beach areas and some coconut palm plantations. Daytime temperatures often exceeded ninety degrees Fahrenheit, and if the mosquitos and bugs weren't too loud, one could hear themselves sweat in the heat with its eighty to ninety percent humidity.

Cody remembered writing a letter to his mother back in Oregon that, after spending his first week in Lagos, he felt like he was melting. Thank God, or whoever invented it, for air conditioning and ceiling fans.

North of this sweltering coastline strip, which extended inland as far as sixty miles (96½ km) in some places, was a lush area of tropical rain forest. Nigerians never referred to this area as jungle. To them, those only existed in the Congo and in South America. Jungles, wild and uncivilized areas, were located in less hospitable areas of the world, not in their country.

This beautiful region of Nigeria extended from the country's eastern border all the way to its western edge and beyond. All manner of palm trees, flowering bushes and trees, ferns, and other tropical plants adorned this segment. It was an area which was a bit cooler and less humid than the denser coastal areas.

Moving farther upcountry toward the Sahara was the Sahel region. This area was where the ancient cities of Kaduna, Kano, Sokoto, and Maiduguri were located. This semi-arid, semi-savannah section was home to a variety of scrub brush, Acacia and Corkwood trees, and a large assortment of grasses. The northernmost border of Nigeria was semi-desert, except for some of the hardier Acacia trees, thorn bushes, and sparse patches of grass. Here, it was hot during the day and cool at night. Such was the nature of the southern Sahara Desert.

The remaining area of the country, the Benue Plateau, was a shelf located approximately in central Nigeria and extended almost to its northern border. The region closely resembled the vast savannahs of East Africa. At 5,000 to 7,000 feet above sea level, the plateau was coated with a combination of woodlands, grasses, vast open areas, and rocky outcroppings. It also had a relatively cool, moderate climate compared to the rest of the country. Daytime temperatures on the plateau were an average of seventy to eighty degrees Fahrenheit with a humidity of around sixty percent. At night, the air would cool off enough to drop the temperature into the sixties and prompt one to don a sweater or light jacket.

Jos, the capital city of Benue State, where Cody and Jamie were headed, was located in the southwestern corner of the plateau.

As they motored on, Jamie and Cody took careful note of the numerous accidents and wrecked vehicles along the way. Both were constantly looking for a pale blue, beat-up Range Rover with the NSC emblem on the side doors. Their count included six accidents and over a dozen wrecked cars, trucks, and other vehicles, most of which looked as if they had been abandoned. This did nothing to ease their apprehensions about Danny until they witnessed a head-on collision between two bicyclists. The tension was momentarily lifted and they had a good chuckle over that one.

Typical for traveling in the Nigerian countryside, the two passed a great number of colorful lorries along the way. Affectionately called "mammy wagons" by the locals, these highly-modified trucks with canopied backs serve as the principal means of mass transportation in the countryside. Always adorned in brightly-colored paint schemes, these means of mass transportation always displayed any manner of items hanging off them. All lorries bore something profound, religious, or memorial, even a song title painted on the front and back for identification purposes. Their open backs with slat seats could provide room for as many as two dozen people, depending on what kind of livestock the passengers were hauling with them at the time.

By American standards, these open-seat trucks were totally unsafe and would have been outlawed in the United States. Especially by the way they were being driven. Since time was money, the drivers of these gaudy vehicles raced from town to town and back again, trying to get in as many trips and fares as possible in a day. They drove fast, erratically, and had a propensity to run other drivers and bikers off the road. Lorries had, over time, earned the unofficial and just title of Nigeria's "Merchants of Death."

The boys arrived, unscathed, in Jos sometime around 2 p.m., having taken their time and making several stops to eat, drink, go to the bathroom, and to take turns driving. They immediately went to the Benue Hotel, located on a hill in the heart of the city, parked the Rover, and headed for the bar. While Jamie was ordering two Heineken beers, Cody went to the lobby and made a quick call to Kenny Wagner at the consulate in Kaduna.

It was Wagner's sad duty to inform the young Peace Corps Coordinator that he had just received word from the United Nation's field office there in Jos that the body of a young white male had been discovered somewhere upcountry, west of Bauchi.

Cody immediately turned pale and started to get sweaty. A knot formed in his stomach, as did a lump in his throat. His worst fears had achieved reality. The hotel lobby grew small, cramped, and very hot. Time crawled. Cody could feel himself getting ill.

Cody finally broke the ensuing silence. "Is it Danny?"

"Don't know," replied the FSO. "There was no identification on the body and it was found all by itself out in the middle of nowhere by an elderly Bashiri tribesman. The remains were delivered to the police there in Jos earlier today and then taken to the local Evangel Hospital. The hospital just sent out a notification and are asking local businesses, the UN field office, our embassy, the Canadian's, and the Israeli's for help with the identification," Wagner added.

Cody stiffened; he knew what was coming next.

"You and Jamie are the only ones who knew him well enough to make a positive ID," Wagner finally said. "You two will have to go to the hospital, take a look, and report back to me. If it is Harper, I will report as such to the embassy, and after consultation with the Peace Corps, make the necessary arrangements for the remains to be transported back to the States and to his family. In the meantime, and until we know something for sure, I'm keeping this information in-house, as should you."

What followed was a long, reflective moment of silence for both parties to the conversation.

"Cody," Wagner finally said, somewhat apologetically, "I know this won't be easy for you two and I sincerely wish there was some other way to do this, but it has to be done and you guys are the only ones who can tell for sure if it's Danny."

Cody swallowed hard as if his world just collapsed around him. His eyes welled up with a teary wetness. He thanked Wagner for the encouraging remarks and said he'd call back from the hospital as soon as he could.

After the one-sided conversation ended, Kenny Wagner hung up the phone and walked out of his office to the reception area. He informed the young marine security guard he needed some air and was going for a walk. Saying nothing more than that, he headed out into the afternoon heat of Kaduna. The next couple of hours, if not days, might not be easy on any of them and he felt horrible at the prospect of losing a young Peace Corps Volunteer under these circumstances.

Jamie didn't like the look on Cody's face when he walked back into the bar. To Jamie, Cody appeared pale and sullen, like he had some bad news to relay.

Jamie never took his eyes off Cody as he carefully sat down, took a sip of beer with a shaking hand, swallowed hard, slowly exhaled, then spoke.

"Kenny Wagner has been informed by the UN field office here that an old tribesman brought in the remains of a young white man from up north," Cody said, sounding deflated. "There was no identification on the body and just about every ex-pat in the area has been asked to take a look."

"Dear God," moaned Jamie. "That can only mean...we're up. Cody...I'm not sure I can do this. The last time I looked at someone who was dead...I almost passed out. I had nightmares for a week!"

Cody didn't even look up from his beer. He didn't want Jamie to see he was just as shaken. The prospect of looking at whatever was left of Danny Harper had unnerved him as well.

The two just sat there, staring at their half-drunk beers. After an uncomfortable period of silence, Jamie looked up and asked if there were any additional details.

"According to Kenny," Cody went on without looking up from his now, sour-tasting beverage, "the body is in pretty bad shape. Something about wild animals getting ahold of it."

Jamie instantly turned white. "I can't do this. You're

supposed to be in charge of us. You do it. It's your responsibility!"

"Shit!" Cody said, slowly twirling his beer bottle in his trembling hands. "I'm not sure I have the stomach for this either."

Both just sat there in silence for the next several minutes, each lost in his own thoughts. They were finally interrupted by a waiter who politely asked if they wanted another beer or possibly something to eat.

Jamie said he felt sick and quickly headed for the toilet.

Cody paid for the two unfinished beers, thanked the waiter, and headed for the lobby to ask for directions to the Evangel Hospital. They were all of about fifteen minutes away from it. At that point, Cody admitted he wasn't feeling all that well himself.

Jamie was in the bathroom longer than Cody expected. When he came out, Cody was waiting for him by the Range Rover. "Want me to drive?"

"No, no," Jamie said shaking his head. "I'm okay to do my part."

Jamie was still of no mind to view a dead body, regardless of who it was or what shape it was in. Cody picked up on the innuendo right away, bit his lip, and just nodded in affirmation.

Jamie took the wheel and gingerly pulled the Rover out of the parking lot, then headed down the winding road away from the hotel. Once they hit a main road, Cody gave Jamie directions to the hospital, then sat back and tried to think.

The drive was short, but for the two Volunteers, it seemed a good deal longer. Neither one said a word as they drove on, each thinking about Danny Harper or how something so gruesome could have happened to him. The anticipation of identifying Danny's remains continued to eat at Cody's insides. His final thought as they were pulling into the hospital's parking lot was that now was as good a time as any to empty his stomach. He almost didn't get the door opened fast enough.

The ECWA Evangel Hospital was pretty much what one would expect to find in this part of the world. Originally built in 1959-60 at the tail end of the colonial days, the 150-bed, public hospital was known locally as Jankwano, meaning "Red Roof" in Hausa. With the exception of the former British Governor's home, the hospital was one of the first buildings in the area to have a corrugated tin roof. It was painted red for easy identification, but then faded and became rusty after its first rainy season. Over the years, the building was kept up and made fairly modern by the Evangelical Church of West Africa (ECWA) and boasted an international medical staff with Nigerian support.

The two-story building also had a partial basement, the coolest area in a hospital which was only partially air-conditioned. Because of this, half of the basement was set up to be a morgue while the rest was used to store temperature-sensitive medicines. Since electrical service from NEPA, the Nigerian Electrical Power Authority (sarcastically referred to as "never, ever, power anytime" by most), was spasmodic and unreliable, this perpetually cool area of the hospital was the most practical place to store the dead. The back-up generator, when operational, was not large enough to serve the entire hospital, but the special cadaver refrigerator in the basement was on its grid.

In this cooler space, Cody and Jamie met the kindly Dr. Gruden.

"Thank you for coming. I am extremely sorry you have to do this," apologized Hans Gruden. "I was hoping for documentation, like a passport or international driver's license, something to identify the deceased. I do not like subjecting family or friends to this. It is very upsetting for everyone."

Jamie and Cody both expressed their acknowledgement and appreciation at the sentiment. They didn't want to be subjected to it either.

"How do we proceed?" a nervous and choked-up Cody tentatively asked.

"I have prepared the body as best I can for viewing," said Dr. Gruden. "Everything has been covered up except for the head and the hand, so it should be fairly obvious if this is someone you know."

Jamie spoke up without even thinking about it. The statement came out almost as an automatic response. "Don't you mean hands, doctor?"

Gruden gave him a sympathetic half-smile and quietly said that one of the victim's hands was missing.

"Oh God," moaned Jamie as he covered his mouth with one hand and reached out with his other for a supporting wall. They had been informed earlier by Kenny Wagner that the body had been mauled and partially eaten by animals. The stark realization of what this might look like hit Jamie hard.

Tears welled up in Cody's eyes again and his lower lip quivered. This was something only he could do. Jamie was in no condition to see his friend Danny this way. It was a heartbreaking situation for the two Volunteers.

Dr. Gruden gave the two boys a few minutes to recover before he politely said, "Ready to go in?"

CHAPTER 6

Sunday Morning, September 21

Washington D.C.

Kenny Wagner wasn't kidding when he told Jamie and Cody that everyone liked to be kept in the loop, especially when it concerned something like a Peace Corps Volunteer who might be missing.

As soon as he notified the U.S. Embassy in Lagos of the situation, the duty officer entered it into the daily shift report and informed the deputy chief of mission, Michael Olvera, at his home. Because Ambassador Murray was in Italy on vacation, DCM Olvera was in charge of the U.S. Mission in Nigeria, which also included the consulates in Ibadan and Kaduna. In addition to his temporary "ambassadorial duties," Olvera was also responsible, directly or indirectly, for all government-sponsored personnel in the country. This included the marine security guard detachment, any representatives of the armed forces, USIS and USAID personnel, and all Peace Corps people.

Olvera was a tall, lanky, mild-mannered Texan in his early fifties who could trace his ancestry back to the days of the Alamo. He was a career diplomat who graduated with honors from the prestigious Georgetown University in Washington D.C. with a degree in international studies. Olvera had a quiet, easy-going, yet professional approach to his role as the day-to-day manager of the embassy. Because of his outgoing personality and management style, he was highly thought of by all those who worked with him.

Because of his distinctive, hands-on approach to his duties, the affable DCM could tell you at any given time who was where and what they were doing. He took pride in the fact he could remember the first names and most of the birthdays of his staff.

Since the Nigerian Peace Corps program was too small to warrant an official field office and staff, DCM Olvera was, to some degree, responsible for the small group of Volunteers who were in-country. Aside from his role as their unofficial supervisor, Olvera had a genuine affinity for all of the Volunteers scattered throughout Nigeria. He considered what they were doing a noble undertaking and was proud to be associated with this particular group. Olvera especially enjoyed the working relationship he had with the in-country coordinator, Cody Armstrong. The sentiment went both ways. The DCM was more of a paternal figure to the Volunteers than anything authoritarian.

Olvera immediately contacted Kenny Wagner in Kaduna to get the whole story and any recent developments. Then he sent out notices to the Consulate in Ibadan, the embassy in Accra (Ghana), the West African desk officer at the State Department in Washington D.C., and the main Peace Corps office, also in Washington. The embassy in Accra passed down the information to the local Peace Corps field office since it had the closest administrative responsibility to the Nigerian program. The Peace Corps director for Ghana, Hampton Belvoe, had to consult his manual as to what was required next.

Belvoe determined that no specific notification to Peace Corps headquarters was required at this point. He was unaware that DCM Olvera had already sent a cable to his parent organization. The Peace Corps manual called for a 48-hour window before a Volunteer could be considered officially missing and/or endangered. Just to be on the safe side, Belvoe sent a message to the West African Peace Corps desk officer in Washington apprising him of what he knew and offered to personally head to Nigeria.

Since there was a six-hour time difference between Lagos and Washington and a five-hour difference between Accra and

Washington, what was sent out Sunday morning from Nigeria and Ghana was received in the middle of Saturday night in the U.S. capital. No one there knew of the situation involving the Peace Corps Volunteers in Nigeria until the weekend duty officer showed up for work at 8 am on Sunday morning, 2 p.m. Nigerian time that same day.

ꝏ

Matt McKnight, the West African Peace Corps desk officer, was enjoying a leisurely Sunday morning breakfast with his wife, Cindy, when the phone rang. The caller was the Sunday duty officer at the main Peace Corps headquarters in downtown Washington D.C. Like all government agencies headquartered in the Washington area, the Peace Corps also had weekend staff in place to monitor and keep abreast of everything going on in their areas of operation. It was the responsibility of these individuals to inform those next in line, following a pre-determined chain of command, as to what was going down at any given time and place.

McKnight, teasingly called "Mac the Knife" by his fellow staffers because of his name and sharp wit, and also to parody Bobby Darin's hit song, *Mack the Knife,* was looking forward to going on a picnic with his wife and friends in the Virginia countryside this day. Because it was the end of September and the hottest part of summer was over, the McKnights thought a picnic in the woods would be a fun way to say goodbye to one season and welcome a new one. With one short phone call, all that changed.

A former Peace Corps Volunteer himself, McKnight jumped at the chance to go to work for the agency when he finished his two-year obligation in Senegal. Having experience in West Africa and a master's degree in international relations made him an excellent candidate for the desk officer's job. Although only twenty-eight years old, he was mature beyond his years. As a white, Anglo-Saxon Protestant from the Mid-west, McKnight was fairly conservative, practical, and pragmatic. So much so, the level-headed Matt McKnight was considered to be one of the best at his position in the agency. But, the position of desk officer meant he was virtually on call 24/7 with regards to the ten Peace Corps programs operational in the West African region at the time.

He was on the phone for all of five minutes with the duty officer before making the decision he should be at the agency to personally work this situation. After explaining to his wife what was going on, Matt insisted she go on the picnic with their friends as planned and to give him a call at his desk when she returned home. The pair finished their breakfast and while McKnight was throwing a few things into his briefcase, Cindy made him a picnic-style lunch to take with him Matt's wife was thinking this might be an extraordinarily long day for her husband.

During the entire eleven-mile, twenty-five minute drive from their rented townhome in Alexandria to central Washington D.C., Matt reviewed in his mind the events of the preceding twenty-four hours in Nigeria. Sunday traffic was relatively light on the George Washington Memorial Parkway and he made better time than he normally did on weekdays. With fewer people on the road came the opportunity to think and plan without having to dodge traffic and irritable commuters.

Taking the ramp onto the 14th St. Bridge toward the Tidal Basin, Matt's thoughts shifted to how Nigeria and Nigerians came to be. The West African Desk Officer needed to know all about the history of the region as well as that of each host country, so he became a student and somewhat of an expert on the area.

In the mid-1800s, while America was itself embroiled in a civil war, certain political and economic events in Europe created a frenzied competition among nations to expand their influence. This amounted to a global land-grabbing era of empire-building and colonialism that stretched around the globe.

Conflicting land claims led to disputes and, quite often, disputes led to armed conflict. Reaching a breaking point, the various new and on-going claims for the African territories were finally settled at the infamous Berlin Conference of 1884-85. All of Africa was neatly split up into colonies of various sizes, shapes, and worth by the five principal European powers in attendance: Great Britain, Belgium, Germany, Portugal, and France. Borders were drawn up that either combined rival tribes or split up long-existing tribal lands and families. The map of Africa had been neatly divided up and colored in to suit everyone except the Africans. As a result, the stage was set for a variety of future problems. Nigeria was no exception.

The new British colony of Nigeria unwittingly combined over three hundred different tribal groups scattered over a diverse landscape of 357,000 square miles. This was an area about the size of California, Nevada, and Arizona combined. Some of the major tribes; Yoruba, Ibo, Edo, Gwari, Hausa, and Fulani either co-existed or didn't get along at all. In fact, many had been warring for centuries. Thanks to a high-stakes international crap game, they were all corralled together into a new European colony.

The groundwork had thus been laid for a future of turmoil once independence was granted. For Nigeria, this included a series of hostile ethnic rivalries, military rule, *coup d' etat,* political assassinations, anarchy, and civil war.

As McKnight headed north, he could clearly see the Tidal Basin and the Jefferson Memorial off to his immediate left-hand side. After another few minutes of driving, he saw the landmark of the Washington Monument off to his left as well. Then the Ellipse came into view along with the back of the White House. When he reached "K" Street, he turned left and headed west to Peace Corps HQ. Three blocks away from the White House, he turned into the basement garage of the organization's nondescript headquarters at the corner of Connecticut and "K" Street.

Since this was a Sunday, McKnight had to be buzzed into the building at the main basement entrance by a security officer. After displaying his credentials and signing in, he headed to his department located on the third floor. He was met there by one of the agency's Sunday duty officers (DO).

Offering Matt a cup of freshly-brewed coffee, the DO briefed him on the cable traffic that came in during the night, which was pretty much what the officer told him on the phone about an hour earlier. The last word they received came from a concerned consular officer named Kenny Wagner who reported that one of the hospitals in Jos had the body of a young white man who fit the description of Harper, yet needed to be positively identified. Wagner said PCVs Armstrong and Hammer were en route to Jos and would check back in when they arrived. Wagner planned on having the two Volunteers verify if the body was that of the missing Danny Harper.

McKnight paced back and forth, trying to sort out all of this in his mind. "Jesus," he quietly said to himself, "what a friggin' mess."

McKnight tried to put a timeline on things. He knew from experience the drive time from Bauchi to Kaduna, via Jos, should only take about four hours, depending on traffic, road conditions, and stops. If Harper left Bauchi early, before it got hot, say around 7 or 8 am, then he should have been in Kaduna sometime around noon or shortly thereafter. Since Harper failed to show up or call by evening, something serious may have happened. Matt's mind automatically went back to the part about the unidentified body in Jos.

The first thing McKnight thought of, Armstrong and Hammer, was Harper was involved in some kind of open road accident. All manner of scenarios ran through his mind. The first two being the most obvious: either his vehicle had broken down somewhere along the way or he had indeed been in a bona fide Nigerian highway disaster. Again, he thought of the dead body in the Nigerian hospital.

Then a chill ran down his spine as he remembered the story of a British contract worker who was beaten to death in one of Nigeria's remote areas a few years back.

If he remembered the account correctly, a citizen of the U.K., who was working on a road development project in the far, northwestern town of Sokoto, was bludgeoned to a bloody pulp by an angry mob of local villagers. Evidently, the poor Brit had stopped to render aid to a young boy he accidentally struck with his truck. One witness claims the boy ran across the road trying to catch a runaway chicken when he was hit. A group of men and women clubbed and stoned the poor bastard to death on the spot. It was deemed to be just another case of "instantaneous Nigerian road justice" by the authorities and no charges were ever brought to bear, regardless of who was at fault.

All of the Volunteers headed to Nigeria were warned about this. They were further instructed that if they ever got into a serious accident or situation not to stop and offer help, but to immediately leave the scene, head for the nearest friendly consulate or embassy and they would be whisked out of the country as quickly as possible. A few well-placed bribes would be made and the whole incident would simply vanish. The last thing one wanted to do was get caught out in the open by a distraught mob out for blood.

McKnight had the sinking feeling the body at the hospital in Jos might be that of the missing volunteer. "What in the hell happened to you, Harper?" he said aloud to no one in particular.

Although there were standard protocols and written procedures to follow in circumstances like this, a good number of things were still left to the discretion of the powers that be. And it all started with the respective desk officer, namely, one Matt McKnight.

McKnight began by consulting "The Book," the voluminous Peace Corps manual, and found what he was looking for in Book #1, Chapter 400, Section 426: Overseas Deaths, Critical Injuries, and Disappearances. He also took a look at Chapter 600, Section 636: Staff Emergency Visitation Travel, just in case he needed to make a quick trip to Africa.

Matt thought it through once again and decided the next thing he should probably do was protect his own butt. What they referred to in government work as "CYA" or "cover your ass," and inform his boss what was going on. He called West African Regional Director, Ronald Gerrard, at his home in Arlington, Virginia and told him what was up. The first question Gerrard asked Matt was if someone had officially started the countdown clock.

The infamous "48-hour clock" was a procedural item that meant no direct or official action would be taken for two days, giving the missing person a reasonable amount of time to resurface before an all-out manhunt was put into effect. In the States, a missing person's report could not be filed for twenty-four hours, but overseas it was extended because of how things typically worked in foreign countries.

"I don't think so," Matt replied.

"I think we should err on the side of caution and initiate that," Gerrard said. "Let's start it at 0900 hours, Sunday, September 21, 1975, our time, which would be 3 p.m., same day, Nigerian time."

"That will give us roughly a forty-five-hour window to see what turns up by 9 am on Tuesday." Matt acknowledged.

"I sincerely hope the situation will have resolved itself by then," Gerrard offered, then subtly added, "I don't think the agency will be too happy about this."

Both men knew the chain of notification within their organization at the end of those two days would also ignite a chain reaction within the State Department and other agencies as well. None of the participating groups would appreciate that.

Once the 48-hour "grace period" had expired, Gerrard was required to notify a bevy of officials, not necessarily in any order: the U.S. ambassador to Nigeria and his regional security officer, the Peace Corps' counseling and outreach duty officer, and the associate director for safety and security. The AD for safety and security would in turn notify the organization's deputy director and the chief of staff for operations. One of those two would brief the director of the Peace Corps on the matter.

Once all the principal players were notified, an action team would be put into place with Matt McKnight, West African desk officer, as point man. Anything and everything would be under consideration at that time: that the Peace Corps Volunteer in question was simply lost somewhere, had been in an accident, was incommunicado with any manner of illness or disease, possibly kidnapped, or even dead. Homicide was also a consideration because it had happened before. If they were lucky, the Volunteer was simply absent without prior notification. In government jargon, this was called AWOL, or absent without leave. On a couple of rare occasions, rogue Volunteers had simply decided to call it quits on their own and either headed for home or took an unauthorized vacation without notifying anybody.

Whatever the reason for the disappearance was, the PCV's next of kin had to be notified. Matt shuddered at the thought, as would everyone else in the loop if it came to that. The parents of Peace Corps Volunteers had a tendency to keep their local newspapers constantly updated on the wonderful work and grand adventures their children were doing abroad. "Positive PR" was both welcomed and encouraged by the Peace Corps organization. Negative publicity had the opposite effect, especially when members of Congress got involved.

Gerrard told Matt to do all of the necessary documentation and to fire off an "Eyes Only" cable to the Peace Corps director in Ghana and the embassy in Lagos informing them when the clock had started. When Matt got off the phone with his boss, he looked at the oversized series of clocks on the far wall, each representing a different world time zone. It was now high noon in Washington D.C. on Sunday, 6 p.m. that same day in Nigeria. They now had less than two days to find Danny Harper before the shit hit the fan.

CHAPTER 7

Late Sunday Afternoon, September 21

Jos, Benue Plateau

The overwhelming smell of formaldehyde in the hospital's morgue coupled with the thought of what was coming next made Cody instantly sick and he retched into a waste can.

Dr. Gruden had seen this sort of reaction before and felt sorry for Cody and his friend. Identifying a dead body, especially one that was in bad shape, was always an unnerving ordeal for those who had to do it. He remembered being part of a team who had to help identify an old man who took his own life with a shotgun. The body was discovered five days later by a neighbor who complained about the smell. He also had a great deal of experience in dealing with the carnage created on the Nigerian roads.

"Would you like to come back later?" he finally asked Cody.

"No." A somewhat embarrassed Cody sighed. He almost envied Jamie and his inability to deal with this sort of thing. It still needed to be done and Cody appreciated the doctor's concern. "Let's get this over with," he said nervously.

The first thing Cody noticed as Gruden pulled the gurney out of the refrigerated storage unit and uncovered the head was how pale and inhuman the body looked. Under the bright fluorescent lights of the morgue, it looked more like a mannequin than anything. The skin was a light grey, almost ashen-color, and lacked the normal lines and creases. Every feature was sharp and clear, making a positive identification by facial recognition fairly easy.

Dr. Gruden had indeed done his best to make the body presentable. From his discreet vantage point, Cody could see the facial and neck wounds were dressed. The rest of the face was cleaned, the hair was slicked back, the eyes were taped shut and, with the exception of the head and an exposed arm and hand, the remainder of the body was wrapped and covered with a pale green sheet.

At first, Cody couldn't bring himself to step forward and look directly upon the face. He just stood there, trembling slightly as he looked over the form under the sheet. He was also fighting back a growing surge of nausea. He glanced up toward the ceiling, as if making a silent prayer before moving closer to the body. Swallowing hard, he felt like he was going to choke on the bile inching its way up his throat. Despite the coolness of the room, little beads of perspiration broke out on his forehead. His palms were already damp and clammy. He glanced around, looking for a waste can if he needed it.

After what seemed like an eternity, Cody took another tentative step closer. Now hovering directly over the body, he momentarily closed his eyes, then lowered his chin and stared at the pale, lifeless face.

The last thing Cody remembered before his knees buckled and he passed out was that he didn't recognize who this was.

It wasn't Danny Harper.

The kindly Dr. Gruden caught Cody just before he could have seriously hurt himself, and gently eased him down onto the floor. After less than five seconds of semi-consciousness, Cody came around and, as expected, asked what happened. Dr. Gruden quietly explained to Cody he had fainted when he saw the face of the corpse. For some, a perfectly natural response.

"No, no. It wasn't that," Cody tried to explain, pale and short of breath. "This is not anyone I know. This is not the person we are looking for!"

"What did you say?" was Gruden's surprised response, now eyeing the body. "You say you don't recognize this person?"

Just then, an extremely distressed Jamie opened the

oversized double door slightly, peeked in and asked how things were going.

"Is it Danny?" Jamie asked rather meekly, as if he really didn't want to know the answer.

"No, it's not Danny!" exclaimed Cody. "It's not Danny!"

Relieved to the point of his knees also buckling, Jamie retreated into the waiting area outside of the morgue without saying a word. Slumping into one of the old beat-up wooden chairs, he started to openly sob with relief.

"Are you absolutely sure?" Dr. Gruden asked Cody.

"Positive," replied Cody, almost laughing in giddy relief. "I don't know who this person is. I've never seen him before."

"Well, alright then." Dr. Gruden wrinkled his brow as his shoulders sloped. "I guess I'll need to keep investigating this." Taking one last look at the body, Dr. Gruden solemnly covered the face and wheeled the gurney back into the cooler.

As the doctor and the two young men walked back upstairs, Gruden asked them to keep an ear out for anything that might reveal the possible identity of the dead man. Both Volunteers said they would and thanked the doctor for his understanding and kindness. Gruden returned the gesture, somewhat appreciative of the fact that he didn't have the body of their friend. Understandably, he was also frustrated at not being able to identify the corpse and be rid of it.

Once back upstairs, a very relieved Jamie apologized to Cody for his lack of fortitude and gave credit to Cody for doing what must have been a very unpleasant task. Cody simply smiled at his embarrassed partner and cheerfully said, "Not to worry, 'Hammerman.' Everything's okay. But you should know this isn't going to look good on your resume."

The ensuing laughter was exactly what both needed.

The two made their way to the hospital's main lobby where Cody asked the receptionist if he could make a call to Kaduna. The young Nigerian man behind the desk directed Cody over to a side cubicle with a phone on a small desk. The call went directly through to the consulate and was immediately answered by Wagner.

"Hi, Kenny, it's Cody," he said into the receiver when Wagner said hello then identified himself. Before Wagner could even ask what they found out, Cody told him the body at the ECWA hospital wasn't that of Danny Harper.

"Well, that's a relief!" was all Wagner could say in response. "Do you know who it is?" came the obvious follow-up question after a short pause.

"No, not a clue. Except that he's white, young, and well-built, just like Danny."

"Okay, that means we should probably start a search then," Wagner said, trying to think of what to do next. "Can you and Jamie do some backtracking, starting in Bauchi, and see what you can find?"

"I guess so," Cody answered. He hoped this wouldn't turn out to be a wild goose chase around northern Nigeria. Understandably, he was anxious to get back to Lagos and the unfinished business with MaryAnn Reed.

"You two," Wagner said with an air of seriousness, "are there, on the scene. You both know the country, the customs, and the people. Working together as a team, you and Jamie, along with what other resources I can muster, have the best chance of tracking down and finding out what happened to Danny. But we need to move fast before the trail goes cold. It's your call."

Cody sighed. Wagner was right. He and Jamie were going to have to mount an expedition to try to locate their lost friend. They were on the hunt already and stood the best chance of finding Danny. It was the logical, most practical course of action and Cody knew it. "Okay," Cody finally said. "Any suggestions or advice you might have for us?"

"It's imperative that you stay in contact and update me every step of the way," Wagner said. "I can also feed you whatever information that comes along from my sources."

"Sounds like a plan," Cody replied. "We'll start in Bauchi then. Since it's getting late in the day and we're worn out from the drive and especially from our visit to the hospital, I think we'll hole up here for the night and start first thing in the morning."

"Anything you need from me before you leave Jos?"

"Yeah," Cody replied. "Could you wire us some money? We don't have a lot of cash between us and we forgot to get some before we left. Since we don't know how long this will take, a little reserve would come in handy."

"No problem," Wagner replied. Cold, hard cash made things happen faster in this country. "How much do you want and where do you want it sent?"

"I think about 500 Naira will do," Cody said. "We'll probably stay at the Benue Hotel, so please wire it there."

Naira was the official currency of Nigeria and was considered to be "soft currency." It was only good in Nigeria. Kenny could have wired the equivalent in American dollars, or about $825 at the current exchange rate, but knew that whoever was making the exchange on the receiving end would take a hefty commission for doing so. American dollars were good anywhere in the world and especially valuable in Nigeria. Wagner knew this "commission" would not be as great if he wired Naira.

Being a late Sunday afternoon, Wagner called a contact he had at a local bank. Fortunately, the man was having a quiet afternoon at his home and took the call from Wagner without hesitation. He was, in fact, the manager of the Unity Bank of Kaduna, the bank which handled all money matters for the U.S. consulate there. Wagner could justify the expenditure and had the money withdrawn from the consulate's petty cash account. The transfer was arranged and Wagner updated his paperwork, then sent messages out to all of his contacts in the area, telling them of the outcome at the hospital and asking them to relay any information they may come across.

For the anxious FSO, it was now a waiting game. The next move was up to the two Peace Corps Volunteers in Jos. He was also hoping the missing Volunteer would surface somewhere, unharmed, and end this situation in a timely manner. He decided he should probably update the embassy before going home.

Jamie and Cody went back to the Benue Hotel, checked in

to a single room with twin beds and headed, once again, for the bar. Both were exhausted from their trip and the emotional strain of their experience at the hospital. They wanted nothing more right now than a cold beer, a good meal, and a comfortable bed.

After they finished drinking and eating, they stopped by the lobby to check on the status of the money transfer. Informed it had been made, the male receptionist had Cody fill out the required paperwork, asked to see his passport, and disappeared into a back office. He returned shortly thereafter with a large envelope filled with cash.

Cody counted out the money to verify it was all there, which it wasn't. The envelope contained only 450 Naira, not the full 500. When asked about the shortfall, the receptionist shrugged his shoulders, glanced back at the office, and said there was a "modest handling fee." Unperturbed and accepting the fact that that was the way things worked in Nigeria, the two Volunteers headed to their room, which was in a separate building.

The single-story, rustic Benue Hotel was a compound of twenty guest rooms bundled into five quad units and included a separate building for the lobby, bar, and small restaurant. The complex had a beautiful assortment of palm trees, ferns, and flowering bushes. During the colonial days of the late 50s and early 60s, it was an elegant place to stay. Although it was still fairly clean, comfortable, and fairly modern, the years and climate had not been kind to it. Still, the hotel's staff managed to keep the cockroaches, spiders, and bedbugs to a minimum. The small swimming pool, however, looked as if it hadn't been cleaned in a very long time.

ஐ

After the two Americans left his hospital, and with nothing else to do, Dr. Gruden decided that now was as good a time as any to do a toxicology workup on the, as yet, unidentified victim. It may have been nothing more than a procedural formality at this point, but Gruden was thinking the microscopic and chemical analysis of the victim's blood, bodily fluids, and various tissue samples would verify exactly how he died, if not provide more clues as to his identity.

Uninterrupted, Gruden worked fast and within a couple of hours had his preliminary results. Contrary to his original thoughts as to the cause of death, Gruden was somewhat surprised to find a high percentage of neurotoxic as well as hemotoxic poison in the victim's blood and tissue samples. If wild animals had ambushed and brought him down, where did he get these deadly substances?

His next step was to consult medical journals specific to West Africa, of which there weren't many in the hospital's library. He also conferred with several doctors on staff who had been in Nigeria longer than him. What he found out came as somewhat of a surprise. It also made perfect sense.

The decedent, what pathologists refer to as the dead, most likely did not die as a result of grievous wounds and blood loss, although those were certainly a contributing factor. The poor bastard, Gruden reasoned, was apparently bitten by a snake, and an extremely poisonous one at that.

According to the journals the doctor consulted, at last count, West Africa was home to at least sixteen varieties of deadly poisonous snakes. Of all the adders, cobras, and vipers, the one species that stood out to Gruden as the most likely candidate was the mamba. Their venom had a high concentration of both types of toxins and when they bite, they tend to inject large amounts.

Neurotoxic venom, Gruden learned, was a fast-acting and powerful poison that blocked nerve impulses to the muscles. It also overstimulated production of key neurotransmitters, which in turn caused a paralysis of the entire nervous system. This initially resulted in drowsiness, blurred vision, and difficulty in speaking and breathing. As the toxin worked its way through the body, muscle cramps and rigidity would cause the victim to seize up. Soon thereafter, the heart and lungs stop working.

Hemotoxic venom was just as ugly. It was also fast-acting and attacked the circulatory system in a unique way: It stopped blood from clotting and caused internal hemorrhaging. The victim's own blood vessels and veins started to leak, resulting in internal blood loss. This was quickly followed by tissue death and organ failure. Both toxins were efficient ways to impair and kill prey or enemies.

Dr. Gruden also learned, through his discussions with other staff members, that many of the handless and footless street beggars he saw every day were probably mamba or other snake bite victims. Apparently, instead of giving up and dying after being bitten, these poor souls decided to employ "machete first aid" and lop off the poisoned appendage. The good doctor was also surprised to find that around 100,000 people worldwide died annually from poisonous snake bites. A fair number of which, happened in Africa. Gruden decided to pay a return visit to his unidentified victim for a closer look.

Typically, an autopsy came in two varieties: the clinical autopsy whereby only an external examination, with minimal lab tests, was performed; or the more extensive forensic autopsy where dissection, organ removal (including the brain), and extensive lab work was done. Forensic autopsies were the norm in criminal matters where homicide was suspected or some other type of suspicious, unnatural death. Due to the condition of the victim and the obvious cause of his demise, Gruden took the clinical approach. Foul play in this case was never a consideration.

Gruden returned to the basement morgue and retrieved the body from the oversized refrigerator. Snapping on a pair of latex gloves and lowering the overhead lamp, the doctor pulled back the sheet covering the body and then completely unwrapped it. Per procedure, he began his examination at the top of the head. Gruden stopped there. It was not necessary to go any further. There, at the top of the head, about one inch behind the crown, were two tiny puncture wounds with corresponding discoloration and swelling.

The doctor silently cursed himself for not doing a more thorough examination at the outset. To him, it seemed all too obvious in his first inspection as to what killed this kid, so he went no further. Now, he was upset with himself for taking the quick, easy path and not being the professional he should have been. Perhaps, he silently said to himself, he was preoccupied more with the identity of the victim than searching for any ancillary causes of death.

Gruden went back to his journals and did more research. Mambas, he found, came in two varieties in this region. There were green mambas and black mambas. Which were not black at all except for the inside of the mouth, the body scales were grey in color. The black mamba was the larger of the two and perhaps the more lethal. Both were fixed-fanged, large (up to three meters or ten feet in length), territorial, aggressive, and fast. They could race along at 10-12 miles-per-hour, which was faster than most people could run. When they bite, which they might do repeatedly, they injected a large volume of venom into their victims. These were usually wild dogs, wart hogs, rodents, bush babies, small antelopes, and other snakes. Mamba venom killed these types of creatures extremely quickly.

Their standard modus operandi was to slither up a tree with a low-hanging branch and wrap their prehensile tail around the limb like a monkey would do. Being somewhat camouflaged by their coloration, when prey or a threat to their territory walked underneath the branch, they simply slid off the branch, swung down, and bit what was below.

That explained the head wound, Gruden reasoned, and how the victim, once infected and incapacitated, could have easily fallen prey to other predators and scavengers. *Poor chap,* Gruden silently said to himself, *he didn't stand a chance once he walked under that tree.*

Dr. Gruden updated his report as to the cause of death and took a variety of photographs to add to it. He typed up a memo to the hospital's director, Dr. Kruger, apprising him of the snake bite discovery. He added that two Volunteers from the American Peace Corps, looking for a missing counterpart, had paid a visit to the hospital. One of the two had viewed the body and declared he did not know who it was.

Back to square one, Gruden thought, as he pulled the

sheet out of his typewriter and placed it in his outgoing basket. It was time to call it a day.

CHAPTER 8

Sunday Evening, September 21

Lagos

After his phone conversation with Cody Armstrong and arranging for the money transfer, Kenny Wagner initially felt inclined to file an updated report to the embassy in Lagos. Because Ambassador Murray was still on vacation in Europe, he typed out a one-page, "Eyes Only" memo for Deputy Chief of Mission, Michael Olvera. After reading it over, he wadded the note up and threw it into the trash can. Considering the DCM's relationship with the Volunteers, he decided an "off the record" phone call would be better.

Ordinarily, DCM Olvera would be at the Ikoyi Golf and Country Club on Sunday evening enjoying a casual dinner with his wife and a card game with friends and fellow diplomats. Today, however, he decided to stay at home and catch up on a few outstanding chores and paperwork. He let the embassy DO, Mark Duffer, know he was home and reachable should anything come up, whether it pertained to Embassy business or news about the missing Volunteer. Duffer, in turn, made a note on the shift report and informed the marine security guard of such before calling it a day himself.

The telephone exchange system in Nigeria was on par with its electrical system. When it worked, the transmissions typically sounded somewhat tinny and distant. Mrs. Olvera answered the phone that evening and after the initial greeting, handed the phone over to her husband, telling him the call was from the consulate in Kaduna.

"Hello, Kenny, any news?" Olvera asked slowly and somewhat louder than normal as he picked up the call.

"Hello, Mike, just wanted to bring you up to date on the latest," Wagner replied. "Cody Armstrong and Jamie Hammer are now in Jos and will be leaving for Bauchi tomorrow morning. While they were on the road, I got a call from a contact I have at the U.N. field office in Jos. He told me an unidentified, male Caucasian body had been delivered to the morgue at the local Evangel Hospital."

After an uncomfortable period of silence, Michael Olvera somberly asked if it was Danny Harper.

"Mike," Wagner quickly assured him, "It wasn't our boy. It wasn't Harper. When Armstrong and Hammer got to Jos around 2 p.m. they phoned in and I directed them to the hospital to check. Cody got back to me right away and said it wasn't Danny, and he didn't know who it was, even though the body fit the general description."

DCM Olvera slowly exhaled a sigh of relief and closed his eyes. After a brief moment of silence, he spoke. "What's our next step?"

"I suggested to Cody that he and Hammer go to Harper's last known whereabouts and see if they can find out anything," replied Wagner. "I sent them money and told them to check in as often as they could. To my way of thinking, they probably have the best chance of finding Harper before the trail goes cold."

"Alright...well done, Kenny. Would you mind keeping me posted on how they're doing?" replied Olvera, trying to picture what the two Volunteers must be going through.

"No problem, chief. Anything else you think I should be doing?"

"No, can't think of anything right now," Olvera remarked, sucking air through his teeth. "But you should know Peace Corps Washington has started their 48-hour "Missing Volunteer" time period on this. We have less than two days to locate Harper, hopefully safe and sound. After that, they will instigate a full scale search effort, which will directly involve us, Peace Corps

Ghana, the Nigerians, and Lord knows who else."

"Boy, I sure hope it doesn't come to that." Wagner sighed. "Cody and Jamie will be heading out first thing in the morning and will start their manhunt at the teaching college in Bauchi, Harper's last known location."

DCM Olvera once again thanked Wagner for his efforts and told him to call anytime, night or day, either at his home or the embassy with any new information, and then broke the connection.

Olvera sat back in his chair, slowly exhaled and reflected on the situation. He still had a missing Peace Corps Volunteer and Washington had started the 48 – hour waiting period before launching an all-out effort to find him. In addition, an unidentified, Caucasian male corpse lay in a hospital up country that could pose yet another problem if it turned out to be an American citizen. "It's going to be a long week," the DCM quietly told himself.

❧

About a mile and a half away from the DCM's residence in Ikoyi, MaryAnn Reed was putting together a pizza and enjoying a beer with the other two Volunteers at the ambassador's residence. She had made the pizza large enough to also feed the two marines on duty that evening at the mansion. MaryAnn was kind of a "mother hen" at times to all of the young marines stationed in Lagos and they appreciated her attentiveness. They also clearly liked their pizza.

Both Ethan White and Monte Reynolds were in disbelief. First, about being in such a grand palace as the official residence and second, about their missing team mate. None of the three were yet aware of the 48-hour "grace period" before things got really serious. To them, it was already a bad situation and they were obviously worried.

Ethan was especially concerned. He was the last one to sign on for a Nigerian coaching slot. It was Danny Harper who encouraged him the most to take the plunge. Ethan's specialty was basketball and he played for a semi-pro team after he graduated from the University of Washington the previous year. He was so genuine and affable, no one would have ever referred to him as a "token" black in an otherwise all-white ensemble. Of medium-size, handsome, and athletic, the good-natured Ethan White took the ribbing about his last name in stride and referred to his fellow Volunteers as Mr. Whitey #1, #2, #3 and #4.

Monte Reynolds was, perhaps, the quieter and more serious of the group. He had a tendency to either question everything or study it to the tenth degree. Out of everyone in the group, he was the one who had the hardest time "acclimating" to the Nigerian way of doing things. On more than one occasion, he put his fellow Volunteers on the spot by his refusal to just "get along by going along" with the Nigerian way of doing things. He referred to the NSC, the National Sports Commission, as the "National Sports Confusion" because of their unorthodox approach to selecting and training athletes. Reynolds was a top-notch swimmer from Boise State University in Idaho and, like Armstrong and White, was stationed in Lagos.

Both White and Reynolds worked full time out of the National Sports Commission complex in Surulere and lived next to the stadium campus itself in a small, newly-constructed, two-story house. Both initially thought they must have been assigned this location either because of their volunteer status, or because they were American. Their house was directly across the street from one of the city's largest goat markets, complete with its noise, bevy of flies and trademark stench.

MaryAnn called the embassy while the pizza was cooking to see if anything new had turned up. Mark Duffer had long gone home and Corporal Simmons had been relieved by another marine security guard.

MaryAnn identified herself by name and by her embassy security password. Once the guard had verified who she was, MaryAnn asked if there was any news from either Kaduna or Jos regarding the Peace Corps Volunteers. After checking the shift report and log entries, he brought MaryAnn up to date on the day's developments.

"What's up?" Ethan was the first to speak up when Mary Ann got off the phone.

"Oh, boy," MaryAnn replied. "I really don't know where to begin." She had already relayed all she knew at the time when they were at Tarkwa Beach.

"This is just plain crazy," MaryAnn began, shaking her head. "While Cody and Jamie were on their way to Jos, a body with Danny's description turned up at a local hospital there. On instructions from Kenny Wagner, the consulate officer in Kaduna, the boys went to check it out. Now, before you guys go ape-shit on me, let me say it wasn't Danny. No one seems to know who it is, but it's not Danny!"

A building of tension had tightened the men's shoulders and faces, followed by an extreme sigh of relief at the news.

"Wait, there's more." MaryAnn held up a hand and continued, "Wagner sent Cody and Jamie off to Bauchi, Danny's last known location, to see if they can find anything. They'll be leaving from Jos first thing tomorrow morning."

Predictably, Ethan spoke up. "Maybe Monte and I should hightail it up there and see if we can help out!"

"Normally, I would be inclined to agree with you," MaryAnn remarked, acknowledging his offer with a nod. "But not this time. Not only will it take you guys a day and a half of driving to get to Jos, but also the exposure you'd be facing on the open road is kind of unwarranted. Besides, what can you do that Cody and Jamie aren't already doing?"

Neither Volunteer could argue with the logic of MaryAnn's thinking. "There's one more thing you should know," she added, lowering her voice to a more serious tone. "Peace Corps Washington has been informed of the situation and has started their 48-hour waiting period before officially declaring we have a missing Volunteer."

Both White and Reynolds knew exactly what that meant. One of the topics covered during their training in Ghana concerned the serious subject of missing Volunteers and subsequent emergency procedures.

Since the Peace Corps began service in 1961, they were told

126 Volunteers had lost their lives in service to their country. Four of those deaths occurred in Nigeria. Two were male and two were female. Of the total number of deceased Volunteers, only twenty-three were reported missing beforehand, and all but four of those had been found during the initial 48-hour period. The group at the Ambassador's residence that evening didn't like either the odds or the statistics.

They decided the best thing for them to do right now was wait until morning, give Cody and Jamie a chance to find out what they could, and get drunk.

ꝏ

While events played out in Lagos that evening, things were more somber in Jos. Cody and Jamie got something to eat and planned on what they were going to do the following day.

The first thing they discussed was the equipment they would need. Thanks to Kenny Wagner and what they had between them, they figured they had enough money. Cash was always king in Nigeria. They had wheels. Jamie's Range Rover was up to the task and could easily handle a couple of days of exploration, provided they could find enough petrol. Clothing was not an issue, nor was food or water, they could simply pick up what they needed or wanted along the way from the small towns, villages, and roadside stands. They had maps and perhaps the most important asset of all, a Peace Corps field survival kit.

Jamie often remarked these little briefcase-sized kits might be their salvation in a country that was fairly inhospitable to Westerners. Housed in a tough, plastic case with a built-in handle, the kits themselves were more of a survival item than anything. They contained everything from ordinary first aid supplies to a field surgical kit with a ton of antibiotics. The kits also had a variety of supplements, antidepressants, antacids, sedatives, amphetamines, and anti-malarial medications. They even contained an oral hygiene kit complete with a fluoride gel. Last, but not least, the kits contained a variety of condoms.

Something that Jamie, for some unknown reason, always had in full supply.

Over their dinner, the two discussed what they were going to do once they reached Bauchi. They decided they were going to talk to everyone Danny had associated with while there, which probably included the patrons of the local bars as well as a few prostitutes. "Knowing Danny," Cody remarked, "that could take up a whole day we really don't have."

Jamie nodded in agreement. "Maybe we should confine our efforts to the teaching college there, the guest house where he stayed, and any known locals he hung out with." Cody admired Jamie's insight and agreed. The two finished their meal, paid the bill, and headed to their room.

They finally called it a night around 10 p.m. Jamie, dead tired from a day of driving and worry, was the first to turn in and was sound asleep within minutes. When Cody came out of the bathroom, Jamie was snoring like an old bear. Cody couldn't help but admire how fast his fellow Volunteer could fall asleep. As he pulled down the covers and climbed into his bed, he noticed his hands were still trembling. It had been a long and tiresome day. First, an early morning flight from Lagos to Kaduna, then a lengthy drive from Kaduna to Jos, and finally, the unforgettable experience at the Evangel Hospital. Despite his fatigue, sleep did not come easy for Cody.

He couldn't help but think about the upcoming day and the upcoming trip to Bauchi. This was foreign territory to him. He'd never been there nor dealt with the indigenous tribes of the area. According to Jamie, over fifty tribes lived on the Plateau, and the largest group consisted of people from the Gwari tribe. The area also accommodated a substantial number of Hausas and Fulanis. The Gwaris, Jamie informed him, were gentle, hospitable, and friendly people comprised of mainly farmers and were a fun lot to associate with.

Most of Cody's experience with the ethnic groups and cultures of Nigeria were with the people of the Yoruba tribe, the predominant tribe in the western and southwestern part of the country. The Yorubas made up roughly twenty-one percent of

Nigeria's population. The majority among all tribes. They were a friendly, colorful, and lively lot who loved their flamboyant clothing, music, and festivals. Depending on their heritage, they would either be Christian or Muslim and practiced, to some degree, tribal scarification. This ancient practice was done for either identification or for "beautification" purposes. Both were usually done to the face by either burning or cutting, sometimes both. One could always tell who was Yoruba by the scars on their face, especially ones from the older generation.

The groups, tribes, and people who made up the remainder of the country were pretty much foreign to Cody. He remembered from his initial training and from what others had told him, the south central area of the country was home to the Edo tribe, black as night and fiercely independent. The southeastern area belonged to the Ibos, where the majority of the country's oil reserves were. That, along with their long-standing rivalry with the Yorubas in the west and the Hausas in the north, was the primary reason for their attempted succession and the ensuing civil war a few years back. The northernmost area was comprised of Kambari, Kanuri, Hausa, and Fulani people. The majority of these were members of the Hausa tribe.

Cody thought of a remark made by one of the soon-to-be departing Volunteers when he first arrived in Nigeria. He was told that in all of Nigeria, the young women of the northern Fulani tribes were perhaps the most beautiful in all of Western Africa. Cody remembered both Jamie and Danny had affirmed this observation since both had spent time in the northern areas.

As he lay in bed and watched two geckos playing a slow-motion game of tag around a fast-turning ceiling fan, Cody hoped he would be fortunate enough to see one of these beauties for himself on this trip. It would certainly make the stressful business of tracking down their missing friend a better experience.

All things considered, Cody acknowledged, he really wanted to be somewhere else right now.

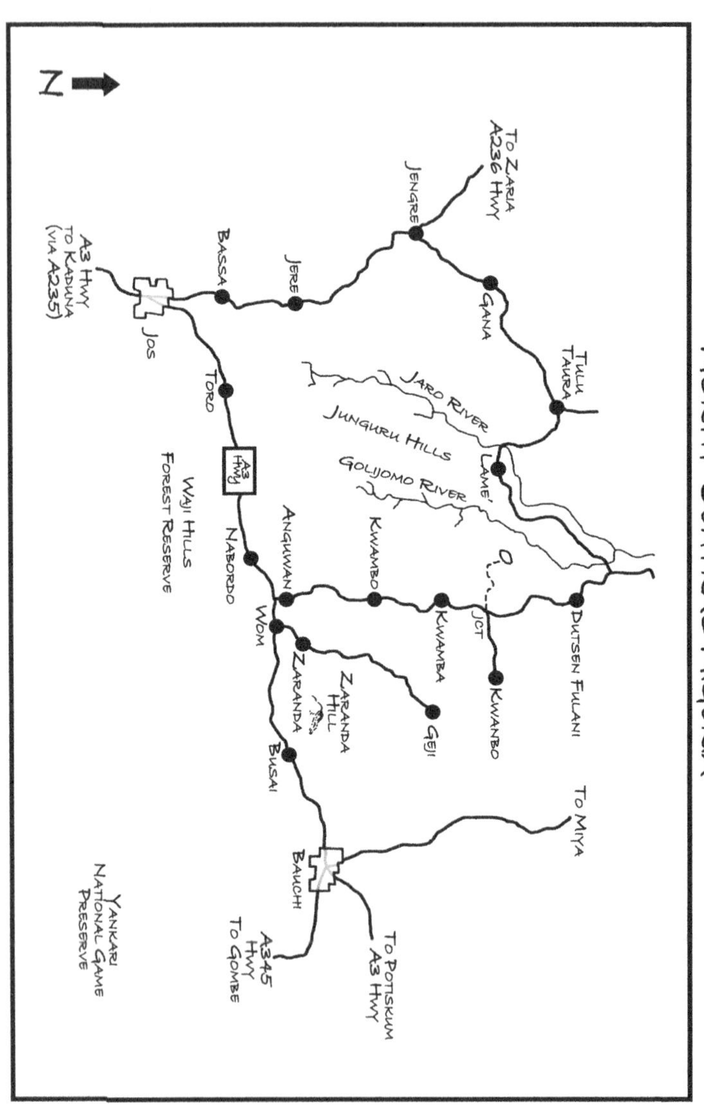
NORTH-CENTRAL NIGERIA
N
TO ZARIA
A236 HWY
JENGRE
GANA
TULU
TAURA
JARO RIVER
JUNGURU HILLS
GOLIJOMO RIVER
LAME'
BASSA
JERE
A3 HWY
TO KADUNA
(VIA A235)
JOS
TORO
A3
HWY
WAJI HILLS
FOREST RESERVE
NABORDO
ANGUWAN
KWAMBO
KWAMBA
JCT
DUTSEN FULANI
KWANBO
WOM
ZARANDA
ZARANDA
HILL
GEJI
BUSAI
BAUCHI
TO MIYA
TO POTISKUM
A3 HWY
A345
HWY
TO GOMBE
YANKARI
NATIONAL GAME
PRESERVE

CHAPTER 9

Monday Morning, September 22

Benue Plateau

Jamie was the first one up, abruptly awakened by a scruffy, angry-sounding rooster right outside their window. His first wish was for a shotgun. He would have loved to put that bird out of his misery.

It was 6 a.m. on Monday morning and the two Volunteers had a fairly comfortable night and a good rest. Both were now wide awake and anxious to get on with the task at hand. Jamie was the first to seize the bathroom and took a quick shower and shaved. Cody had done both the night before, electing to do his personal business before going to bed.

Cody found out soon enough upon his arrival in Nigeria, it was best to shave before calling it a night. Otherwise, if it was done before venturing out into the morning heat and humidity of the tropics, his face would break out. He also discovered, by way of an unpleasant experience, it was a smart move to always flush the toilet before using it, just in case there was something lurking under the rim. On more than one occasion, he had flushed down a variety of cockroaches and spiders. Once, even a small scorpion.

When they were finished and all packed up, they loaded up Jamie's Range Rover and headed for the hotel's restaurant. While Jamie was ordering breakfast, Cody went to the lobby, checked out, then called Kenny Wagner in Kaduna to let him know they were leaving for Bauchi and would check in when they got there.

Wagner subsequently informed the embassy in Lagos that the two Volunteers were now on the road.

Next, he called the National Sports Commission in Lagos to let them know he had gone upcountry to look in on a Volunteer and wouldn't be back until the end of the week.

Having done his check-in duty, Cody joined Jamie for a better-than-average breakfast of fried eggs, imported Canadian bacon, roasted potatoes, and coffee. When finished, they paid their bill then piled into the Rover and headed northeast toward Bauchi. It was 7:30 in the morning and, typical for a tropical country, the streets and marketplaces were already crowded with people going about their daily business.

From where the hotel's winding entrance road met a main avenue, Jamie turned west onto the Old Airport Road. At the intersection of that road and the A3 highway that bisected the city, Jamie turned north on the A3 and stayed on it until it branched off to the main Jos-Bauchi roadway.

As Jamie turned onto the highway and left Jos behind them, both men settled into the drive ahead. The trip to Bauchi, approximately 124 kilometers (77 miles) to the northeast, should take approximately 1½–2 hours. Again, depending on traffic and road conditions. Like on their trip from Kaduna to Jos, the boys took account of all the wrecked roadside vehicles along the way, looking for a blue Range Rover with the distinctive NSC logo on the front doors.

The Jos-Bauchi A3 Highway was pretty much a straight shot and the road conditions were some of the best the two had seen in Nigeria. Along the way, they passed several small towns, roadside markets, filling stations, mosques, churches, and a good number of people out and about. Since it was still early in the day, the temperature outside was fairly comfortable.

The two Volunteers relieved the monotony of the drive by sharing stories of their various experiences and observations while in Nigeria, as well as taking several pee and snack breaks. During a lull in the conversation along a particularly long stretch of open road, Jamie seized upon the opportunity and asked Cody about his "side business."

"Side business?" remarked Cody, not sure which one Jamie was talking about.

"I heard you were pimping a couple of women," Jamie replied quite frankly with a chuckle.

Cody winced. "Where did you hear about that?"

"From one of the marines," Jamie said, matter-of-factly. "I think one of those guys might have been a customer of yours. So, what's the story? Were you moonlighting as a pimp, or what?"

"Yeah, I can understand why some people might look at it that way. But, the truth is, I was the one who was actually being used."

"Oh, I've definitely got to hear this one." Jamie laughed.

"Okay. Just remember, this is not common knowledge, and I'd like to keep it that way." Cody sat back and crossed his arms.

"My lips are sealed," Jamie said with a smirk.

"A couple of months back," Cody began, "I was at my apartment one night, bored to death. So I decided to take the two block walk down the street and grab a beer at the Ikoyi Hotel. As I was walking through the hotel's parking lot toward the front entrance, a group of five prostitutes approached me. At first, I thought they were going to hit me up for some action. Then, the oldest in the group asked me if I would be so kind as to escort them into the hotel's courtyard bar."

"And why would they do that, I wonder?"

"Well, you know prostitution is legal in Nigeria," Cody reminded him. "But it seems 'unescorted' pros cannot go into any of Lagos' international hotels by themselves to conduct business. It's against some city ordinance or law and has serious penalties."

Jamie frowned. "And that's the whole story?"

"No, not quite," Cody said, shifting in his seat. "So, I escorted them in, we got a nice table at the outdoor garden bar, ordered some beer, which they paid for, by the way, and started to chat. The next thing I knew, different British, German, Japanese, and American men started coming up to our table one at a time and asking me how much for one of my ladies."

"Oh, bullshit."

"No, no, it's true." Cody shook his head and chuckled. "I told all these guys the girls make their own deals and I'm just escorting them, which was the truth."

"Really?"

"Yep, absolutely true. So, all of these guys must have just been looking for a quick lay or something, because the girls would all show up, one at a time, back at our table, an hour to two later. All except for one. Alice was her name. She was the oldest and kind of the leader of the group. She stayed at the table with me the whole time and kept buying me beer. I think that was just to keep me there in case anything bad happened."

"So tell me about the money part."

"Well, as each one came back to our table, they gave me a tip, so to speak, for making this a lucrative night for them. I asked Alice what I should do and she said to take the money or it would offend the girls. So I did."

"And how much did you make that night?"

"Oh, about fifty Naira."

"Jesus!" Jamie took his eyes off the road to stare at Cody in disbelief before looking back at the road again. "You mean to tell me you made the equivalent of seventy-five bucks for just sitting at a table with a bunch of hookers drinking beer?"

"Actually, it gets better. Alice and the girls, all of whom were attractive, by the way, asked me if I would like to help them out on a regular basis with similar hotels. And that, my friend, was the start of a nice little side enterprise for me."

"So what are we talking about here?" asked Jamie. "How long have you been doing this and how much have you made so far?"

"Oh, about three months, I guess. To date, I've squirreled away about a thousand Naira, somewhere around seventeen-hundred and fifty dollars."

"Are you fucking kidding me!" blurted Jamie, involuntarily swerving the Rover. "Let me get this straight. All you've done is escort this group to all the big, international hotels in Lagos, sat with them while they kept you happy with beer, and then paid you a nice 'dash' for your efforts? That's just plain insane.

Anybody else know about this?"

"Apparently, a few do. But I'd like to keep it quiet if you don't mind. I'm sure the Peace Corps wouldn't appreciate one of their Volunteers running a string of hookers on the side. That would be bad PR."

Jamie just shook his head. This was just too much to fathom.

Cody's other enterprise, the one Jamie obviously didn't know about, was the black market money exchange he was doing in conjunction with escorting his ladies. As an "official employee" of the National Sports Commission, Cody was paid every two weeks in Naira. In exchange for his signature on a voucher, he was doled out three hundred Naira, approximately $525, in cash. Since he had no housing costs, utility bills, transportation costs, or other real expenses, the only things he had left to spend money on were his food, entertainment, and gratuities for his houseboy. That, added to what the girls gave him, left him with a good bit of discretionary money to play around with, most of which, went into a savings account at a local international bank.

Since he worked part time at the embassy annex, where the American Foreign Service staff was always paid in U.S. dollars, Cody was all too willing to exchange his Naira for their greenbacks. Embassy staffers were always in need of Naira to pay for their domestic help, purchase fresh produce, and to buy other Nigerian goods and services. For them to exchange their dollars for Naira was a hassle that involved several forms to be filled out and sometimes a one – or two-hour visit to a bank. It was much easier for them to ask Cody to make the exchange for them and Cody always gave them a better-than-favorable rate. The kicker to this exchange also meant no paperwork or forms for anyone. It was a win-win situation for all concerned.

Flush with hard American currency that was good anywhere in the world, Cody would give his houseboy, Ahmad, one hundred dollars in cash every week to trade for Naira on the black market. The houseboy would spend an entire day at one of the local open air marketplaces doing business with his contacts and return at the end of the day with a pocketful of

Nigerian currency. It was typically a one-for-one exchange, one dollar for one Naira. At the international exchange rate, one Naira was worth approximately $1.75 in U.S. currency. So when Cody converted his ill-gotten Naira back to dollars he made approximately 75% profit. Naturally, Cody gave Ahmad a generous commission for his efforts.

At the end of each month, Cody would put most of what he had left over from these two moneymaking ventures into his savings account. With the money he saved from his living allowance, the two-thousand-dollar "Readjustment Allowance" he would get from the Peace Corps at the end of his service, and the money he made from his side businesses, Cody was looking to the future.

First, he was planning on spending a month or more in Europe instead of going directly back to the States and home. Then, he was going to buy a nice, affordable car and go back to college and work on his master's degree. At his current rate of deposits, he figured he'd have more than enough money to do it all.

ꟾ

Cody saw it first, somewhere between the small city of Magama and Bauchi. There, way off to the opposite side of the road and rolled over on its top with the front smashed in, was a blue colored Range Rover. His heart sank at the obvious conclusion.

Jamie pulled his own Rover as far off to the side of the road as he could and parked. Without getting out, both Volunteers looked at the wreck on the opposite side of the road. It was a bad one. It also looked like it had been there for a while and there was no National Sports Commission emblem on the doors. It also did not have a Nigerian license plate that began with the letters NSC.

"Nope," said Cody, somewhat relieved. "Let's move on."

Jamie exhaled with a long *whew* then put the Rover into gear and pulled back onto the road.

The two Volunteers arrived at the outskirts of Bauchi at about a quarter past ten. Jamie took the Old Jos Road exit and traveled southeast to the Eagle Roundabout, then got onto the main road of Ahmadu-Bello Way. Consulting the map they brought with them, Cody directed Jamie to stay on that street and head east until they saw University Way. Turning right onto that road, they went about one-half mile south before they spotted the campus of the Bauchi State Teacher's College (BSTC) on their left hand side.

Both Jamie and Cody were impressed with the size and style of Bauchi. Although it was about half the size of Jos, it was still a good-sized city with a population estimated at somewhere around 200,000 people. Set in a savannah landscape surrounded by low-lying hills, the city was not what one would have expected to find in this area of north-central Nigeria. Bauchi's main streets were tree-lined with a median park-like strip separating the opposing lanes. There was still an abundance, however, of streets and roadways of the packed dirt variety. There was also the absence of any grassy areas.

Mixed in with the old, were many modern-looking buildings. Most of the structures were no higher than three stories and still had the distinctive architecture of a Muslim culture, especially the palace of the Emir and the grand Babban Goni Mosque. Both equally impressive. The city enjoyed many European-style stores and eateries along with a small country club, of sorts. The city was like a smaller version of Jos. The campus of the teacher's college was quaint and park-like in places. Both could readily see why Danny liked to spend so much time working here.

Jamie pulled into the first parking area he saw and the two Volunteers decided their next step was to visit with the sports director for the college. After checking in with the receptionist at the administration office, Jamie and Cody were directed to the main sports complex building on the far side of the athletic fields. Crossing the well-manicured lawns of Bermuda grass, the two admired the assortment of flowering bushes and towering palm trees that surrounded the pretty campus.

The BSTC sports director had already left for an early lunch, but his assistant, a perky young Gwari woman, knew Harper well. Jamie and Cody, knowing Danny like they did, could only guess as to how that came about. When asked if she knew where Danny was headed after he left Bauchi, the young woman told the two Volunteers she overheard Harper talking to the director about a camping trip he was planning. Something about a special place east of the Junguru Hills.

"That's a pretty big area and out in the middle of nowhere," Jamie remarked. Cody had to appreciate Jamie's knowledge of this part of Nigeria and was somewhat envious of Jamie and Danny's ability to do all of the traveling they did.

"Do you happen to know how or why he got this sudden urge to go camping way out in Timbuktu?" inquired Cody. Jamie chuckled because he knew what was coming next.

"Mr. Danny," the young woman said rather incredulously, "did not go to Mali. He did not leave Nigeria. He went to the Junguru Hills."

Cody flushed with embarrassment. Timbuktu was the ancient capital of the old Mali Empire, located in the Sahara Desert five countries to the west. The term was an old American cliché commonly used to describe someplace remote and the idiom was unfamiliar to Africans. Cody apologized to the young woman and explained he was referring to "the middle of nowhere."

The young woman nodded in understanding, but remained unsmiling.

"Let me re-phrase my question," Cody said. "Would you happen to know where 'Mr. Danny' got this inspiration to go camping?"

"Yes," said the young lady, "I heard Mr. Danny say he was told of a place called 'paradise' by an ancient Hausa woman in the old marketplace. That is where he intended to go." The way the director's assistant said "ancient" and "Hausa" told Cody and Jamie she wasn't particularly fond of the northern area's predominant tribe. The young woman's Bashiri tribe was but one of the fifty-four minor tribes in a region dominated by the

Hausa and Fulani.

"That is all I know," she concluded.

The two Volunteers inquired as to where this marketplace was and how to get there. The young woman told them the Wunti Central Marketplace was on Abubakar Tafawa-Balewa Way just south of the big stadium. She said the best way to get there was to go back to Ahmadu-Bello Way, turn right heading east, then north on Abubakar road. The marketplace was right next to the A3 highway.

Jamie and Cody thanked the young woman and left the building discussing their next steps. Obviously, they would have to go to the city's oldest open-air marketplace and track down the elderly Hausa woman.

"I bet there's a great many elderly Hausa women in that marketplace – which is probably a maze in itself," offered Jamie as they made their way back across the sports fields. "How will we know where to go or which elderly Hausa woman to talk to?"

"We don't," replied Cody as they walked to the parking area and the waiting NSC Range Rover. "So I guess we'll just have to find our way about and talk to all we find."

"That could take a while," Jamie offered.

"Maybe, maybe not. We'll see,"' Cody said. "Let's find someplace nice to eat and get some lunch before we head over to the marketplace. The last time I ate off of a street vendor, I sat on a toilet for two days."

The two climbed into Hammer's well-used sport utility vehicle and left the campus by the same way they had arrived. Instead of turning right and heading east on Ahmadu-Bello Way as they were directed, they turned left and headed west, back toward the Eagle Roundabout on the western side of the city. Taking the second exit off the roundabout, they traveled for two blocks on the Old Jos Road before turning into the parking lot of the colonial-style Bauchi Club.

Jamie had pointed this place out to Cody as they drove in to the city earlier that morning, mentioning he and Danny had a nice meal at this place some six months back. It didn't take much convincing on Jamie's part for Cody to agree to stop there.

The Bauchi Club was originally built to give the Europeans, especially the British who were living in the area at the time, a taste of home. It was a comfortable recluse, if not an outright escape, from the daily African life just outside its walls. The club was built in the old colonial style, with an oversized British-type bar, a card room, and a small restaurant. Outside, it had a tropical-style patio bar, a nice little swimming pool and three tennis courts. Since it was almost noontime, the place was starting to get busy with ex-pats.

Once seated, both Volunteers ordered a beer and the same luncheon special, the celebrated club sandwich with chips. While waiting for their food, Cody took the opportunity to call Kenny Wagner in Kaduna and update him on their progress. It was now high noon in Nigeria and 6 a.m. in Washington D.C. on Monday, September 22nd. In another three hours, it would be 9 a.m. in Washington and they now had less than twenty-four hours to find their missing friend.

CHAPTER 10

Monday Noon, September 22

Bauchi & Lagos

Kenny Wagner took the call from Cody while he was having lunch at his desk. Monday was a typical weekday work schedule at the Kaduna Consulate.

Cody didn't have all that much to report, only that they made it to Bauchi safely, had gone to the Bauchi State Teacher's College, and found out that Harper was planning to go camping somewhere out in the sticks. After lunch, Cody said they would be going to the Wunti Central Marketplace where they were hoping to find an old Hausa woman who, according to the information they received at the teacher's college, had given Harper directions to some kind of oasis out in the middle of nowhere.

"Good work, Cody," Wagner said. "Do me a favor. If you find this woman, if her information is credible, and you can reasonably pinpoint where this place is, please give me a call back before you go off searching for it."

"Will do," replied Cody. "Anything else?"

"One more thing," Wagner's tone turned serious. "That body that turned up in Jos. The one you and Jamie went to take a look at. It was identified late this morning."

"Anyone we know?" asked Cody cautiously.

"Could be," Wagner responded. "It could very well be someone you or one of your people might have come across during the course of your work. It was a Canadian CUSO

Volunteer from a small town north of Jos called Lame. The Volunteer's name was Wyland Sinclair."

"Wyland Sinclair?" Cody said. "I've heard of him. Both Jamie and Danny know him. What happened, does anybody know?"

Wagner said according to Sinclair's roommate, who identified the body, he took off from Lame on Saturday morning to go fishing somewhere on the Golijomo River and didn't return by nightfall or the next morning. Just as in Harper's case, word got out that he was missing and that led to lots of inquiries from the Canadians.

Kenny had informed the Canadian consul general in Kaduna that an unidentified body had turned up at the ECWA Hospital in Jos.

Shaking his head in disbelief, Cody thanked Wagner for the update and said he'd call back if they turned up anything at the marketplace and then broke the connection.

Cody was turning over in his mind how he was going to break the news to Jamie when he got back to their table. Jamie looked up from his lunch when he saw Cody approaching their table.

"What's up? You have that look again," Jamie said, referring to the expression Cody had when they got the word to look at the body in Jos.

Cody swallowed hard and sat down. "Do you know a CUSO Volunteer by the name of Wyland Sinclair?"

Jamie stopped short and put down the sandwich he was about to take a bite out of. "Yes...why?"

Cody relayed what Kenny Wagner had told him

Jamie just sat there stunned, trying to process what was hard for him to comprehend. "Wow," was all he could say. After a brief moment of silence, he added, "I just saw him not more than two months ago. How could something like this have happened?"

Cody looked at Jamie, searching for something meaningful and comforting to say. He couldn't find the words. Hammer took a long, slow drink of his beer and reflected on the last time he saw Sinclair. Then the thought suddenly struck him: He could have easily identified Sinclair's body in Jos and saved everyone a lot of time and trouble, if only he hadn't been such a chickenshit about looking at a chewed-up dead person.

CUSO, the acronym for Canadian University Students Overseas, was roughly the equivalent of the U.S. Peace Corps. Like their American counterparts, they are part goodwill ambassadors, 100% true professionals, and dedicated to helping those less fortunate. Their declared mission was "to reduce poverty by creating sustainable livelihoods, eliminate disadvantage by improving access to education and healthcare, and combat inequality by empowering people and communities." Just like the American Peace Corps, CUSO Volunteers were all over the globe, most of which were in Africa and South America. Wyland Sinclair was posted to Lame the previous year to work on an irrigation project.

The two Volunteers finished their lunch without further conversation, paid the bill, and silently headed back out to the parking lot and their ride. The fate of the dead CUSO Volunteer weighed heavily on their minds. It was at this point that each one, separate from the other, realized they might be into something which was out of their league. Neither one said so out loud.

❧

While Hammer and Armstrong were leaving the Bauchi Club, Kenny Wagner was placing a call from his office at the Kaduna Consulate to the embassy in Lagos. When the connection went through, he asked to speak to DCM Olvera.

"Hello, Kenny, any news?" said the DCM as he picked up the call in his office.

"Armstrong and Hammer made it safely to Bauchi and got a lead on where our missing Volunteer might have gone," reported Wagner. "They're are going to check it out and see what else they can turn up and then call me back."

"And do you think we should send them out searching if

they uncover anything credible?"

"That was my original thinking, Mike. Do you have another thought?"

"I'm uncomfortable with the notion of sending two unprepared Peace Corps Volunteers on a manhunt out into the bush," Olvera replied. "The nagging thought we could turn one missing Volunteer into three keeps eating at me."

"I hadn't considered that possibility," Wagner said. "When they call back with any additional information, should I tell them to leave it up to the authorities and come home?"

"I think we should keep that option open depending on what they find out," the DCM replied. "Anything else, Kenny?"

Wagner then informed the DCM that the previously unidentified body at the Evangel Hospital in Jos was that of a Canadian CUSO Volunteer. The news did not sit well with the deputy chief of the U.S. mission to Nigeria. Olvera thanked Wagner and asked him to call back the moment he heard anything new. Then he asked his secretary to get his counterpart at the Canadian Embassy on the line.

MaryAnn Reed's and the DCM's secretary's desks were right between the open doorways to the ambassador's suite and Mike Olvera's office. Both women could easily hear the phone conversations going on in the DCM's office.

When Olvera finished his chat with the Canadian minister, he went out into the large common area where the two secretaries worked and sat down in one of the big leather waiting chairs with a heavy sigh. He knew the two civil servants were aware of the missing Volunteer saga and apprised them of the latest developments.

MaryAnn spoke up first when the DCM finished talking. "What will happen if Danny Harper is not found after the 48-hour waiting period has expired?" she quietly asked.

"Good question," replied Olvera, thinking about what that might actually entail. "I'm sure Peace Corps HQ will probably get in touch with the State Department and issue some type of 'all-points bulletin' or something like that. We'll probably be tasked to officially involve the Nigerian authorities on a search, plus whatever we can arrange ourselves. At any rate, I expect a few Peace Corps staff people to show up from some of the other West African countries to lend a hand as well."

MaryAnn's counterpart, Carol Newsome, spoke up next. "Isn't there anything we can do in the meantime?"

Olvera pursed his lips and slowly shook his head. "I don't know what more we can do until we hear from Cody Armstrong and Jamie Hammer. Right now, the ball is in their court."

The three sat there in silence for the next minute or so trying to think of anything that might help. Slowly, the DCM got to his feet and told the two women he was going upstairs to the cafeteria for lunch. MaryAnn and her office mate sat there thinking how hard this must be on Olvera, knowing about his close relationship with all of the Volunteers in Nigeria. The untimely and gruesome death of the CUSO Volunteer added yet another sad dimension to an already tense situation.

ഌ

Cody Armstrong and Jamie Hammer made the cross-town journey to the Wunti Central Marketplace without incident and found a side street in which to park Jamie's Rover. Jamie handed a couple of Naira to a stout-looking young man leaning against a nearby wall and asked him to watch their vehicle. Knowing how things worked in Nigeria, Jamie was essentially pre-tipping, or giving a "dash" to the Nigerian in hopes he wouldn't be the one breaking into his rig.

The two walked approximately two blocks to the marketplace and entered an entirely different world.

The Wunti Central Marketplace in Bauchi was a virtual beehive of color, sights, sounds, smells, and activity. The oversized, crowded, pulsating, open-air market was a place where one could buy anything from Gucci shoes to homemade trinkets. Rows upon rows of wooden stalls with corrugated tin roofs were crowded into the two-square block area. Spices and foodstuffs were displayed in colorful, oversized bowls on tables under shaded areas. All manner of small stalls displayed colorful, elaborate fabrics or products made by artisans. Farmers tried to sell cassavas, yams, peppers, groundnuts, and spices. Butchers had a variety of meats to convey, including cured wild game. As one tried to maneuver through the noisy maze, one was constantly pummeled by frequent calls from traders and merchants trying to lure passers-by to their stalls. A Nigerian marketplace could be half chaotic and half wildly entertaining. Just to stroll around in one was an experience.

Jamie and Cody wandered around for close to an hour trying to find the old Hausa woman's place of business. Jamie tossed a one Naira coin into the bowl of an old crippled beggar who was sitting on a ratty reed mat by a brick and mortar wall that had seen better days. Cody was preoccupied talking to a camel trader across the way.

"Thank you, Master," the old man simply said as he grabbed one of Jamie's hands in both of his and touched them to his forehead, a traditional gesture of appreciation. Then the old beggar, in halting Pidgin English, asked Jamie if there was something in particular he was looking for. Jamie replied that he was looking for the stall of an elderly Hausa woman who might have knowledge of the "wild" area to the north, as he called it.

"Ah, you seek the witch," he simply said. "She goes there." He pointed a long bony finger toward the far end of the marketplace. Before Hammer could ask another question, the old beggar quietly lowered his head in a form of supplication, drew his tattered robe up around him, and said nothing more. Thinking that was a bit odd, Jamie thanked him anyway and hurried over to where Cody was.

"I think I know where she is," Jamie said excitedly as he grabbed Cody's arm

"You do? Where?"

"This way, buddy," Jamie said, leading Cody toward an area of the marketplace that wasn't as crowded or hectic. The two boys walked along a narrow alleyway with just a few scattered stalls. Activity in this section of the marketplace was at a minimum, and the few locals who were milling about gave them curious, as well as suspicious, looks.

Cody spotted the old woman first. She was a small and frail-looking woman sitting all by herself behind a table full of trinkets. She looked like she was keeping herself busy by arranging, then rearranging her wares.

The old hag looked up from what she was doing and smiled at the two approaching foreigners, stood up, and said, "*Matasa samari...maraba*!" From Jamie's language training in Kaduna, he understood this to mean something like "welcome, young white men," in Hausa. But he couldn't be sure.

The woman must have been somewhere in her late 70s, the boys guessed. It was hard to tell because of the darkness of her skin and all the wrinkles. She also didn't have many teeth, but did have distinctive amber-colored eyes, which was about the only part of her they could clearly see. The woman was wearing traditional, Muslim-style clothing: a loose dark robe, called a Jilbab, that completely covered her body and a Hijab that covered her entire head but left her face exposed.

"You buy charm. Make me very happy," she said in her best Pidgin English.

"We are looking for a friend...*aboki*," Jamie said.

"No help you. You buy charm first," she countered.

Jamie selected a small amulet on a leather necklace and asked her how much.

"Ten Naira."

"Really?" Jamie said to no one in particular, knowing full well that was an outrageous price. "I give you two Naira."

"No. You give me ten Naira," she insisted.

"Five Naira," Jamie responded, upping the ante.

"No. You give me ten Naira," the old woman said, sounding more and more irritated.

"Oh, for Christ's sake, Jamie. Give the woman ten Naira and see if she knows anything about Danny," Cody finally said, breaking the stalemate.

"Okay, ten Naira," Jamie reluctantly said, now understanding why the old beggar called her a witch. He pulled a couple of five Naira notes out of his wallet and handed them to the old woman.

"*Na gode*...thank you." She quickly slipped the money into a small leather purse hanging from her neck. Then she looked back up, waiting for Jamie to say something.

"We are looking for our friend," Jamie said, gesturing back and forth between himself and Cody.

"Ah, you look for *kodadde abokin fata*," she replied.

"What did she say?" asked Cody.

"I think she said we're looking for our pale-skinned friend," Jamie said, then turned back to the old woman. "Yes, yes, *abokin*...friend."

Jamie went on to describe what Danny looked like and possibly what he was wearing.

The expression on the old Nigerian's face changed suddenly and turned solemn.

"White boy go to paradise," was all she said.

Jamie and Cody looked at each other. That was the exact term the young lady at the college said she overheard Danny say. Now, they were on to something.

Cody produced a map, handed it to Jamie, and told him to ask the woman if she could point out where this "paradise" was. Jamie opened up the map to the section of the northern part of the country. Laying it flat on the table in front of the old woman, he asked her to show them what she had showed their friend.

The old woman paused, as if in deep thought. She looked first at Jamie and then at Cody as if contemplating what to do. The old crone lowered her head and softly said something to herself in Hausa. After perhaps a minute of muttering softly in her native tongue, she did something quite unexpected. She looked up at the two boys, and then half-smiled. Her voice was clear and unwavering when she spoke.

"Paradise here. Look for mountain of stones." She pointed to a place in the savannah roughly between Bauchi and Lame. It was virtually out in the middle of nowhere. The closest landmark of any consequence was the Junguru Hills far off to the west.

"Go away now...*tafi*." The old woman turned her back on the boys, pretending to be busy with her trinkets. The two

Volunteers wanted to ask a few more questions, but took the hint and left. Jamie put his purchase in his pocket and suggested to Cody they find a phone somewhere.

CHAPTER 11

Early Afternoon Monday, September 22

Lagos & Bauchi

Marine Gunnery Sergeant William "Wild Bill" Ripper walked into the Embassy's 4th floor cafeteria at the same time as DCM Olvera. They each ordered a cheeseburger with fries, fixed the American way, and a Coke. Olvera invited the lanky Vietnam War veteran to join him at a corner table. "Gunny" Ripper was the non-commissioned officer-in-charge of the fourteen marines assigned to provide security for the Nigerian Mission.

"What's the latest, boss?" asked Ripper as he took a mouthful of the greasy burger.

Olivera's mind was still stuck on the dead CUSO Volunteer, the missing Peace Corps Volunteer, and the ensuing manhunt. He brought the marine up to speed on what was going on. Sgt. Ripper, always the tactical thinker, put his burger down, sat back in his chair, and pondered the situation for a good minute.

"Wild Bill" Ripper was a career marine. He entered the service straight out of high school and did two combat tours in Vietnam, one of them earning him a Purple Heart plus a Silver Star. The first decoration was for being wounded while engaged in a firefight with the Vietcong. The Silver Star was for bravery. He saved the lives of three wounded comrades when he pulled them to safety during the same battle.

Standing a little under six feet tall and weighing around one hundred ninety pounds, the thirty-three-year-old bachelor was solid as a rock. Everyone at the embassy joked that the GI Joe doll must have been modeled after him, right down to the short-cropped white hair and square jaw. Despite being a thoroughly professional soldier, Ripper still maintained a sense of humor and had somewhat of a parental attitude toward his boys. Everyone at the embassy liked and respected the Gunny. They also knew he wasn't someone you messed around with.

"Mike, I've got an idea," the sergeant finally said. Olvera was only formal when he had to be and insisted the people he worked with be on a first name basis with him.

"Let's hear it, Bill." The DCM was anxious to hear what the marine had to say, especially since he was a highly-trained combat specialist with a strategic mindset. To Olvera, Sgt. Ripper was the type of person who could face any situation and figure out how to come out on top, regardless of the odds or what he had to work with.

The fast-thinking Ripper laid it all out for him. He suggested sending one of his marines, with the proper equipment, up north to work with the two Peace Corps Volunteers. Since they were already hot on the trail, sort to speak, Ripper's idea was simply to put a trained specialist with Armstrong and Hammer for assistance, support, and as added insurance.

Michael Oliver's face lit up. He liked the part about the added insurance. "Who and with what kind of equipment?" he quickly asked.

Ripper's reply reflected how his strategic thinking worked. "I would send someone who has field survival experience, good tracking skills, and can blend in with the locals. I would equip him with basic survival and tactical items, including a Ka-Bar combat knife, OC pepper spray, a couple of CS teargas grenades, a short wave field radio, several M18 smoke grenades, and a standard-issue, Beretta M9 sidearm."

"Wow, that's a lot of gear," Olvera said. "I hate to show my ignorance, but what, exactly, is OC pepper spray?"

"The technical name," began Ripper, "is oleoresin capsicum. You are probably more familiar with its common name...mace."

"Sounds like nasty stuff," the DCM quipped. "And how would you propose we get your man and all that stuff up north in the shortest amount of time? There is only one flight a day to Bauchi, in the morning."

"But there are three to Jos," Ripper said. "We'd have plenty of time to get him up there on the afternoon flight."

"How would you get him on a commercial airline with that kind of equipment?" Olvera asked. "You know how the Nigerian military checks anything suspicious-looking at airports and checkpoints.

"I'd ask the 'colonel' if he could help us out there. I know he has some high-ranking Nigerian Army contacts who are in charge of security at the airports. I don't think we'd have any problem getting him on a flight with that stuff, even if the airplane is fully booked."

Sgt. Ripper was referring to the embassy's military attaché, Colonel Warren "Bud" Hearst. The State Department made a smart move in talking the U.S. Army into posting this distinguished Vietnam veteran to the embassy in Nigeria. Since the country was governed by the army, it was determined a "full bird" colonel of similar stripe with combat decorations would be well received by the generals and colonels who controlled the country. They were right. Colonel Hearst enjoyed an exceptionally good relationship with any number of high ranking officials, one of whom, was responsible for security at all of Nigeria's airports.

Michael Olvera was beginning to think Gunnery Sergeant Ripper had the makings of a workable idea and said so. "Who do you have in mind and how soon can you get him outfitted and out to the airport?"

"That's an easy one," Ripper replied. "I'd send Jake Simmons. With his skin color, he could easily pass for a Nigerian if he had to. He has all the skills and he's a search and rescue specialist. If one of my men were lost out in the wilds, he'd be my first choice to send looking."

"What authorization do you need to make this happen?" the DCM asked.

"Well," the sergeant said as he rubbed his chin, "You would have to give our regional security officer a written request for use of one of my marines plus approval of this plan. The RSO, in turn, would have to formally authorize it and give me written authority to make it happen. Once I have the documentation in hand, we're all set."

"Let's do it, Gunny! I'll make it happen," Olvera said, popping the table with an open palm. "Just one thing. Lethal weapons are not allowed off premises. So you'll have to forgo the handgun, possibly the knife as well, but I can make a case for the remaining equipment since it's classified as defensive and 'non-lethal.' Sorry, Gunny, but that's the way it's got to be."

Ripper understood completely. In his excitement to quickly put a plan together, he'd forgotten about the rules governing deadly weapons insofar as diplomatic missions on foreign soil were concerned. To carry or use guns of any type in areas that were not classified as "U.S. soil" would be a serious breach of international law, diplomatic protocol, and several treaties. American embassies, consulates, and ambassadors' residences were all considered to be on U.S. soil no matter where in the world they were located and, as such, were exempt from local laws and restrictions. The properties were also a "safe haven" for any American citizen looking for sanctuary or trying to avoid the local authorities.

In Nigeria, the ownership of firearms by civilians was seriously against the law. The only people who were allowed to have rifles, handguns, and the like were soldiers in the Nigerian Army. Security guards and even the police could not have them. There was still too much suspicion and mistrust concerning who possessed firearms, a result of their civil war and the bad blood that still existed between some ethnic groups.

"I'll have the paperwork ready in less than hour," Olvera said as he stood up. Both men left their lunches unfinished and hurried out of the cafeteria. They both knew they had much to do in a short period of time, if they were going to pull this off.

The first thing Mike Olvera did when he got back to his office was have MaryAnn draft a memo to the RCO requesting the temporary use, and reposting of, one of Sgt. Ripper's marines. Then he put in a call to Kenny Wagner in Kaduna.

ↀ

As Cody and Jamie were leaving the Wunti Central Marketplace, they decided to go back to the teaching college and ask around to see if anyone knew something about this place called "paradise" before reporting back to Wagner.

They decided to start in the science department and since this was a Monday, had to wait for the only geography instructor to finish a class before talking to him. They were waiting outside of Peter Onyia's classroom when the last student had left, then walked in and introduced themselves. Jamie took the initiative and explained what they were looking for and why.

The Nigerian teacher found it interesting that an American Peace Corps Volunteer had managed to get himself lost somewhere out in the hinterland, as he phrased it, and hadn't been seen since. He looked at the map the two boys brought with professional curiosity. There, just east of the Junguru Hills and Golijomo River was a large, hand-drawn circle.

"Somewhere in that circle," Cody said, "is some kind of secluded oasis called 'paradise.' That is where, we believe, our friend went to explore and camp out."

"There's really nothing out there to my knowledge," replied the British-educated Onyia, "except for kopjes, grasslands, scrub bush, acacia trees, and assorted wildlife. I've never been out there and neither has anyone I know. It's fairly remote. Sorry, wish I could be of more assistance."

As an afterthought, Jamie asked the teacher if he knew anything about the area at all; something, anything, which might help them. Any information they might obtain about this part of the country could be valuable when it came to finding their way around or dealing with the locals.

"Other than what I've already told you," Onyia said, "the only other thing I know about the area is that it is believed to be part of the original homeland of the ancient Noks."

"The Noks?" Cody asked.

"Yes," responded the teacher, assuming a pedagogical pose. "The Nok culture appeared in this region around 1,000 years before Christ and vanished, under unknown circumstances, around 500 years after his death. They were thought to be very advanced for their period, much like the Mayans and Aztecs of Central and South America."

"Really?" remarked Jamie, tilting his head. "I've never heard of them. Did they leave any evidence of their existence?"

"Oh, absolutely." Onyia nodded. "They left iron tools that demonstrated a high level of knowledge and skill in smelting and forging of various metals. They also created rather unique miniature terracotta statuettes, which are quite expensive on the black market, by the way."

"I don't understand," interjected Cody. "What does the black market have to do with these ancient people?"

"Well," Onyia went on, "the Nok terracotta figurines are some of the oldest known artifacts of West Africa. They are very rare, very beautiful...and, very valuable. That is why looters are always looking for them."

"Do these figurines represent their gods?" asked Jamie, his curiosity somewhat aroused.

"Their purpose is a source of great speculation," the teacher continued, pursing his lips. "But many archaeologists believe their main purpose was either as grave markers or to hold the souls of the dead. Sorry, gentlemen, that's about the extent of my knowledge regarding the Noks and the area. Again, I wish I could be of more help."

"That's okay," said Cody, somewhat discouraged. "Thanks for talking with us, Mr. Onyia, we appreciate your time."
The two sullen Volunteers shook hands with the geography instructor and turned to leave.

"Wait!" Onyia said walking toward them with a finger in the air as if he just remembered something. "I do recall a story that was in our local newspaper a few years back. Something about a pair of British tourists going out into this area and disappearing.

The authorities performed a search, but nothing was ever found...where did you say you got this information?"

Jamie and Cody glanced at each other. "From an old Hausa woman in the marketplace," Cody said. "Why? Is that important?"

"Possibly," Onyia replied, folding his arms. "You said she was Hausa...was she dressed in traditional Muslim garb?"

The young men both nodded. Jamie added, "Yes...yes, she was. Does that mean something to you?"

"Possibly," the Nigerian began again, choosing his words carefully. "In the Islamic culture, paradise is supposedly where a good Muslim goes when they die."

Both Cody and Jamie felt a cold shiver run down their spines.

Onyia's remark left them both speechless for a moment. With the Nigerian teacher's revelation about paradise, all manner of wild thoughts raced through their heads.

"Could it be the old woman intentionally sent Danny off to some remote place knowing he would die there?" Jamie anxiously asked the teacher.

"There's no real way of knowing that," interjected Onyia. "What you are saying is pure speculation and I wouldn't draw any conclusions about it. I think you should go back and talk to the old woman some more, or go to the authorities."

Jamie and Cody once again thanked the teacher and hurried off to find a phone so they could call Kaduna. The receptionist at the entrance to the science building offered to let them use his.

Kenny Wagner was anxiously awaiting to hear from Jamie and Cody. After relating to the FSO what they had found out in the marketplace and from what the Nigerian teacher at the college told them, they were worried and asked Wagner what they should do next.

"Head back to Jos," was Wagner's curt response.

"What? Why?" Cody asked.

"DCM Olvera and Gunnery Sergeant Ripper have a plan to send you a little help," Wagner said. "Jake Simmons is catching the afternoon flight to Jos. You'll need to pick him up, purchase extra gear, and then the three of you can proceed with your search."

"Jake, from the marine security detachment?"

"The very one," replied Wagner. "He was chosen because he could blend in and hopefully give you credibility with the locals. He's also trained in search and rescue as well as field survival. He'll be catching the 3:30 flight, which should put him in Jos somewhere close to 5 p.m."

Cody checked his watch; it was now a little after 2 p.m. If they left Bauchi within the next half hour, they should be able to make the two-hour drive back to Jos in time to meet Cpl. Simmons.

"We're on it, Kenny. Jamie and I will leave immediately," Cody said. "Anything else we should know about?"

"You're aware that by 3 p.m., our time, it will be 9 a.m. on the same day, in Washington," Kenny reminded him. "We have already burned one day on their 48 – hour clock. That gives us one more day to turn up something."

"Hopefully," Cody said, running a hand through his hair, "Jake can put us on the fast track to try to locate this place where Danny supposedly went. One last thing, how are we going to stay in touch if we're out in the bush and bump up against the time limit?"

"No problem. Jake is bringing field gear with him, including a short wave radio set. With our set here in Kaduna, we're in range as far east as Bauchi and as far north as Kano. Whatever you discover, Jake can transmit the information to his counterpart here and we can relay it on to Lagos."

"Sounds like we have a plan. We'll be in touch when we head upcountry with Jake."

Wagner told Cody to have a safe trip back to Jos and broke the connection.

"Guess what?" Cody said to a waiting Jamie Hammer after he hung up the phone and thanked the male receptionist. "We're going back to Jos to pick up reinforcements and then we're heading out into the back country."

"We're doing what?" Jamie said, wrinkling his brow as he

spoke.

"I'll explain on the way. We need to get going...now," Cody said as he led Jamie out of the building and back to the waiting Range Rover.

As they were leaving the parking area, Jamie was hoping his well-used rig would be up to the challenge of off-road travel, if it came to that. Unlike its sturdier cousin, the Land Rover, the standard NSC-issued Range Rover was nothing more than a cheap, mid-sized 4 x 4, sport utility vehicle. The blue-colored Range Rovers that belonged to the NSC didn't have a great deal of amenities or power. Because all of the contract coaches with the sports commission received new Rovers as part of their compensation, the Peace Corps Volunteers and the minor NSC officials got the hand-me-downs. Cody, the one exception, got a fairly new Peugeot compact car, which always seemed to require some type of mechanical attention.

ഋ

Gunnery Sergeant Ripper wasted no time in putting his idea into motion. As soon as he left the embassy's cafeteria, he went straight downstairs and walked into the office of the regional security officer, Al Shannon. Ripper briefed the RSO as to what he and the DCM had in mind and said a request for authorization would be forthcoming within the hour from the DCM's office.

Shannon, already aware of the situation regarding the missing Volunteer, agreed to expedite the paperwork, including a voucher for an open-ended air ticket to Jos and a cash advance for Cpl. Simmons. Shannon said he would enter everything as a TDY assignment for field training purposes and the necessary paperwork and money would be ready by the time they headed out to Ikeja Airport. Ripper thanked the RSO for his help and headed down the hallway to the office of the Military Attaché.

Ripper entered the small office, greeted the colonel and then quietly shut the door behind him. After hearing the Gunnery Sergeant out, Hearst pledged his full cooperation and immediately put in a call to one of his contacts. The Nigerian, a colonel himself, was only too happy to accommodate the American officer after hearing the story of the missing Volunteer coach.

Ripper thanked the colonel for his help and immediately left the embassy and headed back to his barracks-style apartment building, which was affectionately referred to as "The Marine House." He found Lance Corporal Simmons enjoying his day off sleeping under a deck umbrella by the swimming pool.

"Off your ass and on your feet, Marine!" barked the gunnery sergeant as he strode up to Simmons. "We have work to do...and thanks for volunteering!"

Simmons jumped to his feet and assumed a position of attention. Basic training at marine boot camp had instilled instantaneous responses in his body without the mind being fully engaged. Even his words were an automated response.

"Sir, yes, Sir!"

Ripper had to work to hold back a chuckle. Although he half expected a reaction like this, he was not quite prepared for the quick and formal response of the young corporal.

"At ease, Simmons," he said. "You are being tasked with a humanitarian mission of mercy."

"Sir, yes, Sir!" replied the still half-out-of-it Simmons. "May I ask what mission I volunteered for, Sir?"

"I said at ease, Jake...and sit down...and while you're at it, hand me a beer from your bucket."

It was standard operating procedure, "SOP" as the marines called it, to have a bucket of iced beer on deck, the pool deck as it were, whenever one or more of the young guards was at poolside relaxing. It was one of the perks of the duty and they were expected to share.

"What's up, Gunny?" Simmons inquired, trying to shake off his sleep-induced fog.

"Beer first," replied Ripper, "and grab one for yourself; you're going to need it."

Ripper went on to explain the situation to the young corporal and what his plan was. Simmons was well aware of the issue regarding the absent Peace Corps Volunteer. He was, after all, on duty the previous day when the news came into the embassy. Ripper emphasized this was officially a voluntary assignment, sanctioned by the DCM, RSO, and himself and was not a requirement of duty.

Simmons didn't even blink an eye. "When do I leave, Sir?"

The response made the senior marine blush with pride. Ripper told him they had approximately an hour to get geared up and on the road to the airport. The two didn't even finish their beers before they headed straight inside. Simmons went to his room to change and start packing, while Gunny Ripper went to the weapons locker.

CHAPTER 12

Monday Morning, September 22

Washington D.C.

When everything was set in motion, DCM Olvera felt obligated to inform the Peace Corps office in Ghana about their plan, even though they were still within the 48-hour grace period. PC Ghana, in turn, passed on the information to Matt McKnight at Peace Corps HQ in Washington D.C. Although it was already 1:30 in the afternoon in Lagos, it was only 7:30 a.m. and the start of a new Monday on the eastern seaboard of the United States.

ᘓ

Matt McKnight had just checked in with the overnight duty officer that morning when he received the cable, marked "urgent," from the PC office in Accra, Ghana. Matt read the cable twice, to make sure he clearly understood what was in the works. The semi-classified cable simply said PCV Danny Harper was still MIA in north-central Nigeria. Deputy Chief of Mission Michael Olvera and the RSO had approved a plan by Gunnery Sergeant William Ripper to send one of his marines upcountry to join PCVs Cody Armstrong and Jamie Hammer in their search efforts. The marine, Lance Corporal Jake Simmons, was a field survival and SAR specialist and would be equipped with survival gear, a field radio, and non-lethal, self-defense equipment. They were to begin their search starting at Jos and from there, head up-country to an area east of the Junguru Hills. ETD (estimated time of departure) for the search team was 0600 hours (6 a.m.) Nigeria time, Tuesday, 23 September.

Matt glanced at the time zone clocks on the wall. Knowing Nigeria was six hours ahead of Washington, he quickly calculated that by late tonight, around midnight Washington time, Jamie, Cody, and the marine corporal would be on the road at first light, Tuesday morning in Nigeria.

The last paragraph of the cable stopped Matt short. PC Ghana was going to send two staff personnel to Lagos to monitor the situation. Between clenched teeth and under his breath, Matt muttered a disparaging "Sonofabitch!" This was the last thing he needed on his plate right now. The 48-hour clock wasn't even close to being up. They still had another 25½ hours and the PC field office in Ghana was already sending people to work the search. Either they were confused about the timing of the countdown, which started at 9 a.m. on Sunday, Washington time, not Nigerian time, or they were confused about the proper procedure for this type of occurrence.

Matt thought the Ghanaian Peace Corps director, Hampton Belvoe, was either looking for "brownie points" by being pro-active on this, or he was starting to panic. The small Nigerian program was, after all, somewhat his responsibility since he had the closest PC support staff to the Nigerian group. Knowing Belvoe the way he did, Matt guessed it might be a little of both. In-country Peace Corps directors could either be dismissed over something like this or be elevated – depending on the way they handled it. Matt knew that Belvoe had aspirations of becoming either a high-level Peace Corps official or even an ambassador someday and thought his current job was somewhat beneath him. Either way, Belvoe was "jumping the gun" by more than a day and McKnight didn't appreciate it.

After taking a couple of minutes to think things over, and to cool down, Matt called his boss's secretary to see if the regional director for West African programs was available for a meeting. The secretary told Matt the RD had an open schedule for the morning, something he habitually did on Mondays, and told

Matt to drop by anytime.

As fate would have it, Regional Director Gerrard had also received a similar cable from Ghana and was waiting to hear from McKnight. When Matt walked into the RD's office, Gerrard asked him if he would like a cup of coffee and invited him to take a seat. The two made themselves comfortable in the over-stuffed, leather chairs away from the director's desk.

"What's the latest from Nigeria?" Gerrard politely asked, taking a sip of his coffee from the standard-issue, U.S. government mug.

Matt told the director everything he knew, including the information contained in the cable he received that morning. To Matt's surprise, and perhaps embarrassment, the RD told Matt he too, had received a cable from Accra that morning. Comparing notes, Matt started developing the distinct impression that the PC director in Ghana was a first class, self-righteous asshole.

"Looks to me like Hampton doesn't trust you to do your job," remarked Director Gerrard. "Tell me what you think we, as an organization, should do next, Matt."

Matt could tell by Director Gerrard's comment he didn't approve of Hampton Belvoe's jumping the chain of command either. Matt felt partially vindicated and told the regional director what he thought their next steps should be.

"The first thing I wanted to do is send a cable directly to Deputy Chief of Mission Olvera at the American Embassy in Lagos," Matt said. "I'm assuming he's the point man in the search for our missing Volunteer. I'll ask Olvera to provide me with whatever information is available, including any reports from the field as they come in."

"Excellent," Director Gerrard said. "And after that?"

Matt went on to explain he would make arrangements to travel to Nigeria, hopefully to coincide with the end of the 48-hour waiting period and assume the lead Peace Corps role in the search, coordinating the efforts between the embassy there, the upland search team, and the Peace Corps people from Accra .

"Sounds good so far," Gerrard said. "Belvoe probably won't

like it, but I do. I'll approve your travel plans, ticket purchase, and per diem money advance. Anything else?"

"Once our two-day time limit is up and Harper officially becomes a missing Volunteer of record, I will need to inform our key staff members and Harper's family," McKnight added. "I'll ask our people to take whatever steps they think is necessary beforehand. Once we hit 9 a.m. tomorrow morning, our time, I want everyone to hit the ground running if Harper is still missing...including me."

Regional Director Gerrard liked Matt's plan and told him so. But he had one final question: "Matt, does your plan follow our standard protocols and procedures? Will this be done by the book?"

"Absolutely," was Matt's immediate reply.

Gerrard smiled as he stood up, indicating the meeting was over, and asked Matt to update him as often as possible on his progress.

Matt McKnight wasted no time and hustled right back to his desk. He had a lot of work to do before lunchtime. The first thing he did was call the travel department to find out when was the next available flight to Lagos. The travel specialist informed that a Pan Am flight was departing from John F. Kennedy International in New York at 6 p.m. that evening, with stops in Dakar (Senegal), Monrovia (Liberia), and Accra (Ghana) before going on to Lagos. Matt asked what the Lagos ETA (estimated time of arrival) was.

"With stops, you're looking at somewhere around a fourteen-hour trip," replied the young man on the other end of the line. "Your ETA for Lagos should be approximately 8 a.m. tomorrow morning, our time, or 2 p.m. the same day in Lagos."

Matt asked him to book a mid-afternoon commuter flight for him from Washington National to JFK in New York, as well as the overnight Pan Am flight to Nigeria. Matt told the travel specialist the authorization would be forthcoming within the hour. If everything went according to plan, he should be in Lagos about the time the 48-hour window closed at 9 a.m. on Tuesday, Washington time.

With that out of the way, Matt turned his attention to the other details that would be necessary if Harper wasn't found in time. He asked his secretary to arrange a meeting, as soon as possible, between himself, the agency's counseling and outreach duty officer, the associate director for safety and security, the deputy director for operations, and the organization's public affairs officer. The Peace Corps was, in all respects, the typical government bureaucracy. Someone always reported to someone else with a higher pay grade.

Matt phoned his wife to let her know he was leaving for Nigeria later that day and didn't know how long he'd be gone. Cindy McKnight was already well aware of the situation from the ruined plans of the previous day and asked if there was anything she could do. Considering the fact she had a job of her own, Matt couldn't expect her to skip out of work and go home just to pack him a bag. He would have to do with whatever he could scrounge up at a nearby department store as well as what was available at the JFK airport. Money was no problem; he would get per diem cash and traveler's checks from the Finance Department. He kept his passport locked in his desk drawer, just in case something like this ever came up, but needed to get an emergency visa stamp from the Nigerian Embassy to enter that country.

Right about then, his "shared" secretary poked her head into his cubicle and informed him the meeting he requested was scheduled for 11 a.m. in the small conference room on the fourth floor. Matt thanked her and asked if she would place a call to the logistics officer for him.

When the LO came on the line, Matt quickly explained what he needed and why. The LO said he would put in an immediate call to the Nigerian Embassy, fill out the necessary paperwork, and send a courier right up to fetch his passport and World Health Organization immunization record, commonly referred to as a "WHO card." Matt thanked the LO, hung up the phone, and fetched his official government passport and his immunization record from a locked drawer in his desk. After giving them a quick glance to make sure nothing had expired, he put both documents on the corner of his desk by his "out" basket.

A great many foreign countries, especially those in tropical areas, required visitors to have a number of specific immunizations before letting them into their country. Only the little yellow booklet issued by the World Health Organization was universally accepted as proof a foreign visitor wasn't going to infect someone in their country with a potentially lethal disease. Even the United States required an up-to-date WHO card before allowing its own citizens re-entry once they'd been abroad to many of the third-world countries.

Matt had to smile at the thought of all the grumbling new Volunteers made when they learned they needed somewhere between twelve and sixteen shots to be able to serve in West Africa. Matt also impressed upon them that if, by chance, they lost their WHO card, they would have to start all over again with most of the shots. The point, as it were, was well taken.

Before he could organize his meeting notes, the courier strode up to his desk, introduced himself, collected the documents, and disappeared. *The LO runs a tight ship*, Matt thought.

At 11 a.m. on the dot, he strode into the undersized fourth floor conference room. All the other attendees were already present and chatting about what they knew of the situation. A great deal of speculation and rumor were being bandied around.

Once Matt got their undivided attention, he briefed the three men and one woman on what the latest information was concerning the missing Volunteer in Nigeria. This had the potential of being a serious situation for not only the agency, but for each one of them as well. They were, according to Peace Corps protocols and procedures, responsible to do whatever they could to successfully resolve this emergency. They were the responsible officers of the agency when it came to something as dire as this. What each one did or didn't do, with regards to this situation, could have a serious impact on their careers as well as that of the Peace Corps organization itself. Also, all knew Nigeria was a "high priority" experimental program and understood the consequences.

Matt couldn't have asked for a more attentive audience, nor a more enthusiastic group. When all the discussion and questions ended, the forty-five-minute meeting was adjourned and all the participants hustled back to their offices. They immediately went to work on their part of what needed to be done when the 48-hour clock expired.

Matt took a lunch break to go shopping and came back to the office with most of what he needed to make the trip. To his amazement and delight, the courier from the logistics office walked into his cubicle with the visa-stamped passport and his WHO card just as he sat down. Right behind him was a second courier, this one from the travel office with his tickets, which he had to sign for. The courier instructed him that he would have to go down to the "cage," the teller's booth in the finance department, to get his travel money.

Matt made courtesy calls to all involved, thanking them for the rush job, then checked in with his boss. Gerrard was pleased with all Matt had accomplished in such a short period of time and asked him if he had notified Accra and Lagos he was on his way. Forgetting about that little detail in his haste to make travel arrangements and put a plan in motion, Matt said he'd get right on it. Within twenty minutes' time, he had fired off corresponding cables to the Peace Corps office in Accra and to the embassy in Lagos, with copies sent to Gerrard.

He caught the late afternoon shuttle flight to New York in the nick of time. He had worked later than anticipated, trying to tie up loose ends before he left. Matt ditched his car in long-term parking and hoped this trip wouldn't last longer than three or four days. The parking fee wasn't going to be cheap, no matter how long this took.

Since he had nothing more than a carry-on bag and a briefcase to contend with, Matt breezed through the pre-boarding procedures and walked to the departure gate as the last boarding call was made.

The Eastern Airlines 737 made good time and Matt walked off the plane and into the disembarkation lounge at JFK

International with nearly ninety minutes to spare. He decided to head for the international concourse and get an early dinner, Lord knows what Pan Am was serving on their African flights these days.

After having an overpriced and less-than-stellar airport meal, Matt waited for his flight's boarding call in the Pan Am lounge. The lounge was normally available only to first class Pan-American passengers, but when Matt showed the doorman his official U.S. government, maroon-colored passport, he was let in with a welcoming smile. *Working for the Federal Government does have its occasional perks,* Matt reminded himself.

Within thirty minutes, the first boarding call was made for Pan Am's "African Queen" flight. Matt headed for the embarkation area. A final check of his ticket, passport, and WHO Card and Matt was walking down the gangway and into the cabin of the long-range Boeing 707. After finding his seat in the business section and stowing away his bag and briefcase, he sat back and tried to relax. He had been at a dead run for almost twelve hours.

CHAPTER 13

Mid-Afternoon Monday, September 22

Bauchi & Jos

Jamie and Cody wasted no time in getting back on the road to Jos. Once they left the Bauchi Teaching College, they once again went east on Ahmadu Bello Way to the Eagle roundabout. Taking the second exit onto the Old Jos Road, they passed the Bauchi Club on their left, then stopped at a petrol station to gas up the Rover. Two more blocks of driving put them on the A3 Highway heading southwest back to Jos. Jamie took the first stint at driving.

The first town they passed, Busai, was not as busy as it had been when they went by earlier that morning. Since it was now late afternoon and the heat was at its maximum, not as many people were out and about. There wasn't as much road traffic either, which meant clear sailing, for the most part, all the way back to Jos. Jamie mentioned they were making good time and should make it to Benue Plateau's capital city in plenty of time to pick up Simmons and wondered what their next move was going to be.

While Jamie raced the British Leyland-made Rover down the highway, Cody was studying their map which contained the markings for the hidden oasis. About twenty minutes into their drive, the landmark of Zaranda Hill came into view on their right-hand side. Fifteen minutes later, they passed the intersection that connected the highway to the fair-sized town of Zaranda itself, located a short distance north of the A3 on a separate road.

Cody, referring to the map, made a mental note of the little town of Anguwan as they passed by it. Once they picked up Simmons in Jos, they would have to backtrack to this small hamlet, which also sat on the north side of the A3 highway. This is where they would get onto a hard-packed dirt road that would take them north in the direction of the oasis. Anguwan is where their starting point would be in their upland search for Danny Harper.

Cody did some quick calculations in his head. If the marine's flight was on time, and that was a big if, they should be picking him up shortly after 5 p.m. While Simmons was getting his gear, Cody would be calling Kenny Wagner in Kaduna for any updates and further instructions. Add another one and one-half hours to pick up additional supplies on the way out of town and that would put them back on the road somewhere around 6:30 p.m., shortly after sunset. They would have another thirty minutes or so of twilight and dusk before actual nightfall. By Cody's reckoning, that would put them somewhere around the town of Toro. This would not even be halfway back to the turnoff at Anguwan.

One of the questions Cody would have for Wagner and Simmons was if they should spend the night at Toro, go onto Anguwan for the night, or just keep going and get as far upcountry as possible before dawn on Tuesday.

The two Volunteers made good time, stopping only once for a roadside pee break while waiting for a small herd of Kuri cattle and their herders to cross the highway. As they drove on, they passed the time by chatting and reminiscing about some of their experiences and observations since first arriving in-country. The two talked about anything and everything that popped into their heads just to stay alert, and one subject or story always led to another.

Since he was driving, Jamie couldn't help but make an obvious observation. "I've often wondered...since Nigeria is a former British colony, why do they drive on the right-hand side of the road and not the left?"

Cody looked over and casually said, "Well...as I understand it, when the country was granted independence from the Crown, one of the first things they did was to switch sides. They wanted to be in conformity with the rest of the West African countries."

"Maybe that explains the road carnage," Jamie mused. "Since a great number of the vehicles on the roads were still of the right-hand driving type, perhaps they're having a hard time making the switch."

After governing the African colony for over sixty-five years, Great Britain finally granted independence to Nigeria in 1960. Throughout the years since, the British influence remained strong and the Nigerians made English their official language. They also preserved several time-honored British customs. One that neither Jamie nor Cody could fathom, was the tradition of drinking beer at room temperature, or more properly, between 10-14 degrees Celsius (50-57 degrees Fahrenheit). They were told the "Brits" believed cold beer killed its flavor.

Admittedly, both boys had acquired some British customs during their time in the former colony. Jamie picked up the habit of eating with a fork in his left hand and a knife in his right; this was considered proper British eating etiquette. Neither one of the two developed a preference for tea over coffee, but Cody did confess he had acquired a taste for the refreshing drink of gin and tonic. Both still considered beer to be their beverage of choice. Jamie admitted he was developing a taste for goat's milk over that of Nigerian cow, having gotten sick on several occasions from drinking cow's milk. The revelation drew a chuckle from Cody who had a similar experience. Both now referred to gasoline as petrol and both had to learn the metric system and how to convert it to the American Imperial System.

When they were through talking about all things British, they turned their conversation to all things Nigerian. They started with the food. Both readily admitted it took some time to develop an "acquired taste" for the traditional foods of the country. They discovered from the outset that most Nigerian dishes are prepared with a "fair" amount of spices and peppers, usually cooked in either peanut or palm oil. Jamie and Cody both preferred the peanut oil dishes as opposed to those cooked in the rancid-smelling palm oil. Jamie was a fan of the Hausa kabab dish known as Suya, accompanied with fried beans and onions. Cody favored the Jollof Rice dishes and Afang Stew, as long as it included meat and not fish. Both agreed that Dodo, thinly-sliced plantain deep-fried in peanut oil, was a great snack for any occasion. It was also a great complement to a cold beer.

Speaking of food, Cody said he always found it interesting how Nigerians used flat sticks to clean their teeth after eating, even in public, instead of adopting the western use of a toothbrush. Jamie observed that no amount of scraping from these wooden implements could ever remove the orange-brown stain caused by their habit of chewing "beetle nuts," the Nigerian answer to America's addiction to a "chew" or "pinch" of tobacco.

Jamie made the further observation that he found it interesting how Nigerians always seemed to have something balanced on their heads, their traditional way of carrying things. Perhaps, Cody added, that explained why the woman all had excellent posture. They were the ones who were always moving about carrying goods while the men usually just stood around and visited.

Both had a good chuckle over the way Nigerians loved to "dicker" over everything, usually leading to some type of satisfactory compromise for everyone involved. It didn't make any difference whether it was over the price of a stalk of bananas or what should be included in a new bride's dowry. Bartering and negotiating were highly developed skills in the Nigerian culture and the two boys shared their foremost experiences regarding it. They also admitted that this was a skill neither one had quite mastered. In America, one was accustomed to paying whatever the price was on the label, plus a sales tax where there was one. This brought up a comparison of the taxation differences in their states of origin. Oregon, where Cody was from, had no sales tax.

This last line of conversation between the boys invariably led to the controversial topic of the "dash." In Europe, North

America, and similar Western-style cultures, people offered a financial "reward" as a way of expressing gratitude for services rendered. Westerners called this customary gratuity a "tip," which was usually doled out at the conclusion of the service. Waiters, waitresses, hairdressers, bartenders, taxi drivers, and so on all expected a tip as part of their service to their customers. The better and/or the more expensive the service, the bigger the tip.

However, Nigerians expected a "pre-tip" called a "dash," not a post-tip after the service was rendered. Understandably, the size of the upfront "dash" predetermined the level or speed of service. Sometimes, without an adequate "dash" at the outset, there would be no service at all.

Both Cody and Jamie experienced this first-hand their fourth night in Lagos when all of the Volunteers decided to go out to the infamous Can-Can Nightclub for a night of partying. There they were, standing in line, waiting to get in the door and being passed over by just about everyone who showed up after them. They simply didn't understand how the system worked. Monte Reynolds, the uncompromising person that he was, refused to give the doorman a bribe, as he called it, just to get in and spend money. Danny quickly figured out what it took to make things happen and gave the two large Nigerians guarding the entry a ten-Naira note. They were let in immediately. Danny had saved their evening of fun.

Their running conversation took a quiet turn after that story. For the rest of the drive to Jos, Cody and Jamie were pretty much lost in their own thoughts, which mostly consisted of Danny Harper and the future of their program.

Right on schedule, the two Volunteers arrived at the outskirts of northern Jos at quarter to five. They stayed on the same highway, which became the Jingiri Road as it went through the city and at the southern end exited off onto Omama Road. After three kilometers (1.8 miles), they turned onto the entrance to Yakubo Gowon Airport. The two Volunteers had made the eight kilometer (5 mile) trip across town in under 15 minutes. Somewhat of a record.

Jamie parked the Rover in the expansive gravel parking lot and the two headed for the airport's main terminal at a quick-paced walk. They reached the disembarkation area just as Jake Simmons' plane was taxing up to the ramp.

By prearrangement, Jake was met at the plane's stairway by two serious-looking Nigerian soldiers, complete with helmets, combat vests, and Belgian-made FN-FAL assault rifles. The pair probably didn't have a clue as to what was going on and were only following orders. Few words were exchanged and after Simmons showed them his passport and the official-looking documentation, he was escorted to the plane's baggage hold where he unloaded two hefty rucksacks and a suitcase-sized metal container. None of this was inspected by the soldiers nor any of the airplane's baggage handlers or ground crew. For all anyone knew, Jake Simmons, age twenty, United States Marine Corps, could have been carrying a small nuclear bomb. The soldiers were only instructed to provide security and to expedite the arrival of the American soldier. So far, Ripper's plan was working as planned.

Both Jamie and Cody were extremely happy to see Jake. After their initial greeting, Jamie and Jake grabbed a quick beer in the airport's dinky little stand-up bar and briefed each other on the latest developments, while Cody found a pay phone and called Kaduna.

"Hi, Kenny," Cody said when the familiar, distant voice came on the line. "Jake Simmons made it to Jos and got through the airport without any of his gear being checked or ripped off. What's our next step?"

"All three of you have had a pretty long day," Wagner told the Volunteer Leader. "You need to go shopping. Jake has a list. Find some accommodations in the city for the night and get an early start in the morning."

"Why not head back up-country tonight?" asked Cody. "We still have daylight for a couple of hours and can get in at least an hour or so on the road after we're finished picking up what we need."

"Cody," said the sympathetic Foreign Service officer, "you

and Jamie have had quite the day; you're tired, Jake's tired, and you three need rest. Who knows what the next twenty-four hours will bring? You know it's too dangerous to travel those roads at night. Find a place to stay there in Jos, get a good meal, a good night's sleep, and head north at first light."

Wagner was right and Cody knew it. He was indeed tired. The last two days had been pretty hectic and who knew what the next couple of days would bring. What Kenny said made sense despite his eagerness to get back up-country and start looking. Cody agreed with Wagner's advice, thanked the FSO, and broke the connection. He joined up with the other two at the bar, and after a quick beer and conversation, the trio headed out to the parking area.

The three young men left the airport and headed north, back into central Jos. They decided to follow Wagner's advice, orders really, and hole up in the city for the night. It was Jamie's idea to head back to the hilltop Benue Hotel for food and lodging. After two quick stops, one at a department store and the other at a small food market, the three made one last stop to fill up the Range Rover and three "Jerry Cans" with gas, then went straight to the hotel and checked in, paying cash for their room. They ate a light dinner then retired to their room to plan, inventory their equipment, and repack for a fast exit the following morning.

Thanks to the "Gunny," Jake was well prepared for any eventuality. In one of his rucksacks, he had packed a lightweight sleeping bag, mosquito netting, a change of clothing, essential toiletries, and a field survival kit. In the other was a Coleman lantern, a flashlight with extra batteries, a compass, a pair of binoculars, the various non-lethal ordinance agreed upon, relevant maps, and three web utility belts with canteens. The compact shortwave radio set was housed in a separate, lightweight metal case. Jake also had his Ka-Bar knife with him, strapped to the inside of his left thigh under his loose-fitting, cargo-style trousers.

From their short shopping spree on the way to the hotel, they picked up a sleeping bag for Cody, two extra backpacks, a lightweight shovel, an extra flashlight with batteries, matches, a dozen assorted tins of sardines, and other canned meats, crackers, toilet paper, ten jugs of bottled water, a box of granola bars, and two machetes. Cody often wondered why these oversized blades were considered a field tool and not a lethal weapon in Nigeria.

Jamie, on the road as much as he was, already had all of what he needed, including his own machete, packed away in his Range Rover. The two Peace Corps Volunteers also had their standard-issue field survival kits with them. The men wanted to be sure they had everything they needed to survive for a couple of days of roughing it out in the bush, if it came to that.

As they sorted through their supplies and equipment, they divided everything up into two packs apiece, six total, plus a separate box for the food and water. They didn't know if they would need to go hiking or not, but wanted to be ready just in case. They could still work out of the elderly Range Rover for as long as possible and planned to top off the tank with gas when they turned off at Anguwan.

Rather than packing up everything and loading it back into the Rover, Jamie suggested they keep the equipment with them in their room for the night. No sense in risking a nighttime break-in of the Rover and losing all of their gear. The other two agreed that was probably the smart thing to do and stowed away the packs and the rest of their stuff in their room, then they called it a night.

Unable to quickly fall asleep like the others, Jake lay there awake for a while, then did what naturally came to him. He quietly rolled out of bed and ripped off thirty push-ups.

CHAPTER 14

Early Morning Tuesday, September 23

Jos & Anguwan

Jake was up well before dawn, long before any obnoxious rooster could ruin his slumber. He didn't bother to shave or shower; he just got dressed, washed his face, and brushed his teeth. He wasn't trying to be quiet about it either.

Jake's stirrings managed to wake both Jamie and Cody. Neither one had slept all that well anyway and were only too happy to get an early start on the day. Both Volunteers followed the same routine as did the marine and the group was ready to head out the door in less than half an hour.

All three were dressed casually and comfortably: hiking boots, lightweight cargo pants, loose-fitting polo or tee shirts, and either baseball caps or boonie-style tropical hats. They wanted to be comfortable and protected, in either the heat of the day or the cool of the night. They definitely wanted protection from the sub-Saharan sun as well as a bevy of insects. Namely, virus-carrying mosquitos.

When they were finished loading the Rover and left the parking area, it was 5:45 and the eastern horizon was glowing with the pale suggestion of light. Sunrise wouldn't happen for another thirty minutes. Cody suggested they get something to eat on the road, even if that only amounted to a bunch of bananas, since the hotel's restaurant was probably not open yet. The other two agreed and Jamie navigated the semi-dark streets of Jos and onto the main A3 Highway in record time. They were well clear of Jos by the time the sun came up. All three donned their Ray-Ban sunglasses when the sun peeked above the horizon.

As they left Jos behind, Cody and Jake started checking out the roadside stands along the way for some place to stop. Finding nothing that appealed to them, the three decided to push on to Anguwan, approximately one hour away, where they would gas up and try to have some type of breakfast. Jake would also need to test his radio to see if it would reach Kaduna.

Jamie drove his Range Rover at a higher speed than he normally would, considering the volatile traffic conditions of the Nigerian highways. He felt fairly confident in doing this since it was early in the morning, the traffic was light and this was a fairly new highway.

During the fifty-five minute drive, the three young men discussed a variety of things, including how they should proceed once they "turned the corner," as Jamie put it, and started upcountry into the bush.

Jake looked at the map and remarked, "There are a couple of small towns, villages really, along the dirt road we'll encounter while travelling northward after turning off at Anguwan. We should stop at each one and inquire if Danny had passed through or not."

The other two readily agreed.

Approximately twenty-five minutes after leaving Jos, they sailed through the town of Toro and in another fifteen minutes, around seven, they went through the town of Nabordo. In another fifteen minutes or so, they should come to their turnoff point at the small town of Anguwan. They were looking forward to getting something that represented a decent meal, which could possibly be their last for the next couple of days, as well as getting on with their search.

The remainder of the drive was consumed by the on-going discussion regarding all possible scenarios relating to Harper's disappearance.

Jamie suggested, "What if Danny, once he found his oasis, had problems with his Rover and decided to wait out the arrival of help? Knowing Harper the way I do, he'd be more likely to stay put than to venture out into no man's land, especially since he'd be on foot and exposed."

Cody offered a more tragic picture. "What if, carelessly going cross-country in his over-used rig, he suddenly went off the edge of an embankment, crashed, and wound up in a wadi somewhere? He could be trapped and seriously injured in a smashed-up vehicle, perhaps even dead!"

Quickly shaking off that depressing notion, Jake offered a whole list of other possibilities. "Perhaps Harper came down with a serious illness while camping and is incapacitated. Malaria, schistosomiasis, typhoid, and all manner of insect stings and bites are common in this part of Nigeria. There's also about a dozen different types of poisonous snakes roaming about. Or... he could have been kidnapped by a gang of some type, robbed, or simply got lost and is still wandering around trying to find this magical oasis of his."

At the mention of the word "robbed" by the marine, both Jamie and Cody glanced at each other.

"What if," Cody speculated, sitting up straighter in his seat, "Danny accidently stumbled across some grave robbers...looting a remote archeological site in search of Nok artifacts?"

"Is it possible?" Jamie quickly asked, picking up on Cody's line of thinking.

"It certainly would explain a few things...except..."

"Except what, Cody?" Jamie shot back.

"If that were the case," Cody added, "looters are just like poachers. They would be more likely to kill and get rid of any evidence as opposed to being caught. There are some pretty nasty tribesmen out there and this country has very strict laws regarding the theft of relics. The Nigerians are especially touchy about being ripped off when it comes to their artifacts."

"What the hell are you two talking about?" asked the young marine in the back seat.

Cody took the lead, with interjections from Jamie, in explaining to Jake what they had learned about the Noks, their culture, and how valuable their artwork was. Jake could certainly see the viability in such a theory and was beginning to think he should have brought some real firepower with him.

Like the miles, other theories came and went and did nothing to relieve the apprehension and anxiety all were feeling. The last possibility they talked about, the one that probably weighed the heaviest on their minds and concerned them the most, was what if they couldn't find Harper or any trace of him? What if his disappearance was a permanent thing? That scary proposition would leave a lot of people with a lot of unanswered questions and would probably haunt a great number of people, including them, for the rest of their lives.

Of the three, it was the trained soldier and the youngest of the group who seemed to be the most level-headed and focused on the task at hand. Jake informed Jamie and Cody that in a standard search and rescue operation, the first objective was to gain as much "intel" as possible. Having as much intelligence, or information, as obtainable up front would allow the searchers to concentrate their resources and efforts in the most efficient way. Oftentimes, with an adequate amount of information, the simple process of elimination would lead searchers directly to their target.

That was exactly what Cody and Jamie started doing over a day ago without even realizing it. Through their efforts, they had good leads and they knew, approximately, where Harper was headed. One clue always generated another, bringing them, step by step, closer to finding out what happened to their lost cohort. Jake reassured them they were on the right track and doing everything the professionals would be doing. Both Jamie and Cody appreciated the vote of confidence.

Right on schedule, approximately one hour after leaving Jos, they saw the sign for Anguwan and turned off the A3 Highway and drove into the little town.

Anguwan was the typical, small, off-road hamlet one would find along any northern Nigerian highway. All of the buildings except for a half-dozen were single-story and constructed out of concrete blocks or mud and mortar. The town had several two-story buildings and one which was three stories. Almost all of the buildings had either rusty, corrugated tin, or the newer-type tile roofs. Electricity was available in the town since it was just off a major highway and it had a deep well with a functioning water-delivery system, but no real sewer system by Western standards. The town was clean, and well laid out with nice wide streets and was fairly quiet, if not somewhat picturesque with a variety of trees and flowering bushes scattered about.

Once they were into the main part of town, Cody spotted a filling station with a small, open air eatery across the street from it. Jamie swung the Range Rover in next to the solitary gas pump and asked the rather young attendant to top off the Rover with the highest octane petrol he had.

Cody and Jake got out, stretched, and headed for the little restaurant across the way. Cody glanced at his watch. They'd made good time, it was just 7:00 a.m. They had until 3 p.m. that afternoon, 9 a.m. Washington time, to find something credible enough to stop the 48-clock and forestall a heavy-duty manhunt.

An elderly man with a white-stubbly beard came out of the newly – constructed, single-room building to assist the youngster with the petrol. Before he would start the pump, the elder one insisted on a cash deposit before any fuel was administered. That was the way business was done in rural places. Strangers paid up front to forgo any chance of running off without paying their bill. Even money was also the norm. If one only rang up eight Naira worth of gas and gave the attendant a ten Naira note, there would be no change.

The old man was exceptionally curious to see an official NSC vehicle at his place of business and asked Jamie if he was joining the other fellow. Jamie couldn't believe his ears and yelled at Cody and Jake to hustle back over. He wanted them in on any conversation that might relate to the whereabouts of Harper. Believing he might have a solid lead with the old man, Jamie managed to ask a couple of more questions before the other men made it back across the square to the gas station.

Cody couldn't help but make light of the gathering. "What's up, Jamie. Having issues with the locals?"

"No, no. Nothing like that," Jamie said, gesturing towards

the elderly Nigerian. "This man told me a Range Rover just like ours passed through here four days ago!"

"Did the driver stop and gas up?" Jake asked.

"No, no he didn't," Jamie replied with a frown. "According to this old guy, the rig just went through town without stopping. He said it was heading north toward Kwambo."

"Did he get a look at the driver?" asked Cody.

"Nope," replied Jamie, "but he did say there was only one person in the blue-colored Rover. The driver."

"Wow," Cody remarked. "Good work. I think we just got a solid lead. Let's grab something to eat and follow the trail. We already ordered something."

The old man filling the Rover was paying more attention to the three Americans than he was to his job and accidentally over-filled the tank, letting a small amount of petrol squirt out and run down the side of the Rover's fender. "Sorry-o" was all he said as he wiped off the spilled gas with a dirty rag.

Ever since he set foot in this West African country, Cody always found the expressions used by the Nigerians as somewhat entertaining. "How now?" was the usual greeting. "Sorry-o," the standard apology. "Master," the term used to address male foreigners or ex-pats. And if anyone was truly angry with you, they'd call you a "son of a goat," usually in their native tongue, so the insult didn't register with foreigners.

Hammer finished his business at the gas station and relocated the NSC rig across the street and closer to the eatery while the other two walked. Cody and Jake had already ordered breakfast for the three of them: scrambled eggs and shredded chicken meat rolled up with some kind of chunky sauce in a piece of flatbread. It reminded Jake of a lame attempt at a breakfast burrito. Jamie joked he hoped they brought enough toilet paper and antacids.

After they finished their meal which, they had to admit, was surprisingly good and surprisingly cheap, the trio went back to the parked Rover and did an equipment check. This also gave Jake an opportunity to try out his radio set and update the consulate in Kaduna.

The Hughes AN/PRC-104B was a compact, high-frequency shortwave radio set with the capability to reach anywhere within a thousand mile radius, given the right atmospheric conditions. The radio was designed to utilize "Sky Wave Propagation." In other words, bounce its signals off the ionosphere as opposed to using strictly line-of-sight transmissions. With 20 watts of output power, this allowed the radio waves to travel beyond the horizon and was well suited for field work and combat situations. Military operators referred to the set as the "Prick, 10-4 Bravo."

It only took Jake about ten minutes to set up the fourteen-pound set. After unpacking it, he grounded the set with a small alligator clamp to the frame of the Rover then unrolled the twenty-five foot tape antennae and flung one end over a low-hanging branch of a nearby corkwood tree. Finally, he connected the battery pack and turned the set on.

Before leaving Lagos, Sgt. Ripper had assigned the marine guard in Kaduna and Simmons a special frequency and a call sign to use. This wasn't, by any stretch of the imagination, a secret mission of sorts; they simply wanted to be discreet and they were following standard marine radio protocol.

Once the set was powered up and everything checked out, Jake tried reaching Kaduna. "Kilo Charlie One," he announced, "this is Victor Sierra Tango." Simmons was using the International Radiotelephony Alphabet to identify who he wanted to raise and to identify who he was. "Kilo Charlie" meant Kaduna consulate and "One" because that station was home base for the search. "Victor Sierra Tango" meant Volunteer search team. "Keep it simple" was always Gunny Ripper's motto.

Twice more, he made the initial call before he got the designated response. "Victor Sierra Tango...this is Kilo Charlie One...read you five by five." The two Volunteers and the borrowed marine were relieved everything was working as designed. "Kilo Charlie One...team arrived safely in Anguwan and has a positive lead...will travel north to Kwambo...repeat, Kwambo...expect next transmission around noon."

"Roger, Victor Sierra Tango...stand by."

The three listened to ten seconds of muted static before Kaduna came back on line. "Victor Sierra Tango...be advised... Peace Corps people are in route from Ghana and Washington D.C. to Lagos...over."

"Shit!" Cody blurted out, and was thankful he wasn't talking into the headset. "That's all we need right now, PC people all over the place trying to look like they're doing something! Christ, we haven't even come close to our forty-eight hours yet!" To Cody, this represented the notion the organization had little or no faith in his ability to take care of his small contingent of Volunteers.

"Cody," Jamie said, putting his hand on Armstrong's shoulder, "this doesn't mean they have lost faith in you, or in us. This only means they are fulfilling their responsibility to ensure the safety and well-being of a Peace Corps Volunteer lost on foreign soil. That's all. I don't think it's anything personal and, who knows, they might actually be of some help."

Cody thanked his friend and fellow Volunteer for the sentiment and asked Jake to acknowledge the transmission and sign off.

While the marine was packing up his equipment, Cody and Jamie spread their map out over the front fender of the Rover and agreed the next clue probably awaited them in the little village/town of Kwambo, approximately an hour's drive time to the north. It was now 8:25 and they estimated that if all went well, they should be there somewhere around 9:30.

"Let's get going," Cody finally said. "It's starting to get hot and we're burning daylight!"

CHAPTER 15

Tuesday Morning, September 23

North Central Nigeria

The two Peace Corps Volunteers and the young marine left Anguwan in a cloud of dust, literally. The dry, red dirt roads in this part of the country were famous for that.

As they were motoring north, they took notice of several wrecked and abandoned cars and trucks along the way. None were of the Range Rover variety. This stretch of road had a great deal fewer scooters, cars, trucks, and lorries than what they expected. Most of the people traveling on this road were either walking or riding bikes. During the hour-long drive, the three talked about what they were going to do once they reached the small hamlet of Kwambo.

Hammer, behind the wheel as always, confessed he knew very little about this area of Nigeria. Except that the indigenous tribes were primarily Hausa, Fulani, Gwari, and Arawa. "Aside from that, I'm pretty much in the dark about this part of the country." Feeling like he didn't contribute much, he added that he thought the countryside was rather beautiful and saw why Danny would be drawn to it.

Cody nodded in agreement with Jamie's observation then turned around in his seat to ask Jake, sitting in the middle of the back seat, a question he'd been wanting to ask ever since they picked him up in Jos.

"What's the story behind you helping us out on this search?"

The amicable marine leaned forward to talk over the road

noise. "My involvement in this little manhunt came about from an idea the Gunny sold to DCM Olvera. Like all of the marines in our detachment, we feel somewhat of a kinship with you guys. So I think that was part of it, you know, that pledge where no man gets left behind. I also think the Gunny was just itchin' to get in on some kind of action. Embassy security duty can get kinda boring, unless there's a riot or something like that going on."

"I can understand all that," Cody observed, "But why you, in particular?"

"I volunteered. Not so much at Gunny's Ripper's 'suggestion,' but because it sounded like a good opportunity to put my training to actual use. I also like Danny. He's a good guy, a party animal and...I was also a little bored."

Knowing Danny like they did, both Cody and Jamie could agree with the "party animal" part. They could also see Jake was sincere in his desire to help find Harper and that he was happy to lend whatever expertise he could. The three were developing a good working relationship between them. They all got along well and genuinely liked one another. Both Jamie and Cody were glad to have Jake along, and said so on several occasions.

The countryside was almost entirely farmland. In some directions, as far as the eye could see. The farming plots were sporadically broken up by grassland and savannah. It was what one would expect to see in this region of the country. A great number of people, cattle, and goats were out and about, especially on the road, which required Jamie to slow down considerably.

At approximately 9:40 a.m., the blue Range Rover entered the little hamlet of Kwambo. Everyone seemed to be staring at them. Cody made the offhand remark they probably did look a little out of place.

"Maybe they don't see too many people of your 'color' in this neck of the woods," teased Jake.

"Easy for you to say, you fit right in," Cody said, which generated a chuckle out of all of them.

"Maybe it's because I'm the one riding in the back of this

official-looking rig and they think I'm someone important," quipped Jake. "You know, like some high ranking NSC official and you two are my escorts."

"Fat chance of that," remarked Jamie, jumping in on the exchange. "Anyone can plainly see you're not from around here!"

Considering the fact that Jake Simmons was just as dark-skinned as any of the locals, their chuckles turned into outright laughter. With the stress they'd all been feeling lately, it felt good to let go.

As with most Americans of their generation and age, keeping things on the lighter side served a variety of purposes. By trading "jabs," they not only helped to mask any anxieties and apprehensions, but also the joking promoted a sense of bravado. Interjecting an element of humor into an otherwise serious situation also helped to establish an element of comradeship.

Kwambo was home to somewhere around 800 people and its occupants were from a variety of tribes. But as Jamie implied, the population consisted mostly of Hausas. The streets, if you could call them that, were nothing more than packed dirt. Like most Nigerian towns, sidewalks were virtually non-existent. Buildings were constructed of concrete blocks or mud bricks. The larger of the buildings had the ubiquitous tin roofs, while the remainder had thatched roofs. Chickens, goats, and dogs roamed freely in the streets. Kwambo was a postcard of rural African living.

The town was spread out fairly evenly on both sides of the road, which widened considerably as it went through town. On each side was a colorful assortment of stalls where locals could purchase a variety of meats, vegetables, fruits, spices, palm oil, drinks, clothing, and a thousand other items. The main road through Kwambo was, for all intents and purposes, the principal market area for the community and surrounding countryside. On this day, a good many people were out shopping, bartering, and talking.

Jamie pulled the Rover into a small open plot of land that resembled something like a parking lot and turned off the

Rover's engine. The three decided Jamie would walk one side of the street and Cody would walk the other. Jake would stay behind with the Rover and keep an eye on it, as well as all of the equipment they had inside. It didn't take long for Jake and the blue NSC Range Rover to attract attention. Perhaps, Jake thought, Cody was right when he joked about these people thinking he was somebody important.

"You...coach?" asked one youngster, pointing to the National Sports Commission emblem on the door.

Not knowing what else to say, Jake said he was.

"Coach what?"

"I coach fitness," Jake replied, pumping his arms as if he were lifting weights.

"Ah hah." From the wide, white grin, the kid was obviously proud of himself for making first contact with this important visitor. "You coach boys...be strong," the young Nigerian said, nodding his head as he played to the small crowd gathering around them.

Simmons had only been in Nigeria for less than three months and had not yet had the opportunity to get out of Lagos and experience the people and culture of this West African nation. He was instantly intrigued by how open, friendly, and curious these people were. He was also impressed by the fact that even way out here, coaches were held in high esteem. So he seized on what he thought might be a golden opportunity.

"My young friend," Jake said as he knelt down to the boy's level. "Have you seen another car like this one...here?" He pointed at the ground.

"Yes, *Mahori,*" replied the boy. "Sport commission car stop here...four days ago."

"Can you tell me what the driver looked like?" asked Jake, circling his face with an extended finger.

"Yes, *Mahori,*" said the young Nigerian. "Skinny white goat man drive blue Rover. He talk to *tsohon mutum.* Old man over there," and pointed across the street toward an elderly man selling bottled water.

Jake knew he hit pay dirt with the description. Harper

was a tad on the thin side and "goat man" probably referred to his scruffy little chin beard. Jake looked across the way and sighted the old man standing behind a table of plastic bottles in a shabby-looking stall. He thanked the helpful youngster and gave him several, one-Naira coins in gratitude and asked him to watch over their Rover while he hustled across the street.

Jamie was working that side of the market area and saw Jake head for the little stall selling bottled water. Jake made eye contact with Jamie as well and motioned for him to come over.

Simmons reached the stall first, and pretended to be casually looking at the man's merchandise while Hammer caught up.

"What's up, buddy?" inquired Jamie.

"A young boy told me Harper was here four days ago and talked to this man," Jake said as he gestured toward the old merchant.

"Then we should probably find out what he knows," returned Jamie, gently grabbing Jake by the arm and leading him over to the elderly Nigerian.

The man was carefully arranging his one-liter bottles of water in some sort of a geometric display. Dressed in traditional Nigerian tunic-style garb with a pillbox type of hat, the old man was probably younger than he looked, no doubt the result of the climate and a hard life.

The two boys casually walked up to the old man and introduced themselves as coaches from the National Sports Commission. The man's expression was not, what one would call, a warm and welcoming one. Jamie struck up a conversation with him and asked if another coach, like them, had stopped by within the last few days.

"Yes, Master," answered the old one, lowering his head and looking down toward the ground to avoid eye contact.

"A young boy said he talked with you," Jamie went on.

"Yes, Master...*fata fararen fata*...he look for mountain of black stones."

"Can you tell me where this place?" asked Jamie, using his best Pidgin English.

"No go, Master...bad place...bad Juju...no go...no go," quietly pleaded the old man as he slowly shook his head from side to side.

"Please...please, we need to find our friend," Jamie pleaded as he put his hands together in a prayer-like gesture.

The elderly man once again told Jamie not to look for this cursed place. "No go to black mountain...bad spirits...very bad spirits...dangerous place, Master...stay away," he begged as he stole a couple of sideways glances. He was obviously worried someone else might be overhearing this conversation.

Jamie was persistent and said equally bad things could happen if they didn't find their friend. Hammer kept at it, genuinely pleading with the old merchant to help him He was not about to give up on getting all the information he could from the water peddler. He even took two, ten Naira banknotes out of his wallet and placed them on the old man's rickety table.

The old Nigerian lowered his head and looked down at the ground once again, obviously giving Hammer's request serious thought. Finally, he looked up and pointed a bony finger down the road toward the north. The look of anguish lay clear on the old man's face as he quietly told them to turn towards the setting sun when they came to Kwanbo.

"You...go now...go now...no come back," was the last thing he said to Jamie and Jake as they tried to thank him. Then the old man grabbed the money, turned his back to them, and retreated inside of his little stall. The two Americans could only look at one another and wonder what he meant by that.

Cody saw the two walking back toward the Range Rover together and wondered what was up, so he made his way back to the Rover as well. When he caught up with the others at the Rover, they explained to him what they had learned from the old merchant across the way. Breaking out their map once again and laying it across the hood, which Jamie referred to as the "bonnet," because that's what everyone called it in Nigeria, they started planning their next move.

Kwanbo, they saw on the map, was not on the same road as their sister town of Kwambo, where they currently were, or the next small town to the north, Kwamba. The small village-town of Kwanbo was on a separate road that branched off of this main road and headed east, opposite the direction they needed to go.

Jake, well-versed in map reading and cross-country travel, suggested perhaps the old man meant to head west at that point. "Turn toward the setting sun" is what the old man had said. Jake thought if this was where they needed to go, they should turn west when they came to the Kwanbo junction. Jake's theory made sense to the other two and they all agreed that would be their next step.

Cody looked at his watch and made a couple of quick calculations. He estimated a distance of 80-95 kilometers (53-56 miles) to the junction from where they currently were, approximately an hour or more drive time. If they left right away, and it was now after 10 a.m., they could conceivably be at the Kwanbo junction somewhere around a quarter after eleven. That would still give them approximately four more hours to uncover something before time expired on Washington's 48-hour clock.

"Good work, guys. Let's hit the road," Cody announced to his group.

CHAPTER 16

Late Tuesday Morning, September 23

North Central Nigeria

The three made good time on their northward trek toward Kwamba and the Kwanbo junction. The hard-packed dirt road was in reasonably good shape and Jamie pushed the aging Rover about as hard as he dared. Once they left the farmland of Kwambo behind, they didn't encounter anyone on the road except a few stray goats.

"This is strange," Jamie remarked. "You'd think there would be lots of people in this area."

"Not necessarily," Cody said. "Remember what that instructor at the teaching college told us? That this area is fairly remote?"

"It's probably also their siesta time," added Jake. "You know how everything in Nigeria shuts down between eleven a.m. and three p.m. Mid-day heat and all."

With that remark, Cody noticed that his and everyone else's clothes were already stained with sweat and dirt, little wonder since all of the windows were rolled down because the Rover didn't have air conditioning. The outside air temperature was a balmy eight-five degrees Fahrenheit and climbing.

Regardless of the reason for the absence of people, it was still odd to the three young men that they saw no one, no one at all, until they reached the tiny, roadside village known as Kwamba. Even then, they saw very few people. As they pressed on, they were all beginning to appreciate how isolated this part of the country actually was.

They reached the Kwanbo junction with its crude roadway sign after sixty-five minutes of driving, pulled over at what looked like a parking area on the right hand side of the road by the sign, and got out to survey their surroundings.

Cody checked his watch to see how they were doing with time. It was now 11:16. They still had approximately three and a half hours left before the Peace Corps organization went into high gear on an official, sanctioned search. Cody was hoping they could turn up something, anything, to buy them some more time.

Jake grabbed his binoculars from one of the rucksacks and clamored up onto the roof of the Rover. He apologized to Jamie if he contributed any more scratches or dents to the rig. Jamie just smiled and simply told him not to worry. "Anything would be an improvement," he said with a shrug.

From his elevated vantage point, Jake put the high-powered field glasses up to his eyes and scoped out the horizon to the west. Jamie and Cody took advantage of the break and relieved themselves next to the front of the Rover. Neither one wanted to go out into the brush and possibly encounter a snake.

There, far to the northwest of their position, Jake could make out what looked like a large grouping of rocks. He judged it must be at least eighty kilometers (50 miles) away. He invited the other two, one at a time, to come up and take a look while he got down and took a compass heading.

After everyone took a look at what they hoped would be the kopje of the paradise oasis, they crossed the road to find a way to get to it. The three spread out and checked along the west side of the road. They did not find a road, but Jamie spotted tire tracks going off on, what looked like, a trail. "Hey guys. Take a look at this!" he shouted.

Cody and Jake hustled over to where Jamie was crouched down looking at the tire tracks.

"These aren't fresh," proclaimed Jake.

"No, but remember, if Danny did come through here, it was four days ago," Cody reminded them.

Jamie stood up from looking at the tracks and walked back across the road to the parked Rover. He went around to each wheel and looked at the tires. They were all identical. Then he stepped off the distance between the left and right sides. As the other two watched, Jamie then came back to the tracks and took a second look.

"Same type of tire. Same distance between the tracks," Jamie announced. "If I didn't know better, I'd say these markings were made by an NSC Range Rover."

Cody and Jake just looked at each other in amazement. "How in the world did you think to do that?" asked Cody.

Jamie chuckled. "I read about it in a book I finished about a month ago. Some detective was trying to identify what kind of rig was at the scene of a homicide."

"Ingenious," was all Jake could say, shaking his head.

The boys decided before they ventured off road and headed cross-country they should check in with Kaduna. Jake unpacked his "Prick, 10-4 Bravo" radio set and began setting it up as before. Cody checked his watch again; it now read 11:48 a.m. He hoped somebody was still at the Kaduna Consulate and hadn't left early for lunch. Jake assured him his fellow marine would be there regardless and fired up the set.

"Kilo, Charlie, One...this is Victor, Sierra, Tango...over," announced Jake.

After a ten-second wait for a reply, Jake repeated the prescribed call sign then waited another ten seconds before trying again.

Right after his third attempt, loud and clear came the response he was waiting for. "Victor, Sierra, Tango...this is Kilo, Charlie, One...go ahead."

All three quietly exhaled and relaxed a bit.

"Roger...Kilo, Charlie, One...present location for Victor, Sierra, Tango is approximately fifty-five 'klicks' north of Kwambo. Will be heading west, off-road, into open country. Have solid leads and the trail is hot...repeat, trail is hot...over." In the abbreviated, jargon-punctuated language of "milspeak," Jake told his counterpart where they were and that they had positive leads as to where they were heading next.

"Copy...Victor, Sierra, Tango...understand team heading west to open country," was the distant reply, followed by a short pause, "Victor, Sierra, Tango...say next transmission."

Jake looked over at Cody, who looked at his watch, then held up three fingers. "Kilo, Charlie, One," Jake said into the microphone, "next transmission for Victor, Sierra, Tango at fifteen hundred hours...repeat...one, five, zero, zero hours... over."

"Copy...Victor, Sierra, Tango," replied the voice on the other end. "One, five, zero, zero hours...good luck...Kilo, Charlie, One...out."

Jake signed off as well then powered down the radio set. While he was putting it away, Jamie and Cody busied themselves emptying one of the five – gallon "Jerry" cans of gas into the Rover's tank. Jamie locked in the Rover's front wheel hubs, which would enable him to drive with all four wheels engaged for better traction.

Once everyone was on board, Hammer fired up the British-made SUV, made a slight U-turn out of their parking spot, crossed the road, and cautiously entered no-man's-land.

The ensuing ride was bumpy and they were moving along slowly, carefully picking their way across the open stretch of savannah characteristic of the Benue Plateau. Cody looked at his watch and estimated, at this pace, it would take them at least two hours, possibly more, to cover the distance to the isolated kopje.

The three talked very little as they crawled along old animal trails and weaved their way between the Acacia trees and assorted bushes. They crossed a couple of dry river beds and open grassland areas before Jamie observed that the Rover's engine was overheating. They had been traveling for an hour and the "mountain of stones" was still a long way off. Jamie stopped under a tree to let the engine cool off so they could put more water in the radiator. They were all hungry and decided they might as well have lunch, safari-style, while they were waiting.

To be on the safe side, Cody carefully checked out the tree and surrounding area for any signs of unfriendly occupants before getting out. The savannahs of northern Nigeria were home to not only a variety of venomous snakes and poisonous insects, but also baboons, wart hogs, wild dogs, and hyenas. All of which would probably enjoy a change of diet.

Declaring the coast was clear, all three got out of the Rover, stretched, and made their way back to the rear of the vehicle. Jamie opened the tailgate and rummaged through the rucksack that contained all of their food. The three feasted on canned sardines, crackers, and bananas. Other than consuming a granola-type candy bar during their drive from Kwambo to the junction, none of the group had eaten anything since leaving Anguwan.

Having finished his lunch before the others, Jamie popped open the hood of his rig and checked the radiator. The engine had cooled enough to allow him a closer look. Carefully taking off the still very-warm radiator cap, he saw nothing but metal fins inside, which meant the cooling system was dangerously low on water. Then he spotted the problem. The lower hose to the radiator was leaking, leaving a small puddle of liquid under the engine compartment.

"Shit!" was the first word that came out of Jamie's mouth.

Jake and Cody, who were loading up the back of the Rover, stopped what they were doing and glanced at each other, then quickly moved to the front of the SUV.

"I think I must have clipped a rock or something a while back," Jamie informed them. "We're going to have to make repairs to this leaking radiator hose before we can go on. Looks like Murphy's Law is still alive and well, even out here in the boondocks!"

"Do you have a spare hose or anything in your rig we can use to fix it?" asked Cody.

"Maybe," replied Jamie, wrinkling his nose dubiously. "But before we can get to the boot, I mean trunk, we'll need to unload all of our stuff from the back."

Surrendering to the fact they had to unload what they had

loaded up earlier, Jake's expression of "aw, crap" perfectly summed things up. There was nothing left to do but remove all of the gear from the storage area at the rear and check out what was in the tool compartment under a floor hatch.

Once the gear was unloaded, Cody and Jamie rummaged around in the special compartment that held an assortment of tools and the like. Jake once again took the opportunity to break out his binoculars and took a look at the looming mountain of rocks still far off to the northwest. He had read about these unique outcroppings in one of the African reference books they had at the Marine House library.

Kopjes were commonplace and dotted the landscape all over the continent, but Jake couldn't remember any mention of one being this large. He guessed it to be at least the size of the parade ground at Camp Pendleton and quite high as well. It also had an unusual shape and was all alone out here in the middle of nowhere. It was, without question, a mountain of stones, but without a top. To Jake, it looked like a distant and solitary island on the flat sea of the savannah.

Something else about this kopje didn't look right to Jake, something he couldn't quite put his finger on. Giving up on trying to figure it out, he climbed down off the top of the Rover and went to see if he could lend Jamie and Cody a hand.

CHAPTER 17

Tuesday, Late Morning - Early Afternoon, September 23

Lagos

The two male staffers from the Peace Corps Office in Accra, Ghana made the Tuesday morning 9:15 flight to Lagos without too much difficulty, despite the fact that their first plane was overbooked and they had to wait for a second flight.

They were met at the airport shortly after 10:30 by a special liaison person employed by the embassy. The friendly and well-educated Nigerian specialized in expediting and assisting arrivals and departures for the American, Canadian, and British embassies. Something he excelled at thanks to slush fund money and a few friends and relatives who worked at the airport.

The two PC staffers were also met by a driver whose full-time job was to shuttle people back and forth to the airport for the three embassies. The ride from Ikeja International to the American Embassy in downtown Lagos took a little over an hour. The morning traffic, as usual, was heavy and congested. At 11:55, the two walked into the U.S. Embassy, introduced themselves, and were escorted to Michael Olvera's office on the third floor.

Deputy Chief of Mission Olvera met the two in the reception area near MaryAnn and Carol Newsom's desks. After introductions were made, the DCM invited the two Peace Corps people to lunch at the embassy's cafeteria on the fourth floor. By prearrangement, he also had Gunnery Sergeant Ripper and Regional Security Officer Al Shannon join them in a semi-private corner of the dining area.

Over a light lunch of sandwiches and salads, the DCM quietly briefed the two PC staff people on the current status of the search for the missing Volunteer. As expected, they had a great number of questions. Sergeant Ripper and RSO Shannon filled in the details regarding the logistics of what they referred to as "the special operation," a nondescript label they had come up with the previous day.

The three embassy officials got the distinct impression the Peace Corps people were essentially clueless about what had transpired and what was expected of them. Through no fault of their own, Ghanaian PC Director Belvoe had simply told them a Volunteer was missing somewhere in northern Nigeria and they were to get on a plane and report to the embassy in Lagos, then await further instructions.

DCM Olvera and company were uniformly unimpressed with the unprofessional, "knee-jerk" way Belvoe was approaching this situation. The two PC staffers were equally surprised to learn that Matt McKnight, the Peace Corps' West African desk officer, had left the States the previous day and would be arriving in Lagos within a couple of hours.

Although they were rapidly approaching the 48-hour mark, it was Olvera and the two security people's decision to persuade McKnight and the two PC staffers to extend the time period for at least one more day. Their reasoning was based upon the obvious: There was already a search team in the field and they were hot on the trail of the missing Volunteer. One of the members of that team, a marine security guard, was a trained specialist in field survival as well as search and rescue. Having another day to follow their existing leads, without undue interference or fanfare, wouldn't hurt. Who knew what might happen if the Peace Corps and the embassy got the Nigerian authorities, and Lord knew who else, involved.

Olvera knew the two Peace Corps people sent to him from Ghana probably didn't have the authority to make that kind of a decision. The DCM wasn't sure whether McKnight could make that call either. Extending the 48-hour clock to 72 hours or longer would have to come from either Washington or Hampton Belvoe in Accra. Until Matt McKnight could be consulted, they would all have to sit tight.

McKnight's flight went better than anticipated. A tailwind pushed the sleek 707 across the Atlantic faster than anyone could have hoped for. They were way ahead of schedule and pretty much stayed that way as the flight hopscotched its way across western Africa. Matt tried to catch as much sleep as he could so he'd be as alert as possible once he arrived in Lagos. Despite the contribution of several beers and a couple shots of Jack Daniels during the flight across the Atlantic, he didn't get as much sleep as he would have liked.

Just as with the two PC staffers from Ghana, McKnight was met at the airport by the embassy's travel liaison and shuttle driver. Both assisted him through the customs process and had him en route to the embassy within twenty-five minutes of landing. Because it was now early afternoon in the city and the traffic had tapered off, the shuttle driver also made good time and had his passenger to his destination in less than an hour. Matt walked into the embassy's main entrance, introduced himself, and presented his passport and credentials. He was immediately escorted up to DCM Olvera's office. As he walked into the room, the clock on Olvera's office wall said it was 2:10 p.m., which made it 8:10 a.m. in Washington D.C. The unremitting 48-hour clock would expire in fifty minutes.

Crowded into Olvera's office along with Matt were the DCM himself, Bill Ripper, Al Shannon, the two PC staff people from Accra, and MaryAnn Reed. After the introductions were made, the three Peace Corps people settled onto a couch and the rest pulled up extra chairs. Olvera pulled his big leather chair out from behind his desk and joined the group, and then got right to the point. He wanted the 48-hour official waiting period extended for at least another day and explained why.

Matt McKnight shifted in his chair. "I don't have the authority to make that call. That's, more or less, above my pay grade."

"Then who does?" asked Olvera, trying his hardest to

conceal his frustration.

"I think either the in-country Peace Corps director, who would be Hampton Belvoe, or my boss, the regional director for West African programs, Ronald Gerrard."

Everyone in the room exchanged disappointed glances. Most knew if it were up to Belvoe, he would have launched an all-out manhunt days ago, using his people, the Nigerians, UN personnel, as well as any hired guns he could find. He would pull out all the stops and involve whoever he could find. Knowing Belvoe the way they did, he probably would also want to involve the Army, Navy, Air Force, Marines, and CIA as well. He would turn the whole affair into a three-ring circus and would be the self-proclaimed ringmaster. To each member of the group, such a scenario had disaster written all over it.

The embassy's regional security officer, Al Shannon, raised the point of a technicality that would change everything.

"Hampton Belvoe is only the ad-hoc director for the Nigerian program, not 'the' director by legal definition," Shannon began. "Since he isn't in-country with the requisite support staff. Also, no in-country Peace Corps director, wherever they are, 'outranks' the American ambassador or his deputy in that country. This was established back in 1962 so there would be no conflict of interest or jumping the chain of command. Some Peace Corps director in Southeast Asia tried going around the ambassador there and wound up losing his job because of it. When it comes to Foreign Service work in foreign countries, the State Department trumps the Peace Corps."

"In other words," said a now-smiling Olvera, "I have the authority to supersede Belvoe and I can make the call on this?"

"That would be my understanding, Mike," observed Shannon.

The two PC staffers were dumbfounded, but Matt was grinning.

"MaryAnn, please draft a cable for immediate release," ordered the DCM. "Mark it 'Urgent' and 'Eyes Only' for Mr. Ronald Gerrard, Peace Corps regional director for West African programs. Say because we already have an embassy-sanctioned search-in-progress for the missing Volunteer, it is my desire, for which I take full responsibility...that no official action be taken by the Peace Corps organization for an additional twenty-four hours...or until further notice. It is my understanding that under the terms of the joint operating agreement between our two organizations, this action falls under my authority as the deputy chief of mission for the U.S. embassy in Nigeria."

"Oh, and MaryAnn," Olvera added, "don't forget to throw in all that stuff about 'with all due respect' and 'we will keep you informed to the highest extent possible,' blah, blah, blah."

Everyone in the room chuckled at that, including the two staff people from Accra.

As MaryAnn hustled out of the room and back to her desk, Olvera turned to face Matt McKnight and the other two Peace Corps representatives. "Matt, I've got a job for you, which includes our other two guests as well."

The three Peace Corps people quickly realized they were dealing with a true professional and listened intently as DCM Olvera outlined his plan.

"First on the list, I want you to cable Hampton Belvoe in Accra and inform him what's going on and why. Be as diplomatic as possible. I want the Ghanaian PC director working with me for the most part, not against me."

"Second, I want the three of you to set up a command post, of sorts. I'll ask MaryAnn to get you squared away in a small empty office down the hall. All information, search coordination, and planning will now be your responsibility."

The DCM went on to tell the three that he would arrange to have them stay at the embassy's guest apartment in the complex across the street, but wanted someone in the command post around the clock.

"The RSO will provide you with identity cards and embassy passes. I'll direct the consulate in Kaduna and the embassy's Communications and Records section to communicate directly with you as information comes in from the field. Whatever cables you need to send out to Accra or Washington can be given to MaryAnn."

"And last but not least, I want one of you packed and ready to go on a moment's notice if you're needed up-country for any reason."

It was obvious to the three visitors Olvera sincerely wanted to include the Peace Corps in on this to the highest extent possible, but he also made it clear he wanted to be kept up to date on everything that was happening, and that he had the final word.

The three Peace Corps people were elated and excited to be at the vanguard of the search and rescue mission. The two staffers from Ghana were impressed by Olvera's organizational approach and expressed their gratitude. One of them even mentioning that, for a change, it was nice to be working with someone as opposed to just working for them. Matt couldn't help but smile at the indirect shot at the leadership shortcomings of Hampton Belvoe.

To his credit, DCM Olvera had shrewdly managed to make the manhunt a Peace Corps operation and forestall the 48-hour clock, while still being in control of it. He hoped Belvoe and PC Washington would be happy with the arrangement. His three new disciples certainly were.

Olvera turned to Shannon and Ripper. "Al...Gunny...get word up to Kaduna that I've intervened and extended the waiting period by another twenty-four hours so they can relay it to our field team. Also, inform them we would like to have regular updates, and if they don't turn up anything by three p.m. tomorrow, they're to hightail it back to Jos and await further instructions. Have your people in Kaduna relay all field reports to our Peace Corps command center here at the embassy."

"What happens after the extension is up on Wednesday afternoon and our boys don't find anything?" asked Al Shannon, saying what was on everyone's mind.

"Can we send any more of your marines up-country with one of these PC guys if we need to?" the DCM asked the other two.

After a quick minute of thought, Bill Ripper spoke up. "With Al's permission, I could probably free up one more, but you probably won't like my choice."

RCO Shannon's eyes rolled up toward the ceiling. He knew what was coming next.

"And who might that be?" inquired Olvera, half smiling.

"Me, Sir," answered the serious-looking gunnery sergeant.

Olvera stood there in silence pondering Sergeant Ripper's offer for several seconds. Meeting Ripper's steely gaze, he responded with the obvious question, "Anxious to get in on the action, Gunny?"

"Anxious to find our missing Volunteer, Mike," came the sincere reply.

"If it's okay with Al, I'll approve it," Olvera said. "But first, I think we should wait out the extension I've just authorized."

Everyone in the room glanced at the oversized clock on Olvera's office wall, which now read 2:46 p.m.

"First things first, guys," ordered the DCM. "Let's get on the horn with Kaduna before the field team checks in so we can update them. Then, we'll get you Peace Corps people set up in your command post and temporary quarters. Gunny, I think you and Al ought to discuss your next steps and get you prepared to go up-country if need be."

"Yes...Sir," was Ripper's straightforward response.

CHAPTER 18

Tuesday Afternoon, September 23

North Central Nigeria

The only thing Jamie could find in his rig that might work to fix the leaking radiator hose was a partial roll of electrical tape.

Cody crawled under the front of the Rover to see how bad the damage was. It was evident that repairing this tear would take a considerable amount of tape, probably a lot more than what they had. What they needed was a new hose. Which, of course, Jamie didn't have.

"What might work," offered Jamie, "is if we had some sort of flexible sleeve to slip over the damaged area and then we could secure it with tape." Jamie looked at Cody and added, "Do you think that would work?"

A light bulb suddenly went off inside Cody's head.

"Jamie!" Cody said, "you're a genius! Open your field kit and give me all the condoms you have!"

Jamie smiled, automatically realizing what Cody had in mind. It was worth a try.

"You got it, pal!" Jamie quickly moved to the back of the Rover to retrieve his Peace Corps-issued, field survival kit.

Much to Jamie's chagrin, Cody said he needed every one of his "rubbers," which would temporarily leave him without any protection from sexually-transmitted diseases. Not that Jamie had to worry about catching anything way out here. Cody couldn't resist teasing his fellow Volunteer about his almost-full supply of "latex insurance," as he called them. Jamie simply said he was saving them for a "rainy day." The comment generated a few chuckles from the other two.

Cody unscrewed the hose clamp that held the lower radiator hose to the radiator and pulled it free of the flange. A fair amount of water came gushing out from both the hose and the radiator, soaking the ground Cody was lying on. The rust-colored coolant had a distinctive acrid odor.

Cody wiped the hose clean with a rag he had scrounged from the hatch area of the Rover. He had Jamie dip another rag in gasoline and wiped down the hose again. Cody explained this would remove any oily residue and slightly abrade the hose so the tape would stick better.

Jamie opened up the three packages of condoms he had retrieved and cut the ends off each one. Handing them to Cody one at a time, Jamie couldn't pass up a golden opportunity to say something "appropriate" for the occasion. "That one was for Rosalee...that one was for Janet...that one was for the ugly divorcee who lives across the street from me."

Cody and Jake laughed and started trading quips with Jamie. The banter and the levity was a welcome relief.

Cody stretched the opening of the first condom, then slipped it over the end of the hose and worked it down to within a couple of inches from the small tear. The he unrolled it, much like it was designed to be applied, over the tear. As he estimated, the condom covered the tear with approximately a one and one-half inch overlap on each end. The tightly-stretched condom fit nicely around the two-inch diameter hose. Cody repeated this process until he had used all three of Jamie's Trojan-brand prophylactics. Then he heavily taped each end and the center section, giving stability and strength to the patch job.

After Cody finished re-attaching the hose to the radiator, Jamie and Jake fetched a couple jugs of water and filled the radiator back up. By the time they had eaten lunch, repaired the Rover's cooling system, and had everything packed up and were ready to go, they had lost more than an hour. It was now 2:46 p.m. and all three were getting anxious about making the three o'clock call to Kaduna.

Rather than hit the road immediately, Cody decided they should stay put and let Jake set up his radio. They killed the next fifteen minutes by taking turns checking out the distant kopje with Jake's binoculars and by starting up the Rover to see if their handiwork would hold, which it did.

At 2:59 p.m. by everyone's synchronized watches, Jake Simmons made the call to his counterpart in Kaduna. On the second attempt, he got through. Jake had nothing of significance to report. Only where they were, that they had a minor breakdown, fixed it, and were now ready to proceed. The call wasn't so much of a status report as a check-in. If the trio hadn't made the call when they said they would, it would mean something was amiss. All three were extremely anxious about any news regarding the expiration of the 48-hour waiting period, which was to happen as they made their 3 p.m. call.

"Victor, Sierra, Tango...be advised," came the distant-sounding voice on the radio. "...Just received word from Lagos...deadline has been extended...repeat, deadline has been extended...over." The reply from Kaduna was both a relief and a reprieve for the three boys and all exhaled deeply and looked at one another.

"Kilo, Charlie, One..." Jake quickly replied into his headset's microphone, "understand deadline has been extended...by how much...over."

"Victor, Sierra, Tango," came the immediate reply, "extension has been granted...for additional 24 hours...over."

Cody tapped Jake on his shoulder. "I'd like to know by whose authority and if there are any conditions or restrictions."

Jake immediately followed up with Cody's request.

"Victor, Sierra, Tango...the DCM pulled rank on Ghana PC director...no conditions except regular reports...no restrictions except for you to return to Jos after 24 hours...over."

The two Peace Corps Volunteers and the marine looked at one another and then at their watches. They all shared the same thought: "Is one more day enough time?"

The marine who was broadcasting from Kaduna asked Jake when he could expect their next transmission. Again, Jake looked at Cody for a decision. This time, Cody said 6 p.m., or 1800 hours, figuring they should reach their destination by then.

Jake smiled, made the call, and signed off. "I appreciate you making regular reports every three hours. That's very "military" of you."

Cody laughed and accepted the compliment as offered.

The boys quickly packed up their gear and were back on the road by quarter after three. By Jake's estimation, and at their present rate of travel, they should reach their objective in approximately one hour.

Cody said, "That will put us in good shape to report something positive by six o'clock. I'm thinking if we find something concrete to follow up on, and we need more time, we can convince them to extend the timeline further if need be."

All agreed with a nod and climbed back into the well-used Range Rover.

Jamie started it up and once everyone was settled in, slowly built up speed while keeping one eye peeled on the temperature gauge. So far, so good. The needle stayed in the green arc.

From that point on, Jamie did his best to follow, what he assumed to be were the tracks of another Range Rover across the grassy plain. Jamie was also doing his best to avoid rocks and stubs of bushes as he went along. He didn't want a repeat of what happened before. Despite his trepidation, he still managed to keep up a good pace and the looming kopje got ever closer.

The savannah of this part of Nigeria was pretty much what one would expect: dry grasslands punctuated by an occasional Acacia tree, some sandy areas, different types of shrubs and bushes, and the occasional rock outcropping. All three mentioned they saw little wildlife, which they thought strange since there were no people out here.

"Is this the way Africa is supposed to look like?" asked Jake.

Cody deferred the question to Jamie since he had spent most of his posting in this region.

"I don't think so," Jamie said. "Usually, there are either lots of people, or in their absence, lots of wildlife. I've never seen it so dead up here."

"Nice choice of words," remarked Cody.

"Sorry." Jamie cringed. "I don't think this is a normal thing. There's something about this area that's just plain creepy."

"You know," Jake interjected, "I've had a strange feeling about this as well. I've been looking at that oversized kopje we're headed toward and something about it doesn't look right. Somehow, it just looks...looks...ominous to me."

"A soldier's combat intuition?" asked Jamie.

"Maybe." Jake shrugged. "The last time I had this feeling was during 'E & E' training. That would be escape and evade training to you two 'non-coms.'"

Jamie and Cody both chuckled at the label. Although it could have been taken as a derogatory remark, neither Cody nor Jamie took it that way. Jake even made it sound somewhat complimentary.

"What happened?" asked Cody.

"E & E is a simulated exercise where a lone soldier is isolated from the rest of his unit, usually behind enemy lines," Jake began. "He has to escape and evade his pursuers for a 72-hour period and live off the land. It's basically a hunting game where the isolated soldier is the prey. If he gets caught, he gets tortured, and the hunting team has creative ways of simulating the real thing."

"Nice game," groaned Jamie.

"It's a normal part of combat training," Jake added. "It's also an extreme wake-up call for the survival instinct. After the exercise was over, I had nightmares for about a week. I was unlucky enough to get caught. This area and the place we're headed for seems to bring back unpleasant memories."

The conversation carried them to within about eight kilometers (5 miles) of the kopje. Naturally, the closer they got, the larger it looked. For the last several kilometers, Jake had positioned himself to be leaning over the top of the front seat between Cody and Jamie. He wanted to get a better look at the kopje as they approached it.

"Christ, would you look at that!" Jamie said to no one in particular. "This thing is massive!"

Cody tilted his head so he could clearly see it through the windshield. "It looks almost man-made, like a fort of some kind, instead of a natural geological phenomenon."

Jamie shook his head. "The rocks and boulders are too large to have been moved by primitive Nigerians."

Jake said, "Maybe it's the crater of an ancient volcano that never fully developed."

Orientated southwest to northeast, the oval-shaped kopje extended for approximately eight hundred meters, approximately one-half of a mile, across the flat savannah landscape. The outside consisted of semi-sheer rock walls of dark granite and volcanic tuff which rose, vertically, to about 40-68 meters (130-225 feet) in height. The looming structure was indeed impressive. It was also unexpected to find something like this, especially in this part of the country. This kopje was a genuine geological anomaly. It was totally out of place when compared to other rock outcroppings or the surrounding landscape.

Jamie was still following the previous tire tracks as he slowly approached the kopje from the southeast quadrant. Their gazes were transfixed on the sinister-looking monolith as Jamie continued following the tracks, slowly proceeding counterclockwise around the structure to the northwest side. Out of habit, Cody checked his watch to see if they were still on schedule, which they were. His watch said it was a little before five p.m.

They continued looking up at the formidable stone wall as Jamie slowly came to a stop on the northwestern side of the edifice. There, close to the rim, was a distinctive notch in the wall, a sort of entrance which, hopefully, created a doorway to what lay within. Below the notch, a pile of boulders and rocks lay in a tumble. Jake pointed out what looked like a pathway through the boulders.

The low afternoon sun cast a strange light on this side of the Kopje, which made the stones look somewhat oily. Unlike the natural beauty of the surrounding African landscape, this place looked downright ugly and menacing.

Both Jamie and Jake sat there looking at the structure with their mouths partially agape, then nearly jumped out of their skins when an excited Cody suddenly yelled, "Sonofabitch!"

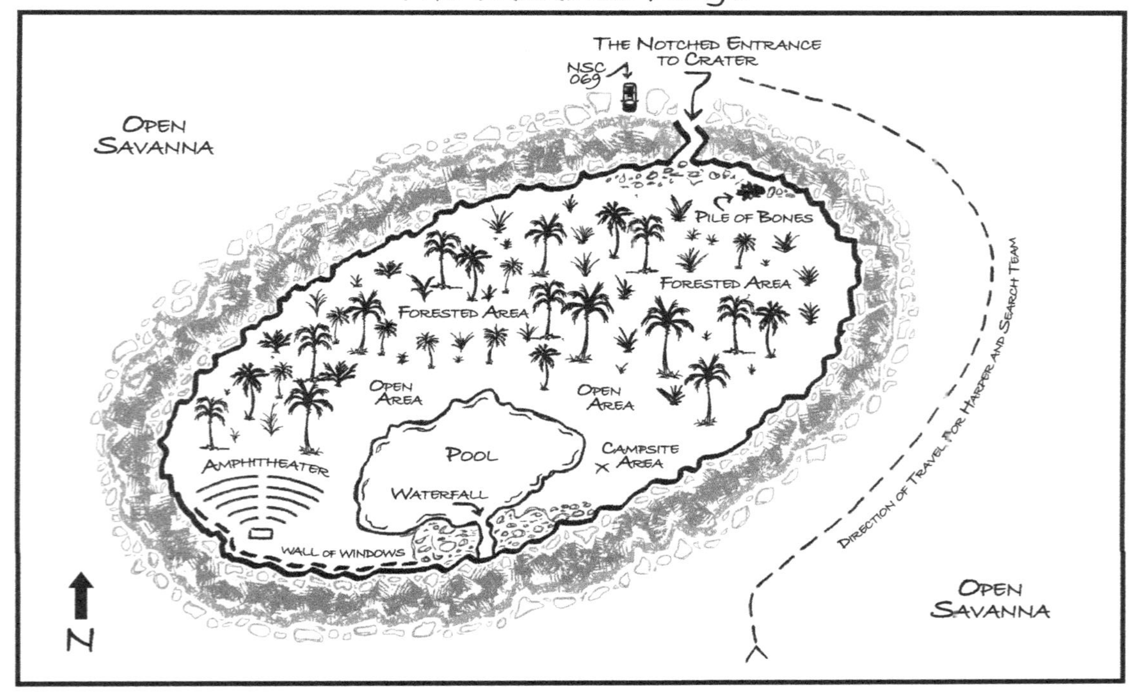
The Paradise Kopje
The Notched Entrance to Crater
NSC 069
Open Savanna
Pile of Bones
Forested Area
Forested Area
Open Area
Open Area
Pool
Campsite Area
Amphitheater
Waterfall
Wall of Windows
Direction of Travel For Harper and Search Team
N
Open Savanna

CHAPTER 19

Late Tuesday Afternoon, September 23

The Paradise Kopje

Cody was pointing a bouncing finger at a pile of bushes between two large boulders by the entrance to the notched area. There, barely visible, one could make out the tires of a blue vehicle hidden by the shrubbery.

"Jesus, Cody!" stammered Jamie. "I almost peed my pants! Don't ever do that!"

"Sorry-o," was all Cody could muster, slightly embarrassed and now realizing how much this place had them all on edge.

The two Volunteers and the marine slowly got out of the Range Rover, their hearts pounding and their senses at maximum. All eyes were on the camouflaged vehicle.

After taking a quick look around, Jake suggested they all don a web utility belt with a full canteen and attach their machetes to it. As they did so, Cody took another quick look at his watch. It was now 5:24 p.m. Together, they decided to check out the hidden rig to see if it was, in fact, Harper's SUV.

Once that was confirmed, Jake would break out the radio, check in with Kaduna and inform his counterpart they had located the Rover belonging to the missing Volunteer. Jake would also report they had not seen any sign of Harper or started a search for him.

It didn't take the boys long to completely uncover the blue, NSC Range Rover with the distinctive emblem on the front doors. The clincher was the license plate, NSC 069. Harper had specifically requested the license from the sports commission just to see if he would get it. Cody had always thought that Danny, being a little on the wild side, might have gone a little too far with this one. He hoped no one from the sports commission, or otherwise, picked up on the sexual reference.

Other than a light coating of dust and grime, along with the usual dents, dings, and scratches on the Rover, nothing was amiss with the rig. It was all locked up and none of the windows were broken. The three agreed Danny's ride had not been messed with in any way.

"Okay, guys, so what do we do now?" Cody asked. "We've only got about half an hour before we need to check in."

"I say we do a little 'recon' before we make the call," suggested Jake. "That way, we might have more information and a plan of action to pass on."

"Sounds good to me, let's do it," Jamie chimed in.

Jake suggested they fan out and walk the perimeter of the kopje for fifty meters (164 feet) in both directions to see if they could pick up any evidence of Danny walking about. Cody and Jamie agreed. They spread out approximately three meters (10 feet) apart and started walking in a straight line abreast.

They covered their intended search area with time to spare and saw only a few footprints on the driver's side and at the back of the Rover. The prints were all the same and led up to the rocky area below the notch in the wall. It looked as if Danny had made more than one trip back to the Rover, probably to check out the accessibility of this spot or to haul more gear. Aside from those prints, no other human or animal tracks of any kind lay anywhere. Something all three thought a bit strange.

What they had found so far led the boys to the assumption that this was, indeed, the so-called paradise oasis. They also assumed the actual oasis itself must be on the inside of this crater of rocks, meaning it would be thoroughly isolated from the rest of the surrounding savannah. What actually was on the other side of this wall was anybody's guess until they scaled this rocky area, breached the rim at the notch, and saw for themselves what lay within. They were hoping Danny Harper would be somewhere inside. Hopefully, safe and sound.

Jake said they should keep to their communication schedule and make the 6 p.m. call to Kaduna before going any further. Cody and Jamie readily agreed and started helping Jake set up his equipment. As they were doing so, they discussed whether or not they should spend the night inside the kopje or outside by the vehicles.

Cody noted that sunset would occur around 6:30, which would be in about forty-five minutes, but it wouldn't be fully dark until about 7:00 or so. This would give them plenty of time to scale the wall, get inside, and set up a camp before night fell. They also had a Coleman lantern, several flashlights, and fire-making material to stave off the darkness, if need be.

Day or night, all were eager to start searching for Danny in earnest. They felt like they were getting close to the end of their manhunt and were anxious to continue. Whatever they decided to do, they had to make the call rather quickly so they could inform Kaduna of their plans.

Jake finished with the final set-up of the radio and made his initial call to the marine manning the same at the Kaduna Consulate. He got his reply on his second attempt. "Kilo, Charlie, One" was relieved to hear from the search party and asked if there were any problems or if they had turned up anything new.

Jake reported they had found Harper's Range Rover at a large, remote kopje, but no sign of the missing Volunteer except for a few tracks. He added they had not yet initiated a significant foot search for him.

As expected, Kaduna wanted to know what the three intended to do and when their next transmission would be.

Jake looked at Cody and Jamie with an expression that said, "Well?" Under his breath, Cody asked Jake to tell "Kilo, Charlie, One" to stand by, which he did.

"Okay, guys. What's the call?" Cody asked his two companions when Jake set down his headset. "Do we spend the night out here and wait until morning, or do we move inside, set up a camp, and start looking for Danny tonight?"

Both Jake and Jamie stuck out their thumbs and motioned

them toward the kopje.

"Alright, guys," Cody said with an air of finality, "let's pack up and go exploring. Jake, would you please inform Kaduna as to what our intentions are and that we'll transmit again at nine?" Jake made the transmission, signed off, and started packing up his radio set.

Jamie took the opportunity to climb back into his Rover and close all of the fresh air vents. Cody thought that to be somewhat of a strange thing to do and asked Jamie why he did that. His simple reply was, "To keep the critters from crawling inside during the night."

Jamie said he had climbed into his rig one morning after leaving the vents open overnight and almost sat on a scorpion. He got into the habit of closing the vents and all the windows at night after that. Cody just nodded, thinking he wished he'd thought of that a time or two.

Once the radio set was packed up, all three started loading up their backpacks and slipped them on. In addition to their own packs, Jake and Cody were carrying the radio set in its combat case between them. Jamie was tasked to carry the extra rucksack of equipment along with his own pack. Each man figured he was carrying somewhere around fifty to sixty pounds and each was convinced he had the heaviest load. The time was now 6:14 and the African sun was getting so low in the west it would soon be touching the horizon.

The three searchers slowly picked their way through the warren of boulders and rocks that littered the area in front of the low spot on the kopje's steep rim. To Cody, this part of the wall looked like it had been partially opened to grant a somewhat easier access to what lay inside. Cody wondered if this was an intentional piece of work or a natural occurrence. Either way, it was still a difficult climb. Made more so by the load each was carrying and the long shadows generated by the setting sun.

It took them over twenty minutes to reach the summit of the notch. Tired from their climb and out of breath, they stopped to take a look inside while they still had daylight and to orientate themselves.

What they saw left them speechless.

On the inside, the long oval-shaped kopje was nothing like the sparse, semi-arid, African savannah on the outside. Completely shut off from the rest of the surrounding countryside, the ecosystem within the confining walls of the kopje was extraordinary.

Even in the low light of dusk, the boys could tell the floor area was level and immense. All three guessed it was bigger than a football field and was, perhaps, at least four to five acres in size. Maybe larger. The inside walls were solid rock and fairly steep. They looked to be anywhere between fifteen to twenty meters (49-66 feet) high and were sporadically covered with a combination of creeping vines, moss, and hanging ferns.

The crater's floor was adorned with a variety of palm trees, rare North African pine trees, Marula trees, large ferns, and assorted flowering bushes. It was, by all accounts, an impressively-adorned tropical forest. At the far end, only slightly visible over the canopy of the forest, the boys could see a large pool of water being fed by a small, cascading waterfall coming out of the rock wall about a third of the way down from the rim.

The whole inside had the appearance of a well-maintained botanical garden or grotto. It was indeed both an oasis and a paradise. It looked like a primitive world one would see in a movie, except this one was real and breathtakingly beautiful.

"Wow! I can honestly say...I've never seen anything like this!" Cody remarked, gazing around in wonder.

"Me either...unbelievable!" added Jamie, drawing out his last expression for emphasis.

"Just your standard oasis, boys...on steroids," quipped Jake.

The comment drew a few chuckles from all three.

"Now, I can see what all of the excitement was about," Jake added. "This place is truly amazing. I'd love to hang out here for a weekend myself!"

"Boy, Danny sure does know how to pick 'em," Cody said. "How in the world did he ever find this place?"

"I'm sure Danny is probably not the first person to ever be here, nor will we be the last. This is too beautiful of a place to be kept secret," Jake said.

After seeing the oasis for themselves, none of the three could understand why all the secrecy and warnings they got regarding this place. To them, this was nothing to be shunned or feared. It was a virtual Garden of Eden.

The three agreed that there was probably only one way in and out of this place and that was where they were currently standing. A curious mix of admiration, excitement, and apprehension weighed heavily on them as they slowly and carefully picked their way down through the boulders and rocks to the inside of the kopje. It didn't take them nearly as long as it took them to make the ascent on the other side, but they still had to be careful. One misstep could easily result in a sprained or broken ankle, or something worse.

As they descended down the rocks to reach the floor, the temperature shifted dramatically. The shaded crater of the kopje was cooler and more humid than the arid savannah outside. Cody made a mental note of the temperature when they were in Kwambo. Eighty-nine degrees Fahrenheit and climbing. Inside the kopje, Cody figured the late afternoon/early evening temperature to be somewhere in the upper-seventies to low-eighties. He suspected it would get even cooler come nighttime.

Once all three had picked their way down to the floor, their next move was to find a suitable spot to set up a base camp. Even though the sky was still light enough to clearly see their surroundings, Jake broke out a flashlight just to be prepared. Nightfall would come much quicker inside this crater than it did outside on the open savannah. The other two followed Jake's lead and retrieved theirs as well. When Jamie turned his on to test it, he spotted footprints in the sandy soil right next to them.

They all assumed these were Danny's and started calling out for him. There was no reply except for a distant, faint echo. Jake suggested they follow the prints, which took off toward the opposite end of the grotto. The tracks themselves were following somewhat of a path and appeared to be of normal stride, neither running nor lagging. This meant, to some degree, that Harper didn't appear to be hurt or in any danger. They tracked the prints for about seventy-five meters (246 feet) through the assorted trees and bushes before coming to an open area surrounding the small pool.

All three dropped their heavy packs and surveyed the area with their flashlights. Jake spotted the signs first. There, tucked away between the inside wall of the kopje and the edge of the pool was a recently-erected campsite.

CHAPTER 20

Tuesday Evening, September 23

Lagos

Matt McKnight was restless. He found it hard to concentrate and pacing didn't help. The other two Peace Corps staffers occupying the same small office found it quite irritating, and said so.

The time was 6:30 p.m. and most of the embassy staff had ended their workday and gone home over an hour ago. With the exception of the swing shift officer in the Communications and Records unit, the marine security guard, and a couple of other staff people working late, the three Peace Corps people were the only other occupants in the complex.

As soon as they received the latest report from Kaduna, Matt was going to send the other two out to get dinner. He planned on taking the first shift, which would last until midnight. The second shift would stay until six in the morning. The last staff member would relieve that person at 6:00 a.m. and stay until noon, and the rotation would start all over again with Matt. Unless something significant turned up. Matt had set up rotating six-hour blocks to comply with DCM Olvera's request to have someone in the "command post" around the clock.

At approximately 6:25, the embassy's junior communications officer walked into their little office with the transcript of Kaduna's six o'clock report from the search team and handed it to McKnight.

Matt quickly read it out loud for the benefit of the other

two. "U.S. Consular Office Kaduna," he read. "Limited Official Use...Internal Communication Only...Twenty-three September, 1975...1815 hours. Field team reported in approximately 1800 hours. PCV Harper's Range Rover found parked next to large, crater-like kopje in open savannah country. No sign of trouble or damage to vehicle. Team located footprints from Range Rover to rocks at edge of kopje. Team planned on climbing rocks and going inside crater by dusk to start immediate search. Next transmission 2100 hours. End Kaduna Transmission."

"I've never heard of a kopje with a crater inside of it, at least not in this part of Africa," remarked one of the PC staff people.

"The transmission did say it was large," remarked the other one.

Their comments fell on semi-deaf ears. McKnight was deep in thought as to what all of this meant and tried to envision what was going on with the search team. After three more minutes of pacing and talking to himself, Matt declared he needed to get to Jos. But first, he needed to talk to the gunnery sergeant.

Matt left the office and headed down the closest staircase for the lobby, where he hoped to find the marine security guard. He found the young corporal in the Communications and Records office located at the bottom of the stairwell, down the hallway from the main lobby. The marine was signing the log book, verifying that the embassy had received the LOU communication from Kaduna and it was given to Matt McKnight at 1825 hours.

After receiving this last field report from the consulate in Kaduna, Matt had a few questions he believed only Sergeant Ripper could answer. Matt asked the young serviceman if he could get in contact with the sergeant right away, saying he needed to talk to him as soon as possible. The marine got on his handheld radio and relayed the request directly to the Marine House and Gunny Ripper.

As expected, the first thing Ripper asked was if this was an emergency. The guard replied with a "negative, Sir" and, per McKnight's request, asked the gunny if he could come back to the embassy. Ripper asked if the 1800 hour field report had come in from Kaduna. "Affirmative, Sir," was the marine's answer. "I believe that's what the Peace Corps people want to talk to you about, Sir."

Ripper thanked his guard, asked him to inform McKnight he was on his way, and broke the connection.

It took "Wild Bill" Ripper only fifteen minutes to stop what he was doing and make the return trip to the embassy's main building. Traffic was fairly light that Tuesday evening in Lagos and Ripper was in a hurry.

"What's up?" the marine asked as he strode into the small office everyone now referred to as "Search Central" and approached McKnight's desk. Ripper stood with his hands on his hips waiting for an answer. The other two PC staffers were still in the office and were busy looking over a map. Matt stood up and handed the just-received report to the sergeant without saying a word. After speed-reading it several times to make sure he didn't miss anything, Ripper looked up and said, "What's on your mind, son?"

"Sergeant Ripper," Matt began, sitting back down, "in your unbiased and professional opinion, are my two Volunteers and your man at risk, any risk at all, by doing what they're doing?"

"I don't believe so," Ripper said immediately, shaking his head. "I have full confidence in Corporal Simmons' abilities to handle unknown situations like this. That's what he's been trained for. Your two Volunteers are no rookies themselves. They're in good shape and by now, have acquired a good deal of experience when it comes to traveling about in this country. The search team is well-equipped and I see no reason to be overly concerned by what they are doing or are attempting to do."

Matt pondered Ripper's remarks for a fast minute, then asked, "Well – equipped how...exactly?" He needed some reassurance to alleviate his steadily-growing apprehensions and especially what was out of his sphere of control.

"In addition to basic camping and survival gear," the dead-serious Ripper stated, "Corporal Simmons also has non-lethal, crowd-control ordinance with him." Ripper went on to remind the Peace Corps desk officer all of this was spelled out in a previous cable to him.

Matt apologized, then asked the gunny to refresh his memory about the "ordinance" he sent with his marine.

"Specifically," came the straightforward reply, "three canisters of OC pepper spray, two teargas grenades, and two smoke grenades. I believe Simmons also took his Ka-Bar combat knife with him. Again, all of which were approved by the DCM and the RSO."

Before Matt could say anything, the iron-jawed Gunnery Sergeant continued, "The guys were also going to pick up some machetes and possibly a few other items before leaving Jos."

"Jesus!" Matt quietly exclaimed, as if realizing for the first time what the sergeant was actually talking about. "Do you realize Peace Corps Volunteers are not supposed to have anything to do with that kind of military-type stuff, especially while on assignment in a host country? It's not only a violation of Peace Corps' policy, it is also in direct violation of our country-to-country operating agreements!"

"Listen to me," quietly explained Ripper. "Corporal Simmons has these items, possibly with the exception of the machetes, not your people. Jake is well-trained, knows how to use this ordinance, and will only do so to protect himself and members of the search team. They're strictly for self-defense and are in his care and safe-keeping. Your people may not even know he has them."

Matt was still paranoid about what was going on and after the sergeant's revelations regarding the non-lethal ordinance, became even more convinced that he should be closer to the search and expressed as much to the gunnery sergeant. Matt McKnight was on the edge and Ripper recognized the signs.

Ripper pondered Matt's request, then fixed a steely gaze at the desk officer and punctuated his words. "We will both be going. First flight out for Jos tomorrow morning. I will talk to the DCM, the RSO, and our people in Kaduna. I'll also make all of the travel arrangements. All you need to do is inform your boss in Washington, along with this Belvoe character in Accra what we're doing and why, then be ready to head out at 0600 hours tomorrow morning…sharp!"

Matt was left somewhat speechless, but the other two PC staffers in the office were inwardly smirking. In no uncertain terms, the no-nonsense gunnery sergeant had made his case. He had stood up for his marine, Cody Armstrong, Jamie Hammer, and the plan he had worked out with DCM Olvera. Ripper was obviously in no mood to be second-guessed.

The three Peace Corps staff people fell silent, and Matt quickly realized, thanks to the sergeant's sternly-loaded remarks, that the United States Marine Corps had something at stake in this endeavor as well. To their credit, the other two Peace Corps staff people just looked at Matt and one another, not daring to say anything. The decorated, combat-hardened marine was obviously in no mood to be messed with.

"Okay, Gunny. You got it," Matt finally said. "Pick me up next door at our temporary quarters at 0600. I'll be ready. Anything else?"

"Negative," was Ripper's curt reply. As abruptly as he had entered the newly-christened Peace Corps field office, the gunnery sergeant did an about-face and was gone. The three Peace Corps staffers stood there in complete silence for a minute. No one was anxious to say anything more, especially if Ripper was still in earshot.

Matt McKnight, the "by-the-book" desk officer for all of the Peace Corps programs in West Africa had just asked for, and committed himself to, an upcountry trip with a bona fide commando in search of a missing Volunteer. He had never done anything like this before and without fully considering what he might be in for, was now into something neck-deep. Something definitely way above his pay grade. He wished he had given more thought to the role the United States Marine Corps was playing in this matter.

As Matt was considering how best to relay this latest development to his superior in Washington and Hampton Belvoe in Accra, Sergeant Ripper was in the Communications and Records office downstairs and on the phone to DCM Olvera at his home in Ikoyi. After a ten-minute conversation, his next call went to RSO Shannon at his home. Finally, he called the logistics officer and asked if she wouldn't mind coming back to the embassy that evening to make the travel and money arrangements for their trip the following morning. Everyone at the embassy knew what the score was regarding the missing Volunteer and all were on board to help out in any way possible.

Satisfied everything was in order, Sgt. William "Wild Bill" Ripper briskly walked out of the embassy at exactly 1959 hours and headed back to the Marine House to prepare for the next day.

CHAPTER 21

Tuesday Evening, September 23

The Paradise Kopje

The campsite the three boys found was a mess. Everything was in disarray and scattered. It looked like someone was rummaging through the stuff and didn't particularly care where it wound up. All three boys called out Harper's name, hoping to hear a familiar voice and friendly reply. There was none.

Jake and Cody set the radio container down and the three shed their remaining packs, but kept on their web utility belts containing the machetes. It was now getting dark inside of the kopje, but the boys could still see the pale remnants of the sunset above the western rim. It had been four days since the last full moon, which meant there would still be light available from the last quarter moon when it rose above the crater's rim. Considering how bright the last full moon was, they anticipated it to be fairly light and not totally dark inside the kopje.

Jake broke out his Coleman 220-J, double-mantle lantern and lighted it anyway. The harsh, white glow radiated in all directions for approximately fifteen meters (49 feet), including half way up the inside wall which was about ten meters (33 feet) away from them. Jake set the lantern on top of the upended case that contained his radio set, which spread the light out even further.

With light to work by until the moon rose, Jake suggested they organize the campsite and check to see if any of the scattered items could be identified as Danny's. The three cautiously spread out and, with the aid of their flashlights and the lantern's far-reaching illumination, started collecting the remnants of the previous campsite. The strewn articles consisted of a sleeping bag, mosquito netting, what was left of a rucksack, a few articles of clothing, assorted foodstuffs, toiletries, an instamatic camera, a small cassette player, a journal, and some fire-making material. Also among the littered landscape was a standard-issue, Peace Corps field kit with the initials "DH" stenciled on the lid.

"Danny was definitely here," Cody announced. "But where on earth could he have disappeared to?" He glanced around.

"I say we don't waste time cleaning up this mess," advised Jake. "I think we should stay together and, starting at this point, work our way around the inside of the wall until we come back to this spot. That way, we won't get separated in the dark and we can orientate ourselves to this place while looking for Danny at the same time."

"How long do you think something like that will take?" Jamie asked, nervously looking at his watch. "Remember, we have to be back here in a little over an hour to make our nine o'clock call to Kaduna."

"Oh, I don't know. How long does it take to walk around an oversized football field?" replied Simmons, light-heartedly. "I think we'll have plenty of time to explore a good deal of it and still make it back in time. If we run short, we just stop where we are and head straight back to this campsite. It should be easy to find with a beacon as bright as 'Mr. Coleman' over there."

All agreed with Jake and they set off exploring the inside perimeter of the kopje. Starting in a counterclockwise direction. With their flashlights sweeping back and forth, the three were not only checking the place out, they were also looking for any signs of Harper.

The interior walls of the kopje were pretty much vertical and seemed steeper on the inside than they looked from the outside. Without proper rock climbing gear, no one was going to get out this way. The ground around the inside edge was fairly navigable. A natural open span separated the vegetation from the rocky walls, making it easier for the boys to make their way around.

Cody and Jake took the lead, followed by Jamie. They walked, more or less, as a group, scanning their flashlights in all directions. After a few minutes of walking, the open path they were following looked more and more like a deliberate trail. It looked as if it was well used, but Cody could see no tracks or prints of any kind. For the time being, he decided to keep the observation to himself.

As they were rounding the northeast corner, just before they reached the notched area where they made their entrance from the outside, Jake made a startling discovery. Piled up amongst a group of large rocks next to the wall, was a rather sizable pile of bones.

"Jesus!" Jamie exclaimed as his flashlight illuminated the pile along with the other two's. "Are those human?"

Jamie reflectively backed off and let Cody and Jake take a closer look.

"Some look like they could be," Jake said, scrounging around the pile and kicking at it with one foot. "But most likely they came from a variety of animals."

"Maybe this whole place is the lair for a pack of hyenas, baboons, or something worse!" Jamie said, nervously flipping his light around the edges of the dark vegetation behind them.

"Unlikely," Cody remarked, trying to keep his friend calm. "If that were the case, we would have known it as soon as we set foot in here. I wouldn't be surprised if this little pile here doesn't contain some of those animals you just mentioned. Besides, predators aren't in the habit of leaving bones neatly stacked up like this."

"Now that you mention it," Jake added, "for some strange reason, there doesn't seem to be a trace of any wildlife in here, except for that pile. I haven't even seen so much as a single animal or bird since we left the outside. Except for the frogs and crickets by the pool, you can almost hear the silence in this place."

As Jake climbed up the mound of bones and continued his

rummaging, his foot slipped on what he thought was a smooth rock. A human skull popped out from under his foot and tumbled down the pile, stopping at Cody and Jamie's feet.

"Jesus Christ!" Jamie exclaimed, training his flashlight on the grisly find. "You can't tell me that's from some damn animal! That's a human skull! Could that be Danny?"

Jamie and Cody stared at the gray-white object for a few moments before Jake, who was half way up the pile, said, "Easy, boys. Don't go radical on me. Danny's only been missing for four days. It takes a lot longer than that to completely clean off human bones, even with help from bugs and such. Besides, if Danny had died in here, we would have known it right off the bat. After twenty-four hours in this heat, a dead body would be giving off a distinctive stench."

The reassuring comments didn't make the two Peace Corps Volunteers feel any at ease. Quite the opposite.

Jake trained his flashlight back on the pile. Scattered around the top half and now readily visible were more skulls in addition to what looked like other human bones. Jake estimated he was standing amongst the remains of perhaps a half dozen or more human remnants. The comment he had made earlier about others finding this place suddenly came to mind. The thought that his group might share the same fate sent a shiver down the marine's spine.

After Jake climbed back down to join Jamie and Cody, the three slowly made their way around the pile of bones looking for any signs Danny could have been there. After several minutes of searching and finding nothing, Jake finally said what was on everyone's mind: "Okay, let's get the hell out of here!"

The disturbing find made Cody paranoid and even more cautious as they headed toward the rocks that marked the entrance to the kopje's interior. Passing the point where they originally entered the crater, the search team silently moved on; however, Cody's thoughts were still on the pile of bones.

The three traversed the western wall of the kopje's interior, their flashlight beams scanning in all different directions while they carefully and slowly checked out this section of the oasis for clues. They walked in a southwesterly direction along the pathway between the wall and the forested area. The path was narrower than before, but still walkable, requiring them to fall into a single file formation. Jake took the lead, followed by Jamie and then Cody. They kept but a meter or two of separation between them.

Approximately halfway down the length of the wall, about seventy meters (230 feet) after they passed the entrance area, the young marine abruptly stopped.

"Find something?" Cody asked.

Jake made a quarter turn to his left so the other two could see his face, then put a finger up to his lips in a shushing gesture and turned off his flashlight. The other two huddled around him and, following his lead, turned off theirs as well.

Whispering, Jake said, "I thought I heard something moving off to our left."

Cody strained his eyes to see if there was anything out there. Slowly, the lighting got better. Having breached the eastern rim of the kopje, the quarter moon slowly illuminated the inside of the crater. His eyes were becoming more accustomed to the dark, but he still could not see anything definitive.

The three stood there, silently for a minute, straining to see what Jake had heard.

"Anything?" Cody quietly asked the motionless marine. Jake shook his head slowly from side to side, his attention still focused on the foliage off to their left. After another minute or two of motionless silence, Jake turned his flashlight back on and the others did the same. All three focused their beams on the area. Nothing was there.

Slowly moving forward once again, Cody asked Jake what he thought he heard or saw.

"I thought I caught a glimpse of movement, but it turned out to be nothing," Jake confessed. "Then I thought I smelled something like really bad body odor. After what we just saw on that bone pile, I think this place is getting to me. I'm starting to jump at shadows."

"It's getting to me too," Cody said. "As beautiful as this place is, there's something not right about it. I can't put my finger on it, but this place is kind of freaky. And for the record, I did shower this morning."

"Guys...guys," interjected Jamie, now bringing up the rear. "I recommend that since it looks like we're directly across from the campsite, we stop here and work our way back so we can make our nine o'clock call."

"Jamie's got a point," Cody conceded. "I'm also hungry. Let's mark this spot and come back to it after we make the call and get something to eat."

The marine agreed and found a couple of small rocks to pile, marking where they would pick back up on their exploration once they'd taken a break. All three broke out their machetes in case they needed to hack their way through thick vegetation or ran into an unfriendly inhabitant. Following Jake's lead, the group turned off the pathway to their left-hand side, making their way southeast toward the distant glow of the reassuring lantern and their campsite.

The hike wasn't bad; the underbrush wasn't too thick and they made good time. The thought crossed Cody's mind that this place was a true wilderness and wondered out loud, "How many people, over the years, knew of this place, but refused to set foot in it?" Then a chilling thought came to his mind: Here was an isolated oasis people refused to acknowledge even existed, let alone visit. Why?

Jamie retorted, "How many people who did manage to stumble across this place wound up on that pile of bones?"

They all fell silent and walked faster after that comment.

Once they broke out of the forest, they moved along the northern edge of the open sandy area surrounding the pool and worked their way back to their campsite. They had circumnavigated over one-half of the kopje's inside wall, with two stops, in about an hour. Cody noted the time as they approached their campsite. It was now 8:41 p.m. They had approximately twenty minutes to set up the radio and report in to Kaduna.

Jake, with his heightened sense of situational awareness,

pointed out that their campsite was not as they left it. When they started their exploration, Harper's stuff was still scattered about, but all of their stuff was neatly organized. Now, it appeared as if someone, or something, had rummaged through two of their packs. Again, Jake wished he could have brought a firearm.

They all stopped short when the crickets and frogs suddenly went silent, followed by a rustling in the dark forested area beyond the opposite side of the small pool.

The boys all looked at one another as if to say, "Did you hear that?"

First, Jamie, then Cody and Jake began calling out Danny's name again, hoping their lost friend had seen the light from the lantern and was stumbling around looking for them. They received no response. Only the sound of something large moving away from them. With the exception of the soft rippling sound of the waterfall behind them, an eerie silence followed. Then the critters around the pond slowly resumed their rhapsody.

After a moment or two of silence, the ever-perceptive Jamie matter-of-factly stated, "Guys...I don't think we're alone in here."

CHAPTER 22

Tuesday Night, September 23

The Paradise Kopje

The three young men stood there, listening for any more rustling coming from the forested area and vainly tried to see past the illuminating glow of the lantern. They heard nothing more, nor could they see anything. The harsh light from the Coleman had all but destroyed their night vision.

"If it wasn't Danny," Cody asked, "what could that have been?"

Jamie and Jake continued staring into the distance and, without saying a word, gave each other concerned looks.

Jake turned on his heels, leaving Cody and Jamie staring off into the void, and quickly returned to where their gear was stowed. The young marine dropped to one knee and methodically broke out the special equipment. Setting the ordinance aside for the time being, Jake unpacked the "Prick, 10-4 Bravo" radio set. The marine worked quickly and efficiently while the other two started picking up the strewn-about gear. As they worked, all three kept a watchful eye on the forested area opposite them.

At 8:57 p.m., Jake was finished setting up his radio and tried raising Kaduna.

At first, he wasn't entirely successful. Although he did manage to make a connection on his second attempt, the reply was weak and crackly. Jake figured it was because of the high walls surrounding them. He asked Kaduna to stand by so he could relocate his tape antennae to get a better signal.

Quickly scanning the rock wall next to their campsite with his flashlight, Jake spotted a small ledge next to, and slightly above, the spring-fed waterfall. He asked if either Cody or Jamie could climb up to the ledge with the end of the antennae and anchor it with a rock. Jake estimated the ledge to be eight meters (26 feet) or more above the kopje's floor, which should give him enough height to make a better connection.

The rock wall was barely scalable, but the nimble Jamie managed to make the climb fairly quickly and without incident, thanks to a pair of good gloves and plenty of illumination from Cody's flashlight. Jake kept a watchful eye on the tree line behind them while he fed out the radio's tape antennae and connecting cable as Jamie climbed.

After ten minutes of carefully crawling his way up the rocky wall, Jamie reached the ledge. What he saw parked at the rear of the ledge when he pulled himself up, clear as day in the quarter moonlight, stopped him short.

"Hey, guys!" Jamie yelled down to his teammates. "You're not gonna believe what I found up here...a cooler with beer in it!"

"Ha," Jake called up, "anchor the antennae, and then toss down the cooler!"

Jamie did as requested and then began the slow, deliberate climb back down to the kopje's floor, again with the aid of Cody's flashlight.

Cody managed, to some extent, to catch and break the fall of the little cooler Jamie tossed down from the ledge. On the lid was painted a skull and crossbones with the warning: **Danger! Do Not Touch! Life-Threatening Chemicals Inside!**

Yep, Cody concluded, this cooler belonged to Danny Harper alright. Only Danny would do something like that to keep people out of his "beer locker," as he called it. To the senior Volunteer, this was additional proof positive Danny had been, or was still, at this location.

By 9:21, Jake had finally managed to establish a clear communications link with Kaduna. "Kilo, Charlie, One" was only too happy to hear from the search team. In addition to the marine operating the radio set, also present on the receiving end was Kenny Wagner, who had been following the boys' progress since day one. The search team was late making contact and that worried the Foreign Service officer.

Jake updated his listeners on where they were and what they had found. He also apologized for the lateness of his call.

The "read back" from Kaduna pretty much summed up the situation: "Victor, Sierra, Tango...understand you have found a ransacked campsite...there is solid, additional evidence Harper was there...you believe foul play may be involved...you think you're being shadowed by person or persons unknown."

"Affirmative...Kilo, Charlie, One," Jake said into his headset. "We are on high alert...have non-lethal protection...will continue our search after eating...expect next transmission on or about 2400 hours...over."

"Roger...Victor, Sierra, Tango," came Kaduna's reply. "Read you loud and clear...be advised...Gunnery Sergeant Ripper and Peace Corps Officer McKnight heading to Jos on morning flight."

After the customary sign-off, Jake looked at the two Peace Corps Volunteers and said, as if he could read their minds, "No big deal, guys. Now that we're closing in, they're probably just staging themselves to be close by if needed. You know, in anticipation of us finding Danny or to be here when our time runs out tomorrow afternoon."

"So what do we do now?" Jamie said, running one hand through his hair and making it stick up.

"We eat," Cody said, "like we agreed on. Then, we pick back up where we left off on the other side of the kopje." Cody turned to face the marine corporal. "Jake, what was that you said about 'non-lethal' protection?"

"Sorry, guys. I probably should have told you about this earlier," Jake said as he reached for his pile of gear. "I was instructed not to break out the equipment or talk about it until necessary."

Cody and Jamie stood there, waiting to hear what Jake was talking about.

"When we got back to the campsite and discovered things were amiss and then heard some movement in the forested area," Jake began, lifting some small items out of his rucksack, "I thought now was probably as good a time as any to unload the 'protection' I brought."

"Which is…?" Cody prompted.

"Three canisters of OC pepper spray, one for each of us, some tear gas, and several smoke grenades."

Cody and Jamie stared at the marine, half dumbfounded and half relieved. At least, Cody thought, they had more than a couple of machetes to protect themselves with if need be.

"And all of this stuff is okay with your boss and Mr. Olvera?" Jamie asked.

"Absolutely," Jake said. "In fact, it was the Gunny's idea for me to bring this equipment. He also wanted me to have a sidearm, but the DCM nixed that idea. The knife was an afterthought."

"Wow," was all Jamie said. "You know, I'm starting to feel a little better about our situation. I think we're pretty much set up to handle any surprises this place might throw our way."

"So, show us what you've got and how to use it," Cody prompted as he stole a quick glance back at the tree line.

Jake gave the two Volunteers each a canister of the pepper spray and instructed them on its use. "Stay upwind, never downwind or you'll hose yourself. Use short bursts. Aim for the face area, specifically the eyes. This stuff is so strong, it will even stop a bear or in our case, a hyena. That's why civilians can't buy it in this concentration."

"Seriously?" Cody asked, trying to imagine what it must feel like to be face to face with an animal like a bear or hyena, and then he inquired about the spray's range and what it actually did.

Jake summed it up with an ugly picture, with emphasis on the fact that this was something not to be messed around with. The two Peace Corps Volunteers listened intently as the marine explained the finer points of using OC pepper spray.

"When you press the trigger," Jake began, pantomiming

how to do that, "an aerosol stream will shoot out about three meters, or ten feet. The spray's chemical compound, 12% oleoresin capsicum, referred to as OC, is an oil-based compound derived from very, very hot peppers. Once it touches the face, the eyes become so inflamed they will swell shut immediately. The mucus membranes of the nose, sinuses, mouth, and throat will also burn and swell, causing the victim to gag and have trouble breathing. Some people also cramp up if they've swallowed it and, oftentimes, will puke their guts out. Since it is oil-based and not water soluble, water alone won't give much relief. A soapy solution is required to remove it, something most people don't carry around with them. That's what makes this spray so effective for crowd control, animal control, self-defense, and for torturing prisoners."

"Torturing prisoners?" asked Jamie.

"Yep, and it's effective at that too. Especially since a prisoner can't wash it off," Jake replied. "I got firsthand experience of that when I was captured and tortured during my 'Escape and Evade' training. That's why I still have nightmares about the experience."

"Unbelievable! How come I've never heard of this stuff?"

"Oh, but you have," replied the bemused marine. "You probably only know it by its common name. Mace."

With renewed respect for what he was holding, Jamie gently set down the canister Jake had issued him.

Satisfied the lesson in self-defense went well, Cody suggested they finally eat something and broke out their provisions.

Under the bright glow of the Coleman lantern, the boys ate a combination of cold Spam sandwiches, bananas, and stale granola bars, all the while sitting with their backs together. Jake had suggested they sit this way so they would have a 360-degree visual coverage of their campsite and surrounding area. Cody once again appreciated having a highly-trained soldier as part of their group.

At approximately 10 p.m., having finished their meal, they got ready to resume their search pattern. With a heightened sense of awareness and sufficiently armed with flashlights, machetes, and OC pepper spray, the boys made their way across the open area and back into the tropical forest. Fifteen minutes later, they were back at the western wall. Cody found the stones Jake had piled up earlier. They were undisturbed, but it appeared as if their previous footprints were partially brushed away.

Strange, he thought, *I wonder how that could have happened*? He decided not to alarm the other two unnecessarily and kept the discovery to himself.

They began the next phase of their exploration where they left off, approximately halfway down the west wall, moving in a southerly direction along the pathway they were on earlier. Again, in a single file.

After ten minutes of walking, the wall was now gently curved to their left, indicating they had reached the southern end of the kopje's crater. By Cody's reckoning, they had now covered somewhere around three-fourths of the interior wall. There was still no sign of Danny, or for that matter, of anything else. They had yet to explore the denser, tree-laden interior of the crater.

They were at the extreme southern end of the kopje when the forested area began thinning out and they could sporadically see the pool and the distant light of their campsite off to their left. Quite unexpectedly and without any prior indication, they stepped out of the tropical forest onto a patch of moss-covered, open ground.

Jake, in the lead, stopped to survey the sudden change. Jamie and then Cody, who was bringing up the rear, stepped into the opening and took up positions on each side of Jake. All were shining their flashlights on the clearing in front of them and against the rock wall just beyond.

After a moment or two of sweeping their flashlights back and forth and silently gawking, a wide-eyed Jamie was the first to speak.

"Oh my God! Is that for real?"

CHAPTER 23

Tuesday Night, September 23

The Paradise Kopje

Covering a wide section of the rock wall on the southern corner, were over one hundred niches chiseled into the granite and volcanic tuff. Each little alcove was no more than a foot and a half tall, approximately twelve inches wide and fairly deep. All were separated, perhaps, by a foot or less in all directions. From their vantage point, the small recesses looked like rows upon rows of tiny arched windows, going from just above ground level up to nearly the top of the kopje's rim.

The cleared area that separated the boys from that unusual-looking wall looked just as out-of-place. Wide open with moss-covered flat stones, the small field was tiered in four, semi-concentric arches that sloped downward toward the wall, like open seats in an amphitheater. At the center of this, adjacent to the wall with its alcoves, was a large block of black stone. The block was roughly the size and shape of a medium-sized desk and looked like it had been chiseled into its present shape.

As their flashlight beams danced back and forth while they surveyed the area, the boys carefully moved in for a closer look. They approached the stone block, bringing the recesses in the wall into better view. Once again, Cody couldn't believe what his eyes were telling him.

In each niche, nestled at the rear and almost out of sight, was a discolored and dust-covered terracotta figurine. Each distinctly different and each absolutely beautiful. They looked like abstract images of little people with oversized heads—all waiting to come to life. They also looked as if they'd been there for a long, long time.

All three young men stood with their mouths wide open in complete awe. Cody had never seen anything like this; it was both mesmerizing and sobering at the same time. Here, at the far end of the kopje's crater, hidden from the outside world, was this ancient and secret place.

A sudden chill ran down Cody's spine. The niches, the figurines, the secrecy of this place, and the dire warnings. He suddenly realized what all of this meant. They were in some sort of a primeval burial ground. This was not any ordinary Nigerian cemetery. This place had all the earmarks of belonging to the ancient Noks.

Cody suddenly remembered what Peter Onia told them about these ancient people when they visited him at the Bauchi State Teacher's College: *The terracotta figurines were thought to hold the souls of the dead.*

All of this now made perfect sense. This was a secret and sacred graveyard. Hallowed ground. One that had gone undetected and undisturbed for perhaps thousands of years, and they, or rather Danny, had accidentally discovered it.

A soft, undistinguishable sound reached their ears that resembled whispering. Jamie's flashlight slipped out of his hand and clanged off the ground. Jake and Cody jumped.

"Sorry…my hands are shaking. Couldn't hold my torch," Jamie said, apologizing for his clumsiness.

"What is this place?" Jake asked.

"This, I believe," Cody replied, "appears to be an ancient Nok burial ground, including seating arrangements and altar for some kind of ceremony. Those little alcoves with their clay figurines inside supposedly hold the souls, if not the ashes, of the dearly departed."

"No shit!" Jake exclaimed. "The same Noks you guys told me about on the drive up from Jos?"

"The very same, my friend. The very same," Cody lamented. "I have my suspicions that this is either an off-limits or a totally undiscovered place. Probably both."

"Undiscovered, and quite possibly, protected," added Jake. "If this place is anything like what you say it is, it's probably similar to the ancient Indian burial grounds back home. Which means we could be in trouble."

"What do you mean, trouble?" Jamie said as he stepped forward to join the conversation.

Jake rubbed his chin thoughtfully. "Lore has it, the Indian burial grounds of North America are protected not only by the spirits of the dead, but by the living as well. In times past, transgressors who were caught were tortured and killed. Sometimes hideously. I remember reading stories about trappers who unknowingly trespassed through a burial ground and were found with either their throats slashed or a war spear impaled in their chests. Some were even skinned or gutted."

Both Cody and Jamie winced. Jake's remarks did nothing to alleviate the growing tension Cody felt.

Jake lifted his hands with wiggling fingers as he continued. "Those who were not caught and killed outright were supposedly cursed for the rest of their lives."

"Cursed, how?" asked Cody, looking around furtively.

"Oh," Jake exhaled a short breath while stealing a quick glance at their surroundings. "You know, the usual stuff. On-going bad luck, crippling or fatal accidents, unexplained illness, stillborn babies, or children born with deformities. Some really nasty stuff."

"You seem to know a lot about Indian culture," Jamie remarked.

"I took a class on it at the junior college before I joined the Marines. It was an elective and probably the most interesting class I took. I also managed to get an A."

"What does American Indian culture have to do with all of this?" Jamie inquired as he swept his hand around the area.

"In this class," Jake continued, "we also learned about the similarities between ancient cultures and practices from different tribes and groups scattered around the world. Almost all of them had some sort of sacred, 'do not disturb' burial grounds. This one seems to fit the profile. Like I said, we might be in trouble, especially if we touch any of those artifacts."

A momentary silence followed Jake's remarks as the three looked at their strange surroundings with renewed curiosity and respect. One at a time, the men exchanged glances as a slight wind blew off of the pool and gave them a shiver. Again, Cody heard the strange noise that sounded like low whispering.

"Maybe this place is haunted or cursed," offered Jamie, wide-eyed. "Maybe it's protected by spirits or ghosts or something like that!"

"Great," moaned Cody. "Let's not get all freaked out. I say we finish checking this place out for any signs of Danny and then get the hell out of here."

The three resumed their exploration of the amphitheater and the wall of windows with their extraordinary contents. Cody took a quick look to see how they were doing on time. His watch read 11:04 p.m. They had approximately fifty-five minutes before they were scheduled to check back in with Kaduna. By Cody's estimation, they had been scouting out this section of the kopje for over twenty minutes and had been away from their campsite for over an hour. He glanced toward the pond and the reassuring light of the lantern just beyond.

The hair stood up on the back of his neck.

The campsite was completely dark.

The other two were too busy exploring their find to notice the lantern was no longer lit.

"Uh, guys," Cody said, the tension rising in his voice. "Has anyone noticed the Coleman has gone out?"

"What? When?" Jamie said as he whipped his head around to look for the light.

"I just noticed it," replied Cody. "The last time I saw it burning was when we entered this place, which was about a half hour ago."

"It could have just run out of fuel." Jake shrugged. "It's been burning for about three hours. I've never run one dry, so I don't know how long that small tank would last."

Cody sighed. "We should head back to the campsite and

either build a campfire or relight the lantern. At any rate, we still have a radio call to make to Kaduna by midnight.

The other two agreed. They carefully made their way out of the burial area, heading north and then made their way around the pool and back to their campsite. It was an easy walk. The ground was fairly open and the whole northern side of the pool was like a hard sandy beach. The grassy campsite area on the eastern side of the pool was a welcomed sight, except it was dark.

The first thing Cody did when they reached their stuff was to check to see if it was as they left it, which it was. Then Jake checked the base of the Coleman to determine if there was any fuel left in the tank. It was about one-quarter full.

Jake shook his head. "I have no idea why the best camping lantern made went out with plenty of fuel left. He pumped the little plunger at the base to pressurize the fuel tank, opened up the top, and relit it. The two mantels flared back to life. Jake adjusted the intensity of the light down to conserve fuel, closed the lid, and stood up, holding the lantern high to illuminate their surroundings.

Jamie and Cody were standing together about two meters (6 feet) away from Jake, intently scouting the tropical forest to the north of their campsite with their flashlights.

"What are you two looking at?" inquired Jake.

"Don't know for sure," Cody said. "Jamie and I thought we heard some rustling in the foliage from that direction, just beyond that line of palm trees and ferns. Whatever it was, it's quiet over there now."

Jake, setting down the lantern on top of the radio case, also trained his flashlight on the area. "I don't see anything," he said. "Just some palm trees, assorted bushes, and some dead snags. There's nothing moving."

"Trust me, someone or something was moving out there a second ago." Jamie's voice was tight, his words came fast. Their experience at the burial grounds had spooked all of them, so naturally, they were seeing and hearing all kinds of unexplainable things.

Finally, the young marine spoke up. "Well, there doesn't seem to be anything out there now...guess I'll go get the radio fired up." After reconnecting the antennae, which was still dangling from the rock ledge above, Jake checked his watch. He prided himself on punctuality and professionalism.

Cody looked at his as well: 11:41 p.m. They had at least fifteen minutes to kill before checking in.

Jake decided to walk over to the spot where Cody and Jamie were watching the forest. He fetched his binoculars from one of the rucksacks and crossed the small clearing. As he approached the two Volunteers, who were still intently checking the tree line, Jake asked if they saw anything more.

"Nope, nothing," reported Cody, relaxing somewhat. "Nothing's changed. All's quiet now."

Jake took a look through his binoculars. "It's hard to see much of anything, even with the aid of two flashlights and a quarter moon."

"Maybe we are just imagining things. You know, starting to jump at shadows and the like," offered Jamie, trying to reassure himself and the other two.

"Maybe. Maybe not," Cody added. "I'm beginning to think Jamie's initial assessment may have been right when he said we're not alone in here."

Jake scoffed. "Come on, guys. Chill out, will ya? You're beginning to scare me and you're starting to sound like the little boy who cried wolf. Let's settle down and not let this place get the best of us. But, just to be on the safe side, I say we stay up all night and continue searching after I've called Kaduna. The last thing I want to do is be caught off-guard while sleeping and wind up on some pile of bones."

Jamie and Cody flinched at the remark, then readily agreed. All three quietly moved back to their campsite. Cody couldn't help but stop and take one more glance behind them at the forest as they walked; all his instincts told him something was there.

CHAPTER 24

Midnight Tuesday, September 23

The Paradise Kopje

Before dialing up Kaduna on the "Prick, 10-4 Bravo" radio set, Jake asked if he should report their discovery of the graveyard and its contents. Both Cody and Jamie looked at each other as if waiting for the other to answer. Jamie quietly shook his head from side to side, indicating he thought they should keep it to themselves, at least for the time being.

Cody pursed his lips and looked down, torn by the decision. After a few seconds of deliberation, he looked up at Jake and asked what he thought.

"No, I don't think we should," Jake began, rather emphatically. "And not just for those scary reasons I mentioned earlier. I'm convinced this place, this whole crater, was selected by some ancient people as a holy, final resting place. A place so revered, so protected, and so secret it has gone for centuries without being disturbed. I think we've crossed the line by even being here and I, for one, believe this sacred ground should remain anonymous and undisturbed for as long as possible."

Cody instantly recognized the meaning and the emotion behind Jake's words. He couldn't agree more. Somewhere, along the course of his class on the culture of the American Indian, Jake had unconsciously made a moral decision to respect and protect one's ancestors. The fact that Jake, a black American, was standing up for what may have been the lost forbearers of his ancestors carried a tremendous amount of weight.

Jake had made his case and now it was time to make the call to Kaduna.

"Kilo, Charlie, One...this is Victor, Sierra, Tango...over," Jake announced into his headset.

After a short delay came the expected response. "Victor, Sierra, Tango...read you loud and clear...over."

Jake had made contact on the first try thanks to an antennae stretched halfway up the crater's wall. "Kilo, Charlie, One... Victor, Sierra, Tango reports a campsite belonging to Harper has been found...repeat, have found campsite belonging to Harper but no sign of Harper as yet. We plan on continuing search through the night."

"Victor, Sierra, Tango...understand you have found Harper campsite but no Harper and will continue searching all night... anything else?"

The three silently looked at each other. Jamie and Cody shook their heads.

"Negative, Kilo, Charlie, One...nothing else to report...expect next transmission at 0600 tomorrow morning."

"Affirmative, Victor, Sierra, Tango...expect next transmission at 0600, Wednesday...good luck, guys...and be careful. Kilo, Charlie, One...out."

The three young men, the two Peace Corps Volunteers and the U.S. Marine, exchanged approving nods as Jake turned off his radio. The decision had been made. All knew, each justifying it in his own way, they had done the right thing. The paradise kopje, with its ancient and secret burial ground, was still unknown to the outside world.

"Now what?" asked Jamie, somewhat renewed by the shared secret.

"We go back to searching for Danny," Cody announced. "We don't leave a stone unturned, and when we're finished, we remove all traces we were ever here. This place must be left exactly as we found it."

Jake put away his radio and made sure the Coleman was charged enough to burn for a while, then he turned to Cody and asked where he wanted to start. This was, after all, a Peace Corps operation.

"I think we should go back to the graveyard," Cody said. "We didn't get a chance to thoroughly search it because I was concerned about the lantern going out. If we don't turn up anything there, we have systematically eliminated everything except the central forested area."

Jake sucked air through his teeth. "That might take a while. We should wait until daybreak before attempting the forest."

Against Jake's better judgment, Jamie agreed with Cody's idea. After securing their campsite, the three set off back around the pool to the corner of the crater which contained the altar and the wall of ancient artifacts.

It was a short hike. It took all of about fifteen minutes to reach the amphitheater. Jake suggested they spread out along the wall and look for footprints or evidence if anything had been tampered with. "Above all else, we shouldn't touch anything. This is a sacred place and nothing should be disturbed. Nothing."

The two Volunteers replied with a simple thumbs up.

Jamie and Cody started checking the ground along the wall and the amphitheater with their flashlights, methodically looking for anything that might give them a clue as to the fate of the missing Volunteer. Jake, standing behind the altar, was looking out toward the amphitheater itself.

"What's up, buddy?" Cody said as he quietly walked up and positioned himself next to Jake. The Marine was deep in thought.

"Oh, I was just wondering what, exactly, went on here. You know, trying to imagine what their rituals must have been like. That sort of thing."

"I know what you mean. All of this," Cody remarked, sweeping one hand around the area, "makes one feel kind of small and out of place. It's a strange feeling to be a witness to this much history. Now, I know how those British archeologists must have felt whenever they opened up a new Egyptian tomb."

Jake looked over at Cody, scrunched his lips together and nodded.

"We should get back to it." Cody turned around and

continued his searching. Jake followed suit.

Thanks to his tracking skills, Jake soon came across barefoot human prints in the sandy soil between the altar and the pool. Upon closer examination, he discovered a combination of several different sizes of footprints, all obscured by something apparently drug across them. As he was trying to sort out the possibilities in his mind, a low whistle came from one of the others.

The sound came from Jamie. He immediately got the attention of the other two and motioned them over to where he was. Jake and Cody simultaneously convened at Jamie's location, where he was shining his flashlight into one of the tiny catacombs. Huddled together, they all shone their flashlights into the void. Jamie had discovered one of the alcoves was empty.

Unlike the rest of the wall, they wondered why this space was empty. Something had been there, and not too long ago either. There was a clear indentation in the sandy floor of the rocky niche. A figurine must have been there and had been removed.

As if that discovery wasn't perplexing enough, right next to it was a second empty alcove. But unlike the first one, it was apparent this one had been emptied a long time ago. There were no marks, just a smooth dusty floor.

As the boys were discussing possibilities, including one where Danny could have removed the terracotta statuette from the first alcove for closer examination, a faint movement rustled in the tree line beyond the back of the amphitheater. The boys instantly wheeled around and froze, then simultaneously brought their flashlights to bear on the green wall of palm trees, ferns, and flowering bushes.

Sweeping their beams hastily back and forth, the boys could detect nothing except for the usual assortment of foliage. Nothing was moving. It was dead calm. Not even a whisper of wind. Apparently, if something had been there, it wasn't there anymore. Cody stood there, transfixed, involuntarily holding his breath. His mind racing. His heart pounding.

Whatever they heard must have quickly disappeared back into the forest. Yet something had been there, just like something had been shadowing them ever since they set foot in the crater. Their imaginations were not running wild. Without a doubt, they were not alone in this oasis. All three were now on high alert.

Jake advised, "Turn off your flashlights and let your eyes adjust to the darkness. Let's see if we can draw out whoever or whatever is in this forest."

Jake did the same. "Remain perfectly still and quiet."

All three were now involuntarily holding their breath.

After roughly a minute of shallow breathing and frozen positions, Cody quietly exhaled as his eyes, with the aid of the moonlight, could make out the line of trees at the back end of the amphitheater. He could now clearly see their immediate surroundings without the aid of artificial light. No one said a word. All senses were still at maximum. The adrenalin surge would keep it that way for some time.

The three stood, silent and motionless for perhaps a total of three minutes, vainly trying to determine what was going on. All manner of possibilities raced through Cody's mind. Were poachers or thieves following them? Was someone trying to scare them away from this hidden place? Was Danny playing a nasty prank on them? Were they being stalked by wild animals, like baboons? Were they in any kind of mortal danger? The vision of finding human skulls in the pile of bones still weighed heavily on him.

During this extended period of silence, broken only by the gentle splashing sound of the small waterfall, a new sound tripped Cody's nerve endings.

Maybe it is just my imagination, Cody thought to himself, *but I thought I heard something that sounded like moaning*. This was a totally different sound than the spooky whispering he had heard earlier.

While Jake and Jamie were totally focused on the line of trees where they detected the unusual movement, Cody's attention was now focused elsewhere. He slowly turned his head from side to side trying to locate the source of what his ears had picked up. Because he was the closest one to the little waterfall, he decided the cascading water must have made the strange sound and dismissed it, just as with the whispering-like sounds they heard earlier. Then he heard it again. This time, it was more distinct.

"What the hell?" Cody quietly said to himself, then half whispered for Jamie and Jake to quietly slip over next to him. Putting a finger up to his lips, Cody tapped one of his ears, indicating he didn't want them talking or making any noise. He wanted them to just listen. The other two complied, momentarily distracted from their vigil of watching for more movement in the trees.

After a few brief moments of hearing nothing but the waterfall, the soft moaning returned and all three indicated they clearly heard it. They instantly turned their flashlights back on and started looking for the source of the sound. It appeared to be coming from the direction of the waterfall itself.

Cody asked Jamie to keep an eye on the tree line for any more sounds or movement while he and Jake checked out this new discovery. The two boys started clamoring around the rocks looking in every nook and cranny they came across. They tried to be as stealthy as possible, but they still made enough noise to cause Jamie to take an occasional, nervous glance back their way. All he would be able to see, was their flashlight beams reflecting off the rocks and the crater's wall.

The three continued to be as quiet as possible, subconsciously thinking any talking would expose them—flashlights notwithstanding. Jake and Cody were being systematic in their search efforts, yet remained somewhat clear of each other's area of operation. In the darkness of the kopje, surrounded by rocks and boulders of all sizes, one also had to be extremely careful.

Cody discovered a large, cave-like crack in the wall almost directly behind the little waterfall. The moaning sound returned, louder this time and appeared to be coming from inside the crevasse.

Cody, and then Jake, carefully moved around the edge of the cascading water and lit up the oversized crack with their flashlights. To their utter astonishment, huddled in a fetal position against the back wall, was the pale and emaciated figure of Danny Harper.

CHAPTER 25

Midnight Tuesday, September 23

Lagos

Matt's relief showed up at approximately 11:55 p.m., just as planned. Matt was grateful for the staffer's punctuality, but informed him he would be staying for another half hour. He wanted to see the midnight report from his three searchers before catching some shut-eye. At around 12:20 a.m., the night duty officer from Communications and Records strode into their makeshift field office with the latest news.

Apparently, more evidence had been found in the kopje that Danny Harper had been there. The report was fairly short, but also stated the three searchers were going to continue searching throughout the night. The next scheduled communication would be at six o'clock in the morning.

Matt sat back and thought for a minute. He wondered why his two Volunteers and the marine decided to keep searching, rather than call it a night and camp out in the Rovers. Possibly, they found something that made them want to stay up and keep looking, but didn't want to raise anybody's hopes or expectations prematurely. Matt thought he probably would have done the same thing under the circumstances.

Then the "worst case scenario" hit him: what if Danny wasn't to be found? Or, possibly he was found, but dead? This was uncharted territory for Matt. In his three years as a desk officer, he had not lost a single Volunteer. He had, in fact, evacuated several Volunteers over the years due to injury, illness, or other compelling reasons, but he had never actually lost one. Not on his watch.

The thought unnerved him and a growing sense of dread crept into his subconscious. The sensation slowly grew and he started to tremble. He had developed a unique relationship with all of the Volunteers stationed in Nigeria, beginning with the interview process in San Francisco. For the month the group was holed up in Washington D.C. waiting for their visas to clear, Matt enjoyed their company on many occasions. They all liked to party. The notion of losing Danny Harper just when this program was on the threshold of success constituted nothing short of a double fault in his mind. The seriousness of the situation, now that it appeared the search team was getting closer to their quarry, was beginning to overwhelm him.

He remembered Gunnery Sergeant Ripper was going to pick him up at their temporary quarters at 0600 hours, 6:00 a.m. civilian time. Which meant he would miss the early morning report. That would not only be a report that covered six crucial hours of searching, but also six hours of being out of touch with his team. That last thought made him even more apprehensive and uncomfortable.

Given this, Matt would prefer to delay their trip to the airport by as much as thirty minutes if need be, just to hear what the threesome found out during the course of the night. He hoped Gunny Ripper would understand this and be flexible. He wished he knew when the first flight out to Jos was and silently cursed himself for not thinking to ask. Hopefully, they could delay leaving the embassy by a half an hour or so and still make the early flight north.

Having done his due diligence and sufficiently worried himself enough, Matt told the relief staffer he was going over to their temporary quarters to pack and try to get in a couple of hours of sleep. He was secretly hoping his jet lag wouldn't be his undoing at this critical phase of the search. It was now 12:44 p.m. He had fourteen hours left on the extended clock before the Peace Corps formally declared they had lost a Volunteer.

CHAPTER 26

12:58 a.m. Wednesday, September 24

The Paradise Kopje

Cody relayed the news to Jamie while Jake wedged himself into the crack to examine Harper. Jamie's knees buckled when he heard Danny had been found, then teared up when told he was alive.

The trio had finally found what they had been searching several days for. The hunt was finally over. Cody checked his watch. The illuminated dial read two minutes to one o'clock. Approximately one hour after midnight on the morning of Wednesday, September 24, Peace Corps Volunteer Danny Harper was missing no longer.

Jake couldn't remember ever seeing someone look so scared, pathetic, and physically wasted. Given his condition, the marine was impressed Harper was even alive, given the fact that he might have been holed up in here for the last four or five days. Jake tried talking to Harper, who was still moaning and spasmodically trembling. He also had a wild, glazed-over look in his eyes, what people typically referred to as the "deer in the headlights" look. Jake could tell he was in shock and probably dehydrated as well, not to mention starving.

With barely enough room to kneel down beside him, Jake gently patted Danny's shoulder while trying to talk to him. Harper flinched at the touch, suddenly coming to life as if waking from a fitful sleep.

"Mmmonsters!" Danny hoarsely stuttered. "Tttree...

mmmonsters! Look out! They're...they're coming! No...no...no!"

Oh boy, Jake thought, *he's so wasted, he's gone psychotic. Poor guy, he probably doesn't even know who he is or where he is.*

Cody asked Jake if he could get Danny out of the oversized crack by himself or if he needed help.

"I think I can get him to his feet, but I'll have to get behind him to hold him up. If you and Jamie wait at the entrance, you might be able to help pull him out from the front side."

Jake worked himself in behind Danny, grabbed his belt in one hand and the back of his shirt with the other. Using the rock wall for support and leverage, he gently lifted him straight up. Harper was so out of it he didn't offer any resistance; he just kept mumbling something about tree monsters. Jake was surprised at how easily he lifted Danny, then remembered he wasn't very big, to begin with, and had probably lost a lot of weight during his ordeal.

The marine also noticed Harper was pretty rancid. In addition to several days of body odor, Danny had obviously relieved himself in his pants several times. Basically, he was a stinking mess. Jake had smelled better outhouses than what he was being exposed to right now. The close, confined area made the stench much worse. Jake gagged from the smell.

Cody couldn't believe what had happened to their friend as he and Jamie gently pulled him from the opening. They held Danny upright by his upper arms while checking him out. Both were speechless. The high-spirited, super-fit Danny Harper had been reduced to this.

Harper was half-trying to stand, but his legs were too cramped and atrophied to hold his weight without help. His head rolled from side to side as if he was trying to figure out who Jamie and Cody were or what was going on.

Jake was still lifting on the back of Danny's belt as the three slowly moved Harper away from the opening and out from behind the small waterfall. Cody noticed Danny was trying to hold on to something rolled up in the front of his shirt.

The three rescuers managed to half-walk, half-drag a delirious Danny Harper out into a small open spot between the pool and the burial grounds before setting him down. Jake, because of his advanced first aid training, started a cursory examination of Danny and asked Cody if he would run back to the campsite and get a bottle of water, a couple of bananas, a blanket, a change of clothing from Danny's stuff, and his field medical kit. A concerned, shaky, and tearful Jamie was preoccupied holding his flashlight on Danny and partially supported him while Jake doled out instructions.

Once Cody took off, Jake continued with his quick, triage-type of examination to see if anything needed immediate attention. Danny was more-or-less sitting upright on his own, with the help of Jamie kneeling next to him. Danny's knees were drawn up against his chest, held in place by his two skinny arms wrapped securely around them. He still looked "out of it" and didn't respond to Jake touching him. He just sat there, gently rocking back and forth mumbling what he had said earlier.

"He's in pretty bad shape," Jake announced. "In addition to being in shock, he's also dehydrated, malnourished, and looks to have either a broken or badly sprained right ankle. Additionally, he has an assortment of cuts, scrapes, and bruises, none of which look to be life-threatening. We're lucky to have found him when we did."

Jamie, now quietly sobbing, kept looking into Danny's eyes and softly started talking to him while rubbing one of his arms. Jake encouraged Jamie to keep talking. He was hoping that Danny would recognize the familiar voice and respond in some small way. Harper just kept rocking and continued muttering something about monsters.

Looking up at Jake, Jamie asked the obvious question, "What was he doing in there?"

"I assume he was hiding from something," Jake offered, thinking about what Danny was mumbling. Not wanting to raise Hammer's paranoia any more than it already was, he said nothing more.

"I don't understand," Jamie quietly prodded. "What could have frightened him like that? What could make him do this to himself?"

Before Jake could answer, the heavy footsteps of something approached them out of the darkness. Cody Armstrong burst out of the darkness and into the lighted area across from the other three, sucking in air from running.

"Jesus, Cody!" snapped Jake, "a little warning would be nice before scaring the shit out of us!"

"Sorry, I guess I forgot where we were." It hadn't taken Cody long to retrieve the items Jake requested and make his way back to the group. Cody had made the round trip in less than twenty minutes. His abrupt arrival, however, forestalled any "atta boys" he was expecting to receive.

"Any problems?" Jake solemnly inquired. "Did you see or hear anything around our campsite?"

"Nope, nothing," Cody reported and unpacked the stuff he had rolled up in a blanket. "How's he doing?"

"Not good, but he could be worse," replied Jake. "He's responsive, which is a good sign, but we need to get food and water in him. We should also get him cleaned up and to a hospital as quickly as we can."

Cody handed Jamie a bottle of water to see if he could get Danny to drink while he wrapped the blanket around Danny's shoulders. Jamie unscrewed the lid, gently put the bottle up to Harper's lips, and let a little of the liquid drizzle out. Danny licked his lips, so Jamie tried pouring a small amount into his mouth. Danny sipped the water at first, then as Jamie introduced more, started gulping it down.

"Not too much and not too fast," cautioned Jake. "We don't want to shock his system."

"How in the world did he survive this long without water?" Cody asked.

"He must have left his hiding spot from time to time and grabbed a mouthful of water from the waterfall," offered Jake.

"How long would he have survived without it?"

"I think the maximum number of days a human can survive without water is somewhere around three to four days," Jake replied. "After that, the kidneys start shutting down and one's own blood turns to poison."

Jamie slowly withdrew the bottle of water from Danny's parched lips and set it down. Grabbing the banana Cody brought, Jamie quickly peeled it and broke off a bite-sized chunk. He gently eased the piece of fruit into Danny's open mouth and watched as he slowly chewed it.

"Asking me to get a banana was a good call," Cody said to Jake. "How'd you know to do that?"

"Something we learned in survival and first aid training," the marine replied. "Bananas are easy to chew, are loaded with natural sugars, and contain sodium, potassium and calcium. A person could virtually live off the fruit, provided you also ate the peel, almost indefinitely."

Cody wrinkled his nose at the idea of eating a bitter banana peel. "You seem to know a lot about bananas."

"Had to live off the little suckers for the entire time of my E & E exercise," Jake moaned.

By this time, Jamie had managed to get Danny to consume half a bottle of water and one whole banana.

"That's probably enough for now," warned Jake. "We need to revive him slowly or we might accidentally kill him. I think we should clean him up as best as possible, then get him back to camp."

Out of habit, Cody looked at his watch. It now read 1:38 a.m. They had been attending to Harper for over half an hour. With the food and water, Danny settled down. He was no longer rocking back and forth but kept his knees up to his chest with his arms still wrapped tightly around them. He was still mumbling to himself. At this point, the boys had to admit Danny looked better than when they pulled him out of the cave-like fissure, but he still reeked.

Jake suggested they get him out of his filthy clothes and wipe him down as best they could with rags made from his shirt. The others agreed. Jake and Cody started working carefully to unfold Danny's arms as Jamie held a flashlight on them and quietly assured Danny everything was going to be alright.

At Jamie's urging, Danny seemed to relax somewhat and slowly let go of his knees. Taking his time, he carefully straightened out his legs, but kept his arms and hands wrapped around his midsection.

Jake and Cody worked slowly and methodically. It took some effort, but they managed to remove Danny's soiled pants and boxer shorts. He wasn't wearing any footgear on his swollen and beat-up feet. They turned their attention to Danny's shirt, but first, they had to untangle his arms.

With Jamie's calming voice and the careful work of Jake and Cody, Danny relaxed his grip on his midsection and dropped his hands to the ground to finally support himself. When he did this, a terracotta figurine fell out from underneath his rolled-up shirt, bounced off his thigh, and came to rest on the ground right next to him.

Jamie, Cody, and Jake all stared at the cherished, symbolic statuette, then looked at Danny and then at each other without saying a word. All three were thinking the same thing: *Now we're totally screwed*!

CHAPTER 27

1:52 a.m. Wednesday, September 24

The Paradise Kopje

Jamie spoke first. "Oh shit, this can't be good," he uttered, his voice cracking.

"We should put it back," Cody said as he reached for it.

"No!" Jake reached out to block Cody's hand. "Don't touch it! Danny removed it, so he's the one who needs to put it back. Remember what I said about curses? Legend has it that whoever removes something like this must be the one who returns it!"

"Look at him, Jake," Jamie pleaded. "Danny's in no shape to do anything right now. One of us has to do it."

"Jamie, please listen to me," the marine quietly said. "Given what we have experienced so far, especially you and Cody these past few days, do you really want to take the chance of defying this sacred place? I mean, why take the risk? We're probably already on somebody's shit list for just being here."

Jamie and Cody momentarily fell silent.

Cody, being somewhat of the group's leader, finally spoke up. "Let's get Danny cleaned up and squared away. We'll leave the figurine where it is and not mess with it, then we'll help Danny return it. Will that work for you guys?"

Jamie slowly nodded and responded with a reluctant "okay."

Jake simply said, "Yep, that'll work for me," and slowly removed the blanket draped over Danny's shoulders.

While Jamie continued holding a flashlight on them, Cody

unbuttoned Danny's shirt. They took their time attending to the grungy-looking Volunteer, all the while being extraordinarily careful not to touch the figurine on the ground beside him

Cody and Jake removed Harper's shirt and then Jake systematically tore it into rags. Cody re-draped the blanket around Danny, who appeared to be more calm and lucid than when they brought him out of the cave-like fissure. Cody gave both Jamie and Danny a sympathetic smile. To Cody, Danny's look of appreciation was a good sign.

While Jamie stayed with Danny and continued to comfort him, Jake and Cody took the rags to the pool and soaked them. Returning with a pile of wet and dripping shirt remnants, the boys started wiping four days of dirt, grime, dried blood, and human waste off a transfixed and sullen Danny Harper.

Being as thorough and careful as possible, it took them perhaps half an hour to do the job, interrupted by repeated trips to the pond to clean off the rags. The final phase of the sponge bath was to get Danny to his feet for the final wipe-down and to get clean clothes on him. Once they were satisfied they had Danny laundered as best as possible, they started getting him dressed. Which, to their surprise, he half-helped them with.

Once they were finished, Cody and Jake coaxed and helped him reach down for the undisturbed figurine. For a brief moment, Danny seemed to snap out of it. He quickly picked up the terracotta statuette, immediately tucked it under his new shirt, and held it there, almost as if to protect it. His swift and deliberate move surprised the other three.

"Why is he so protective of that statue?" Jake wondered. "You'd think it was a baby or something."

"It's kind of strange when you think about it," offered Cody. "I hope he doesn't think it belongs to him or something like that. Which could mean trouble for us if he doesn't intend to part with it."

It was at that moment they once again heard rustling and movement in the tree line at the back of the amphitheater. All three automatically snapped their flashlights up and trained them on the area. But as soon as the lights hit the forested boundary, it went still again.

Danny mumbled something about monsters again and dropped to his knees, still clutching the figurine under his shirt. Jamie knelt to steady Danny while the other two continued to sweep their lights back and forth over the area. Nothing was visible except for what they saw before. No sound and no more movement.

Jamie and Cody helped Danny back up to his feet while Jake continued checking the foliage for any more activity. Seeing nothing, he quietly suggested they should quickly help Danny put the statuette back and then hurry back to their campsite. Although the three searchers still had their machetes and pepper spray with them, Jake said they were too exposed at this location and he wanted more of his "non-lethal" protection at hand. This graveyard also gave him the creeps.

Because they were only about ten meters (33 feet) away from the wall of windows and the empty space that once held the purloined terracotta figurine, it was an easy distance for the four of them to cover, even though Cody and Jamie once again had to support a staggering, shoeless Danny. Harper was still cradling his prize, rolled up in his shirt, and held securely next to his stomach. Jake followed the procession, occasionally shining his light back to the tree line to check for more movement or anything suspicious.

Once at the wall, it took more than a little coaxing by Cody and Jamie to get Danny to part with the foot-tall sculpture. They had to each grip an elbow and forearm and help Danny unroll the artifact from underneath his shirt. Danny held the figurine in trembling, outstretched hands and stared at it as the two boys gently guided him toward the opening.

With one final nudge from the pair, Danny reluctantly set the article down inside of the niche. It was even facing in the right direction. All swore they heard soft whispering come from all directions when Danny retracted his shaking hands.

"Alright," Jake announced, "let's get the fuck outta here!"

Keeping a watchful eye on the tree line, the four made their way over to the pool, then slowly walked around it and back to their campsite on the other side. Jamie assisted Danny by slinging one of his arms slung around the back of his neck to help hold him up. Jake led the procession, followed by Jamie and Danny, and then by Cody, who had picked up everything they had brought including Danny's soiled clothing, all wrapped up in the blanket. They doubted they'd be returning to this area of the crater, so Cody and Jake took great pains to make sure they left no trace of their presence before leaving.

With Danny's inability to walk normally, it took the ensemble a good twenty-five minutes to make the journey back to their campsite. Cody, again, checked his watch. It was now 2:45 in the morning; it had been a long day and an even longer night, and it wasn't over yet. Jake saw Cody check the time and did the same.

"Cody, what time is sunrise?" he asked.

"Six twenty," Cody responded. "We have somewhere around three and a half hours before it starts getting light."

"Not soon enough for my liking." Jake asked Cody to see if he could round up some firewood. Jake also cautioned Cody to stay on the clearing side of the forest, especially where he had good light from the brightly burning lantern. Jamie sat with Danny, keeping him warm while trying to give him more water and another banana. Jake, now down on one knee, busied himself by keeping an eye on Cody and the tree line while unpacking and checking the rest of his ordinance.

Cody returned in about ten minutes with an assortment of dried palm fronds, dead shrubs, sticks and twigs, and several small chunks of bark. With the help of Jake's fire-starter kit, Cody had no problem in building a small fire. He decided to do this close to the edge of the pool on sandy ground. He thought it would be easier to shovel the ashes and unburned remains into the water when they were finished. They had all agreed earlier they were to leave no trace of their occupancy when they left.

The small fire gave off a reassuring warmth and glow. It also gave off a fairly distinctive odor.

"What'd you throw on that fire?" asked Jamie. "It smells like burning hair."

Jake examined a piece of the bark Cody had brought back from the edge of the forest, sniffed it, and then threw it into the flames. As soon as he did that, the fire flared up and the smell got worse.

"Jesus," Cody uttered, "what kind of bark burns and smells like that?"

"Most tree barks don't stink when they burn," replied Jake. "Actually, most give off a more fragrant smell. But this, this bark you found, is nothing like I've ever seen or smelled before. It's different somehow and it feels almost greasy."

"Well, considering where we are, maybe it comes from a new species of tree," offered Cody.

"I don't know," Jake said, shaking his head. "This bark just seems to be out of place in here. With the exception of the palm trees and a few other identifiable species we've come across, the only other thing to consider is those dead snags we've seen on occasion. Add one more thing to the list of unexplained items for this place, I guess."

Not to be left out of the conversation, Jamie chimed in with a semi-serious comment. "What about Danny's 'tree monsters?'"

CHAPTER 28

2:56 a.m. Wednesday, September 24

The Paradise Kopje

Cody stared at Jamie. *What if? What if there is something to what Jamie just said?*

Jake shook his head. "Oh, for Christ's sake, you two. Aren't you a little old to be believing in fairy tale monsters...ghosts and goblins...the boogie man?"

"Okay, okay," Cody replied, "I see your point. But again, how do you explain what's happened to us, or especially to Danny, since we've been in here? I, for one, think there's something unexplainable going on in this kopje. Something that might be protecting this place from outsiders. The skulls we found in that pile of bones tells me we could be into something sinister, if not downright deadly. We've said all along we don't think we're alone in here."

"Well," Jake responded, "I believe we can rule out any predators; they seem to avoid this place with a passion. That leaves only two other possible explanations: One, we've been stalked and terrorized all along by some locals. Possibly like you said, guardians protecting this burial ground. Maybe even thieves or poachers guarding their turf. Second, and I have a real hard time even considering this one, is that there are some type of actual 'monsters' in here with us."

Jamie spoke up next. "If there are local natives in here with us, how do you explain what happened to Danny, and why haven't we seen them?"

"That's an easy one," the soldier answered. "Camouflage. Marine Corps snipers wear what is called a 'ghillie suit' when they are out in the field. These outfits are so good, so natural-looking, that someone wearing one could be standing right next to you and you'd never notice it."

"And Danny," Jamie shot back, sympathetically looking at his friend sitting on the ground next to him. "How do you explain what happened to him?"

Harper was once again gently rocking back and forth with his legs crossed, holding onto the blanket draped over his shoulders.

"Someone in a well-constructed ghillie suit would have leaves, small branches, and all kinds of things hanging off it," Jake explained. "Wearing a similar type of hat with a camo-painted face would definitely make them look like a tree. Since it looked like Danny had been drinking beer and was probably tired from searching for this place, I would guess someone snuck up on him dressed like a tree and, in his condition, literally scared the shit out of him."

"That would account for his condition alright," Cody offered, partially accepting Jake's theory. Then he thought of something else. "But what about the fact he was holed up for days holding onto one of those figurines...as if he were trying to protect it? And what about that foul-smelling bark we've been burning?"

Jamie followed Jake and Cody's back-and-forth dialog with a growing look of dread. "Maybe he wasn't protecting it," Jamie finally offered. "Maybe it was protecting him."

"What?" Cody asked, now focusing his attention toward the two figures sitting by the fire. "What do you mean?"

Jamie took a few moments to organize his thoughts before replying to Cody's question. "Just maybe," he began, "and I say this because of the way he kept holding it in front of him and was reluctant to let go of it...maybe whoever, or whatever, put him into this state was held at bay by the figurine. You know, like a shield because of its spiritual aspects."

"That's a helluva notion, Jamie," Cody said, "and if that

were the case, it would certainly explain why he grabbed it. I doubt Danny would intentionally remove something like this from its altar unless he thought it would save him."

A brief moment of silence fell on the group before suddenly being interrupted by the shaky and weak voice of Danny Harper. "Protect me...statue protect me...protect me...from monsters...afraid of statue."

The other three looked at Harper in stunned silence. Finally, Danny had come around and offered a clue to the mystery. Harper, in his semi-lucid state, had affirmed Jamie's theory regarding the significance of the figurine. One more puzzle solved. That left open the question of Danny's "monsters."

As if things weren't already tense enough, the reassuring glow of the Coleman lantern decided to add another element of intrigue by suddenly flaring out.

Jamie jumped up and all three men simultaneously turned on their flashlights. Scanning the area, they saw nothing. Nothing at all except for the radio case with the dark lantern on top of it and the rest of their gear stacked about. *Just a coincidence, perhaps*? thought Cody. The three exchanged worried glances and brought their pepper spray canisters out, just in case.

Jake cautiously walked the seven meter (23 feet) distance to the lantern to examine it, all the while scanning the area with his flashlight and keeping an eye on the distant tree line. After picking the Coleman up and shaking it, Jake announced to the others it was simply out of fuel, then realized he forgot to bring more.

"Well," quipped a somewhat embarrassed Jake, "looks like I didn't live up to the Corp's primary 'Six Ps philosophy.'"

"And that is...?" Jamie sat back down, clearly relieved that neither ghosts, goblins, nor tree monsters had sabotaged their lamp.

Jake half-smiled as he gave out the answer, "Proper Planning Prevents Piss-Poor Performance!"

The others chuckled and clearly appreciated the humorous reply. The overall mood of the group relaxed.

"That being the case," added Cody, "we should probably

build up the fire and scrounge up enough wood to last us for the next couple of hours."

Jake checked his watch. "It's 3:28. We still have about three hours before dawn. If our mysterious watchers actually exist and are going to make a move, it'll probably be after the moonlight fades, but before dawn. That would be the darkest part of night. That's the prime time to take someone by surprise. Folks are either asleep or too tired to recognize they're in danger until it's too late.

Cody was tired, as were Jamie and Jake. They'd been up since before dawn, approximately twenty-one hours ago. Fatigue was starting to catch up with all of them. There wouldn't be any relief in the near future either.

The marine continued airing his concerns. "Once it gets light enough to leave, we'll high-tail it out of here and get back to Jos. Then get Danny to a hospital. Three more hours until dawn, another hour to get out of the kopje, and then a six-to-seven-hour-drive back to Jos. That'll put all three of us in the neighborhood of over thirty hours without sleep. Straight into sleep deprivation hell."

"No problem," Jamie flatly said. "When I was studying for finals in college, we'd always pull 'all-nighters' and sometimes go several days without sleep."

"No shit?" inquired a doubtful Jake Simmons. "How'd you manage to do that?"

"Easy," Jamie came back with. "All you have to do is pop a "Dexie" every six hours or so and, wham, you're back on top!"

"A 'Dexie?' What the hell is a 'Dexie?" Jake sounded confused, but Cody was quietly smirking.

"Jake," Jamie lectured, nose in the air, "'Dexie' is a slang term for Dexedrine, a prescription amphetamine originally used to treat hyperactive kids. It is also used by long-haul truck drivers, police officers, people working a graveyard shift, and college students to keep them awake and alert."

"Wow, sounds like just what we need. Too bad there isn't a drug store nearby," Jake said half-seriously.

"Ah, but we do," Jamie smugly replied as he reached for his

Peace Corps field kit. "Right here in this little case, we have the envy of many a street dealer. What's your pleasure, little girl?"

All three laughed. Maybe it was the fatigue, the lack of real food, the situation they were in, or a combination of everything. At any rate, they all felt the better for it.

Jamie broke open his kit and found the little bottle he was looking for fairly quickly. He opened the container and took out three, 10-mg. pills and administered one pill to each. Cody asked if they should give one to Danny. Because of his condition, Jake said that would probably be a bad idea, not knowing how the drug would affect him, especially in his semi-psychotic state.

It didn't take long for the little pink pills to take effect. Within ten minutes, all three boys felt alert and refreshed. They also felt like they could conquer the world, which was a common side effect of this class of drugs. It was now time to turn their attention on building up the fire and obtaining enough wood to fuel it for the next several hours. Cody tossed all of Harper's soiled clothing on the small fire, as well as any other unusable, burnable material they had on hand. He wanted to get a good flame going before they left the sanctuary of their campsite in search of more firewood.

While Jamie stayed with Danny by the fire and fed him another banana, Jake and Cody fanned out beyond their camp in search of wood. Jake told Cody they needed to keep each other in sight at all times and not venture any farther than a meter or two into the forested area.

It was perhaps only four meters (13 feet) from the edge of the pool to the campfire and another five meters (16 ½ feet) to the spot where they had their stuff organized. All were in an arched clearing surrounding the pool of water. From where their gear was stowed, it was anywhere from nine to ten meters (approximately 48 feet) of clearing before the tree line that surrounded the open area. In the semi-darkness of the crater, it looked like a longer distance than it actually was.

Because this open area extended most of the way around the pond, one could be on the other side of the water, still be in the clearing, be next to the trees, and be able to keep the fire and campsite in visual range. The problem was the distance. Going around the pool, back toward the direction of the amphitheater would put someone nearly twenty-five meters (82 feet) or more away from the safety of the campsite. That might be a problem in the event of an emergency.

This was where Cody inadvertently found himself while looking for whatever he could find that would burn. He was soon on the other side of the pool and separated from Jake by a considerable distance without either one realizing it.

Bending down to pick up a dried palm frond just inside of the forested area, he caught a whiff of strong body odor. Then, something heavy and sharp latched onto his left shoulder from behind.

CHAPTER 29

3:49 a.m. Wednesday, September 24

The Paradise Kopje

Thanks to the stimulating effects of the Dexedrine, Cody reacted fast and instinctively, dropping flat and rolling over to his right while shining his flashlight straight up and slightly behind him as he did so.

There, in the bright glare of his flashlight's beam, stood a gnarled, tree-like creature with one of its branch-like arms moving up to protect, what Cody imagined, were its eyes. The thing let out a small yelp, then disappeared into the darkness of the forest.

Cody lay there motionless for about five seconds, his heart racing and his mind reeling, trying to comprehend what his eyes just witnessed. Quickly snapping out of the shock-like state, he jumped up and yelled for Jake as he pulled out his pepper spray with his free hand. He was still holding his shaking flashlight, scanning the area where the thing disappeared.

When Jake heard Cody yell, he snapped upright, dropped the fire material he had gathered, and took off in a sprint, un-holstering his machete as he ran toward the sound of Cody's voice. The young marine was approximately twenty-five meters (82 feet) away from Cody, but covered the distance in record time. He wasn't even breathing hard when he reached a trembling Cody Armstrong.

"What happened?" Jake asked, his face full of concern.

"I saw it...I saw it!" Wild-eyed, Cody tried to catch his

breath. "It was...it was...actually a tree...a tree of some kind... it reached out and grabbed me...actually grabbed me...then ran away!" Cody had to force the words out between the panting breaths. He was either really scared or so excited he was hyperventilating.

"Cody...Cody!" Jake said, sinking the tip of his machete into the ground and putting his now-empty hand on Cody's chest. Cody's heart pounded like it was trying to escape from its owner. "Calm down, man. Calm down and breathe slowly. I'm here. Everything's okay," Jake said this slowly and evenly, trying to get Cody to settle down so he could talk rationally.

"Jake, I saw it!" exclaimed Cody after he took a brief moment to swallow hard and collect himself. "I saw it! Danny was right! There is a tree monster in here!"

"Cody," Jake kept his voice calm and even. "Are you sure of what you saw? Remember what I said about the camouflage suits the snipers wear? Are you sure someone wasn't wearing something like that?"

"This was no man in some fucking ghillie suit!" Cody yelled, irritated. "It was a creature of some kind and it looked straight at me! I'm sure of what I saw!"

"Can you describe it?"

"It was big." Cody gestured with outstretched arms. "Tall, like a man. It had branches for arms and hands. It moved on two legs or trunks. The feet looked like roots. I didn't get a clear look at the head because it covered it up with one of its arms, or branches when I hit it with the light. Then it turned and disappeared back into the forest."

"Anything else you can remember...anything at all?" pressed Simmons, now starting to get a little shaky himself.

"No," Cody said, shaking his head. "No. Wait. Wait a minute. There were two other things. I distinctly smelled some type of BO before it touched me and the thing didn't resemble a living tree...it looked more like some kind of a dead snag or something like that."

With that revelation, Jake felt a shiver go down his spine. They had, in fact, seen several dead snags in this crater during the course of the night. Cody remembered thinking they seemed out of place in this lush environment.

"Come on," Jake finally said, "let's get back to the campsite. I'm sure Jamie is probably worried about all this yelling. We'll pick up the stuff I dropped on the way. I've suddenly got a really bad feeling about this place."

"No shit!" Cody said. "I can't believe this!"

Jamie was anxiously waiting for them to return to the campsite. He was on his feet, standing next to the seated Danny, with pepper spray and flashlight in hand. The fire was burning low, which plunged the open area around the campsite into semi-darkness.

Cody and Jake approached Jamie out of the darkness. Forgetting to announce their arrival as they entered the light, a nervous and now trigger-happy Jamie Hammer was a heartbeat away from letting them have it with his pepper spray.

"Whoa there, cowboy. Don't shoot. We're the good guys!" Jake exclaimed when Jamie took aim. "Sorry to startle you. Guess we should have announced ourselves before we became targets."

"You're damn right; you should have!" Jamie shouted, jabbing a finger at the pair. "I heard Cody yell and then heard a lot of commotion on the other side of the pool and freaked out! I thought something bad might have happened to you guys! What the hell is going on?"

Before answering, Jake threw a few pieces of wood onto the fire, making it sizzle and pop. Instantly, the flames leapt up and bathed the whole area in a brighter glow of light.

"Hammer man, you are not going to believe what I just saw!" Cody began, trying to catch his breath. "It was some kind of creature that resembled a tree!"

"You saw the tree monster! It really exists?" Jamie's eyes grew wide. "What the fuck do we do now? We need to get the hell out of this place! Right now!"

"Calm down, Jamie. Take a breath," Jake advised in his most soothing voice. "Just calm down a minute. We need to figure this out rationally and not panic. That would work against us...big time. For us to panic is the last thing Danny needs right now as well."

Jake's remarks seemed to settle Jamie down and bring him "back to Earth," as they liked to say when someone was losing it. Cody took the opportunity to throw additional wood on the fire. In the bright glow of the growing fire, Cody checked on Danny, who was looking better than before and was no longer rocking back and forth. To Cody, it appeared as if he was trying to follow the conversation.

For Jamie's benefit, Jake asked Cody to start from the beginning and describe everything in detail about his experience. Both listened intently as Cody tried to narrate his encounter with the "tree monster," right down to the unusual smell.

A minute or two of dead silence fell after Cody finished telling his story. Jamie was still edgy, but Jake seemed to be contemplating something.

His military mind must be working in high gear, Cody guessed.

Finally, Jake spoke up, looking at Cody but addressing both of his counterparts. "You said the creature lightly grabbed your shoulder, but not in a menacing way, and it didn't come after you. Is that right?"

"That's right," Cody answered, not sure where Jake was headed with this. "When it grabbed my shoulder, I hit 'em with the light, then it ran away. What of it?"

"Suppose," Jake replied, "just suppose for a moment that whoever or whatever this thing is, it's not hostile and means us no harm?"

"What do you mean?" asked Cody, starting to follow Jake's line of thought.

"Suppose we're only being watched, or observed, because this 'thing' is just curious about us," Jake continued. "Maybe it's trying to figure out the same things about us as we are about it."

"And maybe it's studying us because it's looking for a weakness or a good opportunity to strike. Maybe it's hungry!" added Jamie, his paranoia notched up a couple of degrees.

"Jamie," reflected the pragmatic marine, "if it wanted to harm us, it had plenty of opportunities. It has probably been watching us since the moment we set foot in here. We weren't always together and we didn't always have weapons within easy reach. I think there's more going on here than we may realize."

"I'm having a hard time considering that possibility." Jamie crossed his arms. "Look at what happened to Danny. He may never be the same again. We're damn lucky he's even alive for Christ's sake! And what about those skulls we found earlier?"

"All good questions," Jake offered, "but we don't know for certain what actually happened to Danny. He may only have been frightened out of his wits and not actually attacked. He could have hurt his foot while trying to escape from what scared him. We just don't know until Danny comes around and talks to us. As for the skulls, maybe someone just picked them up somewhere and threw them on that pile. The fact is, guys, right now we have more questions than we have answers."

"We still need to keep our guard up," Cody announced, nervously glancing around. "This place is starting to scare me more and more. Whatever happened to Danny is something I don't want happening to us!"

The three unconsciously glanced down at Harper, who was now quietly talking to himself and playing with a stick. Jamie knelt and softly asked him if he wanted more water or something else to eat. Danny didn't respond; he just kept mumbling he wanted to go home.

"So, teammates, what's our next step?" Jamie asked, standing up to face the other two.

Before anyone could offer up a suggestion, rustling and movement came from two different directions in the forest. Stepping out of the cover of the tree line and into the far reaches of the light from the campfire emerged, what appeared to be, two gnarled-looking trees.

"Oh, shit!" exclaimed a startled Cody Armstrong, pointing at the pair. "There's more than one!"

CHAPTER 30

4:05 a.m. Wednesday, September 24

The Paradise Kopje

The two creatures looked menacing.

The pair stood on the fringes of the forest, yet clear of it. They were clearly out in the open, occupying a transitional strip of grass and bushes that separated the trees from the open area where the boys were. They were swaying back and forth, as if shifting their weight from one foot to the other. Looking similar, Cody thought, like a tree moving in the wind.

They were standing approximately five meters (sixteen feet) apart and perhaps thirteen meters (forty-three feet) away from the foursome by the campfire. Too close for comfort for Jake. He was hoping they weren't as fast or as nimble as he or the others were.

Whispering, Jake told the other two not to make any sudden moves and not to turn on their flashlights. Jamie slowly moved sideways and stepped in front of Danny, shielding him from the view of the creatures and instinctively giving him some protection. All three checked that they had their weapons at hand if necessary. The OC pepper spray canisters were in holsters, located on their web belts, as were their machetes.

From what Jake could see in the dim light, they were exactly as Cody described. They did, in fact, look like dead trees, except for the tops, which were definitely shaped like a conical head. *If those are ghillie suits,"* Jake thought to himself, *they're damn good ones*!

The boys stared for perhaps one to two minutes, as did the creatures at the boys. It was a classic "Mexican Standoff." No one, or no thing, made a move.

"What the hell are they?" Cody said to no one in particular, half whispering. "Where did they come from?"

"Maybe they're aliens...or some sort of 'throwback' creatures...you know, like Bigfoot!" offered Jamie, trembling.

"They could be some sort of a mutation," Cody added, "...some genetic cesspool that accidentally created a type of monster."

"Who knows what they are...or where they came from," Jake quietly said, not taking his eyes off the pair. "The fact is...they are definitely real...and we're trespassing on their turf. Whatever they are, they have us at the disadvantage. I wasn't trained to confront monsters."

The thought they could be facing imminent death never registered with the three. In Cody's mind, they were seeing something quite extraordinary and he was transfixed and fascinated by what stood before them.

"Do you think we should try and communicate with them in some way?" Cody quietly asked out of the side of his mouth.

"No," responded Jake, shaking his head. "Let's wait and see. Let them make the first move."

Before anyone could say anything more, the creatures shuffled forward a few meters, stopped, and resumed their swaying motion.

"Okay, they made the first move. Now what?" Cody whispered to Jake, instinctively taking a step back.

"I think they're either challenging us, like a bear or a gorilla would, or they're trying to bait us into chasing them," Jake replied quietly. "Just stand where you are and do nothing to provoke them."

Cody found himself fighting off a growing sense of fear and panic. Even Cpl. Jake Simmons, USMC, who had not yet seen combat or death, wore a look of dread and apprehension.

"It looks like they are either challenging us or studying us," Cody nervously said out of the side of his mouth.

The creatures stood where they were and continued their swaying. Now that they were closer, they looked even more sinister. If not downright scary.

The bizarre standoff soon took its effect on Jamie. He was already stressed out enough as it was and the Dexedrine didn't help matters. He was ready to go ballistic at any time. Cody heard him mumbling something incoherent to himself.

Without warning, Jamie bolted forward and hopped with his arms outstretched into a crouching position and yelled, as if he were jumping out from behind a bush to scare the neighborhood kids. The sudden and deliberate move surprised even Jake and Cody, and in the process exposed Danny to the creatures.

The creatures shrieked and quickly disappeared back into the sanctuary of the trees.

"What the hell?" Cody said out loud, breaking their dialogue of whispers.

"Something spooked them," offered Jake, still speaking in a hushed tone. "Maybe it was Jamie's sudden move or the sight of Danny. Whatever it was, I bet we'll find out in another minute. My intuition tells me they'll be right back. Stay alert, guys. Stay alert."

Jake and his intuition were wrong. The creatures didn't return, at least not immediately. After five minutes or so had passed without their re-appearance, the boys relaxed their defensive postures. Danny was the exception. The sight of the creatures sent him back into the sobbing fetal position they found him in.

"Jesus, Jamie! What the hell were you thinking, pulling a stunt like that?" demanded Cody, not happy with the actions of his fellow Volunteer. "Are you deliberately trying to provoke them? Do you want to wind up on some monster's dinner plate... or bone pile, for God's sake?"

Jamie almost cowered at the remark. "I'm...sorry...I don't know...what came over me. Please, don't yell at me. I just couldn't stand it any longer...staring at us like they were. I guess I just...sort of...panicked."

Neither Cody nor Jake could condemn Jamie for what he

did. The visceral tension of the moment could have made any one of them do what Jamie had done. His impromptu reaction was a totally human response.

"Not to worry, buddy," replied Cody, putting his arm around Jamie. "I think you scared them worse than they scared us. At least, now they know we'll fight back if necessary. Shit... you even scared me!"

Jake smiled approvingly at Cody's effort to console his team mate and nodded. No more words were exchanged, or needed to be at that point. Shaking, Jamie went back attending to Danny, who remained in his fetal position. Cody threw more fuel on the fire and Jake moved away from the campfire and a couple of steps closer to the trees. He was hoping his night vision would return so he could keep a watchful eye out without the aid of his flashlight. For the time being, at least, the three felt reasonably safe and tried to relax.

Danny's relapse had all of them concerned. Jamie did his best to comfort him and offered him more food and water. Jamie's reassuring tone and presence slowly started to have an effect on Danny. He relaxed from his fetal position and sat upright as Jamie offered him a stale granola bar.

Partially out of habit and partially because time was now a serious part of their survival plan, Jake checked his watch. Its luminescent dial read 4:29, approximately one hour and twenty minutes until twilight. Almost two more hours until daybreak. To Jake, the last hour or so seemed to last a lifetime. He made a quarter turn to his right, momentarily taking his eyes off the tree line, and whistled a short note to gain Cody's attention.

Looking up from stoking the small fire, Cody saw Jake pointing at his watch, indicating for him to check the time as well. Cody also couldn't believe only an hour had passed since they went searching for wood. It had been one crazy hour. That was for sure. Cody gave Jake a thumbs up, indicating he recognized where they stood with regard to first light, and put more material on the flaming campfire.

Jake saw Cody give him the thumbs up signal and watched Cody as he returned to his fire-tending. When the marine turned back around to check the tree line, he did a quick double take and his heart skipped a beat.

The creatures were back and standing approximately where they were before, again swaying from side to side. Only they were closer this time.

Jake made another low whistle directed at Cody. Once he had Cody's attention, he pointed at his eyes using two spread fingers, the universal "look/watch sign," then pointed at the creatures.

For an instant, Cody thought his heart had stopped as well. Quickly regaining his composure, he slowly picked up his flashlight without turning it on then retrieved the OC pepper spray from its holster on his utility belt. Cody reached out and tapped Jamie on the shoulder, indicating to him their visitors had returned. Then he stepped forward, joining Jake.

Jamie slowly stood up, took out his pepper spray as well, and picked up his flashlight. Jake silently motioned to both Cody and Jamie to keep them off for the time being. Cody instantly understood why Jake wanted the lights kept off. Based on his own experience from earlier, they could be used to blind the creatures if they came too close.

Cody turned part way around so Jamie could see his face. Cody pointed to his eyes with two fingers as Jake had done and then made a thrusting move with his flashlight. Jamie understood the crude sign language and nodded. Cody was relieved to see Jamie had regained his composure and didn't appear to be in the panic mode he was in earlier.

Cody then turned his attention back to the creatures, who were now standing approximately eleven meters (36 feet) away from them. His heart raced and his mouth was so dry it was getting harder to swallow.

From this distance and with a roaring fire behind him, Cody could see the creatures clearer than before. They still resembled hulking tree snags, but now looked more humanoid. The creatures were fairly tall, somewhere around six feet in height and powerfully built. Their conical-shaped heads were covered with long strands of thick, matted black hair that hung below their shoulders. What could be seen of their faces resembled something totally alien. The sunken eyes looked cold and menacing. There wasn't much definition to the shoulders or upper arms, which were covered with strips of a bark-like substance, as was the chest and torso area. The forearms and hands looked like gnarled tree branches, as did the legs and feet. They resembled a cross between an old oak tree and a willow gone bad. Cody could tell almost immediately these were not men dressed in camouflage-type ghillie suits.

From this close distance, the creatures had a distinctive smell. They literally stunk to high heavens. Cody reasoned the smell explained the intense body odor they caught a whiff of from time to time. He shivered at the thought that one of these creatures had been standing practically right next to him on several occasions and he didn't even know it.

The bark-like substance hanging off the creatures was exactly like the bark they'd been finding lying around all over the place. The same stuff they'd been throwing on the fire. The bark that smelled like burning hair. Cody felt ill.

After an excruciatingly long two minutes of holding their ground and swaying, the creatures unexpectedly shuffled forward.

CHAPTER 31

4:36 a.m. Wednesday, September 24

The Paradise Kopje

The boys steeled themselves, weapons at the ready, expecting to be rushed. In one hand, each had his flashlight and in the other, except for Jake, his canister of pepper spray. Jake was holding his machete at his side, thinking his knife-fighting skills might come in handy. Cody and Jamie had their machetes close at hand as well, stuck point down in the sandy soil next to them. None of the three were planning on going down without a fight.

Jamie slowly took a couple of steps forward, joining Cody and Jake on their left hand side, making a defensive column, three abreast. Danny was still sitting on the ground behind them, next to the fire, with his head down, gently rocking back and forth.

The two Volunteers and the marine were so focused on the creatures in front of them, they didn't realize Danny had gotten to his feet and staggered the few steps to be next to Jamie, who was standing closest to the pool. When he saw the creatures, Danny stood still for a moment, wild-eyed and paralyzed with fear. Then he did what no one expected him to do, but was probably a natural reaction for anyone in his condition.

Danny screamed bloody murder then bolted.

Even with a bad ankle, he managed to quickly disappear in the dim light toward the north side of the pool. All three jumped when Danny screamed and took off in the direction of the graveyard, but no one made a move to go after him. The three boys' reaction time was temporarily on hold. They didn't hesitate out of fear; all were unconsciously waiting to see what the creatures would do.

They didn't have to wait long. The brute closest to the pool quickly disappeared as well, presumably going after the panicked Danny Harper. Without saying a word and before the other two could react, Jamie turned on his flashlight and took off in the same direction as Danny and the pursuing creature.

"Standard divide and conquer tactic," Jake muttered. "Shit! This could be bad. We can't be separated. We need to catch up to Jamie and Danny before that monster does!"

Without waiting to see what the second creature would do, Cody grabbed his machete and turned on his flashlight. Jake followed suit. Then the boys quickly took off in the same direction as Jamie and Danny. From their position in front of the campfire, they darted off to their left toward the north side of the pool. It didn't take them long to get to the sandy area, circumnavigate the pool to its other side, and come out at the backside of the area. The place looked empty.

Jake holstered his machete and retrieved his OC pepper spray from his web belt. Then the two quickly searched the amphitheater with their flashlights, calling out for their two missing members. There was no response. Although only about eight minutes had elapsed since Danny and Jamie had left the campsite, there was no sign of either one in the amphitheater or graveyard. It was as if the kopje had simply swallowed them up.

Cody and Jake quickly scoured the amphitheater and then the tree line behind them with their lights to see if they'd been followed. Nothing there either. Jake suggested they check the cave-like crack behind the waterfall, the one where they originally found Danny. Again, they found nothing.

Stepping out from behind the waterfall and working their way back to the graveyard, they again started calling for Jamie and Danny. This time, a faint and familiar voice off in the distance yelled, "Here! Over here! Follow the wall!"

With flashlights in hand and their weapons reattached to

their belts, the two boys began re-tracing their original route back along the western wall, heading north this time with the rocky wall on their left. Both were moving quickly, yet cautiously, down the one-lane path. They stopped every ten meters or so to call out again. They heard nothing more in response and feared the worst.

As Cody followed the young marine down the trail, he now regarded this once lush and beautiful oasis as a living, green hell. Then the scary thought crossed his mind they could be indefinitely trapped inside this oasis and, perhaps, their lives would end here as well. The notion made Cody shiver.

Both boys kept moving at a steady, yet fairly quick, walking pace. At one point, Jake stopped abruptly. A sharp yelp, like the sound a dog would make if someone had stepped on its paw or tail, ripped through the air. Cody heard it as well and gave Jake a concerned look. Neither spoke. They quickly resumed their pursuit.

They were about halfway along the wall when Jake, out in front, stopped again and stared at something on the ground. Cody was only three steps behind and pulled up alongside to see why Jake had stopped moving.

"Find something?" Cody asked, panting.

"Not sure," was Jake's tentative reply. "Is it my imagination, or do those chunks of bark on the trail look familiar?"

"They sure do. They look like something that fell off of one of our visitors."

"Or was hacked off," added the marine, bending down to take a closer look.

Jake picked up a foot-long piece that roughly looked like a skinny branch. Unlike the ones they'd picked up for firewood, this one wasn't dried out. It was on the greasy side and it smelled awful. It was also bloody on one end.

Both boys looked at each other and then at the bloody "stick" once again.

"Maybe Jamie got a piece of one of them!" Cody offered.

"My thoughts exactly," Jake added, shining his flashlight at the ground. "It also looks like it left a blood trail that goes into the interior."

"So, do we follow the blood or do we stick with the wall?" Cody asked, not sure which direction to take.

"If this thing is wounded, it will be that much more dangerous. Especially since it looks like it headed back into the cover of the trees. Because we've never explored the forested part of this crater, it would have us at a disadvantage. I think we should stick to the wall."

Cody readily agreed with Jake's reasoning and, out of habit, took a quick look at his watch. It was now eleven minutes after five in the morning. The sky wouldn't start to get light for at least another forty minutes and it would stay dark much longer inside the kopje. Jake tossed the disgusting piece of flesh away and the two started working their way around the wall toward the entrance area, occasionally calling out for Jamie and Danny.

The two were perhaps seventeen meters (56 feet) away from the rocky area that marked the entrance notch when they once again heard Jamie's familiar voice.

"Here! Over here! We're over here!" Jamie shouted, alerted to their presence by the flashlight beams bouncing off the kopje's steep wall.

When Jake and Cody emerged from the cover of the foliage, they were within six meters (20 feet) of the rocky pile that marked the entrance to the crater. Jake threw a hand up in front of Cody's chest to halt him. Halfway up the notched area and illuminated by Cody's flashlight, were Jamie and Danny. In the clearing at the base of the rocks, illuminated by Jake's flashlight, stood both of the creatures. One with blood dripping down one of its branch-like arms.

"Shit! What do we do now?" Cody asked Jake out of the side of his mouth as he, too, now trained his light on the creatures.

The two brutes stood there, looking back and forth between the pair marooned up on the rocks and the two who had just emerged from the trees. The pair had strategically placed themselves to intercept anyone going up or coming down from either side of the rock pile, putting them directly in between the two groups.

"Nothing," was Jake's delayed reply. "Don't make any sudden or aggressive moves. I need to figure out what to do next. Can you check on Jamie and Danny?"

The two lumbering creatures could not possibly make the climb up to Jamie and Danny without difficulty, so the two were safe for the time being. The creatures made no moves toward Cody and Jake. Cody couldn't tell if they were held at bay because of the lights they had shining on them, or because they were smarter than they looked.

As long as the creatures controlled their escape route, they would be trapped in this crater for God knew how long. Perhaps they were smarter than he had originally given them credit for.

Cody called up to Jamie. "Hey, Hammer-man. Are you guys okay?"

"I am," Jamie called back. "But Danny's in a pretty bad shape. I think he's had some kind of mental relapse, plus he's boogered up his ankle even worse."

"Jamie, did you take a whack at one of the creatures with your machete?" Jake asked.

"Yep. Sure did. Caught up to it along the wall just as it was about to get Danny. How much damage did I do?"

"Not much," Jake said. "Their bark is pretty tough, but you did draw blood. Can you climb out?"

"I could. But Danny's too fucked up to go any further and I can't leave him behind. Got any ideas?"

"Yeah, stay put until we figure this out," Cody ordered. "I think you guys are safe where you are."

Satisfied his two Volunteers were not in imminent danger, Cody turned his attention back to the monsters guarding the rocky nook. Jake was still alternating his flashlight back and forth between the two. At this close of a distance, the ends of the arm-like branches looked more like claws than twigs. *Shit,* Cody thought, *those could do some real damage if given the chance...so what would be the smartest thing for me to break out right now, the pepper spray or the machete?*

Jake turned slightly toward Cody and told him to take out his pepper spray while he unclipped his machete. Cody checked his watch in the process. Time was crawling. His watch read 5:36. Half an hour until dawn.

The tree-like abominations stood their ground, swaying back and forth like before in the glare of the two flashlights. *That's strange,* Cody thought, *they don't seem to be frightened by the lights anymore.* Then he suddenly realized why.

Both flashlights were getting dimmer.

CHAPTER 32

5:37 a.m. Wednesday, September 24

The Paradise Kopje

Thinking fast, Jake told Cody they needed to hustle back to the campsite before the batteries in their flashlights went completely dead. Jake quietly let Cody know what he was thinking. Jamie and Danny were in a safe spot, but Cody and Jake wouldn't be as soon as they lost their lights. Jake also said he and Cody could move faster than the creatures, if they were to follow. The start of the path which originally took them through the forest to the pool and Danny's campsite was only a couple of meters away. If they took off quickly, catching the two monsters by surprise, they'd have a good head start and could easily make it back to their staging area.

Cody hollered up to Jamie to stay put and keep his guard up. From his vantage point, Jamie had been watching the fading beams of their flashlights and automatically understood what the two needed to do. He gave Cody a thumbs up signal.

"Let's go!" Jake suddenly said.

The two boys darted for the path with Jake in the lead. Both were moving quickly through the vegetation, keeping their focus on the trail in front of them. The last thing they wanted to do right now was trip and fall. A pile-up or injury at this point would be bad. If one of the creatures were to follow them, Jamie would give a shout-out warning. Nothing was heard as the two moved as fast as they dared through the dark foliage.

It took a little over ten minutes for the boys to work their way through the forest and cover the distance, even though the path was somewhat of a straight shot from the rock-strewn entrance to the pool and campsite. The two boys rushed out of the tropical forest and into the open area slightly out of breath. By pre-arrangement, Jake went directly for the rucksack that contained the spare batteries, while Cody kept scanning the tree line with the ever-fading beam of his flashlight.

Jake quickly found what he was looking for, and after fumbling a bit, inserted fresh batteries into his flashlight. Grabbing spares, he joined Cody and kept watch with his light while the Peace Corps Volunteer loaded up his flashlight as well. They now had strong, ample light to check the tree line. Nothing was there. They weren't followed. Both let out audible sighs of relief.

"Should we go back?" Cody asked the marine.

Jake kept scanning and looking at the trees and shrubbery, clearly calculating their next course of action. Civil twilight had already started, making objects distinguishable without artificial light. Although it was still fairly dark inside the crater, the sky above them was definitely getting lighter.

"No, not right now," Jake finally said, looking at his watch. Before Cody could ask why not, Jake continued, "Jamie and Danny should be safe as long as they stay where they are. I think the creatures will stay put for the time being. They seem to know they're cutting off our only means of escape. For the time being, we have time on our side. It's now 5:53 and we need to make the call to Kaduna at six, as expected."

"What are we going to tell them?" Cody asked, anxious as to what their response would be. "We didn't let on about the ancient Nok graveyard. Can we say we're being confronted by monsters?" Cody's heart was racing and his hands were starting to tremble.

Jake blinked a few times then pursed his lips. "I think... we should keep it short and simple. And...like we agreed upon before, say nothing about the graveyard. As for the 'tree monsters'...I don't think we should say anything about them either. Kaduna would either think we've gone nuts or that we're in serious danger. Either way...I don't want to turn this place into a combat zone—or a freak show. We should tell them we found Danny, alive, but in need of medical attention. And...and that we're heading back to Jos at first light and that's it! We can make a follow-up call somewhere along the way, if need be."

The young marine's optimism, as well as his logic, never ceased to amaze Cody. Jake was obviously of the opinion they would, indeed, all survive this this night and live to tell the tale. Cody also thought Jake was mature well beyond his years, and definitely underpaid. He couldn't agree more with Jake's summation and told him so. Nothing more needed to be said.

While Jake broke out the radio and quickly set it up, Cody again kept a watchful eye on the tree line, slowly scanning his flashlight's beam back and forth. Still nothing. They were still safe. Jake's original assumption that the creatures would remain where they were was holding true.

Jake made his call to the Kaduna Consulate precisely at 6:00 a.m., 0600 hours, military time. He kept things short and to the point, stating they had found the missing Volunteer alive and they needed to get him to a hospital as quickly as possible.

Kenny Wagner was listening in on the Kaduna side. He had been with the marine at the consulate the entire night, feeling both a professional, as well as a personal responsibility to be there. He asked the guard who was operating their set if "Victor, Sierra, Tango" needed any assistance.

"Negative," Jake replied.

"Kilo, Charlie, One" reminded Jake once more that Gunnery Sergeant Ripper and Matt McKnight would be heading to Jos on the first flight out that day. Jake said they could meet them at the Evangel Hospital and would possibly make another call while in route to Jos. Kaduna wanted to know the condition of Harper because "everyone" would want to know. Jake simply said Danny was suffering from a bad concussion, was delirious, dehydrated, hadn't eaten in days, was a little beat-up, and had either a badly sprained or broken right ankle. Having nothing more to add, Jake thanked his opposing operator, signed off, and ended the transmission.

Jake was beginning to show the strain of the last two days. He stood up from where he was hunched over his "Prick 10/4 Bravo" radio set and stretched. *Man, I'm going to need some serious R & R after this,* he thought to himself.

Cody checked his watch to see how they were doing on time. The dial now read 6:14. The sun would be peeking above the Nigerian horizon now, though it still wasn't visible inside the kopje.

Jake checked in with Cody to see how he was doing, then started packing up the radio set. He walked over to the wall beneath the ledge and grabbed ahold of the dangling tape antennae. When he gave it a solid jerk, the far end popped free of the rock Jamie had set on it earlier. The twenty-five foot strip tumbled to the ground, as did the rock.

Cody jumped at the crashing sound with a sharp-sounding "Jesus!"

"Sorry," Jake said as he continued packing up the set. When he was finished, he walked over to Cody, who was still watching their surroundings. "Hey, man," Jake said softly, "how you holdin' up?"

"I think I'm gonna need another one of Hammer's little pink pills," Cody responded, chuckling. "I can't believe how tired I feel right now and I'm starting to get hungry. To top things off, we still have a full day ahead of us, provided we make it out of this place."

"Oh, we'll make it out alright." Jake looked up the path toward the notch in the rim. "Those creatures seem to be more concerned with keeping us in here right now than harming us. Time is on our side. We have our ordinance and we outnumber them. They're also on the awkward side, so I think all we have to do is distract them long enough for us to scramble up the rocks to where Jamie and Danny are, finish climbing up to the notch, and then down the other side. Then, we're home free."

"What do you think we ought to do with our stuff?" Cody asked. "It will only slow us down if we try to haul it all out of here, especially up those rocks. That would give those creatures an added advantage."

"We can't leave it. Any of it." Jake shook his head, his voice firm. "Remember what we agreed on earlier? When we go, we can't leave a single trace we were ever here. This is a unique and sacred place. It's been undisturbed for who knows how long and we need to leave it just as we found it."

Jake was right and Cody knew it. There was no point in discussing the matter any further. Everything had to go with them.

The sky was lighter still than when Jake had packed up his radio. Although the sun was now clearing the eastern horizon, the bright orange refection of it shone only along the western rim of the kopje's rock wall; it was still fairly dark inside the crater. Cody checked his watch. It read 6:25 a.m.

Jake continued packing everything else up while Cody kept his vigil. In addition to the container carrying the radio set and the four rucksacks and packs they brought, there was also Danny's pack and cooler. Fortunately, Harper had drunk most of the beer he brought and the other three had consumed a fair amount of the food, so everything was lighter than when they arrived.

Jake stuffed Harper's soiled clothing and all of their garbage into the cooler and securely tied it to the top of the radio's container with the para-cord he brought with him. Next, he made sure their fire was out, and with the little break-down shovel he brought, scattered the remains into the pool of water.

Cody had turned off his flashlight and moved back to where Jake was putting the finishing touches on their campsite. Cody couldn't believe his eyes. Jake was sweeping the area with a palm frond. *Boy, he wasn't kidding when he said leave no trace,* Cody quietly said to himself before he gave Jake an approving nod.

Jake had already divvied up the five packs according to weight. He carried two of the lighter ones plus a heavy one. Cody carried the other two, which were a tad on the heavier side, he grumbled. They carried the radio container between them with the cooler lashed to the top. Jake even took the time and trouble to lash the stem end of the palm frond to the radio container so it would drag the trail behind them. *This guy is pretty anal about leaving no trace,* Cody thought as they started walking back toward the notch and the waiting creatures. *Must be more of that 'Escape and Evade' training he went through.*

It took the two young men twenty minutes to work their way back along the narrow path to the crater's entry point with their heavy load. They had to stop a couple of times to take the strain off their backs and used the opportunity to check their surroundings. Approximately ten meters (33 feet) before the clearing that separated the entrance from the forested area, they stopped and quietly dropped their packs. Jake wanted to scout things out and make a plan before going any farther.

Creeping up to, then crouching behind the last grouping of bushes and ferns, the two could easily see Jamie and Danny still high up on the rocks, thanks to the early morning light. They appeared to be okay and in no immediate danger. Cody had to gently brush a fern branch aside to see the base of the rocks and the place where they last saw the two creatures.

To Cody's bewildered surprise, the two brutes stood in front of them side by side. Standing right in between them was the frail figure of the old Hausa woman with the amber-colored eyes.

The very one who originally led them to this strange place.

CHAPTER 33

5:58 a.m. Wednesday, September 24

Lagos

Matt McKnight was waiting at the entrance to the embassy's temporary staff quarters when Gunnery Sergeant Ripper drove up and popped out of the embassy-issued Ford Bronco.

"Morning, Matt, ready to head for Jos?"

"Sergeant, I was hoping to delay our departure until after we get the six o'clock field report from Kaduna."

Ripper looked at his watch. Matt knew from looking at his it was 6:00 a.m. on the dot. He guessed Ripper already knew what time it was, but was probably looking at the dial and trying to calculate how long they could delay their trip to the airport and still make the morning flight.

Matt saved him the trouble. "We need at least fifty minutes to the airport, another thirty to go through ticketing and another thirty for a cushion. That meant we only need two hours to make the 8:30 flight."

"Okay, Matt," the sergeant said, "but we'll need to leave no later than 6:30 to be safe."

"No problem," Matt quickly said. "I'll meet you in the Communications and Records room." Matt tossed his bag into the passenger seat of the SUV and trotted across the street to the embassy's main entrance. Ripper wheeled the standard U.S. Government-issued vehicle into a U-turn and entered the embassy's oversized parking lot.

Ripper caught up with Matt at the counter that separated the inner workings of the C&R department from its small lobby area.

The graveyard shift duty officer minding the shop that night was nowhere to be seen. Ripper told Matt the staff was probably in one of the secure "comm" rooms in the back receiving Kaduna's transmission as they spoke.

The two waited at the counter for over ten minutes before the duty officer emerged from the back with a piece of paper.

"Either one of you a Matt McKnight from the Peace Corps?" she asked, not immediately recognizing the out-of-uniform gunnery sergeant in the subdued lighting.

Matt stepped forward. "I'm McKnight. You have something for me from the Kaduna Consulate?"

"Yep. Just came in. Here's the transmission." The young woman handed the report to Matt then looked over at Ripper. "Looks like your search team found your boy. A little worse for the wear, but alive. They're headed for a hospital in Jos. Want to send a return message?"

Matt quickly read the report. With a trembling hand, he gave it to the gunnery sergeant.

"I would," Matt responded. "Please inform Kaduna that Sergeant Ripper and myself are still going to Jos and thank them, in every way you possibly can, for all of their help and assistance. I sincerely appreciate it."

"Will do. Anything else?"

"One more thing," added Sgt. Ripper. "Would you update the other two Peace Corps people upstairs as to what's going on, as well as DCM Olvera?"

To the young woman behind the counter, Ripper's request sounded more like an order than anything.

"No problem, Sir."

Ripper and McKnight turned and quickly headed out the door

Ripper knew that the good news would be quickly relayed to Belvoe in Accra and to the Peace Corps organization in Washington. They were well within the 24-hour extension period, which would be of great relief to everyone.

ꙮ

Understandably, Michael Olvera was the first to be notified. The early morning phone call to his home interrupted a leisurely breakfast he was having with his wife. The first thing he did when he put down the receiver was to quietly drop down on one knee, cross himself and murmur the Catholic *Prayer of Gratitude*. True to his heritage, it was said in Spanish.

The news that Peace Corps Volunteer Danny Harper had been found alive and reasonably well spread like wildfire throughout the embassy community that morning. Everyone was in a joyous mood and celebrating as they went about their regular duties. All those directly associated with the search, especially RSO Shannon, were elated. MaryAnn Reed was beside herself with joy and couldn't hold back the tears.

The marine security guard detachment went into high gear after hearing the news. They immediately started to organize an all-embassy celebration when everyone got back to Lagos. If there was ever a time to have the mother of all parties, this was it.

CHAPTER 34

7:06 a.m. Wednesday, September 24

The Paradise Kopje

In the early morning light, the old woman looked unafraid and content standing between the two hulking creatures who resembled dead trees. It was an extraordinary sight.

Speechless, Jake and Cody looked at each other in dismay. *What the hell is going on*? Cody thought. His question would soon be answered.

"Come...come...do not be afraid," the old woman said to the two boys hiding behind the bushes. "Come...I want to speak with you."

Jake and Cody slowly stood, revealing themselves. Not sure what else to do. Not taking their eyes off the creatures and the old woman, they cautiously carried their gear over to an area at the base of the rocks. They unloaded and sat everything down at a spot where it looked like it would be the easiest, if not the fastest place to climb out. Both made sure they still had their weapons on their belts as a precaution.

The two slowly made their way around several medium-sized boulders toward the old woman and the creatures, stopping about five meters (16 feet) directly in front of them.

The old woman was dressed in traditional, robe-like Muslim attire, except her clothes were dirty and tattered. Her head was covered by a desert-style Hijab leaving her face uncovered. Her feet and sandals were covered with dust, as if she'd been walking for a while. In her left hand, she was holding a crooked staff with charms and feathers attached to it. She looked like a desert nomad straight out of a Hollywood movie.

From this distance and in the increasing light of the new morning, Cody could clearly see the creatures who had been taunting them since they climbed into this crater. He had no more doubt, they were indeed human. Sort of.

The pair was without any clothing, dark ebony in color, and appeared to be of the male gender. The two beings looked horrifying. They were completely disfigured with large, ugly, bark-like scabs all over their bodies. Long tendrils of dead flesh hung off them, resembling an old Juniper tree shedding its bark. The growths on their hands and feet made them unrecognizable as such. Their fingernails, if that's what they were, were so long their hands looked like claws. The long, greasy, and unkempt black hair hung down past their shoulders and partially covered their faces, which also had wart-like strips of protruding flesh. They had an abundant amount of unkempt facial hair. Their deep-seated eyes were cold and beady. They were also amber-colored.

They looked like some throwback to leper colonies filled with hideously deformed people, only this was much, much worse. They were probably more animal at this stage than human. The beings were scary-looking as well as repugnant. Cody could not have dreamed up uglier monsters than the two standing a couple of quick steps directly in front of them. He now understood what had sent Danny over the edge.

Cody could also see why there were no tracks or prints anywhere inside the kopje. The feet and lower legs of the two brutes looked like a tangle of roots and gnarled twigs. A condition that would have brushed the ground clean as they moved along.

"With feet and legs like that," Jake half-whispered between clenched teeth, "I don't think they're capable of moving very fast."

"They probably rely on camouflage and the element of surprise to get their prey," added Cody. "Which not only explains what happened to Danny, but how he managed to get away from them."

Although Cody was starting to feel better about their odds of escaping from the creatures, the two sub-humans were still large and menacing. The pair looked as if they could easily kill something, or someone, provided they could get their claw-like hands on them. Cody had never seen anything like this, not even in a horror movie. He couldn't take his eyes off them. They were mesmerizing.

"My sons," the old woman said, answering their unspoken question while lowering her head. It was as if she were ashamed to admit that, even to herself.

Cody couldn't help but stare. The revelation caught him completely by surprise. Jake's mouth hung open as if he was trying to speak. After a brief minute of awkward silence, the two young men regained their composure enough to address the elderly woman. Cody spoke first.

"My name is Cody," he began, looking for a reaction and getting none. "This is Jake and up on the rocks are Danny and Jamie. We're Americans." As soon as he said it, Cody regretted the dumb introduction.

"You...grave robbers!" shrieked the old woman, pointing a boney finger at the two boys in front of her. "You...steal from the ancient ones!"

The woman's vehement and accusatory response momentarily caught the two men off-guard.

"No, no!" Jake squared his shoulders toward the woman. "We came here to find our friend." He pointed up to Danny on the rocks.

"You...lie!" she snarled, taking a step closer. "You...steal soul of ancestors!"

Cody suddenly realized that the old woman was accusing them of stealing terracotta statues from the graveyard's wall. He raised his hands in a conciliatory gesture. "We no lie," Cody said, trying his best to emulate her Pidgin English. "We here to find friend. No take statues. Leave sacred ground undisturbed... understand?"

The old woman glared at Cody for a moment, then at Jake,

as if she was searching for some indication they weren't telling the truth. Unconvinced, she turned to the creature standing closest to her and quietly said something in Hausa to him. The disfigured brute uttered a grunt and nodded, looked at the two men menacingly, then swiftly strode off down the path toward the pool and the graveyard beyond.

"What's going on?" Jake said softly to Cody.

"I think the old woman instructed her 'son' to go check out the wall cubicles to see if any statues are missing."

"We could be up shit creek, you know," Jake placed his hands on his web belt with deceptive casualness. "There was one empty niche when we discovered the place. They know Danny had one, but may not know it was put back."

"We're okay. We're okay." Cody lowered his arms. "When the creature comes back and reports to 'Mama' that nothing is amiss, she'll understand we're telling the truth and all we wanted was to find Danny."

Before either Cody or Jake could say anything more, Jamie's nervous voice rang down from the rocks. "Hey, what the hell's going on down there? Can we get out of here, or what?"

Cody took a step backward and turned toward the rocks so Jamie could see and hear him better. He cupped his hands around his mouth for a megaphone effect. "Be patient, buddy... we're trying to convince these three we didn't steal anything from the graveyard...only want to leave peacefully with Danny."

Jamie didn't say anything in return. He surveyed the situation down below, then gave a big thumbs up signal to Cody and returned his attention to the still-suffering Danny Harper.

Cody turned back to face the old woman and the remaining creature. "Your sons," he said, trying to sound as respectful as possible. "How did this happen to them?"

The old woman took a minute to collect her thoughts and to wipe a glistening tear from her dark cheek. When she began talking, she spoke slowly, carefully choosing her words so Cody and Jake could follow her. The old hag began by saying her boys were being punished for stealing from the dead. After a few more moments of silent reflection, she went on to tell the story of the ancient curse and the sacred artifacts of the kopje.

Jake and Cody listened intently and without interruption as the old woman told her sad, yet bizarre, tale.

When her boys were younger, she began, she brought them to this kopje to teach them about their ancestors, the Noks. As the boys grew older and were exposed more and more to the modern world, they came to quickly understand the value and power of money. Young and naïve, they acquired an appetite for the things money could obtain. They also discovered looters and collectors were willing to pay large sums of cash for the rare terracotta statues. The easy money was too much of a temptation for the two teenagers.

The boys snuck out to the Kopje one night and stole one of the statues from its resting place. They sold it to an unscrupulous collector in Bauchi. The twin brothers were only sixteen at the time.

At this point in her story, the old woman stopped talking and quietly began to sob. Cody couldn't help but feel sorry for her. It was obviously painful for her to talk about what happened to her boys. He also now understood why one of the cubicles was empty.

The woman soon collected herself and continued her tale. By the next full moon, her boys started to develop long, ugly warts all over their bodies, the result of an ancient hex bestowed upon grave robbers. The warts, she explained, continued to grow and grow. Their bodies changing in horrible and disfiguring ways. Then, their minds began to deteriorate along with their bodies.

To isolate and protect her sons, she brought them back to the kopje for sanctuary, as well as punishment. Their life-long sentence for being greedy and for defiling their forefathers was now to act as guardians of the dead. To protect this secret place and all its treasures from the outside world. Here, for over thirteen years, they had remained, living like feral animals. Cursed and forever paying for their sacrilegious crime.

As she finished her depressing, yet remarkable, story, the old woman stepped over to the remaining creature, leaned against it, and gently stroked its arm. Tears slowly working their way down her wrinkled face.

Cody felt for the old woman. Her sorrow and grief must have been unimaginable. Both men stood there for a few moments as they watched this poor woman being a mother to a lost son. It was a heartbreaking scene.

After a few moments of silence, Cody felt compelled to speak up. "I'm sorry for your family tragedy. We have many unanswered questions, if you would, please." There was still the unresolved issue of his group leaving the kopje, hopefully without incident.

The woman slowly regained her composure and invited Cody to speak his mind.

"How did you get in here?" Cody thought there was no way a woman of her age and frailty could make the climb into the crater.

"I have...secret way."

Not wishing to press the issue, Cody accepted her answer at face value.

Jake asked, "How did your sons survive for so long in such an isolated place?"

The old woman looked up at her deformed son and let out a heavy sigh. "Pool have good water...many trees have fruit...I bring food...they hunt game."

Cody suspected the two creatures had also, on occasion, tasted human flesh; remembering the pile of bones they had encountered earlier. He wasn't about to voice his suspicions out loud, however.

Cody appreciated the fact Jake was curious about the survival and lifestyle of these self-imposed monsters, but he needed to focus on getting them out of there. He also had one last question, one last piece of the puzzle he needed an answer to.

"Why...why did you send our friend, and the rest of us to this place?"

"To...save...my sons," she said matter-of-factly. "To save my sons."

"How can we do that?" Cody replied, shaking his head.

"How can you possibly expect us...to do that?"

"You...all of you," the old woman said, pointing her talisman staff first at Cody and Jake, then up at Jamie and Danny.

"...Will take their place!"

CHAPTER 35

7:31 a.m. Wednesday, September 24

The Paradise Kopje

The unexpected and stark answer hit Cody hard.

Here was a mother, who was so distressed about the fate and condition of her children, that she was ready to sacrifice other human beings in hopes of resurrecting her sons.

Cody broke out in a cold sweat. *They have no intention of letting us out of here!*

The other creature emerged from the tropical forest. The brute strode over to its mother and said something indistinguishable. The old woman looked disappointed, if not outright broken-hearted, then dropped her head in silent reflection. After a brief moment or two, she looked up and spoke.

"You...not take spirit of ancestor," she said solemnly. "You... not cursed like sons! You...cannot take their place!"

"We respect your ancient ones...and this place where their spirits are kept," Jake said.

Cody hoped Jake's skin color and words would have an impact on the old woman.

"We leave this place undisturbed," Jake continued. "We will not talk of it. We only want the small white boy to go back...to go back to his mother."

Nice touch, Jake, Cody thought. *Nice touch indeed*!

Jake's attempt to stir a sense of empathy in the old woman had little effect. The disappointed old woman scowled and made a grunting sound.

Cody tried one last approach to stave off, what he perceived, was an escalating, if not ugly, confrontation. He turned his outstretched hands palms up. "Let us leave. We can find help for your sons. Please, let us save our friend and we'll return with help!"

The woman squinted. Her sinister gaze showed she did not trust the foreigners. The white man's medicine could not help her boys. No medicine or doctor could lift a curse.

The anticipated redemption for the sins of her sons had all but evaporated for the old woman. She tapped her staff against the ground and once again, pointed a boney finger at the two boys in front of her and then up at Jamie and Danny.

"We...cannot allow you...to leave," she said coldly.

Without saying a word, Jake discreetly nudged Cody with his elbow to get his attention. Cody took a sideways glance at the marine. Jake was slowly and carefully unclipping the canister of pepper spray from his web belt. He flipped the safety off and held the canister behind his back. Understanding they might be in imminent danger, Cody followed suit.

"We...cannot allow you to leave!" she firmly repeated, staring directly at the two boys in front of her with those cold, amber-colored eyes.

"How...how will you keep us here?" Jake asked.

"Your death...will keep our secret!" she hissed. "You will not leave this place! You will join ancestors...like others before you!"

"You have...killed...others?" Cody asked, swallowing hard.

"Yes...we kill many...before you. It must be done!"

"We? You and your sons?" Cody said, picking up on the innuendo and wanting to make sure no one else was involved.

"Yes...my sons and other keepers," she replied. "We...have many numbers. Many protectors, like sons...but not cursed. We are everywhere. There is no escape!"

The old woman's revelation about their numbers and murderous attitude toward anyone who came in contact with this place sent a shock wave through Cody. He and Jake quickly glanced at one another, determined in what they had to do. They would defend themselves and the rest of their group at all costs. It didn't look like there was going to be any negotiating on their leaving peacefully.

Jamie was doing his best to follow the on-going dialog below him. He and Danny were approximately three-quarters of the way up the rocks and close to the notch, so it was difficult to hear everything being said. He could clearly see the intimidating gestures from the old woman, the departure and the return of one of the beasts, then the threatening body language of the old Hausa woman. From where he sat, things looked like they weren't going well.

Danny and he could have made it the rest of the way to the notch and back down the other side to the waiting Rovers. But he decided the two of them weren't going anywhere until Jake and Cody could join them. It was a tense period of wait and see, which did nothing to alleviate Jamie's growing anxiety level.

"No more talk!" the old woman barked as she took a step back, tapped her staff on the ground, and pointed it at Jake and Cody. "*Kasha 'yan fashin!*" she shrieked.

"What the hell does that mean?" Cody uttered between clenched teeth.

"I think she just ordered her sons to kill us," Jake said, moving into a fighting stance. "Time to take off the 'kid gloves.' Get ready Cody!"

The two creatures looked at one another and then at their mother. Reacting at the same time, the two brothers separated and trudged off to opposing sides, cutting off any escape route up the rocks as well as back into the forest. Jake recognized the flanking movement instantly and told Cody to go back-to-back. Whatever was going to happen, was going to happen right here and right now.

Unexpectedly, the old woman shrieked loudly, then started screaming curses in her native tongue.

From his perch high above, the resourceful Jamie Hammer threw several small rocks at the old hag and her sons. A few found their mark and the woman fell to her hands and knees crying in pain.

The diversionary tactic worked. The two creatures abandoned their pincher movement and shuffled back to the aid of their mother. Jake and Cody simultaneously stepped forward, raised their OC canisters, aimed, and cut loose at close range with two streams of the highly concentrated pepper spray.

Cody caught the creature nearest him dead on in the face, and then for added insurance, squirted the old woman as well.

The reaction was instantaneous. The old hag cried out bitterly while trying to wipe the foamy substance from her head and face. She only made things worse. In a matter of seconds, her red and swollen eyes were watering and partially shut. Clear mucus ran out of her flared nostrils. Her tongue and lips swelled, making speech difficult. She writhed on the ground, incapacitated.

Jake's initial aim was low. His stream caught the second beast in the chest, but he raised it fast enough to hit the creature's face before it could react.

At first, the monsters tried wiping away the stinging liquid. Because their eyes showed no immediate reaction like their mother's had, Cody thought the growths on their faces prevented the chemical from reaching the eyes and the mucus membranes of the nose.

Then both brothers roared in rage. The two creatures dropped to their knees and started scooping up dirt and rubbing it all over their faces. Their attempt to neutralize the effects of the oleoresin capsicum was only marginally successful; they were still in a great amount of discomfort. They were vulnerable, as was their mother, and they sensed it. Instinctively, the hulks grabbed the old witch by her arms, brought her to her feet, and plowed down the trail towards the pool.

"Let's get the hell out of here!" shouted Cody, loud enough for Jamie to hear up on the rocks. Jamie was already in motion with Danny.

"Right behind ya, man!" echoed Jake. "Don't forget our stuff!"

The two boys picked up everything they had brought with them and scrambled up the rocks, dragging behind what they could not carry. They had a finite amount of time to get up and over the notch and then back down to the Rovers before the creatures and their mother recovered. Cody figured they had maybe twenty to thirty minutes, max, before someone would be hot on their trail.

The climb out was definitely easier for them than the climb in. Cody would have thought different since Jamie was half-carrying Danny and he and Jake were packing out what four people brought in. Cody figured it must be a combination of adrenaline and Dexedrine. Whatever it was, they made it up and through the notch and down to the waiting Rovers in about thirty-five minutes.

By the time they climbed down from the notched area and reached the two SUVs, they were sweaty, out of breath, on borrowed time, and they all knew it. The sun was well above the horizon and the heat of the savannah was intensifying. They had no time for "dilly-dallying."

Jamie half-dragged Danny over to his camouflaged Rover and set him down. As soon as Jake and Cody cleared the rocky entrance, Cody hurried over to Jamie and got the keys to his rig, then went back and unlocked it.

While Jake and Cody were hurriedly throwing gear into Jamie's Rover, Jamie was going through Danny's pack looking for the keys to NSC 069. Cody had worried they'd be long lost, but Jamie found them tucked into a zippered pocket. Unlocking Danny's Rover, Jamie helped Danny into the back seat, put a seat belt on him, then started uncovering the vehicle.

It didn't take Jake and Cody long to load up Jamie's rig; they just threw everything in haphazardly. They hustled over to the other Rover and helped Jamie finish uncovering it. Cody asked Jake to drive NSC 069 so Jamie could be in the back with Danny and he would drive Jamie's rig.

Before Jake and Cody got into their respective driver's seats, they did a quick walk around to see if they had missed anything. The place was clean. They agreed Cody would take the lead and Jake would follow. Their plan was to take their original track back to the Kwanbo Junction, making sure to stay off each other's tire tracks. The last thing they wanted to do was create some semblance of a road that led straight to the kopje.

As Cody was climbing into Jamie's Rover, he took one last look up at the notch to see if anyone was there. It was empty.

The two boys started up their vehicles and formed a tandem line, one after the other with Cody in the lead and rolled.

They didn't get far.

Without warning, the old woman stepped out of nowhere and stopped right in front of Cody's vehicle, blocking his path. Cody came to an abrupt halt, as did Jake behind him, locking his brakes to avoid rear-ending the first Rover.

Cody couldn't believe his eyes. Somehow, the old woman had survived the shot that he had given her and managed to get outside the kopje in time to cut them off. Other than her eyes still being bloodshot and swollen, she seemed none the worse for her encounter with the noxious spray. Much to the relief of the rescue team, the old woman's sons were not with her.

"Shit!" Cody said to no one in particular. "I guess she does know a secret way in and out of the crater!"

In the Range Rover behind Cody's, Jake could only shake his head in disbelief. His initial thought was, *What else could possibly go wrong at this point*?

As shadows moved to surround the two Range Rovers, Jake and Cody suddenly realized the old hag wasn't alone.

CHAPTER 36

8:44 a.m. Wednesday, September 24

The Paradise Kopje

It had been daylight on the savannah for almost three hours and it was starting to get uncomfortably hot outside. Considering the circumstances confronting them, it was getting even hotter inside the Rovers for the four Americans.

The two British-made Range Rovers were completely encircled by at least a dozen Nigerians, and they didn't look happy. Both men and women of all ages surrounded them and all had weapons. Several were carrying machetes and axes. Others were holding clubs or rocks. They looked like an angry mob out for blood.

The group had popped up out of nowhere from the surrounding landscape. Obviously, they were out there when the boys came out of the crater and loaded up their vehicles, but remained quiet and hidden. There weren't even any vehicles or beasts of burden to give them away. The old woman stepping out from behind a large bush and into the path of the lead Rover must have been their signal to appear and surround the vehicles, but not to attack.

The ring of people stood no closer than nine meters (29 ½ feet), but they weren't advancing. Not yet. All were periodically looking at the old witch for the signal to storm the two Rovers. To the boys, they looked menacing and determined.

Cody didn't want to run anyone over, if he could help it, but would if their safety and escape depended upon it. He watched the old woman intently and started sweating profusely, and not just from the heat. Peering into his rearview mirror, he saw Jake scanning from side to side to determine how many threats there were. Cody assumed Jake's military mindset must be in overdrive, assessing the situation and looking for a solution to their predicament. Jamie was doing his best to keep calm for Danny's sake, but was clearly edgy and kept telling Jake to just go.

Cody returned his focus to the old, ragged Nigerian directly in front of him. The woman seemed unafraid at the prospect of being run over and stood her ground. It was as if she was waiting for the right moment to command the group to attack.

Cody stole a quick glance in his rearview mirror at Jake behind him. Jake shrugged his shoulders while raising his hands palms up, the universal sign for "well?" Under his breath, Cody quietly said, "Come on 'Mr. Escape and Evade,' think of something quick or I'm going to have to run this old woman over!"

The mob of Nigerians were getting restless and inched their way closer to the two Rovers.

As if he read Cody's mind, the young marine suddenly thought of something. Jake turned in his seat and told Jamie to look in the back for the olive-drab rucksack with the Marine Corps emblem on it. Jamie found it on top of the pile in the back, retrieved it, and tossed it up to Jake.

In the front Rover, Cody was still concentrating on the old woman, wondering when and what her next move was going to be. He didn't have to wait long. The old crone shook a wrinkled fist at Cody and shouted something that sounded like "your children will pay for this!" before stopping to wipe her eyes with the sleeve of her robe. Cody noticed the group of Nigerians were even closer than before.

Cody was at the brink. He revved up his Rover's motor, ready to accelerate straight at the old woman. But before he popped the clutch and hit the gas pedal, he quickly took another look in his rearview mirror, just in time to see Jake step out of his Rover and motion for Cody to roll his window up.

Cody complied and saw Jake fiddling with something. Then Jake lobbed what looked like a can of food on top of his rig. It bounced once then rolled and stopped somewhere above the passenger side. Cody was wondering what the hell that was all about until Jake pulled the pin out of another canister and placed it on top of his Rover, then wasted no time in jumping back into his rig.

Almost simultaneously, the two tear gas grenades went off on top of the two Rovers, with a loud popping noise. They shot out streams of white gas in a 360 – degree umbrella around the two vehicles. It all happened so fast Cody almost didn't get his window rolled up in time.

The defensive tactic worked perfectly. The entire group encircling the SUVs was instantly enveloped in a cloud of expanding tear gas. All, including the old woman, succumbed to the effects of the growing cloud. The chemical elements of the gas had rendered them helpless and incapable of attacking the two Rovers and their occupants. Those who were only mildly affected helped those who were totally incapacitated retreat from the choking effects of the grey-white fog.

"Way to go, Jake!" exclaimed Cody as he put his Rover into gear and took off, swerving around the old woman as he did so. Jake was right behind him, and, not seeing the woman through the smoke until the last second, swerved just enough to miss her on the opposite side. Cody silently thanked Jamie for closing up the Rover's vents, or he would have been gassed as well.

Cody went as fast as he dared for approximately two kilometers (1.2 miles) before he rolled down his window and slowed down. Jake, following about ten meters back on Cody's left hand side, did the same. Then Cody stuck his arm out the window and signaled for Jake to stop.

Both drivers quickly got out of their Rovers, checked to see if anyone was following them, then walked toward each other. Both were half-laughing with joy.

They had made it.

"Man, that was close!" extorted Cody. "You didn't hit her, did you?"

"Nope," Jake said, "but I think I gave her a good scare. What's up? Why'd you stop?"

"For starters, I needed some air," Cody replied, puffing out his cheeks on a big exhale. "I'm drenched and I couldn't handle the heat of that cabin any longer. I also needed to unwind. My heart rate must be off the charts!"

Jake thought of something when Cody said the word "heat." He climbed up on the Rover's running board and looked on top of his rig. Resting against one of the tie-down racks, he found the spent canister of tear gas. He retrieved it, still warm to the touch, and threw it inside the Rover. "Can't have spent ordinance with U.S. military markings on it just lying around."

Cody climbed up on his running board as well and retrieved the canister Jake had chucked on top of his Rover, which now had scorch marks on its roof. *Oh well,* Cody thought, tossing the empty canister to Jake. "No trace, means no trace," he said out loud to no one in particular.

Jake tossed the second spent canister into the Rover, then walked over to Cody. "What did that old woman shout at you as you dusted her?" he asked.

"Something about our children will pay. Or something like that. I really didn't catch most of it." Cody shrugged. "I was pretty wired at the time."

"Stupid woman." Jake shook his head. "I don't have any children...at least none that I know of."

Cody grinned and then started to laugh. He couldn't help himself. It was the perfect comment to relieve the tension. He walked up to Jake, still chuckling, and put a hand on Jake's shoulder. "Thanks, man," Cody said with all sincerity. "We couldn't have pulled this off without you. I mean it."

Cody reflected on their harrowing experience and the twelve long hours spent inside the kopje. A newfound bond, born out of kinship and mutual respect, had grown between him and the young marine.

Before another word could be said, Jamie stuck his head out from the second Rover and shouted, "I hate to break up this tender moment, but does anyone else think we need to haul ass outta here?"

Cody took a deep breath and slowly exhaled. "Okay, partner," he said to Jake. "Let's hit the road!"

As both Rovers made their exit and headed southeast across the open savannah, Cody occasionally glanced in the rearview mirror back at the paradise kopje. The monolith, as before, stood out from the surrounding landscape, though mired in a hazy fog on the north end.

As they drove on, he couldn't help but reflect on their harrowing adventure. He had mixed feelings about their experience and what they had to do to escape. They hadn't killed or injured anyone, and that was the important thing. Even Jake, the trained soldier, had said he was relieved he hadn't been forced to take an innocent life. They were all alive and well and the sweet joy of finding Danny, as well as being homeward bound, greatly overshadowed any regrets. They had accomplished their mission. They had found the missing Danny Harper, and he was alive.

With a short stop to put the last of the petrol they brought into the tanks of the two Rovers, it took them two hours to get back to the Kwanbo junction. It had not been an easy trip, either. Cody and Jake were careful not to create any ruts by driving in each other's tracks and the boys went at a slower speed to avoid doing any damage to their Rovers. Neither wanted a repeat of a damaged radiator hose or something worse. Danny was holding his own. Being out of the hidden crater and away from the kopje seemed to have a calming effect on him and he slept for most of the way. Jamie, still paranoid, repeatedly checked on him to make sure he okay. He also kept glancing back to see if anyone was following them.

The two Rovers pulled out of the bush and back onto the dirt-packed road sixteen meters (62 feet) north of the Kwanbo junction. By following their previous track and looking at landmarks, Cody did a fairly good job of navigating and getting them back, more or less, to where they started.

First, Cody, then Jake, entered the road. After traveling a short distance, they pulled off in the open area next to the sign marking the junction. The two got out and stretched. Jamie joined them after checking on a still-sleeping Danny. They were all hot, sweaty, thirsty, hungry, and extremely tired. Cody checked his watch; it was now a quarter after eleven. It would be another two-and-a-half-hour drive to reach Anguwan and another one and a half hours of driving to reach Jos.

They shared their last jug of water and each ate a banana; they didn't want their stomachs to give them any grief when Jamie doled out the last of his Dexedrine tabs. They figured on driving through Kwamba and Kwambo without stopping. Their petrol situation would require them to stop at Anguwan for gas. It would also be a good place to get something decent to eat before continuing on. Jake said he'd also like to make a radio call to update Kaduna and see if Sergeant Ripper and Matt McKnight made it to Jos. With stops, Cody figured they should reach the city somewhere between 4:30 and 5:00 p.m. By that time, they would have gone for over thirty-four hours without sleep.

Before heading out, they took great pains to erase all evidence of where they originally pulled off the road and entered the open savannah two days ago, as well as where they re-emerged at the junction.

After that, the three boys, having eaten something, quenched their thirst, and relieved themselves, continued their journey. Cody and Jake again checked their watches. It was now 11:47. Once they were underway, they kept a keen eye out for any signs of being followed.

Forty minutes later, they found themselves going through the village of Kwamba. They only slowed down enough to safely go from one end of the town to the other and tried to be as inconspicuous as possible. Approximately thirty-five minutes after that, they entered the northern edge of Kwambo. Again, they felt as if everyone was watching them as they passed through. After they were well clear of the small burg and picked up speed, Jamie nervously leaned over the passenger seat in front of him and asked Jake if he saw anyone with amber-colored eyes. Jake said he did not.

The two beat-up and dust-covered Range Rovers were

running on fumes as they entered Anguwan from the north at 2:35 p.m. All things considered, they had made reasonably good time since escaping from the mob at the kopje at nine that morning.

The pair of Rovers pulled into the only gas station in town. The very one they stopped at on their way upcountry two days prior. The same old man and young boy again serviced their rigs. The elder Nigerian acted half-surprised to see them, but said nothing.

Once they were filled up, Cody paid for the petrol in cash and left a nice "dash" for the pair. Then he and Jake drove their rigs across the road to the open square and into the parking area, pulling up next to the little eatery where they stopped before going up country.

Cody got out and stretched. Thanks to the "Dexie," he felt better than he should have, as did Jake and Jamie. They still needed a break and definitely some real food. Jamie helped Danny get out of the Rover and, along with Cody, led him over to one of the shaded outside tables at the little eatery. A polite and energetic little boy brought them out a stack of plastic glasses and bottled water. He quietly asked if anyone would care for a Star beer. All declined.

While the other three were relaxing and looking at the tattered menu, Jake unpacked his field radio and set it up on the tailgate of Jamie's Rover. Again, he pitched one end of the tape antennae over the branch of a nearby Acacia tree, startling the assortment of colorful birds occupying the upper branches.

Jake raised Kaduna right away. He didn't have much more to tell them than what he had before. Saying they had reached Anguwan without incident, Jake told his counterpart in Kaduna they had stopped for gas and to get something to eat. Yes, Danny Harper was still okay; he had slept most of the way, but seemed in good spirits when awake and wasn't in as much pain. He reiterated their plan was to go directly to the Evangel Hospital when they hit Jos. He also learned Sgt. Ripper and Matt McKnight missed the morning flight out of Lagos, but managed to catch the early afternoon one and landed in Jos around 1400 hours, or 2:00 p.m.

Jake signed off after the five-minute report, retrieved his tape antennae and packed up his radio set, then headed over to the little café to join the rest of the group. Cody and Jamie ordered essentially the same thing they had for breakfast the day before. Which now seemed like a lifetime ago. Jake followed suit.

Danny ate, but didn't act like he was aware of what was going on. He remained fairly quiet and withdrawn, lost in his own world.

While they were eating, Jake felt inclined to speak up and asked the million dollar question, "So, what are we going to say, officially, about this...this rescue, guys?"

CHAPTER 37

3:14 p.m. Wednesday, September 24

North Central Nigeria

"For openers," Cody said in between bites, "if we tell the truth, the whole truth, nobody will believe us...so why bother?"

That brought a genuine chuckle out of the other two. Although Cody meant it as somewhat of a joke, it also made perfect sense. All things considered, his reasoning was sound. It was an insane type of logic.

The three were facing a moral, ethical, and professional dilemma. To fully reveal what they had experienced since entering the kopje was their duty. It also had a ton of implications. A full disclosure would undoubtedly generate an investigation coupled with an official report, possibly followed by an official complaint being filed by the American Embassy. This, in turn, would probably lead an official board of inquiry to investigate the matter on the part of the Nigerian government. Given the fact that American citizens had been assaulted by Nigerian citizens, and "questionable" self-defense measures were taken by Americans against Nigerians, things could get complicated, if not messy, real fast.

Obviously, because of the mysterious and bizarre aspects of the rescue, such an investigation and ensuing report would be quickly picked up by a whole host of others, especially the media. And not just the Nigerian press either. The secret kopje would be exposed, explored, and probably exploited. The Nigerian government would confiscate and remove all of the sacred terracotta statues and either put them on display in a museum or lock them away in a vault somewhere, unless grave robbers beat them to it. The two deformed brothers, as well as their mother, would be taken into custody and possibly put on trial for any number of things, murder notwithstanding. Who knew what the eventual outcome, or their fate, would be. The end result, regardless, would probably mean the end of the sacred burial ground. More than likely, it would be gone forever. The last vestiges of a lost culture once again victimized by modern men.

The next set of implications would be for the boys personally. If the Peace Corps didn't send the three Volunteers directly home, probably without any benefits, the possibility existed they could wind up in a Nigerian prison on a variety of charges. Given Danny's unstable condition, that outcome might be tantamount to a death sentence. Jake would have to face an official board of inquiry, could lose his job as a security guard with the diplomatic corps, receive a less-than-honorable discharge from the marines, and possibly even be court martialed. None of which would be good for his future plans.

The media would continually hound them for their side of the story. There would be no peace or privacy for an interminable period of time. Danny would be held up as a pathetic and unfortunate victim of an innocent adventure gone terribly wrong. Poor Danny would be put in the spotlight and hounded for exclusives, possibly for years to come. He would have to relive his horrible experience over and over again.

As the three boys discussed the possible scenarios with all of their ramifications, Jamie finally spoke up in favor of honesty.

"We need to tell the whole story," he said in all seriousness. "No half-truths, no white lies. It is our duty...our responsibility to be forthright, candid, and to give full disclosure to what happened to Danny and to us. We have to tell the whole truth!"

A perplexed look crossed Jake's face as if to say, "*Are you fucking crazy*?"

Trying to muster his best "calm, cool and collected" voice, Jake spoke his mind. "I've been thinking about our 'little' adventure ever since we left the kopje." He finished his last bite and continued, "Only the four of us know what transpired. I'm not sure anyone would believe Danny in his present state; besides, he only knows a part of the story."

"What do you mean?" Cody asked, wishing he had ordered a beer to complement the seriousness of the discussion.

"No one knows what actually happened but the three of us," Jake continued. "We can choose to tell what we want, all true and all verified by our radio reports to Kaduna. But between us, we must be absolutely consistent with our story...what we tell and what we don't. Having said that, I sincerely believe we have a moral responsibility not to say anything about the old woman, her deformed sons, or a secret oasis with an ancient burial ground. I, for one, do not want to be responsible for destroying thousands of years of history. The Noks deserve to rest in peace."

"What about Danny?" Jamie interjected.

"The case could be made that Danny was so delirious from his concussion he imagined all sorts of things," offered Cody, picking up on Jake's line of thinking. "Look at him. I'm not sure he even knows who he is or where he is. Whatever he says, which could be anything, may or may not jive with what we say. But, as Jake says, as long as our story is the same, I don't think whatever Danny says will have much credibility. Especially if he keeps talking about tree monsters."

The diminutive Danny Harper, the focus of the entire search and rescue saga, sat oblivious to the discussion, quietly eating his food. His attention was focused, not on the topic at hand, but on a group of birds fighting over crumbs on the next table.

"I've been giving some thought to this as well," Cody continued with a heavy sigh. "First of all, we originally agreed not to disclose the burial ground because we thought it was the right thing to do at the time. I still believe that. It was the right thing...and the human thing to do. We didn't want to expose the place, with all of its secrets and artifacts, to the outside world. Based on everything we've talked about, it's my honest belief we should not divulge everything we know. Besides, we gave our word to the old woman. It was a sincere promise, not something said just so she and her sons would let us go."

Jamie sat quietly for a minute, obviously turning over in his mind what Cody and Jake had to say. Finishing his meal, he cleared his throat and looked across the table at Jake. "What about your Marine Corps honor code? Doesn't that require you not to lie, among other things?"

"I'm not going to lie," Jake clarified. "I'm simply not going to reveal all the details. I'm basically going to say we followed the leads you and Cody uncovered in Bauchi. We found Danny's mysterious camping spot out in the middle of nowhere. We found him hurt and traumatized, probably from something done by the same angry mob we escaped from. Which would also explain the use of the tear gas and pepper spray. According to what we heard, this mob assumed we had violated some sacred place. In the face of real personal danger, we accomplished our mission to find and rescue a missing Peace Corps Volunteer, all within our allotted time frame and...without breaking any laws or suffering any ill effects. Period. End of story."

"So," added Cody, reflectively, "we can either be heroes or we can be goats. Which way do we go?"

"I will always vote hero," Jake announced with a wry smile.

"Me too," added Cody, looking at Jamie to see if he was on board.

"You two have made some really strong points regarding what we should do and what we shouldn't do...and why," Jamie said. "You're not asking me to lie, which I like. I can also see that Danny has gone through enough and I don't think he needs to suffer anymore. Also, the thought of desecrating and ruining that spiritual place doesn't sit well with me either. The one thing that worries me the most is that by spilling our guts, we could wind up in some Nigerian jail...for who knows how long. I've always believed when you're in a hole, you don't keep digging. So, I guess I'm in."

Cody Armstrong smiled at his fellow Volunteer. "Jamie," he softly said, "I'm proud of you. This is the right thing to do."

ꕥ

While the boys were still in Anguwan discussing what they were going to do, Sgt. Ripper and McKnight safely arrived in Jos on the mid-day flight from Lagos. They caught a cab and, forgetting which hospital to go to, asked to be taken to the largest one in Jos. Out of sheer dumb luck, the driver took them directly to the Evangel Hospital in the central part of the city.

After paying for the ride, the two walked into the main reception area of the hospital and asked to speak to someone in charge. They were led to the office of the hospital's director, Dr. Henrik Kruger. After introductions were made, Matt explained to the doctor that the purpose of their visit was to forewarn the hospital and to make arrangements for a special emergency case, which they hoped would be arriving at this place sometime later that afternoon. Matt and Sgt. Ripper took turns explaining what had transpired over the last several days and what the known condition of the injured Volunteer would be, mentally as well as physically.

Dr. Kruger, already having knowledge of the event from dealing with the body of the Canadian Volunteer they had over the weekend, said he would instruct his staff to make all necessary preparations. He didn't want a repeat of Sunday's fiasco.

From the hospital, the pair took another cab to the Benue Hotel. Matt remembered the name of the place from reading earlier reports. They figured their search team would probably be exhausted from their ordeal and would want something to eat and plenty of rest when they hit town. Because they had time on their hands and missed their own lunch due to the noontime flight, they figured this would be a good opportunity to get something for themselves.

Before going to the hotel's restaurant, however, Matt used his government-issued American Express credit card to pay for a double room for Sgt. Ripper and Jake Simmons, a second double room for Cody and Jamie, and a single room for himself, figuring Danny would probably spend the night in the hospital.

After they finished a nice meal of stewed chicken served over Jollof rice and vegetables, the two hailed a cab and went back to the hospital to wait it out.

ꝏ

According to Cody's watch, the group left Anguwan at 3:44 p.m. Later than they planned. They had stayed at the little café longer than expected, sorting things out and ultimately agreeing on their story. With about a ninety-minute drive ahead of them, Cody figured they should reach Jos sometime around 5:30. Well before sundown. Understandably, he didn't like driving the Nigerian highways after dark, especially as tired as he felt.

With Jake, Jamie, and Danny in the second SUV and behind him, Cody pulled onto the A3 highway and headed southwest. Driving Danny's Range Rover all by himself gave Cody a significant amount of time to reflect on the past five days and what might lie ahead.

What they did would have been impossible without the help of the young black marine and the support of the embassy. Cody also believed that, thanks to Jake's perseverance and "can-do" attitude, he was an inspiration to the two Volunteers. To Cody's way of thinking, Jake Simmons was the true hero of their saga.

As the miles wore on and the fatigue crept back in, Cody vainly tried to sort things out in his mind regarding their little "adventure" and what was to follow. Although realizing the three boys had shared an extraordinary experience together and came out on top, he still couldn't seem to get the old woman's last words out of his head: *Your children will pay for this!*

Shaking off that image, his mind turned to that of MaryAnn Reed. He admitted to himself he genuinely liked the alluring woman and couldn't wait to see her again. Daydreaming about MaryAnn was more comforting than reliving their experience or the worrisome thought of what was going to happen next.

CHAPTER 38

5:19 p.m. Wednesday, September 24

Jos

The boys entered the city of Jos at approximately 5:19 p.m. and headed directly for the Evangel Hospital located in the middle of town. As they pulled into the parking lot, they saw Ripper and McKnight exiting the building and walking quickly toward them. The two men, hoping they had the right place, had been keeping a watchful eye out for the group's arrival since getting back to the hospital around four.

Jamie and Jake helped get Danny out of the back and steadied him on his feet as a couple of orderlies came rushing out of the hospital with a wheelchair.

Ripper went directly up to his marine, who started to salute, but was stopped cold when the sergeant grabbed his hand and shook it earnestly while resting the other on the young man's shoulder. The gesture was not military protocol, but "Wild Bill" Ripper didn't care. He was extremely proud of his boy and he showed it. Besides, he thought, they weren't in uniform.

Matt McKnight strode up to his three Volunteers and, after taking a quick look at Danny Harper, turned to the other three rescuers and simply said, "Thanks, guys. Thanks for finding him and bringing him back." Matt, who Cody swore had a tear in his eye, put a hand on Danny's shoulder as the orderlies got him into the wheelchair and wheeled him toward the main door. Matt accompanied them inside the building without saying another word. After everything that had happened and after what he and everyone else had gone through, Matt was having a hard time keeping his emotions in check.

Ripper, regaining his military composure, congratulated the three on a job well done and asked if there was anything he could do to help out. The boys looked at each other, shrugged and shook their heads, too tired to respond. Picking up on their condition, Ripper told them rooms were awaiting them at the Benue Hotel.

The three wanted nothing more than to head straight to the hotel, grab a hot shower, a quick bite, and then go directly to bed. Ever the Boy Scout, Jamie thought they should first see how Danny was doing before heading to their lodging. Ripper and the three young men made their way into the hospital and were directed to the emergency station, located down the hall from the reception/receiving area.

They drew a few stares along the way, which was to be expected since all of the boys were unkempt, dirty, smelly, and in need of a shave. They found the waiting area for the emergency station across the hallway from where Danny was being attended to. Matt was already there, leaning against a wall, observing what was going on in the exposed area across the way. They had a clear view of the work-in-progress in the open, oversized Emergency Station No. 1.

A doctor, two nurses and an orderly, all Nigerian and all extremely attentive and professional, scuttled around Danny poking and prodding. Since he was somewhat dehydrated, the doctor had one of the nurses put an I.V. into Danny's left arm to administer fluids. This was connected to a clear bag filled with a purified water solution containing small amounts of sodium bicarbonate and potassium chloride to help stabilize any electrolyte imbalance.

The other nurse, per the doctor's on-going instructions, took a blood draw to have the lab check Danny's red and white cell count. This was a precautionary measure in case his various bruises, cuts, and scrapes were becoming infected. Septicemia, more commonly known as blood poisoning, a generalized infection of the blood stream and fairly common in tropical climates, could result from even minor scrapes and cuts.

The doctor himself was focusing on Danny's vital signs while performing basic triage. Checking him out from head to toe to determine the extent of his injuries and what needed attention first. Although Danny was running what the doctor called a moderately high fever, none of the medical staff in attendance seemed to regard it as life-threatening and decided to wait on the blood test to tell them more. After about twenty minutes of Danny being treated and hovered over, the male orderly wheeled him down the corridor to X-Ray. The doctor wanted a picture of his swollen ankle.

The middle-aged doctor followed the white-clad attendant out of the emergency room and crossed the hallway to where the group was waiting. Nobody was sitting. All were focused on the doctor, who was obviously educated abroad, with concerned interest. They were hoping for good news.

"Your friend," began the Nigerian physician, "is banged up pretty good. There are no traumatic, life-threatening injuries. He has suffered a fairly serious concussion and it looks like he may have a severely-sprained or even broken ankle. I want to keep him overnight so we can get more fluids into him and run a couple of routine tests. He should be okay to leave tomorrow by noon unless the tests tell us otherwise. Are there any questions you might have I may answer?"

Matt took a step forward, introduced himself, and asked the question that seemed to be on everyone's mind. "He seems delirious...like he's gone psychotic. Is that a temporary thing or a sign of something more serious?"

The doctor placed his hands in his lab coat pockets, the thumbs hooked to the outside. "As I said, he has suffered a pretty good bump on the head. That, coupled with his other symptoms: fever, dehydration, malnutrition, fatigue, and shock has, in my professional opinion, manifested into a type of traumatic stress condition."

"I don't understand." Matt frowned, waving a frustrated hand toward the corridor where they'd taken Danny. "How can all this make him so...so out of it? He acts like he's lost his mind!"

"I'm not a psychologist," the doctor calmly said, "and we don't have one on staff to perform an evaluation, but I would guess he has had what you Americans typically call a 'nervous breakdown.' Probably brought on by a sudden and extreme stress-related incident."

Jamie, Cody, and Jake knew exactly what the good doctor was implying, but remained silent. This was the first test of their mutual understanding to not reveal any more than they had to regarding what happened. Jamie unconsciously lowered his head and bit his lower lip as if he was lost in thought and was thinking about saying something, but didn't. Thankfully, the gesture went unnoticed by McKnight and Ripper.

"Will he recover? Be normal...be his 'old self' again?" Matt asked, not sure if he wanted to hear an honest opinion or not.

"I cannot answer that, I'm afraid." The doctor shook his head. "I would suggest you get him to a hospital that can run a full set of diagnostic tests on him, including an EKG. Only then will you know if there is any damage to his brain. Something which could explain his behavior. I'm afraid we don't have the expertise or the equipment to perform those tests or make a credible diagnosis. Sorry."

The doctor shook hands with everyone in the group, excused himself, and started off down the hallway toward the X-Ray department.

Matt looked at the sullen faces of those assembled around him.

"I was hoping I wouldn't have to do this," he said. "But, given what I've seen so far and just heard, I'm going to make arrangements to medevac Danny to Germany as soon as we get back to Lagos."

Medical evacuation, or "medevac" was the system the U.S. government used to transport wounded, severely injured or sick government personnel, especially members of the armed forces, to American-type hospitals while serving overseas. For the most part, they were military-operated installations either on or adjacent to a military base. The two most prominent ones on the European continent, which also served Africa and the Middle East, were located in Wiesbaden and Landstuhl, West Germany.

When a Peace Corps Volunteer was "medevac'd" for any reason, it typically meant the next stop was home. Rarely did a Volunteer return to the host country after treatment to pick back up where they left off and finish out their two-year commitment. The Peace Corps simply did not want the responsibility nor the liability associated with returning a Volunteer back to the source of his or her problems.

Matt's announcement came as no surprise to Cody and Jamie. They were told what the score was pertaining to emergency evacuations while in Accra.

Jamie sighed, looked at the floor again, and said, "I hope Danny will be okay, once he gets out of Nigeria."

It was for the best, yet it still seemed like a bad break for a kid who was doing so well with his first assignment as a Peace Corps Volunteer.

Ripper assured Jamie and the other two, "I'd do the exact same thing if I were in McKnight's shoes. It's the smart thing to do."

Without saying much after that, the group quietly left the hospital and walked out to the parking area in front.

Jake took the opportunity to quietly ask his boss something which had been on his mind since Anguwan. "Is this rescue going to generate an 'AAR?" Jake was inquiring if the standard "After Action Report" was necessary for this mission, knowing full well such might put him in a tight spot.

Ripper, after a moment's thought, said, "No...no, it won't. The involvement of the Marine Corps in this 'humanitarian' effort doesn't really require one. Especially since only the use of non-lethal ordinance was involved and this wasn't combat or a similar situation. Because this was primarily a Peace Corps operation, McKnight will be the one tasked with writing any official report on the event. That's how I see it."

A relieved Jake Simmons smiled and nodded. True to his nature, Gunnery Sergeant Ripper hated writing reports.

The two Rovers had seen better days, but no one was

complaining. They did the job they were asked to do. The gunny rode with Jake and Jamie in Hammer's Rover. There wasn't a lot of chatter on the short drive. Cody, driving Danny's rig, followed close behind with Matt McKnight riding shotgun. After checking into the hotel, the group unloaded all their gear from the two SUVs and separated it into two piles. One for Jake and the Marine Corps, the other for the Volunteers. The boys moved the stuff to their rooms, then each took a nice long hot shower, shaved, and put on clean clothes.

The group rendezvoused after seven in the hotel's restaurant for a round of beer and a light supper. The previous four days had aged everyone, except of course, Bill Ripper. He was the only one who seemed to still have life left in him. Under normal circumstances, they would have been celebrating their success. But Danny's condition plus the ordeal of the last several days had drained them of all energy.

During the wait for their food, Matt asked the boys to "walk him through" the entire search and rescue effort. They complied, each contributing to the story. Even while they were eating, they kept talking. Matt took copious notes, interrupting only to get clarification on some of the details. For almost seventy minutes, the boys relayed their extraordinary experience, right down to their escape from the angry mob and the trip back to Jos. All three were careful to tell only what they had agreed upon and kept it straightforward and simple.

The three searchers were too tired to finish eating. Satisfied they had given Matt what he wanted to hear, they excused themselves and headed for their rooms. All retired early and were fast asleep as soon as their heads hit the pillows. Matt McKnight and "Gunny" Ripper stayed behind, enjoying a quiet beer in the little bar next to the dining room while comparing notes. Fifty minutes and a second beer later, they called it a night themselves. Matt was satisfied he had enough information to write a detailed report and conclude the successful operation.

Perhaps, because the day was catching up with them or they were suffering from the effects of the alcohol. Because neither McKnight nor Ripper thought to ask the boys to pinpoint the kopje on a map or why it took them so long to get Harper out of the place once they found him.

CHAPTER 39

8:00 AM Thursday, September 25

Jos

Everyone slept in later the next morning than they would have liked, especially Ripper. They all joined up for breakfast around eight-thirty and talked about what was going to happen next.

The decision was made to have Jamie return to Kaduna and pick back up with his work there, continuing on with his previous assignment. Cody was to drive Danny's Rover all the way back to Lagos and return it to the National Sports Commission. Cody needed to inform the principals at the National Sports Commission and Danny's contacts in Maiduguri that he was going home, but planned on keeping the reason short and to the point. He also needed to make arrangements with the Maiduguri people to have all of Danny's belongings packed up and shipped to the U.S. Embassy in Lagos. Cody would then have Danny's personal effects sent on to his home in California. The Peace Corps, as well as the Nigerian National Sports commission would want what belonged to them separated out.

Jake and Sgt. Ripper would fly back to Lagos that day on the next available flight, where both would resume their duties at the embassy. As soon as Danny was discharged from the hospital, Matt and he would also fly back to Lagos, hopefully that same day and on the same flight as the two marines. From there, Matt and Danny would grab the next available flight to

West Germany. Matt planned on initially staying with Danny in Germany to determine how serious his condition was and how soon he could fly back to the States.

That was the general plan and everyone was on board with it.

The last items Matt had to deal with were the closure of his "command post" at the embassy, and to brief the two staffers from Ghana and send them back to Hampton Belvoe. He also needed to spend time briefing, as well as thanking, DCM Olvera and RCO Shannon. The last thing he would need to do was write his report. Matt didn't particularly like writing reports, but the paperwork came with the job and he was looking forward to getting this "little" episode behind him. He wanted to get home, back to his routine and, especially, back to his wife.

Everything went off exactly as planned. Danny was discharged shortly before noon with a temporary cast on his foot and ankle. His tests were inconclusive, but to be on the safe side, the doctor gave him a tetanus shot before he left the hospital. Although he looked and acted better, he still wasn't quite the same Danny. The two marines, Matt McKnight and Danny Harper, all caught the mid-day flight back to Lagos and, upon arrival, were met at the airport by the embassy's liaison officer and shuttle driver. The two Nigerians managed to get the entire group through the airport and back to the embassy without incident.

ஐ

The goodbyes at Yakubu Gowon International Airport were all short and to the point, except for Cody and Jamie's, as they had one last beer together at the airport after the others took off for Lagos. The two still couldn't believe they'd pulled it off, and hoped Danny would be okay. Having a shared a remarkable experience, each Volunteer had a renewed admiration and respect for the other. Jamie's final words to Cody pretty much summed up how he now felt about the Peace Corps Volunteer Leader: "You're the man, Cody. You're the man."

After a final handshake, the two young men got into their SUVs and went their separate ways. For Jamie, it would be a three-hour, 282 kilometer (175 miles) drive back to his post in Kaduna. Cody's trip to Lagos would take considerably longer. The 983 kilometer (610 miles) drive would take him approximately fourteen hours. He decided to break up the trip into two days' worth of driving and spend a night at a guest house in the small city of Ilorin, which was approximately at the half-way point.

ꟷ

The "report," such as it was, didn't amount to much. For all intents and purposes, it was nothing more than a formality, a bureaucratic requirement to explain what happened and how, and to justify the time and expense of finding the missing Volunteer. The "red tape" of government needed something in writing, anything, to be able to conclude the event and file it away.

Matt drafted the report on the six-hour flight from Lagos to Frankfurt and on the forty-minute commuter flight to Wiesbaden. While Danny Harper spent two nights in the hospital undergoing tests and follow-up procedures on his injuries, Matt put the finishing touches on a second draft and wired it to Gunnery Sergeant Ripper and DCM Olvera for their input.

Ripper only filled in a couple of details related to the Marine Corp's involvement and the legitimate use of non-lethal ordinance. Olvera simply added the extent of the embassy's involvement, clarification on a few items and an explanation as to why he overrode Belvoe. Both asked for a final copy to share with their superiors. All would put their final, personal notations on the report before it was moved up the chain of command. The marked-up second draft from Lagos was waiting for Matt on his desk when he got back to Washington D.C. three days later.

He dutifully sent the final, official version to his boss at Peace Corps headquarters the following week. Only a few people actually read it and signed off on it. A copy was forwarded to the State Department where it was shared with the embassy in Lagos. The report was eventually archived without any follow-up requirements. The perfunctory, eleven-page, double-spaced document was never released to a Congressional oversight committee, to the media, or to the general public.

The last person to read a copy of the document, one month after the fact, was Kenny Wagner in Kaduna. Wagner played a key role and had been instrumental in all aspects of the search for Harper from the beginning and his eventual rescue, so it stood to reason he was interested in what the "official" report had to say.

Everything was concisely detailed, right down to the on-going radio traffic between the team in the field and his office in Kaduna. Nothing, to his knowledge, had been omitted. The only part of the report that seemed unusual was a couple of paragraphs about Harper's "high levels of anxiety, paranoia, and fear" and his insistence about being attacked and pursued by what he called "tree monsters" while trapped inside of a kopje called "paradise."

"Bullshit," Wagner said aloud, slowly shaking his head that such an absurd thing was even entered into an official government report.

Wagner initialed the document, date-stamped it, and slipped it back into its return envelope. Placing the packet in his "out" basket, the career Foreign Service officer went back to work reviewing visa applications.

EPILOGUE

The old Hausa woman's twin sons were not cursed in the Biblical, mythological, or magical sense. They suffered from an extremely aggressive version of the medical condition known as Epidermodysplasia verruciformis, or "EV." This rare genetic disorder creates a heightened susceptibility as well as a radical reaction to the human papilloma virus, commonly called HPV. The disease is characterized by the obtrusive and rapid growth of long, horrifying, bark-like warts all over the body.

The condition, referred to, years later, as "Tree Man Syndrome," produces its distinctive and disfiguring effects with no known cure. The two boys contracted HPV, as well as syphilis, shortly after they turned sixteen from sharing a prostitute in Bauchi. Ironically, some of the money they obtained from selling the stolen Nok terracotta statue was used to pay the infected woman for her "services." The two boys only lived another two years after their encounter with the Americans—dying at the ripe old age of thirty-two in the paradise kopje, where they were buried by person or persons unknown. Their mother simply disappeared sometime afterward and was never seen again.

Cody Armstrong finished his two-year commitment to the Peace Corps program in Nigeria. Cody did what he could to get Nigeria's best athletes scholarships to American colleges and universities where they could get the training and competition they needed. He also made up for lost time with MaryAnn Reed. Following his exit procedures in Accra, he followed through with his plans to backpack his way through Europe before returning home. Thanks to the money he had acquired during his service, he went back to school and received a master's degree, with honors, from Oregon State University two years later. While working for an electric utility company, he met and married a vivacious younger woman and returned to the family farm with his new wife after his parents passed away.

Lance Corporal Jake Simmons was promoted to corporal after he finished his one year posting to Lagos. He also received commendations from the Marine Corps, the State Department, and the Peace Corps for the role he played in the successful rescue of Peace Corps Volunteer Danny Harper. His next posting was to the U.S. embassy in Geneva, Switzerland. After spending a year there, Simmons was promoted to sergeant and finished up the last part of his four-year commitment to the military as an instructor for future USMC security guards at Quantico, Virginia. He eventually wound up back in California, attending UCLA on the G.I. Bill. He later became an instructor for cultural anthropology at a community college.

Jamie Hammer left the Peace Corps approximately one month after his experience at the paradise kopje, cutting short his two-year commitment by six months. He was joined by two other Volunteers, Ethan White and Monte Reynolds. In their exit interviews, they simply stated they thought the Nigerian coaching program had too many insurmountable problems and was a waste of time and taxpayer money. Jamie also said he didn't feel safe and thought Nigeria was a dangerous country for the Peace Corps to even be in, given the assortment of lethal tropical diseases and absurd driving conditions. He returned to his home in California, found the right girl to marry, and eventually got a job teaching and coaching at one of the high schools in his home town of Chico.

Danny Harper was never the same after his experience. Once discharged from the U.S. joint-forces military hospital in Germany after a two-day stay, he also returned to his home to California with nothing more than a cast on his broken ankle and a ton of psychology reports to show for his ordeal. Diagnosed with a traumatic stress disorder, he needed on-going therapy, counseling, and support, most of which he received from his beloved mother, whom he lived with for a number of years. Jamie Hammer would occasionally make the cross-state trip to visit his friend, but only managed to do so for a couple of years. Because of his disability, Danny received money from the federal government and worked a part-time job at McDonalds until his suicide in 1985.

Michael Olvera submitted commendation proposals for Lance Corporal Simmons and Gunnery Sergeant William Ripper for "above and beyond the call of duty" participation in the rescue of Danny Harper. Olvera continued serving as the deputy chief of mission in Nigeria for one more year before receiving an appointment as ambassador to the north African country of Morocco. After two years there, the ambassador served out the remainder of his career with the State Department as the assistant secretary of state for West African affairs before his eventual retirement to Florida.

Kenneth "Kenny" Wagner also received a commendation from the State Department and the Peace Corps for the key role he played in the search and rescue of Harper. Wagner went on to serve in several embassies over the next five years as the principal officer in the consular section and finally received an appointment as the deputy chief of mission for the U.S. Embassy in Kenya.

Gunnery Sergeant Ripper, in addition to his commendations, received a promotion to First Sergeant after he completed his tour of duty in Nigeria. Ripper applied for, and was granted, a posting as a Drill Instructor (DI) at the Marine Corps Recruit Depot in Parris Island, South Carolina. He left the Marine Corps after serving his twenty years with an outstanding service record and the rank of Master Sergeant. He took his retirement pay and started a successful business in security consulting.

MaryAnn Reed, thanks to Cody Armstrong, thoroughly enjoyed her time in Lagos until the Peace Corps Volunteer left Nigeria. After her one-year stint as one of the executive secretaries for the ambassador and the DCM in Nigeria, she got a two-week vacation before her next posting, which was Paris. MaryAnn had several other short postings before she met and married a younger man, who happened to be a junior diplomat from Canada. She gave birth to twin daughters and retired into motherhood with grace and happiness before turning forty.

Matt McKnight continued to work for the Peace Corps

organization for a number of years following his trip to Nigeria. He also received a commendation for the role he played in the search and rescue effort. McKnight received several promotions over the years and eventually reached the rank of his former supervisor, the West African regional director. Matt was distressed upon learning of Harper's suicide. In 1986, the McKnights, along with their daughter, welcomed a new baby boy into their family. A rambunctious little tyke they decided to name Danny.

Hampton Belvoe continued on in Accra for an additional stint as the Ghanaian Peace Corps director, but did not receive any additional postings after that, nor did he ever get his coveted appointment as an ambassador or as a high-ranking Peace Corps official. Disappointed and bitter by the outcome of his public service career, he moved to upstate New York and started a business more attuned to his style of doing things: a used car dealership.

Although the three members of the original search team: Cody Armstrong, Jake Simmons, and Jamie Hammer, all went on to lead relatively normal and productive lives, they never could fully put their experience behind them. And, as agreed upon, never spoke of it. All had occasional nightmares, anxiety attacks and, on occasion, found themselves "looking back over their shoulders" for dark-skinned people with amber-colored eyes. They kept an eye on the news to see if anything ever turned up about the Noks or the secret kopje in northern Nigeria, but nothing ever did. The three managed to stay in touch for a while, but time and distance slowly eroded their connection and they lost all contact over the years. None of them ever returned to Africa and none ever knew Danny had taken his own life. The "paradise kopje," however, left an indelible mark on all three. Much to their anguish and misfortune, none of the three were ever able to father a child.

ACKNOWLEDGEMENTS

I owe a great debt of gratitude to many people for the production of this story.

Starting with my "beta" readers. I appreciate their time, contributions and encouragement in the writing of *Nigeria*. Thanks to Bill and Cheryl Standley, Fred and Lisa Kroon and to Meredith Mason—all of whom thought that this story should be published and continually encouraged me to do so. An additional thank you needs to go out to Meredith—who did some preliminary editing for me and gave me some ideas I probably wouldn't have thought of on my own.

I am also deeply indebted to my principal editor, Kelly Schaub, as well as my publisher, Kim Cooper Findling. Kelly kept me on track with my story line and gave me more corrections and suggestions than I could keep up with. The woman is a master at her craft. Kim shepherded me through the maze of everything which needed to be done to see this work published. She saw something in my writing she thought was worthy of sharing. And for that, along with everything else she does, I am deeply grateful. I can't thank these two ladies enough for all they have done. Their hard work, assistance and guidance is much appreciated.

Finally, I've got to admit, this work would not have been possible without the support, encouragement and patience of my wife Charlie—who deserves a medal for all that she put up with during the year it took me to write *Nigeria*. I couldn't have done it without my rock.

ABOUT THE AUTHOR

Tom Wangler was born and raised in the high desert country of Central Oregon. A graduate of Oregon College of Education with a Bachelor's degree in physical education, health sciences and journalism, Tom embarked on a teaching career—which eventually landed him a two-year stint in Africa with the Peace Corps.

After returning stateside, he obtained a Master's degree with honors before moving on to enjoy a variety of careers—including working as an account manager for a utility company, general contracting work, commercially flying helicopters, serving as a facilities manager for a certified aircraft company, and teaching at a residential high school.

Tom currently lives with his wife, Cheryl (AKA Charlie) and their two German Shepherds in the resort community of Bend, Oregon, where he is working on his second novel.

Made in the USA
Monee, IL
14 March 2023

29881552R00174